LOVE'S BITTER RIVALRY

"Rhys is a grown man. He surely has no need of a keeper," Jessamyn said.

Eluned clenched her fists. With great control, she kept her hands down against her velvet gown. "Neither has he any need of the likes of you," she spat, her knuckles whitening as she spoke.

"I didn't seduce him."

"Men don't need to be seduced. Their and night. I'm ordering you to stay aw

"You've no right to order me to do here. Or have you forgotten?"

"Rhys is mine! And don't you forget th her face close to Jessamyn's. "Don't thin your ruses to keep him here with one ex

"Don't be ridiculous. Jealously must sense. Besides, I don't dictate what Rhy me to you, surely that's his choice."

"That's where you're wrong. Rhy choice years ago—he's betrothed to m

Other *Leisure Books* by Patricia Phillips:

NIGHTINGALE
THE ROSE & THE FLAME

WOODLAND

THE CONSTANT FLAME

PATRICIA PHILLIPS

LEISURE BOOKS NEW YORK CITY

A LEISURE BOOK®

June 1993

Published by

Dorchester Publishing Co., Inc.
276 Fifth Avenue
New York, NY 10001

Printed in the United States of America.

To my husband, Charles, and to my daughter, Catherine, who from the beginning have always had faith in me.

Chapter One

As Jessamyn Dacre rode along the castle causeway, the cold wind blowing off the river whipped at her gray wool cloak. Quickly she adjusted her hood to keep out the cold, pulling the drawstring tightly around her high-cheekboned face. Now her thickly coiled auburn hair was completely hidden, making her look even more like the lad she pretended to be. She found this peasant garb of homespun wool far more comfortable than her usual figure-hugging gown and surcoat. Jessamyn had borrowed a shirt, tunic and hose from the son of the castle steward; her knee-high deerskin riding boots were her own.

Increasing skirmishes throughout the Welsh Marches made Jessamyn's disguise prudent. By dressing like a peasant boy astride a plain chestnut cob, she hoped that if she met any soldiers she would pass unnoticed. Whether the men followed the king, or the Welshman, Owain Glyndwr, made little difference—a woman alone was an easy mark for marauding troops.

The Welsh border had become more dangerous during this year, 1401, the third year of King Henry's reign. The Welsh continued to raid the lands of the English Marcher lords despite all efforts to stop them.

Picking up speed, the chestnut cob slithered down the last few feet of sandy track leading to the water's edge. Jessamyn glanced back at the massive bulk of Curlew Castle, its red sandstone battlements mighty against the gray November sky. Overhead curlews circled, giving their distinctive cries of *coorwi, coorwi*. The birds had long favored the marshy ground beside the river as a nesting place, their presence suggesting the castle's unusual name.

Forming a natural moat about the castle walls, a narrow tributary of the River Dee curled like a gray serpent about sandstone bluffs before heading north to join the tidal river's race to the Irish Sea. The gray water frothed unceasingly as it tumbled over boulders. The sound of the river, mingled with the curlew's cries and the screech of gulls, was the song of home.

A shallow river crossing lay several yards upstream.

Lifting the trailing edges of her cloak high above the water, Jessamyn plunged her sturdy cob into the surging river. She was soon safe on the opposite bank. Ned, her large brindled dog, trotted behind her. Of doubtful ancestry but of unquestioning loyalty, old Ned had leaped after his mistress, bounding over rocks, swimming when the water deepened. Now he shook himself, showering her with a fine spray of water. When Jessamyn praised him, his shaggy tail wagged happily. Then, with Ned resuming his customary place at Merlin's heels, the trio set out for the riverside settlement of Morfa Bach.

Jessamyn followed the narrow track which curved through spongy meadows and stands of willow and alder. Littlemarsh was the name by which this settlement was known in her ancestors' day. In recent years, its Anglicized name had been discarded in favor of the original Welsh. This change served as an unsettling reminder of the fervent patriotism on this, the Welsh, side of the river.

Here the path turned abruptly, affording Jessamyn an unobstructed view of the castle. She was filled with pride as she surveyed the stone gatehouse and the four smaller, round towers guarding the castle's pentagon-shaped ward. Curlew Castle was not a mighty fortress; it was merely a small lordship castle granted to her great-grandfather by King Edward in reward for his service in the second Welsh campaign. Though it was considered strategically insignificant, Jessamyn could not have been prouder of Curlew had it been the mighty Tower of London.

Regionally, there were far more impressive fortresses, Lord Grey's castle at Ruthin being the most important. Reginald Grey of the Red Castle was Marcher lord of Dyffryn Clwyd, his territory stretching farther than Jessamyn had ever traveled. Fortunately, the mighty Lord Grey had never coveted little Curlew, allowing the Dacre family to reside there in relative peace.

Lord Grey had not been so generous with his Welsh neighbor, Owain Glyndwr. Their bitter dispute over a stretch of land lying between their estates threatened to plunge the region into civil war.

Jessamyn's soft red mouth hardened to a determined line as she considered the sheer impossibility of remaining neutral in this quarrel. Sooner of later, Curlew would be forced to take sides. Owain Glyndwr had ignited a flame of Welsh patriotism which threatened to engulf the land.

To accept the yoke of a powerful master was contrary to Jessamyn's nature. She had always cherished her independence. Being born a woman in a man's world had never daunted her. Jessamyn usually did as she pleased, making few concessions to convention. Surprisingly, her father, Sir Hugh, had never tried to stamp out his daughter's willful ways. When his heir Walter was born, it would have been natural to push three-year-old Jessamyn to the background. Unfortunately, Sir Hugh's longed-for heir was born with a withered leg. As if being a cripple was not blow enough, before he was five, Walter developed a malady characterized by high fevers, convulsions and long periods of unconsciousness.

Feeling sorry for her sickly brother and wanting to help him, Jessamyn had set out to master all his lessons, anxious to help him learn the skills required of a young lord.

Under Jessamyn's guidance, Walter learned to read Latin, keep accounts, and play chess. Unfortunately his physical achievements were less spectacular. Though Walter learned to draw a bow and wield a sword, he became physically ill at the sight of blood. Furthermore, he could stay in the saddle for only short periods of time before the constant movement made the pain in his deformed hip and leg unbearable. It soon became apparent that young Walter Dacre would never follow in his father's footsteps by leading men into battle.

Jessamyn's hazel eyes moistened as she thought about her gruff father. Sir Hugh regretted that it was not she who had been born the son. And though his neighbors criticized him for favoring a girl, he always took little Jessamyn with him when he rode about their land, proud of his daughter sitting so tall and straight on her black pony. His heart was heavy when he thought about his heir lying abed, immobilized by a strange malady. Early in the spring, Sir Hugh had died from complications of a wound he received whilst fighting for King Richard in one of his many dynastic squabbles with his cousin, Bolingbroke, who was now England's king in Richard's stead.

Ahead, the thatched dwellings of Morfa Bach clustered along a curved track running uphill from the river. The tenants of Curlew Castle were self-sufficient. The village had common grazing land for cows and sheep; the pigs rooted in the mast of the thick oak woods ringing the cultivated land. Fertile acres tilled by the villagers yielded sustenance for the castle; the land was worked in payment for the lord's protection. This prosperous village boasted three dovecoats, a duck pond, a smithy, a small inn, and, atop a grassy knoll to the east, its crowning glory—a splendid Norman church whose tall spire pierced the gray November sky.

As lady of Curlew Castle, one of Jessamyn's duties was to oversee the welfare of their tenants. William Rhees, the castle steward, usually informed her of those in need, or in failing health. Today her saddle bags held yarrow gargle to ease the swollen gums of the innkeeper's wife. She also brought pots of salve to lessen the pain of old Agnes's rheumatism. The old woman lived with her idiot daughter at the end of the village street; the women wove baskets to earn their keep. Lately, Agnes's hands had become so gnarled that she could scarcely ply her trade. Sixteen-year-old Maeven was of little help. Though smiling and cheerful, the girl had not the wits of a five year old. An image of Maeven's smiling, moon-round face flashed through her mind and Jessamyn frowned, acknowledging the probable reason behind Maeven's unfailing cheerfulness. A young child had not the intellect to grasp the consequences of civil war. Maeven enjoyed a fool's paradise. Her simple-mindedness gave Jessamyn an added concern: a half-witted girl was always fair game for passing soldiers. Whether Morfa Bach was entered by men following the Welsh dragon or King Henry's stand-ard, it mattered not—Maeven would probably have been raped by men from both armies.

Jessamyn whistled a shrill command to Ned before she turned onto the track running behind the houses. Swiftly the old dog changed course. She smiled down at him affectionately, sadness creeping into her heart. Her childhood companion would not be with her much longer. For some time, Jessamyn had known that Ned was going blind. Those soulful brown eyes, which had always gazed at her with such adoration, had turned milky-blue with age. The old dog compensated for his failing sight by relying on his sense of smell, and by following the sound of his mistress's voice.

Jessamyn stopped outside Agnes's door and slid from the saddle. This last house in the village was larger and better constructed than the rest, attesting to the skill of Agnes's late husband. This fact was a constant source of jealousy amongst the other vil-lagers who, at times, had spitefully accused Agnes of witchcraft. Jessamyn had angrily defended the old woman, shaming the others into a sullen truce.

As the daughter of Gwyneth of Trevaron, Jessamyn had been instructed in the herbal remedies handed down through her mother's family. After her moth-er's death, Jessamyn had carried on her work, caring for their tenants and the inhabitants of the castle. Though Lady Gwyneth's herbal lore had been extensive, she had never been able to cure Walter's affliction. To her delight, Jessamyn had recently developed a brew containing mistletoe and peony root which lessened the frequency of Walter's seizures. A second mixture of sallow willow and yellow gentian root reduced his fevers. These two remedies had done much to make Walter's life more normal.

As she entered Agnes's low-ceilinged dwelling, Jessamyn threw back her hood. The haze of bluish smoke in the room stung her eyes. A cloud of wood smoke hung about the rafters before slowly filtering through the chimney hole in the thatched roof.

Agnes huddled over the hearth, a heavy wool shawl around her shoulders. Maeven sat at her feet, her chapped hands skillfully weaving a rush basket.

"Oh, my lady, you surprised me!" Agnes gasped, startled as the door opened to admit a sharp blast of wind which sent a column of wood smoke dancing crazily about their heads. "Too cold today for you to be out, my lady. Oh, you brung my salve. God bless you!" Agnes's apple-cheeked face beamed happily. "Since it turned cold, me joints is murdering me."

Maeven gazed up in wonder at the beautiful lady from the castle, awed by her very presence; then, at a sharp word from her mother, she obediently returned to her basket weaving.

Agnes creaked to her feet, her ancient garments wafting a pungent odor of mingled dirt and the residue of herbal salve constantly rubbed into her aching joints.

"I've brought a big pot this time. Get Maeven to help rub it in wherever it hurts. Are you feeling any better?"

"I soon will be, my lady. Our Tom's been giving me some stuff he uses on the ailing sheep. It smells terrible, and doesn't work no better. Now this—I'll be well away with this."

When Jessamyn dropped her thick wool mittens on the bench by the hearth, Agnes took her slender hand in her own gnarled brown one.

"You're a saint, Lady Jessamyn, a true saint—as was your lady mother before you. Thinking about me, and you with your own sorrows," Agnes added sadly.

Jessamyn glanced down uncomfortably at the matted rushes, knowing Agnes referred to her father's passing and to her brother's ailment, even more of a burden now that he was lord of Curlew Castle.

"As the good Father often reminds us, we all have our crosses to bear," Jessamyn repeated piously, anxious to change the subject.

"Crosses is the right name for it, lady, and no mistake. Will you sup with us? I've a good stew cooking."

"No, Agnes, I won't take your food. You're going to need what you've got to see you through the winter. It promises to be an early one if today's an example. The wind's like a knife."

Agnes drew Jessamyn out of Maeven's hearing.

"Lady Jessamyn, I don't know if this is something to worry about, but our Tom keeps seeing soldiers. He can see for miles on the hillsides. Are we in danger?"

Jessamyn swallowed, her heart beginning an uneasy thud. That close. She had hoped they would not be touched by the hostilities before summer.

"Whose men are they? Glyndwr's or the king's?"

"Tom's not to know that now, is he, lady?"

Jessamyn bit back the sharp reminder that he could have noted their banners, or if they were close enough, their way of speech. She had forgotten that Tom was barely more advanced than his sister. Idiocy in her children had been one of the crosses Agnes had been forced to bear.

Jessamyn smiled reassuringly as she clasped the older woman's hand. "Don't worry, Agnes. At the first

sign of trouble, you and the others must come inside
Curlew. You can come now, if you'd feel safer."

"Nay, lady, I won't leave me own things—not till I
have to. This is all I've got, built by my man's own
hands. I'll stay here a while."

Jessamyn understood. She gave Agnes a comforting squeeze, holding her breath against the accu-
mulated odors wafting from her garments. As she
turned to leave, she said, "I'll come back tomorrow with the infusion for your swellings. It wasn't
steeped enough to bring today."

"Not if it snows, lady, don't you come out in that."

"I won't. Though it's getting colder, I don't expect
snow so early on."

Agnes stood in the crack of the door waving as
Jessamyn mounted her horse. Ruffling old Ned's
fur, Agnes admonished him to keep good watch
over his lady. She stood a few moments longer at the
open door, feeling strangely uneasy as she watched
the slender figure in gray bend against the north
wind.

Later, when Jessamyn left the inn where she had
delivered Sal's yarrow gargle, she was surprised by
Margery, the village beauty, who eagerly ran up to
her.

"Lady Jessamyn, wait up. See, that hair rinse
worked lovely," she cried, pulling off her shawl to
display a head of shining yellow locks. "Jack says
its bright as buttercups." Margery ducked her head
self-consciously as she revealed the latter.

"What a nice compliment. When's the wedding?"

"Tuesday week," Margery replied, all smiles. "Oh,
my lady, if that Jack don't get back in time, I'll die
of shame."

"Of course he'll be back. He wouldn't miss his
own wedding, you silly." Jessamyn laughed at the
idea, aware that Jack the Drover was eager to wed

15

his pretty sweetheart. He regularly drove stock to Chester; this was his last journey before the big Christmas Market.

Margery blushed and, with eyes downcast, confided, "I'm that eager for him. We waited, lady, no bun in the oven for me."

Jessamyn patted Margery's shoulder. "You've a right to be proud, Margery. See, I've brought something for you."

From her saddlebag Jessamyn took a ribbon-trimmed wreath filled with aromatic herbs to sweeten the newlyweds' chamber.

"Oh, Lady Jessamyn—it's beautiful!" Margery exclaimed in delight, fingering the satin ribbons in bright shades of pink and blue. "I'll treasure it. Reckon this will be the second-best treat to enjoy in our bedchamber." At this, Margery laughed, her cheeks flushed with expectancy.

Jessamyn laughed with her and waved goodbye as she turned out of the inn yard. But as she rode slowly along the village street, her mood soured. Margery's candid expectations of the pleasure of her marriage bed had not offended her, for it was the custom to speak forthrightly about such matters. The unmarried were not kept in ignorance of the relationship between men and women. Because there was scant privacy in either castle or cottage, there was little mystery remaining to the act. For Jessamyn, the greatest mystery lay in the deep human emotions of lovers.

When her father had returned from his last campaign, he had brought back a book about courtly love. On the homeward journey, Sir Hugh had bartered his armed protection to a merchant in exchange for sundry silks, ribbons and laces and this illustrated romance, all for his pretty Jessamyn.

Though the words were difficult to understand, Jessamyn was delighted with the book's pictures. Delicately drawn and brightly colored, these illustrations depicted minstrels and knights serenading beautiful ladies. These lavishly dressed, courting couples were seated beneath rose-decked trellises, the like of which she had never seen. The only flowers Jessamyn knew were the pinks and wall-flowers growing in the flower bed inside the south wall. There was the castle herb garden and the wild flowers which carpeted the countryside in summer, but though she saw briar roses twined about the hedges, nowhere had she ever seen roses with petals like red velvet and a heady fragrance to make men swoon. She doubted that Margery and Jack had much in common with these elegant lovers, yet Jessamyn was surprised to admit that she envied Margery her pleasure with the man of her dreams.

Jessamyn tossed her head impatiently and straightened her shoulders, making an effort to shake off her maudlin mood. Man of her dreams indeed! In her experience, men were either ineffectual weaklings or benevolent tyrants. No man of her acquaintance ever spoke poetic verse, or knelt to kiss the hem of her gown. True, she had never actually been courted, but the local gentry bore little resemblance to those long-faced, soulful-eyed gallants in the rose garden. Her only brush with betrothal had ended with her father's passing. When Sir Hugh discussed betrothing her to his distant relative in Cater's Hill, near Shrewsbury, she was greatly distressed. Her mouth turned down even now at the mere thought of Sir Ralph Warren. Father had not been able to tell her what this man looked like, not having seen him since childhood. In his typical bluff fashion, Sir Hugh had dismissed her questions by telling her she would be happy with the man, whatever his looks, for he would care for her and father her children. Jessamyn had quickly reminded him that she did not want children—she wanted Sir Ralph even less. There the matter had rested.

Wistfully she allowed her thoughts to stray to her favorite picture in the book, wherein a gentleman played a lute whilst gazing soulfully into his lady's blue eyes. The trellis framing the picture was bowed down with goblet-sized roses, the red petals forming a fragrant carpet at their feet. Father had said that Sir Ralph had been to court. Could it be possible he was such a romantic figure? No. Sir Ralph Warren would be fat and pompous, and worst of all, he would seek to *tame* her. Her mouth curled at the thought. She would like to meet the male who was *man* enough for that.

With a sharp cry, Jessamyn kicked Merlin's flanks, urging him to a gallop. Poor old Ned raced after them, valiantly trying to keep pace. Overhead, alarmed gulls and curlews screeched, startled by the sudden flurry of movement. The wind whipped the blood to her cheeks, stinging her flesh with its ferocious chill. Jessamyn's cloak billowed like a sail, flapping and startling the birds circling above, calling in distress.

No Sir Ralph for her. She was free and she intended to stay that way. Guiltily, Jessamyn realized that she was almost glad Walter was not like other young men, for then he, too, would have tried to bring his sister in line. As it was, he lectured her about riding abroad alone, telling her of the danger and disgrace of such behavior. And, as usual, she ignored him. Jessamyn's one concession to safety was in wearing this wool peasant garb. There was no real penance to that compromise, for she enjoyed the freedom of this clothing. From now on, she intended to dress this way every time she left the castle, even after the hostilities were over, if she chose.

Plunging back in the river, Merlin sent up a wall of spray and, despite herself, Jessamyn shrieked as the cold water slapped her face and penetrated her clothing. Wildly she shot through the shallows, soaking poor Ned, who was struggling to keep up. *"Free, free,"* the birds called overhead. Free as the wind and the rain, as the frothing river, the hills, the woods . . .

Brought up short by the castle's stone causeway, Jessamyn was forced to curtail her mad race. Exhilarated by the wind and the fresh air, she now felt more able to return to being the lady of Curlew. At least for today.

The walls of Curlew Castle's Great Hall were blackened by years of smoking torches and blazing logs. Shabby and functional best described the appointments of the huge room with its scarred trestles and rush floor.

Walter waited at the lord's table on a raised dais before the blazing hearth. While he waited for Jessamyn's return, he nursed a goblet of ale— wine was kept for special occasions—and he fumed at having to wait for his meal.

The gloomy sky, visible through the arched window openings high in the wall, looked more like twilight than midday. How could Jessamyn ride abroad on such a bitter day? As if the old wives couldn't wait for more clement weather to receive their potions. For some time, Walter had suspected that his sister used ministering to the tenants as an excuse to go beyond the castle walls. Any excuse was good enough for Jessamyn, who had always chafed at having to sit still and appear ladylike.

Walter sighed. Now that he was lord of the castle, he was responsible for his spinster sister's welfare. How was he to manage such a woman? It was all Father's fault. Had he brought Jessamyn in line as he should have years ago, she would be as gentle as other women. At her advanced age, Walter despaired of ever marrying her off. She was years past marriageable age. Locally, she was called a saint for the healing she dispensed. Saints were allowed to make vows of chastity, not the lady of Curlew Castle. Jessamyn needed a husband and Walter needed a valuable ally. Curlew cried out for a man with a well-trained army who could fight if the need arose, not a poor excuse for a lord who couldn't even ride about his estate without weakening.

Walter ran his hand down his shriveled thigh, disgusted by his affliction. The times were dangerous and he knew that they were ill prepared against an outbreak of hostilities.

The gloom of his thoughts matched the gray day. As he stared broodingly into the leaping flames, Walter drained his ale goblet. He motioned to a page to refill it. When his problems appeared insurmountable, ale soothed his mind. Sometimes, when the pain in his hip was almost too strong to bear, he mixed a herbal potion in the ale to bring relief.

A flurry of movement, followed by the crash of a door being flung open, jerked him to the present. A slender, gray-swathed figure appeared in the Hall, shaking moisture from her cloak. Jessamyn had returned.

"Well, about time. I was tempted to dine without you, sister," Walter called, sitting straighter in his chair. When he was alone, it was all right to slouch, to favor his deformed hip and leg. When Jessamyn was present, she expected more from him—too much at times.

"You knew when I'd be back," she retorted, pulling off her cloak. Ned padded beside her as they approached the hearth. "Do you want me to change, or may I sup like this?"

Walter shrugged. "Would it make any difference what I want?"

"Not really." She grinned at him and reached for a piece of bread. "The cold makes me hungry. Is there ale, or did you drink it all?"

Walter scowled. That was another thing. Jessamyn was forever making veiled references to the amount he drank. Come to think of it, they weren't always veiled; sometimes she was downright accusing.

"Help yourself. There's plenty more where that came from."

"It's supposed to last us through the winter, Walt, which it won't, at the rate you're going through it."

"Then I'll drink wine, Jess. It would be far more pleasant."

"Sorry," she mumbled, reminded that Walter did not like his name shortened. Calling her Jess in return was his way of evening the score. Still, she didn't mind being called Jess. The name was far more workmanlike than the flowery Jessamyn her mother had chosen.

The mistress's return was the signal for the servants to serve the midday meal. A serving girl brought forth a steaming platter of sliced mutton accompanied by a pewter tureen of thick, savory gravy to moisten the meat. Jessamyn lifted the lid off a pottery dish already on the table and sniffed its contents; braised turnips, beans and peas in spiced sauce were today's accompaniment to the main course. First, a fragrant herb pottage of cabbage and apples was placed before them. In readiness, their wooden bowls held thick slices of barley bread over which Jessamyn now ladled the steaming soup.

Brother and sister ate in silence, both occupied with their own thoughts. Presently, Jessamyn said, "I heard something in the village which worries me."

"What's that?"

"There've been bands of soldiers sighted nearby. The shepherd saw them. Do you suppose it's King Henry's soldiers coming to punish us for not answering his call for levies last year?"

"He can punish all he wants. Father was bedfast; we could spare no men, and desperate or not, I doubt that King Henry wanted me in his battle. No, he'll just have to realize there was no one to fight and that's that."

"I'm afraid he won't see it that way, Walter, dear. Kings never do."

They went on eating. Thoughtfully Walter speared a chunk of mutton with his hunting knife. "I've told you before, I'm lord of Curlew now. It's my place to worry about things like that. You're just a woman. Leave such matters to men to solve."

Jessamyn stared daggers at him, but she forced her tongue to silence. Walter very much wanted to act the part of the lord of Curlew. She still felt sorry for him, yet she had to admit that she had liked him far better as a crippled boy. He had matured into a short-tempered, sometimes overbearing man who was growing far too fond of the ale barrel.

"They could be Welsh raiders," Jessamyn suggested, pouring ale from the flagon. She did not offer any to Walter.

"Look, once and for all, let me worry about our protection. Anyway, long before Christmas, our worst concerns will be behind us. Do you think the Welsh will hold off that long?"

"Possibly . . . what's Christmas got to do with it?"

"By then we'll have all the help we need."

Jessamyn set down her horn spoon. "There's something here you're not telling. Out with it. Let's stop playing games. Who's going to help us? Or are we to expect miracles at the holytide?"

"Very funny." Walter dismissed her words sourly, pouring his own ale. "A relative will be here with supplies and men to aid us. That's the miracle we can expect."

"Relative? I didn't know we had one who could afford to provide us with such bounty."

"I wrote to Sir Ralph Warren and told him of father's passing. I also mentioned how poorly garrisoned we are. A messenger came from him last week when you were off gallivanting to one of the outlying farms."

Jessamyn stared at him in shock. "You wrote to him and you never told me?"

"There was no need. I wanted to surprise you when he arrived."

"Oh, I'm surprised all right!" Jessamyn cried, banging down her cup. "Whatever possessed you to do such a fool thing?"

"There's no need to be angry just because you didn't think of it first," he said smugly, cutting himself a chunk of bread.

"I'm not angry for that reason. Sometimes, Walt, I wonder where your sense is. By contacting Sir Ralph, you've laid us open to takeover. Don't you understand? Now he knows Father's gone, that we have few men, and our supplies are too scant to withstand a siege. What do you expect him to do?"

"Will you stop shouting at me! It's not befitting a woman," Walter snarled, annoyed by his sister's angry reaction. "He'll come with men and supplies, and let us borrow what we need to see us through the winter—he said as much."

"For what price?"

"The price of kinship."

"Oh, by all that's holy, haven't you learned anything? Powerful men don't do favors out of the goodness of their hearts. Sir Ralph may bring supplies and men, but he's going to extract a price for it, you can be sure of that. And his price won't be to your liking."

"What do you mean by that?" Walter asked, paling, though he still refused to actually believe his action was unwarranted. "What price?"

"He'll likely take over the castle, brother dear, and we haven't the power to stop him. Or didn't you think of that?"

Jessamyn was aware of her flushed cheeks and pounding heart. At her feet, Ned stirred, conscious of his mistress's heightened emotion and made uneasy by it. Jessamyn brushed his rough back with her toes in a clumsy caress.

"Nonsense!"

She seethed. Nonsense had become one of Walter's favorite dismissals when she had an idea, or a suggestion he disliked. Usually, she managed to endure his scathing comments with patience, always aware of his deformity. On this issue, however, patience was very hard to come by.

"Let's hope it is nonsense," she said, trying to quell the anger in her voice. "I just wish you'd consulted me first, at least given me a chance to discuss matters with you. We mightn't have an abundant larder or cellar, but with care, we can manage. There was no need to go begging. Why didn't you tell me what you were going to do?"

"Because you wouldn't have helped. You'd just have stopped me writing to him."

"Well, at least you could have consulted William Rhees. Surely the steward's advice would have been acceptable, seeing that he's not a woman."

Walter's face flushed, yet he stubbornly refused to admit any fault in the matter. "Maybe Sir Ralph will reopen negotiations on your betrothal whilst he's here."

Aghast, Jessamyn stared at him. "What! Surely you didn't mention that. You didn't tell him . . . Walter!"

"No, no, just a chance thought," he dismissed, grinning as he drained his alecup. "You have to admit, Father was considering it at one time."

"Aye, and thank God it died with him."

"Look, Jessamyn, most girls are betrothed long before they're fifteen. You're not going to be easy to settle at your age."

"Thank you, brother dear, but I'm not exactly eager to be *settled*. Just mind your own affairs. If, and when, I choose to marry someone, I'll select him myself."

"No one will have you unless you mend your ways."

"Good. Then if I carry on in this fashion, I can be assured of keeping my freedom. You've given me valuable advice, Walter."

With this, Jessamyn pushed back her chair.

"Now listen here," Walter began, sitting straighter in his chair. "You can't speak to me like that—you're my sister."

"I'm going up to my chamber whilst I still have one."

"You're making far too much of this, as usual. The way you're acting, anyone would think I'd asked the man to take over the castle. Have you forgotten? He's a kinsman and friend."

"Don't you understand, Walter? You may have done just that. Now all England knows we're vulnerable and under-provisioned. You may have opened us up to threats from someone even less

25

desirable than Sir Ralph Warren."

"All England—what utter nonsense! As if anyone really cares about a little place like Curlew. Would you have us starve in our pride?"

"Well, at least then, we'd still be masters of our own land. A better choice by far than rotting in some relative's dungeon."

Walter threw up his hands in disgust. Turning his back on Jessamyn, he stared into the flames and refused to look at her when she spoke. It was always the same every time he tried to exercise his right as lord. He could do nothing but his sister had something to say about it. The servants must have heard her criticizing him so often that even they believed he was an ineffectual fool.

"I just wish you'd thought about all this before you wrote to Cater's Hill, that you'd mentioned it to me."

"A man doesn't need the approval of his sister for everything he does," Walter countered, consciously trying to make his voice deeper. "If I were to listen to you, I'd have to report every time I fart."

Jessamyn sighed. They were getting nowhere. This discussion had worn out its welcome. "I wish you hadn't written to him, but since you have, let's hope for the best. If the weather changes, perhaps Sir Ralph won't come at all. Does William Rhees know?"

"Yes . . . I told him."

"And?"

Walter spun about, his face set. "If you must know, his reaction was almost as angry as yours. Neither one of you are prepared to let me be lord. He, with his advice; you, with your criticisms. I'm master here. At least give me credit for *some* brains."

"Aye, that I'll do, Walter. Would that you had sufficient brains to make wise decisions," Jessamyn snapped unkindly as she left the table. "Good night, brother," she added as she crossed the Hall, her boots sinking into the rushes as she strode from the room.

Chapter Two

After she had slept on the unwelcome news of Sir Ralph's impending visit, Jessamyn felt more hopeful. Why should Walter be wrong? She prayed that, just this once it was her own sharp assessment of the situation which was at fault.

Afraid that their heated words had made Walter vulnerable to one of his *turns,* as the servants referred to his seizures, Jessamyn sent a servant with a cup of peony root brew to his room. As she expected, Walter was sulking, and his body servant said that his master would see no one.

She shrugged indifferently, determined not to be put out by her brother's childish behavior. She knew that she had been unkind to him, insulting his intelligence and scolding him like an alewife. Yet, she grew so tired of having to baby him, of always needing to remember that he was not quite like other people, to constantly make allowances for his affliction. Walter's ongoing struggle to establish himself as actual ruler of the castle, as well as its titular lord, was proving more trying than Jessamyn had anticipated.

William Rhees had said little when she questioned him the previous night, though she could tell that he shared her fears about Sir Ralph taking advantage of their vulnerability. A wise man, William Rhees was hesitant to take sides against his lord. After all, Walter was master of Curlew. Jessamyn could only hope that, in his thickheadedness, her brother had discovered a glimmer of hope they had both overlooked.

Dressed again as a peasant lad, Jessamyn set out for the village, taking with her an infusion to ease Agnes's dropsy and the ingredients for a poultice to draw the innkeeper's boil. This morning she found her prearranged visit a blessing. Now, she need not be reminded at every turn of Walter's sulks and his probably disastrous stab at establishing himself as master of Curlew.

Just the idea that Sir Ralph Warren might reopen negotiations for her betrothal brought a cold sweat to her brow. She was horrified at the idea of traveling to some foreign place, of being beholden to a stranger, of needing to bow to his will in both Hall and bedchamber—the latter being especially distasteful. Jessamyn shuddered at the thought. Although she had never set eyes on Sir Ralph, the expectation of his coming to court her had produced not a glimmer of anticipation. Margery could speak of her marriage night with excitement, for she already knew her husband-to-be. Jack wasn't some rich stranger who would consider his suit an immense favor for which she must be eternally grateful. Peasant girls were free to be themselves. There were more restrictions placed on ladies, especially on someone who might have become wife to Sir Ralph Warren of Cater's Hill—courtier, influential landowner, supporter of the king.

"Blast Sir Ralph," she muttered angrily, setting her heels into the cob's flank as she urged him toward the river. "Blast you too, Walt, for doing this to us," she added defiantly.

The day was gray; the wind was still. The river still frothed, but the water flowed almost sluggishly. It would rain before morning, or sleet, if the wind turned back from the north. The heavy gray sky seemed to wait expectantly.

When Jessamyn entered Agnes's cottage, she did not receive her customary greeting. Agnes huddled over the hearth with Maeven at her feet, but surprisingly, the girl's hands were idle. When Agnes turned to speak, Jessamyn saw that her face was gray with worry, and her eyes were red-rimmed with weeping.

"Agnes . . . whatever is it?" she asked in concern. She put down her package and hastened to the old woman's side.

"No need for you to worry, lady—nothing to bother you about," Agnes mumbled, her toothless gums working on in silent speech.

"They's going to smoke out me and Mam," Maeven volunteered cheerfully, repeating what she had heard.

Agnes hissed at the girl to be quiet, but Jessamyn had already heard. "Who's going to smoke you out?" she demanded.

"The others." Agnes motioned vaguely towards the cluster of dwellings to the east.

"What's happened?"

"A couple of cows sickened. Idrys swears I bewitched them. Then, the widow's son's still sickening too, they blamed me for that as well."

30

"They say Mam even put a spell on the young lord at the castle, made him so's he can't walk proper . . ."

Maeven earned a slap on the face for her latest news. She subsided, whimpering, to the rushes, nursing her reddened cheek.

"Surely they're not saying that! Oh, Agnes, tell me it's not so. What a preposterous . . ."

"Nay, lady, I swear, I done nothing," Agnes protested indignantly, tears starting to her eyes. "Lady Gwyneth was a saint. I'd never hurt her babe. Please, lady, you've got to believe me."

"Of course I believe you. What I can't believe is that they should be so cruel. I know you'd nothing to do with Walter's sickness. There, Agnes, don't cry."

Jessamyn took Agnes's hand to comfort her, wondering how best to quell this latest round of spite and jealousy.

"Cows don't get sick because of spells, they should know that. They're just a lot of superstitious alewives, and Idrys is the worst of the lot! When I see him I'll give him a dressing down. Now, don't you worry. I'll see what can be done. Would you feel safer coming back with me?"

"Nay, I'll stay. They've always had their eyes on me bed—if I leave, it'll be gone before morning." Agnes glanced proudly at the big oak bed with its rope-slung mattress. That splendid bed was the envy of every goodwife in the village.

Jessamyn gave Agnes a linen bag of herbs and a small flask of steeped liquid. "Here, you can mix your own tea when that's gone. Steep two days, heat to boiling, then strain."

Agnes nodded as she thrust the packet of herbs into the battered pouch at her waist. "Thank you, my lady. What would I do without you? You mustn't worry about me—they've been at me a dozen times

31

before," Agnes assured her, wiping her eyes. "Now, we've finished your baskets. Will you take them today?"

Proudly, Agnes brought out the rush baskets they had made in gratitude for Jessamyn's medicines. There was a shallow, wide-topped basket for carrying flowers and herbs, a deeper round one for eggs, and a firm-bottomed willow laundry basket. Surprised by the gifts, Jessamyn thanked Agnes profusely, taking care to praise the excellent workmanship and practicality of the baskets.

Jessamyn was soon back on her horse, the baskets slung from her saddle, making her look like a peddler. As she had expected, when she rode down the village street, no one came to the door to greet her. They would guess that Agnes had already told of their threats and, being cowards, they all chose to stay indoors rather than face chastisement from Lady Jessamyn. She hoped this latest burst of hostility would blow over like the rest, aware that the outcome would depend on whether the cows lived.

Instead of going to the inn, Jessamyn turned to the east, heading up the gentle slope to the parish church. A few words with Father Paul about Agnes's potential danger might stave off future trouble.

The priest greeted her warmly, offering her a cup of mulled ale as he led her to the blazing hearth. The small adjoining rectory was comfortable, the house kept spotless by Hester, a young widow from the village. The locals gossiped that Hester was far more than housekeeper to the priest.

Father Paul's face creased in worry as, between sips of the warm spiced brew, Jessamyn confided what she had just learned from Agnes.

"These villagers are narrow-minded and superstitious. The old beliefs still linger, despite my efforts to sway them to the Christian viewpoint."

The priest sighed, brushing back his thick, graying hair. Repositioning his large paunch, he stretched on his seat, placing his feet near the fire. "Rest assured, Lady Jessamyn, I'll keep old Agnes in my prayers. And in my sight, too, as best as I can."

Jessamyn thanked him and, nodding goodbye to Hester, went back to her horse. Though she knew that she should have been reassured by her brief meeting with the priest, she was not. To her detriment, she was sure, Jessamyn had never received much solace from the church. Father Paul was a kindly man, yet she could not overlook what was said about his relationship with Hester, nor his undue liking for the ale cup. His appetite for feasting was legend. Indulgence in these very human failings seemed completely at odds with his clerical vows. Yet, now that Father Paul was aware of the villagers' threats against Agnes, he would lambaste them from the pulpit for their wickedness. Soon, all Morfa Bach would be quaking as the priest bent their healthy fear of God's retribution to his own purpose. The church had always been adept at that tactic.

To Jessamyn's dismay, she found the inn yard swarming with strangers and their horses. A couple of supply wagons blocked her way, and she had to squeeze Merlin past them to enter the yard. Her heart skipped a beat. Gradually she reasoned herself out of her fear. These could not be Sir Ralph's men, for traveling due north from Shrewsbury, they would have no need to cross the river. Later, as she heard their speech, she discovered that they were Welshmen, probably followers of Owain Glyndwr, the self-styled Prince of Wales.

Jessamyn had to push her way through the crowd. Assuming she was an unimportant peasant lad, no one made any effort to move out of her way. Jessamyn smiled ruefully, pleased that her disguise had worked, yet not pleased with the lack of respect it prompted.

After an especially fierce struggle to pass a couple of burly men in worn leather jacks who blocked the doorway, she reached the inner room where the innkeeper and his wife lived. Those louts had purposely barred her way, quite enjoying the tussle, she thought in annoyance, as she rubbed her bruised shoulder and side where she had taken the brunt of their resistance.

"The master be busy," snapped a serving girl when first she saw Jessamyn. Then, suddenly recognizing her as the lady of the castle, the girl gulped and stared wide-eyed at the unexpected transformation of Lady Jessamyn. Finally, remembering her manners, she dropped a swift curtsy. "Oh, my lady . . . I never recognized you done up like that," she gasped in apology.

"Good . . . let's hope that rabble out there won't recognize me either. I've brought a mixture to treat your master's boil. In the flask there's gargle for your mistress. I'd best be going before the soldiers steal my horse."

"Soldiers," the girl repeated, mystified. "Oh, you mean they who's out there supping? Oh, they's not *real* soldiers."

"They look real enough to me. And they certainly act real. I've got bruises from trying to push my way in here."

"They're guards traveling with a Welsh lady and gentleman wot's going to Chester. Oh, and beautiful she looks, like the window in the parish church!"

Taken back by the girl's flowery compliment, Jessamyn thanked her and headed back to the common room, determined to see this vision for herself.

The room was so noisy that Jessamyn put her hands over her ears to shut out the racket. The large party of men supped amidst much laughter and raucous speech. Welshmen, without a doubt. She discovered she could understand little of what they said. This was a surprise, for Jessamyn had always prided herself on her ability to converse with their Welsh tenants. These men must have come from distant parts, for their accents were unlike any she had heard before.

A party of ladies was seated before the hearth at a specially prepared table. Jessamyn stood in the window embrasure, where she had a perfect view of the strangers. Though the women were dressed for traveling she could see brightly colored gowns peeping from under their heavy cloaks. On closer inspection, only two of the women were ladies; the other women's homespun gowns marked them as servants.

One of the ladies turned about to speak to someone and Jessamyn gulped in surprise at her perfection. This was the golden vision stepped down from the church's stained-glass window! An unexpected wave of envy spread over her as she studied the woman's fine blonde hair, delicate facial structure, and bright blue eyes. She swallowed hard. Not merely a vision from the church window, this gentlewoman could have stepped from the pages of her beloved romance. So unlike herself in appearance was this woman, Jessamyn's belief that the romance had been written about a separate race of creature was reinforced. This lady was dainty and feminine. Her pale skin and eyes, her delicate gown of cinammon silk, made her look breakable as precious glass. Jessamyn was unable to squelch the prick of disappointed tears at her unexpected discovery. She had hoped someday to find a key to unlock the door to that secret garden, so that she, too, could enjoy such beauty and romance. Now she knew that would never be.

Shouldering her way back through the crowded taproom, Jessamyn headed for the door. She had intended to stay to eat a hot mutton pasty before she left; now, she found her appetite gone. Pushing her way past the supping Welshmen, she kept her wool hood pulled forward to shadow her face. They never even spared her a second glance.

Ned began to bark as soon as she entered the stableyard, his bark more an alarm than a greeting. Fondling his rough head, Jessamyn glanced about for possible danger. Several soldiers had charge of the travelers' horses, but they paid no attention to her. Putting Ned's peculiar behavior down to his advancing age, Jessamyn untied Merlin's reins from the rail. Old dogs were probably much like old people, forever sensing danger where none existed.

As she swung into the saddle, Jessamyn felt unduly irritable. She had been surprised and annoyed by her unexpected reaction at the sight of that noblewoman. Roast meat and a roaring hearth had greeted the woman's arrival, which meant she was either an important traveler, or that she carried much gold. In either case, she would be assured of good treatment.

Jessamyn narrowed her eyes against the wind which had risen whilst she had been indoors. The wind buffeted her with a searing blast, heavy with the smell of burning hearths. She had to call twice for Ned, who seemed determined to head in the other direction. Pulling her cloak tighter about her body to cut out the wind, Jessamyn rode down the village street. Her worry about Sir Ralph's impending visit, combined with fear for Agnes's safety, had left her vulnerable. Envy, jealousy, whichever name she gave her emotional reaction, it was not pleasant. It was so foolish to be envious of that woman's appearance. She had silk gowns of her own had she chosen to wear them. After all, few noblewomen rode about the countryside dressed like a peasant lad. Envy of the woman's probable lifestyle was even more foolish. Even had the gorgeous creature spent her days beneath a rose-covered trellis, serenaded by an army of courtiers, it did not matter. All her dreams inspired by the book were unchanged, for they had not been real in the first place. Curlew Castle and this wild country were her reality, not walled gardens overflowing with roses.

Jessamyn paused, turning in the saddle to glance at the inn, puzzled by her violent reaction at the sight of the strange woman. Something caught her eye. Color showed between the buildings, moving, glowing—Fire! Ned barked again and tried to head back. Instantly she was alerted. She knew the source of that blaze: Agnes's house was on fire!

Turning about, Jessamyn galloped back towards the burning house. Ned ran beside her, barking an alarm. Whilst she had been inside the inn, someone from the village must have set the house on fire. It was stretching the imagination to think this was a coincidence. Perhaps one of the cows had died, forcing the peasants to action.

The fire had a good hold; flames were already roaring through the back of the thatched roof. The past weeks had been unusually dry, the autumn sun further drying out the thatch, creating the perfect conditions for fire.

Out of the corner of her eye, Jessamyn saw a couple of dark shadows close to the wall, then the two figures ran into the trees edging the village. Unfortunately, the men had been running away from her, so she could not identify them.

To her horror, when she reached the house, Jessamyn saw that the entrance was ablaze. By the screams of fright coming from inside, she knew

Agnes and Maeven were trapped inside. Desperately, she leaped from the saddle, almost falling into the water butt at the corner of the eave.

Jessamyn plunged a bucket in the rainwater, struggling to lift it. She flung the water on the blazing doorway. The fire sizzled, emitting a huge blast of smoke, before starting up again. She heaved more buckets of water in a futile effort to put out the fire so she could open the door. If she could just dampen the blaze long enough to get inside, she might rescue the trapped women.

The villagers crowded about, dumbstruck at the sight of fire. Some ran back to their own dwellings to dampen down the thatch before the fierce wind blew the flames the length of the village street.

Jessamyn turned to the gathering crowd, shouting for them to assist her. Several men and women stepped forward to do her bidding, while the rest stood watching the blaze. Furious at their inaction, Jessamyn railed at them, but only succeeded in pulling two more from the enemy ranks to aid her. Together they formed a human bucket chain.

Growing desperate, she sent the blacksmith's lad back to the inn. "Get the soldiers to help," she shouted. "Go as fast as you can."

Obediently Chad took off, his soft-shod feet flying.

The water butt ran dry. Jessamyn sent men to the stream at the end of the garden to fetch more water. This new source of water took precious time to draw, and the fire gained rapidly on them. The blaze around the door had died down, though now the entire roof was roaring, great tongues of orange flames leaping into the sky. Smoke billowed around them, choking lungs and burning eyes, making it almost impossible to see.

Not wanting to take any men off the bucket brigade, Jessamyn took a firelog and tried to batter open the charred door. It wouldn't budge. Agnes must have barred the door.

"Here, lad, give that to me," commanded a man at her elbow. Through billows of smoke, Jessamyn saw a tall figure in a dark cloak. Not waiting for her to obey, the man wrenched the log from her arms and began to batter the door. Other men came to his assistance, and together they put their shoulders against the door.

Suddenly, the door gave way under their combined weight, pitching them inside, where they landed in a heap on the floor of the burning house. Coughing and choking in the confusion of smoke and flame, the men scrambled up.

"Does anyone live here, lad?" the commander asked her, as he grasped Jessamyn's arm and yanked her to her feet.

"An old widow and her daughter."

"Are you sure? I can't see a damned thing in this smoke."

"I heard them screaming when I got here. They must be inside somewhere."

A man shouted that he had found someone when he stumbled over a bundle of rags on the floor. Others came to his aid, and they were soon dragging Agnes and Maeven's inert forms outside, into the fresh air. The house blazed ever more fiercely as the wind whipped the flames and a shouted warning that the roof spars were about to go sent everyone bolting to safety.

In the ensuing mad scramble, Jessamyn was nearly trampled underfoot. Safe outside she leaned against an apple sapling beside the house, dodging the blazing splinters of wood and pieces of burning thatch raining down around her.

"Where's the lad?"

Jessamyn recognized the man who had first come to her aid.

"There you are, lad. The old woman's still alive. I'm not sure about the other one. She's been hit on the head."

Jessamyn ran after him. A crowd of villagers were crouched over the two bundles of rags on the ground. Agnes was stirring. Maeven had a huge bruise spreading from her temple across one eye and down her cheek.

Kneeling, Jessamyn felt Maeven's wrist, then her neck, where she detected a faint pulse.

"She's still alive. Let's get them to the castle. Will you help?"

The man nodded, rubbing his sooty face on his sleeve. Sweat trickled over his brow, forming grotesque patterns in the soot. He sent several of his men back to the inn for a wagon.

When they found Agnes still alive, the villagers backed away. No mortal could have survived such a blaze. They were even more convinced that she was a witch. Without a word, they melted away to their homes, leaving Jessamyn to tend the injured women. When she realized she could expect no aid from the villagers, Jessamyn became so angry that her hands shook as she smoothed back Agnes's straggling gray hair and cleansed her face with the corner of her cloak.

Jessamyn looked back at the burning house, its blackened roof gaunt against the sky. All Agnes's treasures were gone. That charred, smoking wreck was all she had left of her life. Rage, directed toward the others for their superstition and senseless jealousy, roared through her, bringing tears of anger to her hazel eyes. Jessamyn dashed away the moisture, unthinkingly tossing back the hood of her cloak.

A few minutes later the wagon arrived. She could hear the man in charge giving his men directions. The serving girl had said that he was a gentleman, yet he did not dress as one. Instead of fine silk or velvet, he wore a dark cloth doublet beneath a worn leather jack, his traveling cloak reaching to the tops of his hide boots.

"All right, lad, which way?" The man stopped speaking to stare down at Jessamyn in shock. "By God, you're not a lad!" he muttered, his gaze on her thickly coiled bright hair falling in plaits down her back. Catching himself, his voice turned gruff when he said, "Well, girl, then which way? Where do we cross the river?"

"There's a safe crossing nearby. I'll show you."

The man held her cob's reins. Ned had been jealously guarding Merlin throughout the turmoil and now he stood growling, wary of this stranger.

After seeing that Agnes and Maeven were carefully lifted inside the wagon where a makeshift bed had been made amidst the kegs and boxes, Jessamyn mounted her horse. Pulling her hood back over her hair, she hoped no one else was aware of her gender change.

Waving to the others to follow, Jessamyn moved forward, leading the party along the village street to the river.

A small crowd, comprised of villagers, the innkeeper and the other travelers, had gathered outside the inn. The lady and her women clustered in the doorway, out of the wind, curious about the cause of all the excitement. As the wagon drew abreast, the blue-eyed lady called out, asking where they were going.

Answering her in Welsh, Jessamyn's rescuer commanded the ladies to follow them to the castle. At least that's what Jessamyn thought he said. It seemed strange that the captain of these men-at-arms should be speaking in such a familiar manner to his lady.

Riding ahead of the others, Jessamyn went down to the water's edge. The wind whipped the river into gray waves that cascaded in frothing torrents over the boulders. She showed the men where to cross, waiting until the wagon was safely mid-stream before she went on ahead, sending up a great spray of water as she struggled through the current to reach the opposite bank.

Movement and fluttering color on the battlements warned her that Curlew's sentries were alerted. It would be well for her to ride on ahead; she did not want any unpleasant incidents marring this mercy mission. The sight of so many mounted men and wagons would naturally be cause for alarm.

Motioning for the others to stop, Jessamyn rode forward, shouting a greeting to the soldiers who manned the gatehouse battlements. Though the men were surprised to see her with strangers, there was no mistaking their lady, or her horse and dog. Reluctantly, they lowered the drawbridge. Until recently, the bridge had been kept down during the day; but recent concern over the warlike climate had made this new defensive measure wise.

"They are friends," Jessamyn shouted to Simon, whose grizzled head poked curiously around the small door cut in the large one.

"Who be they, lady?"

Nonplussed, Jessamyn shrugged. She had not bothered to ask. Turning, she cantered back to the captain.

"Who seeks entry?" she asked, unconsciously using the official demand.

"Lord Rhys of Trevaron and the Lady Eluned Glynne," the man replied gruffly, his voice carrying to the men on the battlements. As he spoke his gaze roved over the walls, his hand hovering about the knives in his belt.

Uncomfortably, Jessamyn noticed several of his men had already unslung their bows, preparing to defend themselves if need be.

"The garrison's understandably tense because of the recent fighting. Don't worry, you're safe with me," she said, giving what she hoped was a reassuring smile. These troops were a little too hot-headed to suit her. If one of them let fly, she'd be caught in the middle of a pitched battle. "Order your men to show more caution."

He blinked at her sharp, authorative command, began to take issue with it, then reconsidered. Swiftly he gave his men a hand signal and their bows were lowered.

Jessamyn clattered ahead over the drawbridge. Along the causeway, the rumbling wagons and clopping hooves made such a racket that it echoed back tenfold from the stone walls.

"It's old Agnes. Surely you must have seen the fire," Jessamyn explained tersely when Simon planted himself firmly in the middle of the doorway, his grizzled face set.

"Agnes?" he questioned, watching the approaching troops over her shoulder. "What's she got to do with it?"

"Someone set fire to her house. These men were passing through the village and they helped put out the fire and rescue Agnes. The least we can do is to show them hospitality."

Duly chastised, Simon stood aside and waved the troops inside the ward. When they had spotted the fire, followed soon after by the appearance of armed men, the castle garrison had naturally assumed they were about to be attacked. Since Lord Walter had taken to his bed, as Captain of the Guard, Simon was in charge. Assuming that these soldiers were responsible for the fire, he had intended to fire a warning volley when they reached the causeway. That was the plan until he had seen their lady riding with the strangers.

Simon rubbed his gray beard, uneasily contemplating the thirty well-armed men. By their speech, he had discovered they were Welsh and therefore to be considered dangerous. Whether Lady Jessamyn believed them to be friends or not, he was determined to keep a close watch on them.

Agnes and Maeven were carried indoors.

Aware that some of the servants had relatives in the village who might have revealed their suspicion that Agnes was a witch, Jessamyn chose her most trustworthy women to nurse the injured.

William Rhees, the castle steward, bustled outside to greet the travelers, his face flushed with importance. He formally offered the castle's hospitality for the night.

"We thank you, but we'd expected to break our journey with kinfolk. Gwyneth of Trevaron lives hereabouts, does she not?"

Unsure how to answer that question, the steward turned appealingly to Jessamyn, who was instructing a groom to rub down Merlin.

When she heard the question, Jessamyn stopped in surprise. Of course—Lord Rhys of Trevaron. She had not paid close enough attention to the name before to make the association. Though the connection was probably distant, knowing they were even remotely related to her mother's people made her warm even further to the Welshmen.

"This was Gwyneth of Trevaron's home. Though I don't remember her ever mentioning a Lord Rhys."

It was his turn to be surprised. "*Was* her home? She's dead then?"

"Yes . . . several years ago."

"I'm sorry. Of course, we hadn't heard. I didn't know the actual name of the castle where she lived, just that it was in this area. She probably never knew about me. I'm nephew to her brother's wife."

"Well, Lord Rhys, now that you are at the right place, we'll ask you again—will you accept Curlew's hospitality for the night?"

He smiled down at her, the change in his face startling.

Jessamyn caught her breath. The sternness, the hardened mouth, the grim visage melted, as if by magic. He appeared ten years younger.

"Tell your mistress we'll be pleased to accept her hospitality, girl. See if she can make some suitable arrangements for the Lady Eluned and her women, will you?"

"Of course, my lord. I'll tell the mistress to do just that."

Jessamyn turned away, uncomfortable beneath his piercing gaze. This was the first time they had actually looked closely at each other. And when they made eye contact she wished they had not. Lord Rhys made her uneasy. It was not an unpleasant sensation, far from it. When she looked into his dark eyes she felt deeply disturbed. That slow smile which had curved his generous mouth and brought a sparkle to his eyes was the cause of this unusual emotion. When they had spoken, his hand brushed her shoulder in a fleeting gesture of friendship, creating an unexpected sensation of warmth. Jessamyn had quickly stepped away from him.

She marched inside the castle. Jessamyn was glad of the gloom because her cheeks glowed with color. The cold was responsible for that, she reminded herself. The man had stared at her so insolently that she smarted with indignation to recall it. His attitude had definitely changed once he discovered she was not a lad. Thinking her some easy kitchen wench, he probably intended to lure her to his bed. Gleefully, she contemplated his shock when he discovered his mistake. There would be quite a surprise in store for Lord Rhys of Trevaron.

Chapter Three

Darkness fell early in November.

The torches had been lit for hours when Jessamyn finally came from her chamber. She paused at the bend of the stairs to glance at her reflection in the polished steel disk which served as a mirror.

Tonight, she had taken unusual pains over her appearance. Naturally, fighting the fire had necessitated bathing and washing her hair, she told herself, yet it had not demanded the half-cup of precious essence of roses that she had added to the water. She knew that the nicety had been solely to impress the Welshman. Her cheeks flushed at the reminder.

The light from a nearby sconce added gleaming bronze highlights to her thickly plaited hair. She had even wound pearls and blue ribbons through her plaits before firmly anchoring the coils over her ears with bone pins. The blue satin ribbon fillet about her head matched the deep sapphire of her gown. This was her very best gown, sewn from material brought from York. The figured velvet sur-coat worn over a long-sleeved blue silk gown was trimmed with silver ribbon. The luxurious fabric made her feel like a queen. This garment was so special that she had worn it only twice before, Cur-lew Castle not lending itself to lavish festivities.

The reflection which peered anxiously back at her showed the strain of recent days. Jessamyn held her mouth wide to relax the tension in her jaw before carefully composing her full pink lips into a charming smile. Though she was not quite sure of the source of her tension, had she been wholly honest with herself, she would have admit-ted Lord Rhys of Trevaron was a major factor in the emotion. Jessamyn's large hazel eyes looked black in the polished mirror. She quickly smoothed her thick brows in a futile effort to minimize them, aware that fashionable ladies plucked their brows.

"Ready at last, are you?"

She turned to find her brother waiting for her at the foot of the stairs. In honor of their unexpec-ted guests, Walter too had dressed in his best—a saffron velvet gown over red-and-white-striped footed hose. A decorated gold belt was slung low on his hips. Because of his crippled leg, Walter often wore far older styles than were usual for someone of his youth. The fashionable short doublets and skin-tight hose so popular with the young drew too much attention to his disability.

"Shall we go into the Hall?" Jessamyn asked, bit-ing her lips to redden them.

"What's all this commotion for—wearing your best, bathing, washing your hair. Anyone would think the king himself had come to sup."

"I fought a fire, Walter. I was covered with soot and ash," she explained tersely, annoyed by her brother's attitude. "Besides, it's only hospitable to present our best to guests."

"Aye, I have no quarrel with hospitality, but must it include the best wine and the best food, too?"

"I'm serving wine only at the lord's table. Would you have them think we eat like peasants?" she hissed, in an undertone as they moved closer to the Great Hall.

"I don't particularly care what the Welshmen think. I'm more concerned with the expense of entertaining them."

"They rescued Agnes and Maeven, put out the blaze—surely we owe them something."

"Bread and ale in the courtyard would have been well enough for me. They'll eat us out of house and home."

"Not to worry, dearest. Remember, Sir Ralph will be arriving before the holytide laden with gifts for us," Jessamyn reminded Walter sweetly as they stepped inside the Great Hall.

"Bitch," Walter muttered under his breath, yet loudly enough for her to hear.

At their approach, the guests at the high table glanced up. Lord Rhys and his two lieutenants stood to greet the lord and lady of Curlew Castle.

"Welcome to Curlew," Walter said, extending his hand as he limped up the steps to the dais. "I am Walter Dacre, lord of Curlew, and this is my sister, Lady Jessamyn."

He took great pains to conceal it, but she was too quick for him. Jessamyn saw Lord Rhys draw in his breath in a strangled gasp when he recognized her. His gaze was fixed on her face and she felt a glow creeping into her cheeks. Wanting to hide her emotion, Jessamyn quickly curtsied to him and to the beauteous Lady Eluned, whose greeting was not as rewarding. She betrayed no recognition at all.

"Thank you for extending your hospitality to us," Lady Eluned said in a sharp, almost shrill voice. "In this remote area, accommodations are usually very primitive."

"Yes, they do tend to be," Walter agreed amiably, his lip curling scornfully as he glanced over their female guests. Pretty, but of little consequence. Too fluttery and senseless by far. Then he smiled as he realized he was comparing them to his sister, who could hardly be called typical. In fact, the very traits these women exhibited were exactly what he always had wished Jessamyn would display, the better to attract a husband. Remorseful, he took Lady Eluned's white, seemingly boneless hand, and pressed it to his mouth.

"We are most honored to have you sup with us, my lady."

Eluned smiled charmingly, her porcelain pale cheeks flushing prettily. She fluttered her long eyelashes whilst she quickly took note of Walter's youth, his good looks, and his unfortunate physical deformity.

Jessamyn wore a fixed smile, anxious to avoid Lord Rhys, whose dark gaze followed her every move. She noted the red fringed cloth on the table, the fire well stoked, the horn and pewter serving pieces in place. It was all as she had ordered. Pleased, she turned about and signaled the servants to bring out the food and wine.

At such short notice, the feast would not be sumptuous, but it would be adequate, going well beyond Curlew's usual fare. The meal began with a fragrant vegetable pottage, thickened with day-old bread. The huge, steaming tureen went first to the high table before being passed to the men-at-arms seated at trestles lower down the Hall, far from the fire's warmth. A keg of ale was tapped for the men; at the lord's table burgundy was served.

A crackling brown haunch of venison followed, along with dishes of spiced meat and fish pasties, baked sturgeon and salted herring accompanied by loaves of soft white bread, baked especially for the feast and still fragrant from the oven. Dessert offered a choice between cinnamon spiced apple flummery and a pink almond milk mold.

Walter was seated in the center of the table at the high chair, his back to the fire. Lord Rhys sat on his right hand, the Lady Eluned on his left. Jessamyn was glad she had not been seated next to the dark-eyed Welshman. As it was, her appetite was not nearly as good as she had expected. She was far too conscious of his admiring glances to enjoy her meal.

Though the men spoke about armaments, provisioning the garrison, and the state of the land, Walter did not ask the Welshman whom he supported in the current struggle. Jessamyn was thankful for small favors: she did not want to become embroiled in a political argument. Doubtless the man would fight for Glyndwr if it came to a choice. Better for him not to question where lay the loyalty of Curlew.

When the meal was almost finished, several of Lord Rhys's men came forward to sing ballads and play harp music. Jessamyn was delighted by the unexpected treat. They had never had a minstrel at Curlew. Their only chance of hearing such entertainment was to offer hospitality to any wandering minstrel who would sing in exchange for a meal and a bed on the rushes beside the hearth. The two young men began to sing, their voices blending in a beautiful, pure melody. Now she recalled that the Welsh were sometimes scornfully called "the singers" by some of the English lords. Whenever they marched, or fought, or worked, they invariably broke into song, blending their voices in harmony until the hillsides echoed with their music.

Quickly bored by the entertainment, Walter excused himself. He had never had any interest in music. He stared daggers at Jessamyn when she sat unmoving, enchanted by the beauty of the song, for he had expected her to follow his lead. She purposely refused to meet his angry glare. This was the most pleasant evening she had spent at Curlew in a long time. She was not going to exchange it for her cold chamber just because Walter was bored.

To her dismay, Jessamyn found that her brother's departure was a signal for Lord Rhys to voice his unspoken questions. When she moved to a bench closer to the singers, he followed her. For the first time, she was forced to meet him eye-to-eye and engage in conversation.

"Why did you not tell me you were lady here?"

"It was more amusing to let you think me a serving wench."

"Not even a wench—at first I thought you were a lad. Lady Jessamyn, I apologize if I didn't treat you with proper respect. You must understand, a woman who rides abroad dressed like a boy must expect to be treated as one."

She smiled, trying to stay attentive to the music. How she wished he would go away. Though if she were honest, she must admit she had craved his attention; unfortunately, it had turned her foolishly dumbstruck. All the brilliant conversation she had silently rehearsed seemed to have flown away. Instead, she could only smile up at him, quickly dropping her gaze when the expression in his warm, dark eyes turned increasingly more intimate.

"Will you forgive me for my rudeness?"

"Of course. No offense was taken."

"This is such a pleasant surprise. I was expecting to sup with a young lord and his spinster sister, not with such a vision of beauty."

For the first time in her life that she could recall, Jessamyn blushed deep red. In horror, she clapped her hands to her flaming cheeks, as if to erase the embarrassing color. This was ridiculous!

"I thank you for your compliment, my lord," she mumbled, her voice cracking. "I wasn't trying to deceive you this afternoon. Soldiers have been seen in the area, and I thought it wiser to play the boy."

"And a charming boy you make," he added with a grin. "A wise move, though you were ill-advised to ride alone. You should have taken someone with you. Where were your servants?"

"I'd only been tending old Agnes. On such a short ride, I usually don't take servants with me."

His dark brows raised. "How independent of you."

His tone was not condemning, merely amused. She swallowed and finally allowed herself to look fully at him, not expecting the bolt of excitement which shot through her veins when he returned her gaze. She swallowed again and clenched her hands in her skirts.

Tonight, he was a far more polished and elegant figure than when he had come to her rescue during the afternoon. His green velvet doublet was plain, but of good quality. The bright green made his thick, curly hair appear even blacker. In the torchlight, his smoothly tanned skin was golden. His open-collared white shirt emphasized his strong throat where the smooth skin disappeared inside his doublet. A sudden urge to touch his exposed throat, to slide her hand inside the intimate warmth beneath his shirt, made Jessamyn start in alarm. What was the matter with her? Such thoughts had never entered her head before. Nor had she ever before studied a man's mouth with such intensity, imagining what it would feel like to have his firm, warm lips pressed against hers, or to feel his strong arms slip about her shoulders . . .

She sat straighter on the bench, forcing herself to pay closer attention to the musicians. Not making her task any easier, Lord Rhys settled himself comfortably in a cushioned chair before the hearth, stretching out his long booted legs to the blaze. Inside his black hose his thighs were muscular and well defined; his tall riding boots were so supple and soft that they fit like a second skin. As he laced his hands behind his head, Jessamyn stared at his strong, olive-skinned fingers. His hands were not softly white like Walter's, but nicked and roughened from traveling. How would it feel to be touched by those warm strong hands, to feel his caress against her neck, her face, to have him press the length of his broad-shouldered frame against hers?

Dear Lord, she must be going insane! Jessamyn was relieved when the song ended and a round of applause followed. The minstrels bowed. Next, they played a duet on their small harps. The lovely music rippled through the black raftered hall, echoing off the stone walls. When the piece was finished, the men-at-arms began to call for more familiar tunes and, with their lord's permission, the minstrels left the dais to move amongst the trestles in the body of the Hall.

"Their music is beautiful," Jessamyn said, forcing her voice to sound calm and even, though her heart raced wildly when he smiled at her.

"Yes, they're skilled musicians. Good fighting men, too."

"They're not minstrels?"

"In a way, but they're also bowmen from the Llys Valley, brothers who enjoy making music for our entertainment. We've several others among us who are equally gifted."

Jessamyn was amazed. No wonder the Welsh were called "the singers".

"You seem surprised! We Celts have an inborn love of singing and music . . ."

"And also of warm beds and soft mattresses," Lady Eluned interrupted him. "Am I to expect such luxury here, or is that too much to ask of so small a fortress?" She had come to stand beside them, her scarlet gown and fur-trimmed surcoat a bright splash of color in the gloom. Uttering a weary sigh, Eluned ran her slender hand across her brow, feigning fatigue.

Though the woman had not actually insulted her, Jessamyn understood that some insult was implied. She found her temper rising in a renewal of the mixed emotions she had felt when first she saw this lovely noblewoman. Though undeniably beautiful, Lady Eluned was cold and demanding, suggesting that perhaps her beauty was merely skin deep.

"Your chamber has been prepared with all the normal comforts. It formerly belonged to my mother. I'm sure you'll find the bed adequate and the fire well-stoked."

A flicker of a smile played across Lord Rhys's face at her sharp reply. "There, Eluned, you have your answer."

"With some insolence to boot."

"No greater insolence was intended by my answer, lady, than was given in your question."

Lady Eluned gasped in indignation, her delicate features coloring. "So, you dare call me insolent . . .

55

me! I'm not used to being treated so—Rhys?" She spun about, as if expecting him to leap to her defense.

"Lady Jessamyn has answered your question. Leave it at that."

"Oh, what can I expect from you! A pretty face, a beckoning smile—you men are all the same."

"Enough!" He rose quickly, his face set, his voice gruff. "If you're tired, I suggest you go to your chamber."

"Tired, insulted, and my throat's on fire. If the room's not warm enough, I'll likely catch my death of cold. Then we'll never arrive in Chester for Christmas. My sister will be celebrating a funeral instead of. . . ."

Tired of her whining monologue, abruptly, he signaled for Lady Eluned's women to come to her assistance.

Mistress Lloyd, her chief attendant, bustled forward and draped a wool blanket around her lady's narrow shoulders.

"Traveling's unpleasant for one of such sensibilities," the older woman snapped angrily. Her dress indicated that she, too, was of noble station.

Raising his hands in a gesture of conciliation, Lord Rhys shrugged. "Mistress Lloyd, this journey was undertaken at your mistress's request. I had naught to do with the arrangements. I'm merely here to provide protection. No one pretended traveling in mid-November would be pleasant. Cold is a necessary evil. Your lady, and you, also, should be most grateful to Lady Jessamyn for showing you such hospitality, or we all might be sleeping in the wagons."

"Oh, a man can't be expected to understand our problems, Lloyd," Lady Eluned dismissed, her mouth tightening.

"I understand far more than you give me credit for," he countered. "And if you can't show better manners to your hostess, then I suggest you go
to bed. Perchance tomorrow your mood will have
sweetened."

Lady Eluned's deep blue eyes rounded in shock,
tears glimmering instantly in their depths. Hand to
her heart, she gasped piteously, "Rhys, how cruel
you can be! Ladies are frail. We cannot be treated
like fighting men."

"Good night, Eluned. Sleep well. We'll continue
our journey tomorrow."

"My lady's throat may be too inflamed for that,"
snapped the older woman as she led her charge
away.

"If you wish, I can mix a potion to soothe your
ills," Jessamyn offered, stifling her annoyance. "I've
many remedies."

"That's kind of you," Lady Eluned said stiffly,
sniffling and blinking back tears which had been
shed in vain. "As ill as I'm beginning to feel, I'll
probably be glad of your expertise."

With that the five women swished away. Jessamyn
quickly directed a servant to show them to their
rooms in the south tower. She was glad to see their
backs.

"Let me apologize for Eluned's behavior," Lord
Rhys said gruffly, sighing with relief as the women's
brightly colored gowns disappeared in the gloom.

"There's no need. It's none of your doing," Jessamyn said, smiling at him. "I'm aware Curlew's not
the most luxurious of residences, and the lady's tired
and unwell."

"You're a very generous soul."

"I also have to apologize. I never thanked you for
helping me fight the fire. Without you and your
men, Agnes and her daughter would surely have

57

died. Poor old woman, they set fire to her house because they think she's a witch. Of all the superstitious nonsense."

"Is she?"

His question took her back. "Of course not. Surely you don't believe such superstition. The church . . ."

"I know what the church teaches. I also know there are things not easily explained away by religion. As there's great power for good in the world, there's also great power for evil. Do you not agree?"

"Yes, admittedly there's evil in the world, though just because someone's cow sickens isn't cause to supect witchcraft."

He grinned, seeing that she was determined to argue the case.

"Ah, I never expected to be having such a serious discussion with a beautiful woman in the firelight," he said, his tone dropping low and inviting. "There are far better pastimes for a cold November night."

She stiffened, immediately on guard. "Such *pastimes* are not looked upon kindly in this household, my lord."

Far from being put out by her stern tone, he threw back his head and laughed heartily at her indignation.

"A prude to boot. Who would have thought it, lady, and you so beautiful." He shook his head in mock dismay.

His bantering tone was quickly rousing her anger. In fact, everything he did, or said, seemed to affect her emotions. Jessamyn wanted to strike him, to vent her feelings. The very heat of her emotion surprised her when she considered that only an hour earlier, she had nursed far gentler thoughts about him.

She stood, determined to have an end to this thoroughly confusing evening. She was dismayed to find

58

her legs trembling, purely out of aggravation, she was sure.

Lord Rhys stood very close, his face in dark shadow, for his back was to the fire. Without speaking he looked down at her, smiling, though not in amusement. *That* she could have dealt with. Jessamyn swallowed uncomfortably. Though it was normal for him to be a head taller than she, tonight even their discrepancy in height annoyed her.

"We lead a very quiet life. You come from a different country, so perhaps our ways here seem strange . . ."

"Oh, lady, spare me the lecture," he snapped, his smile fading. "I'm a Welshman, it's true, yet I'm not fresh out of the hills. I've lived in London, studied at Oxford. I'm no hayseed. Your patronization is unwelcome. If you also wish to go to your bed, I'll gladly excuse you."

Indignation, anger, and shame crystalized in a wave of embarrassment as Jessamyn struggled to make amends. "I didn't mean to . . ."

"I know exactly what you meant. I assure you, my men won't approach your women, unless they are invited. We'll be models of decorum. You have my word."

Stiffly she thanked him, feeling there was little left for her to do now but retire to her chamber.

"Good night, then."

"Good night, Lady Jessamyn." He smiled slightly, his hand hovering a moment about her shoulder as if he would touch her, then, changing his mind, he dutifully clasped his hands before him. "Don't be put out by Lady Eluned's lack of manners. She's always led a life of indulgence, never required to do more than her current whim dictated. She's beautiful— but sometimes her beauty's a trial for she uses it like gold to buy her way. I can see that you, on the other hand, are a very different woman."

"Thank you, my lord, for your kind words."

Jessamyn smiled stiffly and turned away. The walk across the Hall seemed endless. The rushes beneath her soft-soled slippers became stumbling blocks as her ankles turned and she tripped over her skirts. She could feel his dark gaze piercing her back and she longed to turn about to see his face. Only at the doorway, which was almost too far away to determine his expression, did she look back. He stood where she had left him before the hearth, his dark head slightly cocked, mouth unsmiling. The disturbing sense of loss she felt at leaving him came as a great surprise. Why? He had mocked her, teased her, argued with her: he admired her. That she knew was fact. Though unaccustomed to men's adoration, Jessamyn was woman enough to instinctively sense when it was given.

Lord Rhys was handsome, intriguing, annoying, infuriating, the more words she found to describe him, the faster she walked. She gritted her teeth, feeling cheated. She had wanted to escape his disturbing presence, yet she had also wanted to stay to enjoy his admiration, his touch . . . his love!

Shocked by the admission, she stopped and leaned against the cold stone wall. In a way, she wished that she had never laid eyes on Lord Rhys of Trevaron. Before his arrival, she had been content. All these disturbing emotions had lain dormant inside her body. Now, by his very presence, he had aroused sensations she had not known existed.

She pushed open the door to her chamber. A fire glowed in the hearth and its welcome warmth spilled forth invitingly. Here, in her turret room, she was safe from that disturbing masculine presence below in the Hall. Jessamyn's face flushed. When she had just pictured him standing before the hearth, she was shocked to realize that she longed to return to him, to allow him to lead her down whatever path he chose.

"I'll undress myself, Mary," she said, her voice unsteady with emotion. The maid curtsied, only too glad to be excused from duty. Jessamyn could not allow another to intrude on such intimate thoughts. She needed time to master her wayward emotions.

Later, she stood in her shift, staring out at the dense black sky, shivering in the draught seeping between the stone wall and the windowframe. This was the only window in the castle, placed in a former arrow slit especially for her by Sir Hugh. He had brought the precious horn window all the way from Shrewsbury by pack horse for Jessamyn's chamber. From there, she could see across the river to the Welsh hills, watch the trees bud in the spring, the leaves turn yellow and finally fall to the ground. And from there she had dreamed, content to be shut off in her own private world. No longer. Now she wanted to live in the real world, to share it with him!

The tears which had begun to trickle slowly down her face could not have been tears of self-pity. She wept at the memory of her father. Only in her heart did Jessamyn admit the truth. Her tears were shed for something she wanted but could not have. She wept for a taste of love and excitement in the arms of Lord Rhys of Trevaron!

Shocked, she turned from the window. If he were here tonight, if he took her in his arms and kissed her, would the ache in her heart be stilled?

Jessamyn picked up her beloved romance, studying the colored pictures by candlelight. Could she picture herself and handsome Lord Rhys in the secret garden? No. Abruptly she closed the book. Far from soothing her, tonight the book's illustrations were a shocking reminder that all the women in these pictures looked like Eluned Glynne. A woman like Lady Eluned was a suitable mate for a noble- man, not someone who fought fires and rode abroad dressed like a boy.

Tears of self-pity and denial flowed from her eyes until finally Jessamyn gave in, fighting them no longer. Presently, she felt better. The tears were long overdue. She had not cried like this since Father died.

Nestled in her bed, warmed by a pan of hot coals, she listened to the howling wind. Rain sluiced against the stonework. Jessamyn slid lower inside her covers, pulling a feather pillow into her arms, nestling close as if she embraced a lover. Finally she drifted to sleep. Jessamyn entered the secret garden, willing handsome Lord Rhys to court her with laughter and smiles beneath the rose-covered trellis.

Chapter Four

"Damn, what a night! I thought the heavens had opened and we'd all drown," Walter remarked as he looked up from the table, where he had been going over the castle accounts with William Rhees.

"Yes, I heard the storm," Jessamyn commented absently, glancing around the Hall for their guests—or more specifically, Lord Rhys. This morning, she was confident that she had overcome the baffling affliction which had plagued her the previous night, which had probably been caused by overtiredness, or the distress of the day's dramatic events. If he stood before her, she was confident she would be able to speak to him without any change in emotion. Some of his men-at-arms sat talking amongst themselves, but of him there was no sign.

"Where are our guests?" she was finally forced to ask.

"Lying abed, I suppose. Thank heavens they'll be gone today, unless the roads are impassable," Walter added, recalling the night's storm. He looked glumly at the castle steward. "Is that what you were trying to tell me earlier?" he asked sheepishly.

"Yes, my lord, but you wouldn't. . . ."

"I know, I know." Walter scowled as he absently poked old Ned with his soft-soled boot. "Can we afford to keep them another day, providing my sister doesn't insist on treating them like royalty?"

"Lord Rhys has offered us supplies from his wagons."

"How very generous of him," Walter scoffed, glancing towards the Welshmen who kept to themselves at a single table.

"I should have thought that offer would please you," Jessamyn snapped, out of patience with her brother's peevish attitude. "First you say we can't afford to keep them, then, when they offer to pay their way, you're still not happy."

"Sister dear, I'll be happy only when the Welshman and his troops are on the road to Chester. Would you have us taken over by them? You're so worried we'll be overrun. Have you given any thought to that possibility?"

"No, I haven't."

"As it is we'll be lucky if we can come through the week without the Welsh dragon flying from the ramparts. The man could easily claim the castle for Glyndwr, because, fools that we are, we simply opened our doors to him and his men."

"Oh, have sense, will you, Walt."

Jessamyn went to the hearth where she crouched to rub Ned's ears.

"Why are you so taken with the man?" Walter asked sharply. "I suppose he's your idea of a knight in shining armor, bowling you off your feet."

"What if he is? I'd think you'd be pleased. You considered me unmarriageable a couple of days ago."

"Unmarriageable, not unbedable—there's a big difference."

Jessamyn chose not to reply. He was right. There was a difference, only at this point she did not care to debate it.

"I think you're jealous of him," she snapped, coming back to the table, where she spread a slice of barley bread with fresh churned butter and thick yellow honey.

"Why should I be jealous of some Welshman?" Walter said scornfully.

But the deepening flush on his cheeks told Jessamyn that she had been right. It was unkind of her to point out Walter's failing and she patted his arm remorsefully.

Just then, the Welshman in question came inside the Hall. He strode towards the High table, stopping to greet his men as he passed.

Walter and Jessamyn exchanged polite greetings with him.

"They tell me the road's awash," he said tersely, clearly annoyed that they must delay their journey. "For how long does the water usually lie?"

"Not long. A couple of days—unless we get more rain."

"It's sleeting now."

"Or snow," Walter added glumly. Dear Lord, the Welshman might still be here come Christmastide. What would he say then to Sir Ralph, who would not take kindly to having one of Glyndwr's probable lieutenants under their roof. "There's an alternate route over higher ground. Out of your way, but you can pass there. My sister knows it. She'll show you the way."

Jessamyn began to protest, but Walter glared fiercely at her, shaking his head, so she held her tongue.

"Yes," she agreed pleasantly, "if you wish, I can show you. We'll ride there after we've supped. My brother finds riding difficult," she added, as Lord Rhys looked askance at Walter so warmly ensconced beside the hearth while suggesting his sister brave the elements to show them the new route.

"I see. We'll take some men with us—not many, we don't want to make the natives nervous," he added with a grin, well-aware their presence was not met with great joy.

Jessamyn smiled, thrilled that, so far, she had managed to maintain her emotional distance from this man. His appearance was just as appealing this morning, though he was wearing his workaday clothes of worn leather jack over a dark gray doublet and hose.

They made polite small talk. There was still no sign of the ladies. Jessamyn washed down her honey and bread with a cup of mulled ale, suggesting Lord Rhys do the same. When he bent over the hearth to warm his flagon with a poker, she was amazed to see Ned's tail thumping slowly in pleasure.

"Ned seems to like you."

"Oh, so that's his name. Yes, the old fellow was my companion for a few hours last night. We shared the storm together, here beside the hearth."

Jessamyn hated the fact that she somehow felt betrayed by her canine friend. Usually, Ned befriended no one with such open-hearted trust. To her amazement, he rolled on his back, big legs waving, tail thumping whilst Lord Rhys rubbed his belly and laughed in amusement at the old dog's antics.

"I'll dress for riding, if you'll excuse me, my lord," Jessamyn announced sharply, to which he merely nodded and settled beside the hearth with his cup.

The clothing she had worn the previous day was not yet dry from washing. Jessamyn took from her clothes chest a homespun green wool skirt and bodice. Quickly, she laced the garments over her cream wool shift. It was so cold in her chamber, she wondered how it would feel to be riding through the countryside. She would probably freeze. Out of the chest she took her warmest surcoat of purple wool trimmed with rabbit fur. Fortunately, her boots were dry and she eased them over her wool stockings. Her heaviest cloak was lined with rabbit fur; there was a gray wool hood to match.

Jessamyn picked up her gloves of butter yellow leather before hurrying back downstairs. Though not luxurious, her clothing had not been ill-chosen. The colors complemented her peachy complexion and deep auburn hair, bringing warmth to her skin and a sparkle to her eyes.

When she went inside the Hall, Jessamyn found Lord Rhys already booted and spurred, his heavy traveling cloak swinging about his broad shoulders. He had been waiting for her.

"The horses are already saddled, Lady Jessamyn. I took the liberty of ordering that done," he explained, as he strode towards her. Four of his men followed.

Walter barely looked up as they left, glad that he need no longer entertain their guest. He pulled up a chessboard and motioned for William Rhees to join him. If he were extremely fortunate, maybe that whining flock of women would keep to their rooms until departure time.

"Play, William, it's your move," he said.

On their way to the stables, Jessamyn stopped by the room off the kitchens where Maeven and Agnes were being tended. Neither of the women opened their eyes when she spoke to them; Maeven lay so still that Jessamyn began to wonder if she was still alive.

67

Tassie, who was acting as their nursemaid, shook her head doubtfully when questioned.

"Now the mother be coming round nicely, spoke to me last night, she did. T'other one's a different kettle of fish."

Jessamyn assured her she would come back to see them on her return. Just the sight of the two women rekindled her anger towards the villagers. She had not yet devised a fitting punishment for those responsible for the fire, but she would be sure to find one before much longer.

As if he read her mind, Lord Rhys suggested, "You should have them rebuild her home. She'll need a place to live, unless you intend to keep her here."

Jessamyn glanced up at him in surprise. "That's a good idea. That should take weeks. It'll keep their memories fresh and be useful to boot.

He strode ahead of her into the ward.

Jessamyn realized that the true test of her reaction to this Welshman lay ahead. Though he was bringing some of his men, for the next few hours they would ride together. Though she had no wish to return to the bantering intimacy of the previous night, neither did she want to complete their journey in stony silence.

Lord Rhys politely offered his laced hands to help her to mount. He knelt on the damp cobbles, his face upturned to hers. He looked so much younger and more vulnerable that Jessamyn felt her stomach lurch and her heart began to quicken in excitement. So perfect was his bone structure, his strong features appeared to have been chiseled from stone. His high cheekbones, strongly pronounced nose and a determined chin were softened by firmly inviting lips and large, heavily lashed dark eyes. He smiled as she fitted her foot into his laced hands. A mounting block stood before the stable, yet he had purposely led the horse into the center of the ward, as if he wished to play the groom.

"Remember . . . my name's Rhys."

Rhys. Jessamyn repeated the name to herself as she sat in the saddle, adjusting her cloak and skirts to keep out the wind. Should she extend the same courtesy to him? Perhaps he did not expect to be asked to call her Jessamyn.

The noisy cavalcade clattered over the draw-bridge. Instead of turning back along the riverbank, Jessamyn led the riders east, following a narrow track skirting tangled elder thickets. The track was marshy after the rain, and the horses' hooves sank in the mud. The leaden sky was darkly forbidding behind the castle battlements. Even the curlews were silent, though a few gulls circled and screeched as they rode by.

The churning river spilled over its banks. White-caps broke against boulders and drooping sallow willows. The marshy water meadows were soon left behind. The track led higher, until finally they overlooked the highway to the north, where water lay gray and sullen across the road. The strong north wind tugged at their clothing, stealing inside the smallest gap. Jessamyn was relieved when the road finally changed direction, turning out of the direct blast. Here, straggling oakwoods shielded them from the elements. The night's storm had lashed the trees, stripping autumn leaves from their branches to form a sodden carpet beneath the horse's hooves.

"Jessamyn, tell me, how many miles out of our way does this route take us?" Rhys presently asked, drawing close beside her to speak.

"Not more than three, though this road won't be as easy for the wagons," she replied. When he spoke her name in his lilting speech, it sounded almost foreign. Though she had never been fond of the name Jessamyn, he made it seem one of the loveliest names she had ever heard.

They rode on, skirting windswept farms and pastures where cattle huddled out of the wind. At last, another road became visible, threading like a pale ribbon around the rocky, tree-dotted hillside.

Jessamyn reined in.

"Follow that road. It drops over the side of the hill, then sweeps about to cross the river upstream. There's a bridge there that's generally dry."

He nodded, his dark eyes slitted against the wind as he surveyed the surrounding countryside. "What's the settlement called?" he asked, pointing to a huddle of graystone and thatch at the crest of the hill.

"Holly Ridge. There's an inn, though I doubt you'll need to put up there for the night. You should get as far as Carshalton before nightfall, unless the weather turns bad."

Jessamyn stiffened as she felt his hand closing over her arm; the small squeeze of affection he gave her set her nerves jangling.

"You're a godsend to me, Jessamyn Dacre. Now, in return for your good deed, if you promise not to take offense, I've written a few suggestions on how you can better run Curlew."

"Thank you, my lord."

"Rhys."

"Rhys, I admit we do need help, as you probably observed. Why else would you bother to make suggestions. Father always handled the matter of defense, and most other matters as well. Without him the guards are at a loss. Walter's little help on that score."

They turned their mounts back onto the road.

"Why don't we stop at Holly Ridge? My men'd be glad of a warm hearth and something hot to drink."

"The Two Feathers is a reasonable hostelry."

"Excellent. And perhaps, over a cup of ale, you will tell me what makes your brother so damnably churlish."

When they were seated on the oak settle beside the hearth, a trencher of hot bread and gravy and mugs of spiced brew before them, Jessamyn doubted that he had much interest in hearing about Walter's peevishness.

The blazing fire was a welcome sight. Though her woolen clothing was warm, in the first hour the wind had cut through to her flesh. Jessamyn's feet and thighs felt like blocks of ice. Had she been alone, she would have taken off her boots and spread her toes to the blaze.

At his insistence, Jessamyn told Rhys about her father's death, Walter's ailment, and his recent desperate bid to become actual lord of the castle. While they talked, she made an unsettling discovery; the supreme control over which she had prided herself that morning, was gone. Sitting beside him on the oak settle had been her undoing. Whenever he moved and brushed her arm, or more disturbingly, her thigh, the heat from his body kindled a surge of warmth in her limbs which had nothing to do with the fire.

"And now all that's out of the way, tell me why have you no husband?" he said suddenly, leaning his dark head against the corner of the settle. He studied her face, prettily flushed from the warmth and his close proximity.

"Because I never wanted a husband," she declared firmly. "Father suggested betrothing me to a relative, fortunately, naught came of it. I like being free to do as I please."

"So you and your brother will remain lord and lady of Curlew until he takes a wife. What then?"

71

That was something Jessamyn had not considered. She shrugged. "Walter's never shown much interest in marrying. I admit, it's a possibility. If he marries, I suppose I'll continue to be what I am now—his spinster sister."

Rhys laughed heartily at her unflattering description. "Anyone would think you cross-eyed, middle-aged and straight as a stick. You must be kinder to yourself, my sweet."

My sweet! The endearment had probably slipped out unconsciously, yet Jessamyn could not dismiss it so casually. If, for the rest of her life, she could have this man calling her sweet, life would be sweet indeed! Gulping, she quickly squelched that pleasurable thought.

"In fact, Jessamyn, I know a number of men who, had they known such a beauty was locked away in Curlew Castle, would have come courting long ago."

Her heart began to thump erratically. Would he come courting if she encouraged him? Though she had never wanted a husband, if this man offered himself as such, she would definitely consider him— nay, not merely consider—welcome him! Jessamyn's eyes widened at the honest admission. She moved as far away from him as she could to the other end of the settle.

"Husbands don't want women with minds of their own. I'm no malleable little chit who bursts into tears twenty times a day," she announced defiantly, unconsciously trying to errect a barrier to protect herself.

"Do I detect a reference there to Lady Eluned?"

She had to smile, for that was exactly who she had pictured when she made her speech. "She's very beautiful, isn't she? I've a French romance with pictures of ladies like Eluned Glynne. How often I've wished I looked more like that," she revealed in a small voice, unsure whether she should even mention such secrets to him.

Almost without her knowledge, Jessamyn discovered that his hand had slipped about hers. As he laced his warm fingers in hers, her arm was on fire.

"No, Jessamyn Dacre, never envy Eluned. You're unique. Not all men are enraptured by milksops. There are those who like spirit and courage in their women. And your beauty far surpasses hers."

So stunned was she by his speech, she could not answer. Jessamyn grew so deliciously uncomfortable, she could no longer look into the depth of his dark eyes. She stared nervously at their locked hands, enjoying the sight of his hot, strong fingers around hers, studying the smooth back of his olive-skinned hand, where corded veins were visible under the skin.

"And with that, before I overstep my welcome, I think we should set about our return journey," he said abruptly, in an unusually husky voice. Quickly, he disentangled his hand from hers. "Are you ready to leave?"

Swallowing, trying to gather her wits, Jessamyn finally looked up at him, forcing herself to meet his dark gaze. "Yes. If we get home in time, you can load your wagons and make ready for morning while it's still light."

"Strange," he said a few minutes later as they stood at the inn door, surveying the bleak, rain-drenched countryside. "This morning I was angry because the road was washed out. Now . . ." he turned to smile down at her, his mouth softening. "Now, I'd be content to stay here forever."

Giving her no chance to reply, he strode across the innyard and untethered their horses.

His words created a growing warmth inside Jessamyn's body, a warmth which curled from her stomach, stretching languorous as a cat to envelop her limbs.

All those notions she had prided herself upon had been nothing but delusions. Now, the terrible realization that he would be gone tomorrow stabbed sharp as a knife. He would be gone from her life and she would never see him again. She doubted that she would ever travel to the Llys valley where his stronghold lay, nor even to Chester where he would spend the upcoming Christmas feast. They would not meet again. This fact was so devastating, the breath choked in her throat. Today, tonight, would be all she would ever have of him!

The homeward journey was made in relative silence. Jessamyn could find no safe subject to discuss. Whenever he smiled at her, or rode close, so that their knees almost brushed, she was overcome with unexpected emotion.

Rhys told her about his horses and his dogs, never once speaking about his probable involvement with the Welsh patriot, Glyndwr. Jessamyn was glad. She did not want to destroy her illusion that they could become friends, or even more than that.

Her cheeks flushed when she considered him as her lover, and a shiver of delicious anticipation sped along her spine. The sensation was so unexpected, she could hardly believe she had felt it. She had never felt this way before in her life. It was unsettling to no longer be in control of her emotions.

When at last they clattered back inside the castle ward, Jessamyn quickly made her excuses and headed indoors. She needed time to think and she could not do it in his presence. Her disturbing thoughts centered on him and what she intended to do about her current insanity. Could she be falling in love with this man? Impossible. She hardly knew him. Yet her heart ignored such sensible reasoning. When she had glanced back at him one final time before going indoors, her heart had fluttered as she watched him talking to his horse, gently patting the animal's neck.

How tender he could be with animals, a trait strangely at odds with the other side of his character. His face could harden like stone, his dark eyes burn, his mouth set. Thoughts of his mouth led her to imagine what his kiss would feel like and her heart began to leap and thunder at the exciting promise.

"How ridiculous," she said aloud to the dank stone wall, desperate to convince herself it was true. Such romantic thoughts were more suited to flighty peasant girls in the throes of first love than to the lady of Curlew.

But in the sanctuary of her small room, gazing through the greenish tinted glass at the outside world, Jessamyn knew it was far too late to talk herself out of such foolishness. For her, perhaps love was to last one day, two at the most. Was this all she would ever know of it? A smile? A handclasp?

A whole hour had passed before she felt able to venture downstairs to join the others in the Great Hall.

To Jessamyn's surprise, she found the ladies already grouped around the hearth. As usual, their demanding mistress was being cosseted and coddled by her attendants.

Before she had left that morning, Jessamyn had told Alys at the castle infirmary to provide their guests with whatever herbal remedies they required, naming a couple to relieve Lady Eluned's ills. Apparently, the women had availed themselves of her offer. Lady Eluned sat with her feet in a bowl of steaming water; her head was swathed in a linen covering. She alternately sipped a spiced drink and complained to her women about her ills. Yet, despite her indisposition, Jessamyn found, to her irritation, that Eluned Glynne still looked ravishing. The ivory linen cloth was swathed into a fashionable turban about her golden hair, while the unaccustomed color in her flushed face complimented her peach gown and brown, fur-tipped surcoat. Even her long, narrow feet managed to appear dainty, though they were immersed in unappealing brown water.

"So you see, Rhys dearest, I'm absolutely unable to travel for several days, new road or not," she was saying to Rhys as Jessamyn drew near. "You do understand, don't you?"

"Well, naturally I'm disappointed, Eluned. After just damned near freezing for the last couple of hours trying to find us an alternate route, I'm not thrilled by the change. Still, what else can I do? If you're too ill to travel, we must beg further hospitality from our hosts."

Jessamyn stopped beside the dais. He did not sound in the least disappointed; in fact, he sounded pleased not to have to leave tomorrow. Her heart leaped, and she felt blood pounding in her ears as she wondered if his changed mood was because of her. Rhys had confided he would be content to stay forever, and she did not imagine his change of heart was because he found at Curlew such delightful accommodations.

"Oh, Lady Jessamyn, I didn't see you," Eluned Glynne said, smiling wanly at her. "You heard, I suppose?"

Jessamyn nodded, coming to the hearth to warm herself.

"What's the nature of your illness, lady?"

"Nature of it? How should I know? All I know is that I feel dreadful. Traveling is always such a trial. I probably won't feel well enough to take to the road before next week, at the earliest."

Then a most surprising thing took place. When she glanced up, Jessamyn caught Rhys's eye. He was standing behind Lady Eluned, his face grave; yet, when she looked at him, he grinned and winked at her. Flustered, Jessamyn looked away, her cheeks growing hot. Was he telling her Eluned's ills were only in her imagination, or was it more that he wanted to convey his pleasure at being able to spend more time with her?

She turned away, overwhelmed by the possibilities this change presented. Desperately she looked about for Walter, needing someone to save her from herself. Her brother was nowhere to be seen.

"Where's Lord Walter?" she asked the serving woman, who had brought fresh water for milady's footbath.

"Gone to his room. Needed a bit of quiet, I expect," the woman confided with a grin.

Thank you, Walt, Jessamyn thought angrily. Obviously no one was going to help save her from herself.

"Lady Jessamyn, perhaps you'll show me that book we spoke about," Rhys suggested. He offered her a pillow for her back, for she had perched uncomfortably on the edge of the settle beside the hearth.

"The book," she repeated, caught off guard, trying to arrange her thoughts into a more normal pattern. "Oh, the romance . . . 'tis up in my room."

"Oh, then, some other time," he said. Turning, he snapped his fingers for Ned's attention. The big dog had been resting his head against his mistress's skirts and he rolled his eyes upwards, as if seeking her permission to transfer his attention.

"This water's too hot, you fool! Would you scald me?" cried Eluned, slapping at the serving woman when she poured a steaming refill into the basin. "Are we to eat soon, Lady Jessamyn? Or was that brief meal all we get for the day? Of course, I myself don't have much appetite, having such a sore throat. It's Lloyd and the others I'm thinking about."

"I'm sure we'll eat soon. Since I came back I haven't given any orders to the kitchen."

"Oh, so you showed Rhys the way." Eluned narrowed her blue eyes as she critically studied Jessamyn. "You're such a brave wench, riding abroad in all weathers. I've been raised in a more delicate fashion," she added with a smug smile. "Rhys can attest to that." Not waiting for his reply, Eluned placed her slender white hands to advantage on her lap, so that the light from the candles winked dazzling prisms from her rings. "Why, imagine my surprise to learn you were the peasant lad we met yesterday. I thought you some basket seller." Eluned gave a high-pitched laugh, aware that Jessamyn was not overjoyed with her recital. "After all, wearing such rough clothing, what else was I to think? Had anyone suggested to me you were lady of this castle . . ."

"Eluned, I think you should rest your throat," Rhys suggested sternly.

The frown on his face silenced her.

"There's much to be done here," Jessamyn replied. "A lady who sits all day simpering before the hearth would be no good to Curlew."

Rising, she motioned to Ned who came to her.

Eluned glared at her, aware that she was the lady to whom Jessamyn referred, yet not choosing to take issue with the statement. She knew when she had been bested at her own game.

"I'll show you the book now, if you wish, Lord Rhys."

Jessamyn began to walk away, Ned at her heels. Was Rhys following her? Before she reached the buttery she heard his heavy-booted tread behind her.

"It's this way," she said, her voice sounding small and unsure.

On their way to the north turret, she told the cook to serve the day's main meal within the hour. This done, she felt more protected. She could not spend much time alone with Rhys, for they would be expected to come back to the Hall to sup.

Though he did not say much, Jessamyn was highly aware of him walking beside her. Ned stayed between them, acting as chaperone, pleased to have their attention.

"Ah, yours is a turret room. Just like a fairy-tale princess." Rhys laughed as they headed up the short, winding staircase.

Ned lay down on guard outside the door.

Jessamyn swung the door wide to reveal her small, simply furnished room. The large oak bed took up most of the space; a carved chest and wooden bench beneath the window comprised the rest of the furniture. The walls had recently been whitewashed to add light. A sheep's pelt made a soft rug at her bedside. The garnet wool counterpane added a warm glow to the small circular room, pleasingly lit by a crackling fire in the hooded fireplace. In the fire's glow Jessamyn noticed her hurriedly discarded cloak and boots lying on the floor beside the bed. She had not been expecting company.

"May I look through your window?" he asked, grinning at her as he spoke.

Not knowing how to answer his teasing question, Jessamyn merely gestured towards the window.

Rhys strode forward and stood admiring the panoramic view of river and woodland, framed by the distant Welsh hills. He remarked in admiration on the luxury of this novelty, for few houses, and even fewer castles, had glass windows. He had already told her he had two glass windows at his manor of Trevaron, which was considered the height of luxury in his remote valley. Apparently, at Lady Eluned's house they had a whole room of windows. Jessamyn had expected nothing less.

She lit the candles beside her bed with a taper from the hearth.

"And now the book," he suggested, turning away from the window.

Jessamyn held out the hand-lettered parchment book, feeling rather childish when she recalled with what rapture she had told him about her secret pleasures. He held the book to the light. With difficulty, he tried to struggle through the prose until finally he abandoned the task, French not being his strongest language. With a sheepish grin, Rhys resorted to admiring the pictures. They sat on the bench which he had carried over from the window and set before the hearth.

"This is my favorite picture of all," Jessamyn said, showing him the illustration of the lady and her lover beneath the trellis of gorgeous red roses. "Are there really flowers like this—or is it just in the story?"

He smiled and patted her hand. "Oh, Jessamyn, there's so much I'd like to show you . . ." He stopped, withdrawing his hand. "Yes, there really are roses as large as this, with perfume so heady, it makes you swoon. I've seen trellises laden with color, very like this, but not in Wales. It's the English who are so enamored of flower gardens. Someday, you'll travel there and see for yourself."

Her eyes shone as she anticipated seeing such lovely gardens; then, sadly, Jessamyn came back to earth.

"No, I'll probably never travel more than ten miles from Curlew—unless I have to marry someone."

"Wouldn't it be worth it just to see gardens like this?" he asked, hiding a smile.

"No," she cried, "never, not for all the wonders of the world. I don't ever want to be ruled by someone—by a man who takes away my freedom."

"Wouldn't you relinquish your freedom for love?"

Her heart skipped a beat. "Women don't usually love their husbands. They're often strangers who keep a mistress . . ."

"Not always," he said, his face grave. "Some women marry for love. Didn't you know that?"

She shook her head. "Not daughters of knights. We have to marry for power, or possessions."

He sighed and nodded agreement. "You're right. Sometimes, I, too, can be a romantic. I forget that we live in the real world. There's little room for romance in ordinary people's lives. There's such a lot of living that seems to get in the way."

He stood abruptly and crossed to the window.

Jessamyn sat looking at his broad back, wondering what thoughts troubled him. For, when he had stood, his face had tightened, the brightness gone from his eyes. Apart from the sputter and crackle of the logs, it was quiet in the room. Surely it was almost time to sup. Yet, she had no wish to leave. If only she could find the right word to unlock his reserve, to make him open up his heart to her. She smiled. Childishly, she was still looking for a key to the secret garden, only this time it was not just an imaginary place in a picture. The garden was this man's heart.

"Why are you smiling?"

She started, unaware that he had turned and caught her.

"That's a secret. You must allow me to keep a few secrets."

He held out his hand to her. "I want to know those secrets. You've shared your book, your window . . . but not your heart. What secrets lie there? I can't really believe you're so unfeeling that you wouldn't want a lover, that you'd cherish freedom above all things, all men."

"Not all men," she whispered, hardly able to believe her own words.

As she spoke Jessamyn had taken a few steps closer to him and he caught her hand, drawing her to him.

"Dare I hope I'm one who'd meet with your approval?" he asked guardedly, still not sure enough to cast aside polite convention. By being alone with her they violated rules enough.

They stood close. Jessamyn became aware of her toes pressing against his, the hard leather of his boots cutting into her soft velvet shoes. Time stood still. They were alone in her room, as if they were the only two people in the world. Jessamyn swallowed. How she longed to be able to tell him how she felt. Such candor would never do. Perhaps she could hint, suggest . . .

His hands moved to her shoulders. The heat from his body enveloped her in a wave. "Tell me, sweet."

"What—that you find approval with me? You know that already."

He smiled and some of the tension left his face.

"Aye, I play a game with you. Is it to be our hearts, or our sense which calls the tune?"

Jessamyn felt her legs trembling as he drew her closer. She could see how thick were his black lashes, discovered that his eyes were not a solid color, for the candle's flame sparked flecks of gold and green in the brown. His skin was fragrant with the fresh scent of the wind and the countryside, so warmly inviting.

His mouth closed over hers. Jessamyn shuddered in delight, her emotion so intense that she thought she would fall. He tightened his embrace and she rested her weight against him. How safe she felt in his embrace. She turned up her mouth again for his kiss. This time, when their lips met, she kissed him back, reveling in the hot fragrance of his mouth. Her senses swam. She could not think. Her arms stole around his neck of their own accord and she shuddered at the delicious feel of him pressed against her, at the marvelous hot substance of his muscle and flesh.

Jessamyn realized if she were to die now, here, in his arms, her life would not have been in vain. These wonderful sensations she enjoyed, so alien, yet so welcome, were worth a thousand deaths.

Their eyes opened and held.

"Now your eyes are all soft and tender. 'Tis the first time, sweet."

" 'Tis the first time you've kissed me," she whispered, nestling her cheek against his face. She moved her mouth gently against his warm skin, her tongue tracing along his hard jawbone. He shuddered and gripped her so tightly, his fingers bit into her arms.

"Stop," he commanded gruffly.

Hurt, she stopped. "Why, don't you like it?"

"Oh, Jessamyn," he groaned, smiling down at her. "I want you to stop because I like it too well."

"Then I won't stop, though we might be disturbed when they come looking for us," she teased, giggling. "Surely by now it's time to sup."

"This food's much more to my liking," he confided huskily, lifting her slightly off her feet, holding her up so their faces were level. "You're the most beautiful, confusing woman I've ever met. Jessamyn Dacre, are you weaving a spell over me? I've never felt quite like this before."

"A spell so powerful, you'll never escape," she whispered, lightly kissing his nose before he set her back on her feet.

"May Lady Eluned be ill for a month," he said,[1] grinning as he slid his arm about her narrow waist. "Mayhap I'll stay here through the new year."

"Not if Walter has anything to say about it."

"And does Walter run the castle?"

She smiled and shook her head.

"That's what I thought. Do you really want to go down to sup?"

Jessamyn shivered deliciously at the thought of what he might propose instead of the meal, though her own good sense overruled her emotions. "Yes, we must. You know they'll expect us."

"We could say we were lost," he suggested lamely, pulling her back into his arms. "Oh, Jessamyn, I want to hold you, to kiss you, love you . . ."

She slid out of his embrace, her heart beating frantically.

"Let's go down to sup."

On the way back to the Hall, she hurried ahead of him, her heart pounding, her head spinning. He had said "love you", and she guessed what he meant by that was to "make love" to her. He had never actually said, "I love you", but he would. She was convinced of it.

They walked casually into the Hall, careful not to betray by word or glance what had just taken place between them. Yet Jessamyn's conscience troubled her to such an extent, she thought everyone must know. She saw them glance up, their expressions varying. Did they not see her flushed cheeks, her lips still burning from his kisses? She had not even looked to see if her hair was escaping from its chaplet, or if her plaits were coming unbraided, or her dress crushed.

"We thought to send out a search party," Walter snapped, putting down his alecup.

"Lady Jessamyn was showing me the book her father brought her. It's truly a treasure."

"Oh, that thing—can't see what she sees in it. Romantic nonsense. Although, I must admit, I don't read French very well."

"Neither do I—the pictures are treasure enough. It's a valuable piece."

Walter grunted and waved his sister to her place. He glanced sharply at her, but she set her expression, determined not to reveal any secrets to him.

Lady Eluned smiled charmingly. "Your presence more than makes up for the Spartan fare, Rhys," she voiced sweetly, indicating the steaming tureen of soup. Thick slices of bread, cold mutton and gravy were the only accompaniments to the dish.

"I thought your throat was too sore to eat," Jessamyn retorted hotly. "Had I known your health was restored, we could have supped more grandly."

Even Walter grinned. When he caught his sister's eye, he gave her a rare nod of approval, knowing that she had been stung into retaliation by the other woman's continuous veiled insults.

"You'll soon learn that no one on earth can satisfy Lady Eluned's wants," Rhys remarked evenly. "Just when you think you've mastered the game, she changes the rules."

There was a buzz of laughter around the table. Eluned did not join it.

"Speaking of games, Lord Rhys, do you play chess?" Walter asked, rinsing down his food with a great gulp of ale.

"Yes—probably not as well as you, my lord. I've not had much time to practice lately."

"We'll see about that when we're done. I'm tired of playing William Rhees, he keeps making the same moves."

"Before we play, there's something I want to show you. A list of measures to improve your defenses and the general running of the castle. Your sister said you would both be grateful."

Walter shot Jessamyn a quick warning glance, but she pretended not to see as she concentrated on her trencher.

"Well, yes, I admit, we could use a few good suggestions," he grudgingly agreed.

"Good. You'll be pleased with the changes, for they aren't costly or hard to implement."

"Hmm, all right, show them to Walter Rhees at the same time, then I won't have to go over them with him. And don't make the lecture too long . . . always hated long lectures. My tutor used to bore me to death, always talking, talking . . ." Walter refilled his own alecup, not waiting for the server to get around the table.

Eluned sat in stony silence throughout the meal. The other women spoke to each other, but did not include Jessamyn in their conversation. Walter monopolized Rhys, interested now that a game of chess was in the offing. The two Welsh lieutenants did not understand English. Jessamyn felt like a pariah. She did not know what she had been expecting from the evening, but it had not included Rhys playing a long game of chess with her brother.

As she sat there simmering in resentment, common sense gradually overcame her disappointment. What could she possibly have hoped for? They were bound to stay here in the Hall. She had also noticed that Eluned kept a very close eye on Rhys. There would have been small chance of sharing a private conversation with him. Though Jessamyn knew he was being wise by speaking only casually to her, just as he had done that first afternoon—was it really only yesterday?—it seemed as if weeks had passed. In fact, so polite was he toward her, had she not known it as fact, Jessamyn would have doubted that the stolen romantic meeting in her room had even taken place.

The table was cleared. The other ladies produced needlework and pulled their benches close to the fire. Walter eagerly set out the chessboard, anxious to move from the more practical discussion to his all-important game. The Welsh lieutenants joined their comrades at throwing dice. Again Jessamyn was ignored.

In self-defense, she fished some crumpled embroidery out of a chest in the corner, something she worked on only when she could not avoid the occupation. At this rate, it would take until doomsday to finish the altar piece.

Someone began to sing, and soon the song was taken up by the others. The men kept glancing towards the High table, almost as if they expected Rhys to take up the verse. The song being sung was all in Welsh; Jessamyn had never heard it before. Aware of the sudden lull in singing, Rhys glanced up from the notes which he had spread before him on the table. His men shouted something to him and he half stood, signalling for the musician to strike again. Then he began to sing in a ringing baritone.

Jessamyn listened, spellbound, as he finished the verse, and bowing slightly to the others, he sat, allowing them to continue with the roisterous chorus. Elbow resting on the table, Jessamyn leaned on her hand, grinning at her own foolishness. A few moments before she had been admiring his closely written script, the concise manner of his suggestions. From that she had gone to the unexpected appreciation of his singing. Had the man no end to his talents?

She was madly in love with him. There was no other explanation. Yet how could she be in love with a man who had come unexpectedly into her life just a day ago? And a Welshman at that! Impossible . . . but true.

Chapter Five

Jessamyn reined in, pausing to catch her breath. The bright morning sun sparked diamonds on the frost-coated meadow. Where the river flowed beneath overhanging trees, white mist still shrouded its banks. Jessamyn filled her lungs with the stingingly fresh air. This morning was so beautiful, she was overjoyed just to be alive.

It was Wednesday, the third day, she thought, with a grin over her biblical turn of phrase, inspired no doubt by the Mass she had heard this morning. It was one of the days Father Paul said Mass in the gatehouse's small chapel. Though at first, it had been pitch dark in the bone-chilling stone chapel, once the candles were lit, bathing the priest's vestments in golden light, everywhere she looked seemed holy.

Blasphemously, she wondered if her newly awakened religious fervor owed more to the presence of Rhys of Trevaron, than to any spiritual transformation. Jessamyn grinned at her unholy thoughts and she clicked to Merlin, urging him forward. This morning she felt revitalized; last night's miserable frustration had disappeared.

Jessamyn had just come from the village. She had asked Father Paul to administer Extreme Unction to Maeven, and the poor girl had died soon after. Filled with righteous indignation, Jessamyn had deemed this the perfect time to lash the villagers' collective conscience.

Arriving in Morfa Bach when it was barely light, she had roused several of the village's important men from their snug cottages, herding them without ceremony into the inn's common room, where she told them that she knew the villagers had set fire to Agnes's house. She also told them that she was holding them responsible for building Agnes another house as soon as possible. And, if they did not comply with her orders, she threatened them with prosecution at the next Lord's Court. Though it had been over a year since such a gathering had been held at Curlew, the villagers' memories were long.

The headmen agreed to carry out her command. Not once did they ask, "What does Lord Walter have to say about this," nor did they refuse to take orders from a woman. Sheepishly turning tail, muttering among themselves, before they left the room, they had already named the parties responsible for the fire.

Jessamyn smiled at the recollection. She was the power here, more feared than Walter, also more respected, for it was she who healed them when they were ill, or settled their disputes. To rule the manor of Morfa Bach and the surrounding acres must be her life's vocation, not to live as the pampered wife of a fighting, carousing nobleman.

But her smile turned wistful when she recalled

what Rhys had said yesterday—that some women married for love. It was hard to accept that someone of her station could be allowed to choose her husband. So far, her only defense against matrimony had been to delay any plans for as long as she could. This was a tactic she would continue to employ until she was so old and decrepit that no one would seek her.

Spurring Merlin forward, Jessamyn broke into another gallop. The wind tore her hood from her head, sending her auburn hair streaming in a bright banner behind her. She began to whistle out of sheer joy. Whistling was an accomplishment she had learned years ago, admittedly not a very ladylike skill, yet she cared nothing for that. Today, she was free to do as she pleased, to gallop Merlin to her heart's content, allowing this pure bracing air to fill her lungs. In every direction, this land belonged to her—and to Walter too, of course—she thought belatedly.

A man's shout echoed across the meadow. Finally slowing her pace, Jessamyn turned about in the saddle to see who had hailed her. Her heart turned a somersault. She instantly recognized the big black horse slicing a path through the frost-silvered grass. She hesitated a few moments, waiting until the rider was close enough to be certain the man was Rhys, then she bolted. Digging her spurs into Merlin's side, Jessamyn sent him lurching into a mad, careening gallop.

As the icy wind seared her face and whipped her hair, Jessamyn gritted her teeth, setting a course for open country. She had no idea why she was trying to outrun him. A sudden primitive need for flight had possessed her. Much as she wanted to stop to speak to him, she was also afraid of her own feelings.

Had she stopped to reason, she would have known

91

the task she had set for herself was impossible. Though her sturdy mount was superb in rugged terrain, Merlin was a traveler, not a racehorse. The big black stallion could easily outdistance him. Desperately, Jessamyn tried to pull ahead, turning down another trail which brought her floundering to the edge of the woods which stretched to the foothills of the Welsh mountains.

Skidding on the muddy ground, Rhys cut her off, his big horse panting great clouds of steam.

"Hold, Lady Jessamyn. You're captured."

Reluctantly she consigned defeat, letting the reins go slack. Aware of poor Merlin's heaving flanks, she let him regain his breath.

"Didn't you know who it was?" Rhys shouted as he maneuvered his big horse alongside hers.

"I knew."

She saw the puzzled frown on his brow. His hood was pulled over his head, the dark folds shrouding his face. As she looked at him, Jessamyn was reminded of a cowled monk; the unusual headwear made him appear alien and slightly sinister. Then, she was struck by the humor of her comparison, and her unease dissolved in laughter.

"What's so funny?"

"That hood makes you look like a monk."

"I assure you, lady, I'm no monk."

Though he laughed as he spoke, there was a warning in his statement which increased her unease. Her heart thumped loudly, until she was sure he must hear it, too.

"Riding out alone? What have I told you?"

"Just into the village. Your idea worked. There wasn't a peep of dissent when I told them they had to rebuild Agnes's house."

"You should've waited. I'd have come with you."

"When I saddled Merlin, you were nowhere about."

They fell easily into step as they skirted the mist-filled woodland. Jessamyn shuddered. This morning the silent, gray-shrouded woods appeared threatening; she was suddenly glad of his company.

"I was discussing some points with your steward and the captain of your guard. I don't want you to be caught unawares. Your brother seems more concerned with his chess game than instilling order and discipline. These are hostile times—you know that, don't you?"

"Yes," she agreed, hoping he was not going to enter into a political debate with her. "How's Lady Eluned?" she asked brightly, anxious to change the subject. "I noticed she didn't attend Mass."

He grimaced at her question. "She says now she's so much restored, she would be about our journey."

Jessamyn gasped. His words came as a shock; she felt as if she had been struck. Her heart began to pound but it was not in pleasure.

"But . . . she said . . . I thought . . . several days, at least."

He slowed his horse to a walk as they moved up a slope into the sunlight. Sparkling grass and leaves formed a shimmering crystalline frame through which to view the distant landscape. It was a beautiful sight. But Jessamyn appreciated it not.

"Are you leaving today?" she asked, caring for naught but the pain of his imminent departure.

"No, how could I have left without saying good-bye? I'd no idea where to find you. I told her we couldn't possibly travel at such short notice. The wagon needs repair. We'll leave on Friday."

"Two days?"

"Two days."

She chanced a look at him, flustered when she found he was gazing intently at her. His face was grim, his mouth set.

"And then? Will I ever see you again?"

He reached out to grip her hand, his clasp comfortingly warm through his gauntlet. "Of course. Surely you don't think I could desert you. No, Jessamyn Dacre, you won't be shut of me that easy."

Then a remarkable thing occurred. Though she had not intended to say it, her heart somehow overruled her common sense. "I don't want to be shut of you at all," she said.

His face broke into a smile, the tension slipping away. He looked younger, gentler. "How you do continue to surprise me. Oh, sweet, only two days! So little time. Come, let's walk. There are so many things I want to say to you."

He sprang from his horse and helped her down from the saddle, placing his hands around her waist. The warm strength of his touch thrilled her, enveloping her in heat. Then, all too quickly, Jessamyn found herself set down on the frosty grass. She was wearing Perkin's clothing again, looking exactly like a boy were it not for the mass of bright hair spilling down her back. Once her real identity had been revealed to him she felt strangely vulnerable by being clothed so simply. When wearing her best raiment, she had felt more able to compete. Yet why did she always feel she must compete with Lady Eluned? He was here with her, not back at the castle with Lady Eluned.

They had begun to walk along the path when Rhys caught her arm and stopped her. He was standing very close, looking down at her unsmiling. He pulled off his gauntlet to brush back the thick strands of hair which fell across her brow. His hand lingered. Gently he fastened his fingers in the soft gleaming tresses.

"Such lovely hair," he whispered, lifting a handful of the perfumed silky hair to his lips. "I'll remember the perfume of your hair for many years to come."

She moved even closer, until their clothing touched. His back was to the road, cutting off the sunlight. No man had ever said anything nearly so romantic to her. Jessamyn was deeply moved by his pretty speech, yet the practical side of her nature reminded her that it could have been just that—a pretty speech. His hands moved down to her shoulders, then up to her face, gently caressing her. Jessamyn responded to his touch. A wave of heat sped like lightning through her veins. Alarmed by this unexpected rush, she fought desperately to regain control of the situation.

"You probably say that to all the girls, Lord Rhys."

He smiled lazily. "Only to the pretty ones. And why Lord Rhys, this morning? Did I dream of that time in your room, when you kissed me back with such eagerness?"

"No, but you must stop. Today my senses have returned."

"Are you telling me you didn't enjoy it?"

"I didn't say that."

"Then what are you saying, Jessamyn Dacre? Do you want me to go and leave you in peace, for likely I can salvage the wagon and travel this afternoon . . ."

"No, no, don't do that," she interrupted, afraid that he meant what he said, for he had turned about, as if preparing to remount. "Rhys, I want you to stay with me forever."

He turned back. The hood had fallen from his head and sunlight gleamed on his crisp black hair. She was struck by his beauty, an overwhelming surge of emotion washing over her as she looked at him. How her heart ached at the thought of losing him, of having their love finished before it had begun.

"Would that I could," he whispered, his arms reaching for her.

Jessamyn hesitated a moment, then moved into the circle of his embrace. How warmly comforting it felt to be held against him, to become aware of his heart thumping against hers. Rhys bent to kiss the top of her head, gently holding her as he spoke.

"I love you, Jessamyn Dacre, far more than I should."

At first, she was not sure she had actually heard him. How she had longed to hear him speak those words. So much that she was afraid she had imagined it. Wide-eyed, she gazed up at him, aching to stay in his arms, to be held and loved for all time.

"Oh, Rhys, I love you, too," she whispered, her voice shaking with emotion. "I've never said that to anyone before."

His lips came down on hers, the hot fragrance of his mouth blotting out all thought, all sense. He kissed her again, his mouth on fire. Tenderness and passion overwhelmed her. She kissed him back with even more intensity than she had shown the previous night. Rhys was leaving, and she did not know if she would ever see him again.

Her mounting involvement struck a responsive chord in him. Now he no longer held her gently, but pressed against her so that his steel-hard muscles cut into her quivering flesh. She could feel the tremors coursing through his limbs. Rhys grew more insistent and demanding.

"Jessamyn, sweetheart, I want you," he breathed into her ear, his voice husky with passion.

Desire shot through her in an overwhelming wave as she heard, then understood, his words. She blinked in surprise, looking up at him. His dark eyes burned, dense, black pools of light. Their gazes locked and he knew that she had not mistaken his intent. A yellow gleam flickerd across her hazel eyes, now dilated with passion.

"I want to make love to you, Jessamyn. I've wanted you from the first. Dear God, what a vision you were that first night. I couldn't take my eyes off you. Oh, sweetheart, say you'll love me, for there's not time for a long courtship, for caution and slow progress."

Jessamyn placed her fingers against his lips, silencing his words. Though she greatly desired him, long conditioning forbade the action she contemplated. The breath choked in her throat as she pictured the wonder of making love with him.

Lightly Rhys kissed her fingers, patiently awaiting her response. He forced himself to control his eager body, not used to self-denial. Rhys moved his mouth from her detaining fingers and buried his lips against the base of her throat where the pulse raced, shuddering the delicate white flesh.

At the searing touch of his kiss, fire sped through Jessamyn's body. Purely physical aching beset her; she thought she would fall, her legs grew so weak. Sensing her total yielding, he held her against him, keeping her on her feet.

"Come, sweetest, say yes," he urged again, his lips softly moving against her cheek.

Basking in the arousing, unfamiliar scent of his body, Jessamyn buried her face in the heated hollow of his neck. The rough folds of his wool hood scratched her cheek. She strained to taste the sweet delight of his flesh. Her tongue brushed tantalizingly over the golden smooth skin until he gripped her arms, forcing her to stop.

"Don't," he gasped, holding her at arm's length. "You're an arch temptress, woman. I'm trying hard to honor you. Why must you keep tempting me beyond endurance? Come, delay no longer . . . say you want to love me."

Jessamyn's emotions were in a whirl. She wanted him desperately; she had always wanted him. Yet, still she vacillated. She was a lady. A lady would say no to this arousing Welshman. She did not want to say no; she wanted him to teach her the mystery of lovemaking. But to put him off, to delay the inevitable was her only defense.

"I've already said I love you."

Rhys found little humor in her teasing words. His eyes hardened, his mouth was grim. "Enough games. Are we to go back now? Or will you yield to me?"

The ultimatum. She understood that he would no longer allow her this defensive ploy. Panic beset her as she fought desperately to ignore her own body, to deny the yearning, yielding emotion flooding her limbs. She ached with desire until her knees grew weak. Love, desire—she no longer knew where one ended and the other began.

"There's no place," she said lamely, glancing about the deserted landscape.

He seized her and clamped his mouth over hers. All the gentleness was gone from him. His mouth had turned demanding. The heated pressure pried open her lips. A sizzling wave of passion shot through her as his tongue probed her mouth, hot and seeking. He mimicked the act he longed to complete. Jessamyn shuddered, trying to withdraw from the forbidden delight, but he held her fast.

"I want you, Jessamyn. I won't take no for an answer. I know you want me too. Oh, you've not said as much in words—only your body speaks the truth."

Her breathing quickened with the knowledge that she was betrayed. Was it that obvious to him? She knew it must be. He was no young, inexperienced boy, and though she had tried to check the impulse, her thighs had strained against his, seeking the iron-hard strength of the arousal he could no longer hide.

"I'm . . . afraid."

"Nay, sweet, don't be afraid. Remember, we love each other. Making love is the most natural thing in the world. Say yes . . . oh, sweetheart, please . . . say yes."

Time stood still on that frosty incline. Everything about the moment was printed indelibly on her mind. In the lonely months to come, when he was gone from her life, she would remember how it had been, how the sun sparkled like diamonds in the grass, how the air was icy cold, how the scent of autumn woods and rain-drenched leaves . . .

"Yes. Oh, Rhys, love me," she whispered against his cheek, burying her face in the warm hollow of his throat, tracing her tongue over his tanned skin until he forced her face up and his lips seared against hers. Jessamyn almost swooned in his demanding embrace, no longer trying to check the eager straining of her legs, curious and, at the same time, afraid, of what she would discover about that ultimate surrender.

"Oh, God," Rhys groaned, shuddering, desperate to possess her. "How much you tease, you witch. Will we go back to the castle, or stay here? What's yon shed through the trees?"

Jessamyn hated to take her face from his, to force her brain to action. She could scarcely breathe, let alone think.

"Shed?" she repeated, trying to catch her breath. "What shed?"

He pointed to a dark shape beyond the first line of trees. Slowly her brain responded and Jessamyn

realized he was referring to the lean-to where fodder
was stored for the winter.

"In there?"

"Yes."

The building seemed a hundred miles away. On
pain-wracked legs she stumbled forward, her mind
befuddled. What a fool she was. Her senses shrieked
a warning. *Fool, he'll soon be gone. Then what are
you to do?*

But she was intoxicated by the sweetness of his
kiss. She reveled in the warm strength of his arms
as he bore her up when she stumbled on mounds of
sodden autumn leaves stirred up by their boots. In
a few minutes, they would be one. And all she could
remember was how much she loved him. He was all
that she wanted in life, the fulfillment of her dreams.
Finally, the door to that secret garden was unlocked.
Shortly, she would step inside its walls and her life
would never be the same again!

The fodder shed was stacked waist-high with
fresh hay covered by hessian sacking to keep out
the rain.

Waiting no longer, Rhys pulled her to him and
they fell together on the sweet hay, bouncing before
sinking deep, as if they lay in a feather bed.

All doubt flown, Jessamyn dismissed the nagging
voice of her conscience. She was with the man she
loved. For what other reason had she saved her
virginity than to give it to him as a gift? Mounting
confidence in the knowledge that she was doing the
right thing flooded over her. Jessamyn giggled as
they fell together. Eagerly he swept her in his arms,
pressing her against his body, showering her with
ardent kisses.

"Oh, sweetheart," Rhys breathed, "how much I
love you . . . want you. Oh, Jess, Jess, come to me . . .
come to me."

She marveled at the strength of his limbs, so tense and hard against hers. His hands remained gentle as he caressed her face. He kissed her thoroughly, his thumb grazing her cheek. Rhys drew back slightly to gaze down at her, his hands still cupping her lovely face.

"Dearest Jessamyn, you're the loveliest woman in the world. At this moment you're the only woman. I've been waiting a lifetime to find you."

She lay against him, giving up the fight for control. Straining against the heat of his body, she shuddered as his hand moved from her small waist to explore her breast. When Rhys cupped her breast, she groaned in delight. A molten rush of heat sped through her veins; the nerve-tingling sensation lodged in that secret place between her legs. Unconsciously, she strained into his hands, eager for him to explore further. Rhys slid his hands beneath her tunic, and soon the welcome heat of his fingers engulfed her bare flesh. As he lovingly fondled the full, white orbs, encircling her errect nipples with his thumbs, Jessamyn moaned again, not wanting the pleasure to end.

"You have the loveliest breasts in Christendom," he whispered, bending his head to bestow a trail of kisses across her aching flesh. When Rhys finally slid his tongue around her nipple, Jessamyn cried aloud in passion. She squirmed with pleasure beneath his caresses, sinking her hands into his black hair, begging him not to stop. The aching between her legs intensified, until she thought she could not endure it. She had never dreamed his caresses could create such havoc with her senses; she cared for naught beyond the man in her arms.

In the half-light of the lean-to, Rhys marveled at the beauty of her full breasts, taking their weight in his hands, cupping them, gently stroking her pink nipples until she begged him to stop. How she ached to have his mouth on hers, to taste again the delight of his kisses.

When their mouths met, there was no holding back. She kissed him deeply, joyously, tasting the heated fragrance of his mouth. She reveled in the passion, eagerly anticipating their bodies being joined, as had their mouths.

At first she was shy about seeking him intimately, for though she longed to discover the secrets of his flesh, she did not deem it fitting to be so bold. Impatiently, he grasped her hand, fitting her fingers around the thick pulsing brand which ached for her caress. When at last she touched him, exploring the throbbing thickness beneath his clothing, Rhys showered her with kisses. Suddenly he stilled her hand. And Jessamyn, not understanding, was put out.

"Unless you would have it over before it has begun, give me a few minutes to regain my wits," he whispered, his mouth hot and eager against hers.

She marveled that her touch could create such passion, for she had never been with a man before. Caressing was surely a skill that must be learned. Yet, when she shyly revealed this notion to him, burying her face against his neck, he chuckled at her naiveté.

"Oh, dear heart, 'tis not something you must be taught, though there are many other things I'll delight in teaching you."

He fumbled with the lacings of their garments, untying her points, then his own, slipping down her wool tights to expose the silky smooth whiteness of her firm thighs. With pleasure, he admired her rounded hips, bisected by a silky bush of auburn hair. His sweeping caresses followed the passage of the garment as it slid to her knees.

From her navel, Rhys traced a line with his tongue across her stomach. Jessamyn gripped his head, sinking her fingers in his crisp hair, fondling his smooth neck. At first, she tried to keep his mouth above that secret place. Insistent, his tongue followed the exploration of his hand. Tremors of passion vibrated through his arms. Jessamyn gripped his shoulders, stroking their square breadth. Reaching inside his shirt, she slipped her small hands over his back, finding his flesh hot as fire inside his clothing.

"Oh, Rhys, you're all I ever wanted," she said throatily.

Impatiently he pulled open his jerkin and pushed it aside. Together they unfastened his shirt. Jessamyn smiled in wonder at the breadth of his chest, matted with curling black hair. How hot, how smooth was his flesh. Thinking to create pleasure for him, she fondled his brown nipples, taking the erect flesh into her mouth, tonguing him as he had shown her.

Rhys gripped her face, his hands sinking in her hair. He shuddered. She could not ignore his swollen manhood, pressing like steel against her thighs. The moment she had longed for, yet dreaded, had arrived. She wanted to look at him, to touch him, to discover the secrets of his body.

Eagerly Rhys helped her to roll down his sleek, fitted hose, to pull aside his fine linen shirt. His waist was narrow, his hips lean. A furred black triangle began below his navel, disappearing inside his clothing. At this point Jessamyn stopped, suddenly shy. With an impatient grunt, Rhys pushed down his clothing all the way, releasing the burning, throbbing treasure she had longed to touch.

Jessamyn gasped at the reality of him. For though she was no convent-reared wench, she was not wholly prepared for the changes passion made in a man's body. His pulsing, engorged flesh promised both delight and punishment. She drew back slightly in surprise.

"What, are you afraid of me?" he asked lazily, eyes half-closed, watching her reaction. "Do you not want me, now you've seen what you're getting?"

At first she did not know how to reply. The soft stroking of his hands along her back slipped over the white curves of her hips, warming her to boldness.

"I didn't know quite what to expect," she confessed. Tentatively she caressed his velvet-smooth flesh which leaped anew at her touch. She shivered, her anticipation tinged with fear. "Please, Rhys . . . try not to hurt me."

He smiled at her. "I'll try," he promised, drawing her against him.

The feel of his hair crinkling against her breasts aroused her. Jessamyn nestled close, fitting the strength of his organ between her legs. When her thighs closed around the throbbing delight, her own passion accelerated to such a degree that she no longer questioned what he would do, or if it would hurt. His mouth covered hers while his hand sought that secret place, sliding his fingers gently inside, penetrating until he felt resistance. The combination of his exploring hand and the solid heat of his body between her thighs worked a miracle.

Jessamyn gasped with renewed passion, clutching him, straining her breasts against his chest provocatively. Rhys fondled her throbbing breasts, caressing the aching flesh until she sobbed deep in her throat with desire.

"Jessamyn, darling, I'll love you forever," he vowed intensely. "Wherever I go, whatever I do, always remember that. Promise me."

"I promise," she gasped against his hot mouth, unable to think clearly. The force of passion drove her on, controlling her actions.

Gently, but insistently, he probed the portal between her thighs. Jessamyn could no longer endure the temptation of his throbbing organ pressed invitingly against the most sensitive part of her body. She spread her thighs wider, swept along in the heat of desire. Rhys fitted himself against her. And he thrust.

Jessamyn gasped in surprise, her eyes flying open. The searing penetration took her breath—pain, delight, heat, all mingling inside her. Tears sprang to her eyes and she cried out. Rhys held her, kissed her, absorbing her cries with his mouth. He tasted the salt of her tears. For the moment he lay still. Still kissing and caressing her, he fondled her full breasts, eager to arouse the desire momentarily stolen by pain. Gently he kissed her closed eyelids, where tears escaped beneath the thick lashes.

"Oh, sweetheart, I love you so. Come, try to take pleasure with me," he urged, kissing her mouth tenderly.

Jessamyn gradually relaxed. As he lay still, she stroked his smooth back, allowing her pleasure to be reborn. Very slowly he began to move inside her, carefully gauging her response. They exchanged words of love and Jessamyn shuddered repeatedly as the heat of his skillful lovemaking revived her desire.

Not knowing what to expect, Jessamyn tried to check the driving sensation which swept her along. She suddenly became aware of his change of pace. No longer did Rhys consciously lead her, for passion had finally overtaken him. The pace of his lovemaking grew more intense, the force more driven. Jessamyn realized she could not hold out against that swirling, twisting sensation, for her body no longer obeyed her will.

Mouths clamped together, bodies moving as one, Jessamyn allowed Rhys to take her to the point of no return, climbing to the pinnacle and beyond. With a cry of ecstasy, she cast aside all restraint, plunging deep into the star-spangled darkness of total fulfillment. With ease and confidence he had led her, guiding her through the first bewildering journey, knowing that ever after, she would be a seasoned traveler on the road to love.

For some time after she had plunged into the abyss, Jessamyn reveled in the warm dark pleasure of completion. Pressed close against Rhys, loving him intensely, she had never known such peace. Very slowly she drifted back to consciousness. When she finally opened her eyes, his face was close to hers. She smiled as she admired the black half-moons of thick fringed lashes against his suntanned cheeks. That terrible tension she had seen in his features was gone. His face was softly vulnerable in the aftermath of passion.

"Rhys," she whispered, gently kissing his chin. The black lashes fluttered open and she looked into the soft, brown velvet of his dark eyes. He smiled at her so lovingly, her heart leapt for joy.

"You've made me the happiest man in the world. At this moment, I'd not switch places with the king himself," he whispered, a bemused smile playing about his firmly chiseled mouth.

Jessamyn shivered in pleasure as she gazed at him, hardly able to believe he was hers. She admired afresh his hard, muscled body, slipping her hands over the slim hips and lean flanks of his lithe, horseman's frame. Still a little shy, she stole a glance at his formidable weapon, diminished somewhat, but still slightly intimidating. Jessamyn marveled anew as she realized she had contained him inside her body without lasting damage.

"Now, are you still afraid of me?" he asked teasingly, intercepting her furtive glance. When she shook her head and smiled at him, he reached out and hugged her. Tenderly he stroked back her thick hair, which fell in shining waves, enmeshing them in its net.

"You did hurt me," she half-accused, taking his hand and pressing her mouth against his palm.

"Sorry, sweetheart, it couldn't be helped."

"You don't sound very sorry."

He drew her down beside him, chuckling, the sound rising from deep in his throat. "No, not very. I wanted your happiness, but I knew a little pain could not be helped. Tell me I'm forgiven."

"All right, I forgive you."

He kissed her face, his mouth gentle. For the moment, the driving purpose to his kisses had flown.

"You're every bit as wonderful as I dreamed you'd be," he confided huskily as he caressed her breast. "In fact, Lady Jessamyn Dacre, you aroused me to new heights."

"Oh, you're teasing me."

"No. Would I tease about so sacred a subject, my love? And you are that . . . my love. Promise you'll always be so, for all time."

"I promise . . . you must do the same."

His tongue tormented the sensitive flesh of her earlobe. "You have my word, my dearest, sweetest angel. Forever and a day, you will be my love."

Tears stung her eyes. She had never expected to know such bliss. And as she listened to his husky voice whispering endearments, and felt the gentle, arousing pleasure of his kisses, Jessamyn thought her heart would burst with joy.

Chapter Six

The ride back to Curlew seemed all too short. In no time at all, they were back inside the castle walls.

Jessamyn's heart raced when she looked at Rhys and relived what had taken place between them such a short time ago. So perfect, so totally consuming had been their lovemaking, it all might have been a wonderful, arousing dream.

After the horses were stabled, they walked slowly across the ward. The castle's towering stone walls cast the area in chilly, blue shadow. The first gold rays of morning sunshine crept shyly over the grass.

Outside the door to the north tower, they stopped. Rhys held out his hand, smiling invitingly at her. Quickly Jessamyn clasped his warm fingers, shuddering with pleasure at the touch which sent tremors along her arm.

"Why so modest, sweet?" he teased, drawing her closer. "Are you turning virginal on me?"

"No, but we don't know who's watching."

"Am I concerned who sees?"

She smiled at his reckless declaration and allowed him to draw her inside the privacy of the shadowed doorway. Eagerly raising her face in anticipation of his kiss, Jessamyn trembled with expectancy. His demanding kiss was hot and passionate, making her soft lips quiver.

Rhys glanced up the twisting stair. "Isn't this your tower, Princess? What say we steal upstairs and . . ."

"And," she prompted huskily, her heart pounding so hard that she was sure he must hear it.

"Have you so little imagination? Come."

He caught her against him and kissed her again, his eager embrace robbing her of breath. Not stopping to weigh the recklessness of their action, Jessamyn longed to race upstairs, so as not to waste a precious minute of stolen time.

"My lord."

His arms dropped from her shoulders and Rhys turned about. There, in a shaft of sunlight, stood two of his men. Directly behind them was Eluned Glynne.

The discovery of this unexpected audience brought a guilty flush to Jessamyn's cheeks. Flustered, she swallowed hard, trying to gather her wits. She did not know if the men had seen them embracing, for their faces remained impassive. She hoped that Lady Eluned had been too far away to distinguish much in the deep shadows.

Rhys cleared his throat as he briskly stepped away from Jessamyn. "What is it?" he asked gruffly, making an effort to master his annoyance, for they could not have arrived at a more inopportune time.

"A barrel rolled off a wagon, my lord. Alun was trapped underneath."

Rhys winced. "I'll come. Is he badly hurt?"

The soldiers gravely nodded in unison.

"Perhaps Lady Jessamyn can give him some potions to ease his pain," suggested Eluned, her voice raised to make herself heard above the general clamor in the castle ward.

Swallowing and quickly patting her hair in place, Jessamyn stepped out of the shadowed recess. It was no use trying to hide: Lady Eluned had seen her. What else she had seen remained a mystery. Yet, did it matter if Eluned Glynne saw her in Rhys's arms? Jessamyn thought defiantly. What they did was none of her business.

Rhys and his men had already crossed the winter-browned grass, leaving the women alone.

"I just came in from a ride," Jessamyn explained uncomfortably, aware of Eluned's critical scrutiny of her drab clothing.

Eluned smiled thinly. "So it appears. Did Rhys ride with you?"

"I met him outside the walls and we rode back together," Jessamyn explained, keeping her tone casual. "Where's the injured man?"

"They took him to the infirmary."

Jessamyn headed in that direction; to her surprise, Lady Eluned had not followed her.

The man was unconscious. His arm was twisted at a curious angle; the chest of his padded jambeson was dark with blood. The barrel had rolled off the wagon, knocking him down, and landed on his chest. A jagged rib bone poked through his clothing.

Jessamyn quickly conferred with Tassie and Alys, the castle's most skilled nurses, about the injured man's treatment. Once they had agreed which medicines to use, Jessamyn took down several earthenware jars of herbs from the shelves ringing the room to prepare a potent painkiller. After pounding the leaves to dust in a marble mortar and pestle, she brewed a stout drink to deaden his pain.

Meanwhile, the soldier's comrades had loosened his clothing, cutting away the torn fabric and extracting shredded, wool padding from his open wounds. The man's cries of pain assured Jessamyn that he was still alive. His cries soon became screams when someone tried to move his twisted arm to pull off his shirt.

The following hours were harrowing. Jessamyn supervised the positioning and setting of the soldier's shattered arm. The man's pain was so intense that he would not keep still. Before she could even begin, Jessamyn had to force a large quantity of painkiller down his throat, holding his head so that he would not gag. Rhys watched her work, lending his strength when needed to hold the patient down. The herbs worked swiftly and the man soon lost consciousness, making her task far easier. Jessamyn realigned his arm and splinted it. She bathed the jagged, torn flesh in his chest and applied a healing salve. She then firmly bound his ribs with broad linen bands.

"He'll rest more comfortably now, but he won't be traveling to Chester with you."

"He's one of my best bowmen."

"I hope his arm will knit well enough to use a bow."

Rhys nodded, his face set. All thoughts of romance had flown. "Thank you from the bottom of my heart, Lady Jessamyn," he said gravely, aware of the many listening ears. "You'll be a welcome companion if we ever go into battle. Remember, the offer's open."

"That's not a very tempting offer," Jessamyn said with a smile, not sure if he had spoken in jest.

Rhys gave her an answering smile before he turned and, beckoning to his men, strode from the room, leaving Alun to the women's care.

The main meal was a plain offering, for Jessamyn had been far too busy to give any special orders to the kitchen. A cauldron of hearty soup accompanied by thick slices of barley bread, sliced cold mutton, and ale were brought to the table. Spiced, stewed apples with cream, honey, and butter and a dish of salted fish paste followed.

Lady Eluned remained strangely silent. Jessamyn could hardly believe her good fortune, for she had expected a string of complaints about the Spartan fare. The men ate with their usual hearty appetites, for though plain, Curlew's food was good.

Walter had finally deigned to leave his chamber. He slumped in his chair, greatly displeased by the news of the injured Welshman.

"I suppose this means your journey will be delayed," he ventured at last. "The injury's bad, too, so they tell me."

"There's no need for delay."

All eyes turned upon the speaker. Lady Eluned had made this surprising declaration in an unusually determined voice. Twin spots of color burned in her pale cheeks and her eyes were steely.

"Alun can't travel for a while yet," Rhys explained quickly. "It's impossible to move him."

"Then leave him here. I'm sure our kind host and hostess will have no objections. If I leave a purse of gold to pay for his board, you won't be out a farthing, Lord Walter. We can stop for him on our way back."

Walter readily assented to the proposal—one Welshman under his roof was far preferable to thirty.

Rhys shrugged, trying to appear nonchalant, though inwardly his heart lurched with dismay. Unfortunate as the accident had been, it had provided a heaven-sent opportunity for delay. Eluned's stubborn insistence that they resume their journey as planned had caught him off guard.

"As you wish, Eluned—after all, this is your pilgrimage."

"How kind of you to remember," Eluned snapped, thrusting aside her cup as she stood to leave.

Rhys watched her walk away without bidding anyone's leave; his eyes narrowed. Damn her! He knew that they could manage well enough without Alun; yet, with more warning, he could have manufactured a sound excuse to stay put. As it was, at such short notice, no plausible objection had come to mind.

Dusk crept across the bare countryside.

Jessamyn paused to survey the bleak winter landscape through an arrow slit in the west wall. Beyond the distant Welsh hills, sunset's rosy hues washed the sky with light. For the past few hours, she had been occupied with myriad duties in the kitchen, laundry and infirmary. Despite Rhys's exciting presence, castle life continued, and it was her job to direct it, Walter being little or no help. Rhys had been busy with his men, for she had only seen him in passing. Though she had hoped they could spend some time alone, the prospect grew dim. Walter had already informed her that he intended to finish the chess game begun with their guest the previous night.

"Lady Jessamyn."

Startled by the unexpected voice behind her, Jessamyn spun about to see Eluned Glynne standing in the shadows.

"Lady Eluned—how may I help you? Do you need another potion for your throat?"

"Nay, my throat's well enough. I would speak with you."

They both stood aside to allow a serving woman to pass.

"Privately."

Surprised by the request, Jessamyn gestured towards the narrow stair leading to a curtained alcove off the Great Hall's upper story. This small, well-lit room was used for sewing and reading.

"Will this be private enough?"

"It'll suit. I intend to be brief."

Jessamyn waited expectantly, hands folded against the rough hessian apron covering her russet gown and surcoat. Why did she have the feeling that this meeting with Eluned Glynne was not going to bring her joy? It was the same uneasy sensation she had felt when she saw the noblewoman at the inn.

"First let me enquire as to whether you've recovered from your morning ride?" Eluned began sweetly.

"Recovered? Aye, I daresay. Why do you ask?"

Eluned's thin lips curled scornfully. "How sweet, how innocent . . . the affect's lost on me. I ask because Lord Rhys has a reputation for hard riding, my lady."

Jessamyn swallowed uneasily. A nervous tremor began in her legs. She had the distinct impression Eluned Glynne spoke not about their morning canter but inferred another, more suggestive meaning. "Our ride was slow enough. You speak in riddles."

"No, I speak from experience. I've very keen sight, Jessamyn Dacre," Eluned hissed, taking a step closer. Her blue eyes glittered cold and malevolent. "I watched you out riding this morning. Oh, you'd be surprised what a splendid view there is from the south tower. One can see beyond the woodland, inside which, I might add, I saw you disappear for some time. I'm not fool enough to think he took you there merely to chat. When I saw Rhys kissing you in the doorway, I naturally assumed he was

114

continuing something he began outside the walls."

Jessamyn gasped at the other woman's knowledge, and her audacity in speaking of it. "How dare you spy on me, then accuse me . . . ?"

"Oh, save your outraged modesty for someone else. It's wasted on me. I'd have to be blind not to see how taken he is with you. He could hardly keep his eyes off you that first night. And do you really think I believed your pretense of showing him a French romance?"

"The book's still in my room, if you care to see it," Jessamyn countered, her anger mounting. "And even were your accusations founded, what possible business is it of yours what I do?"

"What *you* do concerns me not at all. It's what Rhys does that interests me."

"Rhys is a grown man. He surely has no need of a keeper."

Eluned clenched her fists. With great control, she kept her hands down against her velvet gown. "Neither has he any need of the likes of you," she spat, her knuckles whitening as she spoke.

"I didn't seduce him."

"Men don't need to be seduced. Their blood runs hot day and night. I'm ordering you to stay away from him!"

"You've no right to order me to do anything. I'm lady here. Or have you forgotten?"

"Rhys is mine! And don't you forget that," Eluned hissed, her face close to Jessamyn's. "Don't think I can't see through your ruses to keep him here with one excuse after another."

"Me!" Jessamyn gasped, finally running out of patience. "Do I have the power to direct storms? Would I stage an accident that nearly took a man's life just to keep Rhys here? Don't be ridiculous. Jealousy must have robbed you of sense. Besides,

I don't dictate what Rhys does. If he prefers me to you, surely that's his choice."

"That's where you're wrong. Rhys already made his choice years ago—he's betrothed to me!"

The unexpected news struck Jessamyn with the force of a physical blow. She reeled in shock, her hand flying to her mouth. Eyes rounded, she stared at Eluned, hardly believing what she had heard.

"Betrothed . . . he's betrothed . . . to . . . to you?" she finally stammered, stunned by the revelation.

"Why else do you think he escorts me to Chester? We've been promised to each other most of our lives. All that remains is the ceremony to bind us. So, you see, Jessamyn Dacre, he's using you like some peasant woman to quench his lust. There's no grand romance to it."

Eluned took a step backwards, rewarded by the utter devastation she had seen in Jessamyn's face before she fought to regain her composure.

"How do I know you're speaking the truth?"

"Ask him."

"Oh, I intend to. Now, if this unpleasant discussion is over, I've many tasks to finish."

Jessamyn spun on her heel, steeling herself to keep a smile fixed on her mouth, to contain the tears burning behind her eyes. By betraying how deeply this news had wounded her, she had already given Eluned cause to gloat.

More by instinct and touch than by sight, she negotiated the narrow, winding stair, aware that Eluned Glynne followed close behind her. Tears blurred her vision. Refusing to look back, Jessamyn marched away, back stiff, head high.

It was only when she had rounded the second bend in the corridor, well out of Eluned Glynne's sight, that she dared stop. So devastated did she feel that she struggled to stand on weak, shaking legs.

Eluned had lied—she must have lied! Rhys would never have made love to her if he belonged to another, would never have declared his heart were he not free to do so. Would he? Miserably she conceded the two did not necessarily go hand in hand. Though her knowledge of men was limited, even she knew that all was considered fair when a sexual conquest was at stake. And with her, he had made a swift sexual conquest. So swift that she blushed to remember how readily she had given herself to him.

"Please, Lord. Please, don't let it be so," she whispered, resting her head against the cold stone wall. The darkness wrapped around her like a comforting blanket. Her heart thundered in distress. After a few more minutes of self-pity, she straightened up, drawing back her shoulders and steeling her jaw. What a fool she was to be downed by the first salvo. She had no assurance that Eluned spoke the truth. Rhys said he loved her; he had pledged her his heart. She was doubting him solely on the strength of a spiteful woman's word? The only person who could confirm or deny this hateful news was Rhys.

Then why did she not go in search of him?

With great reluctance, Jessamyn forced her feet forward. Feeling her way along the cold stone wall, she soon reached the bend where a sputtering torch shed dim light down the passage to the kitchens.

What if Eluned spoke the truth? What if Rhys had deceived her? Her heart plunged at the very thought. Jessamyn miserably conceded that it was far too late to reconsider her position. She had already given him her heart and body, treasures put into his safekeeping. Pray God that her trust had not been misplaced.

Through an endless chess game, Jessamyn waited. Her miserable attempts at needlework only led to speared fingers, until she finally abandoned the task in disgust. And still she waited. Had she not known better, she would have thought Rhys was deliberately avoiding her. He seemed in no hurry to meet her questioning gaze, nor did he speak to her, beyond a few pleasantries.

Eluned and her ladies chose to retire early, with Eluned making a great show of bidding her hostess good night. The Welshwoman's blue eyes glittered in triumph when she saw Jessamyn's downcast face.

Now the ladies were gone, perhaps she would have a chance to speak to Rhys alone. But no, there was yet another round of ale, and more debating over a crucial move in this hotly contested chess game. Jessamyn could have screamed with frustration. When she tried to interrupt, Walter angrily shouted at her to hold her tongue. Finally, unable to stand the ordeal, after giving the men a very frosty good night, she forced herself to walk slowly from the Hall. They did not even seem to notice that she was leaving.

Jessamyn endured a long, sleepless night. Even filled with doubt as she was, she entertained the feeble hope that he might slip away to join her. But Rhys did not come.

The following morning, a pale, wintry sun washed the castle battlements with light as Jessamyn stood surveying the surrounding countryside. Eluned was right: the south tower offered a perfect view of the woods. From this vantage point, she could have watched everything. Or had she merely guessed why they disappeared into the trees? Jessamyn tried to recall where Rhys had first embraced her. Even the fodder shed was visible, shielded by trees, it was true, but on their hasty journey to the shed, they must have walked out in the open.

Shuddering at the idea of Eluned watching their most intimate embraces, Jessamyn turned about. Snapping her fingers for Ned, who waited beside her, she began to walk around the battlements. The cold wind was sharp, and she drew her hood closer about her face to cut out the blast. She quickened her pace, angrily striding along while she mentally rehearsed what she would say to him. Like it or not, this morning Rhys would answer all her questions. Could he have guessed Eluned saw them kiss? Did he suspect she had given him away? Was that why he had been avoiding her?

When Jessamyn finally descended the battlements near the stables, she saw Rhys emerging, an empty bucket swinging from his hand. He had been tending his horse.

"Jessamyn, are you going riding?" he asked, pleased to see her.

"No, I was looking for you."

"And now you've found me. Oh, lady, you don't beat about the bush." He chuckled in amusement as he reached for her. But Jessamyn quickly sidestepped his arm. "What is it?" he asked sharply, sensing her ill-humor.

"We must talk. Can you spare me a few minutes?"

"What a question? I can spare *you* the rest of the day," he said, his tone huskily inviting.

Jessamyn winced as her heavy heart leaped. She had to remind herself of the purpose of their talk, lest her resolve be swept away by his charm.

"There's a bench in the sun, inside the walled garden. Come on."

Without further preamble she led the way, striding as fast as her blue wool skirts would allow. In the past, this sunlit spot had always brought her pleasure; today, she wished she were anywhere but here.

119

His expression was puzzled, but, thinking that perhaps this was a new courtship game, Rhys remained affable.

"Now that we are dutifully seated on the bench, what's this important thing you want to say?"

She had intended to build up to it, to give him the chance to trap himself in her cleverly placed snare. But she had not the stomach for it. Miserably, she looked at him, her heart lurching with love as she gazed full upon his handsome face, framed by thick, black curling hair. How inviting were his firm lips. Inviting . . . and quite possibly deceiving!

Jessamyn swallowed and, gathering her wits, she said, "Eluned told me that you and she are betrothed. Is that true?"

For just an instant his dark eyes wavered and Jessamyn felt a knife deep in her heart. Before he ever spoke, she knew that her worst fears were well-founded.

"Well, in a way. Yes, she . . . she's right."

Dear God, at least he had the good grace to stammer! Angry tears stung her eyes. As the pain of betrayal mounted, her heart thumped slow and deep as a base drum. Fighting the pain, searching for breath, she gasped, "It's true—then you are betrothed?"

"Jessamyn, sweet, we . . . we were betrothed in the cradle."

"Oh, Rhys, how could you deceive me?"

"I didn't decieve you," he countered angrily. "Every word I said to you was true. When I said I loved you more than any woman alive, I meant it. This doesn't alter that. In fact, it has nothing to do with it."

Jessamyn was so amazed by his logic that she could scarcely believe what she was hearing. "Doesn't alter it? How can a man pledge his heart to two women at the same time?"

"I never pledged my heart to Eluned Glynne." Angry now, he grasped Jessamyn's hands and would not let her pull free. "Listen to my side before you condemn me. It's true, we're betrothed. It was done long before we were old enough to talk. The understanding that someday we two would wed meant that there was never any need to pledge my heart to her . . ."

"Because she owned it already."

"No . . . never! I've been in no hurry to wed Eluned, I can promise you that. Don't you understand? There's never been any love between us."

"She loves you."

"No, she considers me her possession, nothing more. I've never courted her, never offered my love. We've never even exchanged more that a polite kiss of greeting. Oh, Jessamyn, have sense. You're making far too much of this. Anyone would think I'd deliberately misled you."

"And haven't you?" she cried, longing to strike him for his stubborn insistence that he was in the right.

"No. I may never marry Eluned. Besides, even were she already my wife, it wouldn't alter my feelings for you."

"Oh, spoken like a true man!"

Now he allowed her to pull free. Jessamyn paced back and forth between the brown rows of harvested herbs, and though her skirts swished angrily, her feet still did not move swiftly enough to suit her mood. Finally he grabbed her and stilled the ceaseless pacing.

"So, you think I lied to you, that I merely wanted to seduce you," he spat, pulling her about, forcing her to look at him.

"You told me you loved me. In that, you deceived me."

"No . . . it's true. I do love you."

"You're not free to pledge love to me. You're already promised to her."

"That doesn't stop my loving you."

"You're not *free* to love me. You've already got a promised wife."

He grabbed her arm and pulled her close. Anger hardened his face. "I didn't ask you to marry me."

"No, that you didn't. Only I was too foolish to know the difference. I thought people who loved each other . . ."

"Oh, come on, Jess, stop lying to me. You yourself said daughters of knights didn't marry for love," he reminded her. "There's marrying and loving—they're not the same."

Fighting to regain her composure, Jessamyn took a deep breath. "Whatever clever logic you use, it still remains that you deceived me when you said all those . . . lies." Her voice cracked as she recalled how very sweet those lies had been, how gentle, how seductive. "You seduced me," she cried.

He looked at her, his face like stone. "There was no need of seduction. As I recall, lady, you seemed most eager."

"Damn you! Need you remind me of my weakness?" she spat, her eyes glittering with tears. "Well, you'll never have the chance to say that again! Go back to your betrothed, you Welsh liar! I'll have no more of you."

"What of your great love for *me*? You already seem to have forgotten it. Was that just a meaningless promise?"

Mustering her faculties, Jessamyn raised her head, face white, eyes blazing. His fingers were like a vise about her wrist. "You can put that vow down to temporary insanity, my lord. Rest assured, it won't be repeated."

They stared at each other, standing so close that her skirts wrapped about his legs. Jessamyn was aware of the enveloping heat of his body, the fragrance of his clothing, smelling strongly of musk rose. He must have worn his black doublet for her approval, for it had been stored in a chest and not aired. Her heart lurched as she reluctantly conceded how handsome he was. For one insane moment she was tempted to yield, but then she regained her wits.

"We only have today," Rhys reminded, his voice softening. "Let's not quarrel."

"I'm sure you've much to occupy your time, though I'm sorry you've wasted such a fine doublet on me. Mayhap your betrothed will enjoy the handsome sight of you in your finery," Jessamyn remarked.

With supreme effort, she stepped back, immediately aware of the loss of his protective heat, for even here in the garden the north wind blew cold. She noticed him glance down at his velvet doublet, almost as if he had forgotten he was wearing it.

"Jessamyn . . . don't."

"You have no need to avoid me. Oh, don't deny it. Last night, it would have taken a thunderclap to get your attention. You guessed that Eluned had given you away, didn't you?"

"Jessamyn, stop being a fool. Would you have had me bend you across the table for all to see? I took care not to give our love away, to preserve your reputation, that's all."

"Well, you'll have no further need of playacting. From now on, there'll be nothing more that polite acquaintance between us."

Anger flashed across his stern face and like lightning, he was beside her, grasping her arms and pulling her into his embrace. Jessamyn fought against him but he was too strong for her. Relentlessly he bent her to him, his mouth seeking hers in a smothering kiss. Her will to resist dwindled dangerously low as she almost responded to his caress. Then, mustering the last of her strength, Jessamyn steeled herself to stay aloof.

"Won't you change your mind?" Rhys asked, his voice warm and low against her ear. "Say you'll forgive and forget for these last few hours. Please, sweet, say yes. Don't be so cruel."

"No."

"Did our love mean so little to you that you can turn away like this?"

He tempted her almost beyond endurance with his persuasive voice and strong, comforting arms. Making the supreme effort, she resisted, shutting out her clamoring senses, remembering only that he had deceived her.

"It means so little, my lord, that I never intend to set eyes on you again," she spat, fighting back tears. "Goodbye, Rhys of Trevaron. May you and your betrothed have pleasure in your visit to Chester. Now, if you'll release me, I've much to do."

He stared at her in disbelief, then moved his arms from around her. Inwardly Jessamyn mourned the loss of that welcome warmth, all the love and arousal which had never rightly belonged to her.

"Very well, lady, if that's what you want, I'll oblige. Thank you for your hospitality to me and my men. And I promise not to bother you further."

With that, he spun on his heel and strode away.

Appalled, she stood there, hot angry tears spilling from her eyes. Jessamyn ground her hands together, groaning deep in her chest as she tried to keep her grief inside. It was supposed to be she who made a grand exit, marching away, while he stayed in the garden, all forlorn amidst the stalks and debris of seasons past. Their vows rightfully belonged in this place, for they were nothing more than useless compost. To Rhys, their love had meant no more than a quick harvest of passion—to her it had meant a lifetime.

Chapter Seven

To fill the long hours until Rhys's departure, Jessamyn launched into a flurry of activity designed to occupy her mind and tire her body. Several angry marches about the castle precincts, taken as fast as her legs would allow, proved not near punishment enough.

Taking advantage of the sunshine, she supervised the castle maids as they carried out sleeping pallets and floor coverings. The pallets and rugs were then slung over a washline, where they were beaten with poss sticks. When the women complained, Jessamyn took on the task herself, wielding the wooden implement like a fiend. She found some relief in beating the straw pallet, imagining it was his face and body she pummeled, dealing blow after blow in payment for his treachery.

After that, she undertook much scrubbing and sweeping to burn off her nervous energy. Jessamyn's aim at the end of the day was to be weary in body as well as spirit.

"By all that's holy! What's the matter with you, sister? 'Tis not spring. Why all this flurry of cleaning?" Walter grumbled, put out that he had been denied the use of his chamber for several hours whilst the household tasks were performed.

"Stop complaining. Would you have the castle like a pigsty when our noble kinsman arrives?" she said, swishing past him none too gently and almost upsetting his alecup.

Walter stared after his sister. Though not overly attuned to her moods, even he could not ignore the change in her. Her flashing eyes, tight mouth, and flushed face; a veritable whirlwind of energy—what possessed her? Then he smiled as he finally understood. Tomorrow, the Welshman was leaving. Could this renewed energy be her way of trying to forget their handsome guest? He would have had to be blind not to have noticed the current of interest between them. So, Jessamyn was not impervious to male attentions, after all. He was surprised, for he had thought his sister long past flirtations. Yet, in a way, it would make his future easier. There was always the chance she would find Ralph Warren equally attractive. With a brother-in-law like Sir Ralph, his troubles would be halved. Pray God, the man was presentable. True to form, Jessamyn had a woman's eye for male good looks.

Later that evening Walter rashly chose to mention his discovery. He began innocently enough.

"Rest, for heaven's sake. You'll be ill abed if you keep up this pace," he said, after the candles had been lit and they shared a companionable snack before the hearth.

"No. I've still got to visit the infirmary before I'm finished," she snapped, picking at the warm meat pasty she held in her linen napkin. Walter's appetite

127

had not diminished for this fresh-baked snack, yet tonight Jessamyn found the flaky pastry as delectable as a hunk of stale bread.

"Look, Jessamyn," Walter began, moving closer, thinking to set his sister's mind at ease. "There's nothing wrong with fancying a handsome man. And though I hate to admit it, the Welshman is that. You're just a normal woman. As I've suspected all along, what you really need is a husband."

"What do you mean 'fancy'? I don't *fancy* any man. And I certainly don't want any part of our Welsh guest, so you can stop that simpering, indulgent smile! I'm not, nor will I ever be, in the market for a husband. Just because I take advantage of a sunny day to turn out some cobwebs doesn't make me lovelorn, Walter. I assure you, the departure of Rhys of Trevaron and his betrothed will grieve me not at all."

"Betrothed?" Walter repeated in surprise. "I didn't know she was that. Did he tell us?"

"No, that was his little secret..." Jessamyn paused, noting several of the soldiers' heads had turned. Even her brother was eyeing her curiously. Her voice had sharpened, betraying her bad humor. She swallowed, realizing she was about to give herself away. "Mayhap I'd have treated the lady kinder, had I known," she ended lamely.

Walter pursed his lips, his hazel eyes bright. So the truth was out. Jessamyn fancied the Welshman far more than he suspected. She was angry and disappointed to learn he was not a potential suitor. Walter nodded, a knowing smirk flitting across his face.

"Ah, ha, so now we have it. You wanted the man to court you, and you're jealous because he's already spoken for."

Jessamyn turned on him, her hazel eyes flashing.

"Hold your tongue! You have no idea what you're talking about. I wanted him to court me? You must be mad!"

She stood, her face hot with anger.

"Tut, tut, not a pretty scene, sister dear. You'll have to learn to curb that temper, or no man will want you."

"For all I care, Rhys of Trevaron can go to hell! And you can go with him, Walt." And with that she stalked away.

After a final visit to the infirmary to check on her patients, Jessamyn retired to her room. Walter's discovery of her interest in Rhys was an unwelcome development. Though she had scathingly dismissed his suggestion, she was not sure Walter believed her. All day, she had fought the urge to say goodbye to Rhys. Now she knew that she could not give Walter further cause to gloat. If she did not come down to bid Rhys farewell, that would help put an end to his foolishness.

Friday morning dawned gray and chill.

Jessamyn broke the fast in her room, feigning indisposition. Though, in truth, it was not all fabrication: her head ached, her stomach churned, and her heart felt like a lump of lead.

Soon Rhys would be gone from her life forever. Was she being foolishly stubborn by keeping to her room? Perhaps she would go out onto the battlements to wave goodbye. Surely he would look up at her window. She knew he still thought about her, because the previous night he had sent her a note, which she had angrily thrown into the fire. Now she wished that she had read his message. A despicably weak part of her character would have taken comfort from his words of love. Enough! She would not say goodbye and she would not wave to him from the battlements.

Her absence would cause no breach of hospitality, for Walter could see their guests on their way. He would be only too glad to be shut of the Welsh. Of course, Eluned Glynne would gloat in triumph, but that could not be helped. Jessamyn did not think she could meet Rhys face to face and remain calmly detached, despite her brave declarations to the contrary. Once he was on the road to Chester, she would set about forgetting that he had ever existed.

It would not be easy to resume her former life, she thought, leaning against the windowsill to gaze across the wintery gray landscape. Compared to being with him, her daily life was colorless and boring. Rhys had opened her eyes and her heart. How she would miss the coursing of her blood, the throb of passion.

Abruptly, she turned away. It was no use tormenting herself. He was gone forever. She must get used to the idea.

Within the hour, Jessamyn heard hoofbeats and the rumbling of wheels. Her heart lurched as she saw a column of men and wagons moving along the causeway. The lead rider wore a dark traveling cloak, and was riding beside a lady swathed in a fur-trimmed, garnet cloak. Clenching her hands, Jessamyn watched the horses pick up speed as they neared the highway. She stared after the column until it was reduced to the size of ants. He was gone. And he had never even looked up at her window. Though angry with herself for wallowing in self-pity, somehow Jessamyn was unable to stop. Did he not care? Was she that easily forgotten? Perchance he was a man who collected women like some men collected rings, or hawks. Eluned had said he bore a reputation for hard riding. That spiteful statement probably meant that Rhys took his pleasure wherever he went. She must face the fact that she had been his pleasure at Curlew Castle. It was as simple as that.

With lips grimly compressed, Jessamyn brushed her hair and laced her cinnamon wool gown. The pain took some getting used to. But she would overcome it. With Rhys safely on the road, she could now resume her life.

When she held up the mirror, her pale, pinched face stared back at her. During the night, she had wept copious tears for all her lost dreams. In all honesty, she could not say *lost love,* for it was possible that Rhys had never loved her. She had wept hard, causing her face to swell. Cold compresses over her eyes had helped reduce their puffiness, but Walter would be sure to notice. Let him, she decided angrily. He thought he was so clever, ferreting out her secrets. Unfortunately, his discovery might accelerate his interest in finding her a husband. Walter desperately needed an ally. She dreaded his attempts at matchmaking. Her anger mounted to encompass Walter, too.

A pox on all males, she thought mutinously, crossing to the chest to blow out the candle. The dull thud of Ned's tail against the floor made her smile, softening her anger.

"You're an exception, Ned, love," she whispered, crouching to pat his brindled coat. "But from this day forward, you and Merlin are the only males who have a place in my heart."

Her defiant statement made her feel better. Jessamyn snuffed out the candle and snapped her fingers at Ned. She was lady of Curlew. It was time to go downstairs to resume her life.

It did not matter that Rhys was gone. She had lived without him before, she could certainly do so again. In fact, it would be far less complicated and more enjoyable to return to her former state of chastity—how she lied! The bitter sting of tears as she dwelled on his broken promises told her that much.

Jessamyn grudgingly had to give Walter his due: sensing her distress during the following days, he was too kind to dwell on the subject. Her brother's rare understanding tempered her anger toward him.

As if making an effort to lift her spirits, even the weather changed for the better. The overcast skies cleared and the sun appeared, pale and wintery, to be sure, but warm enough to dispel the frigid air.

Slowly Jessamyn came back to life, though now a more subdued version of her former self. When she dwelled on the situation, the word *bitter* came to mind. She did not like to think of herself as growing bitter. Maybe older and wiser would be a kinder assessment.

Both infirmary patients gradually gained strength. It was a shock to Jessamyn when she realized Rhys must return to Curlew, if only to collect his man-at-arms. But that would be long after Christmas. By then, her bruised ego would be fully recovered, she told herself with newfound confidence, and if it were not, the Lord of the castle could attend to the visitors.

The first week passed, and she had survived the pain of her loss. The week had not been easy to endure. Margery and Jack the Drover had been married in the parish church. Their mutual bliss and the anticipation of their wedding night had rubbed salt in her wounds. Her loss seemed all the more acute in the face of their happiness. She was relieved when, after the first hour, she and Walter excused themselves from the festivities, allowing the villagers to enjoy their celebration unencumbered by the sobering presence of their lord and lady.

*   *   *

Jessamyn reined in her horse on a knoll over-looking the windswept valley, pausing to survey the wintery, sun-splashed countryside. It would soon be Christmas. She must start planning for the upcoming festival. She had decided already that this year they would fashion garlands of holly and bayberry cut from the nearby woods. In the Hall chest were a dozen bright red candles that she had hoarded from more prosperous times, and a bundle of tinkling silver bells. This year, their austere Hall would be filled with Christmas cheer.

Shielding her eyes from the sun, Jessamyn looked towards the hills across the valley, her attention caught by moving specks of color and flashes of light. For a few minutes, she studied the move-ment before deciding it was a column of horsemen. Her heart lurched at the discovery. Could Rhys be returning sooner than expected? Had he left Eluned Glynne in Chester? Was he returning to Wales? Angry with herself for allowing her heart to leap with joy, she quickly dashed that hopeful thought. This party traveled from the south, and it was an army, not merely an armed band of Welshmen. The soldiers must be the king's men, for they traveled in too orderly a fashion for Glyndwr's followers, their perfectly aligned, twin columns unbroken as they rounded the hillside. Here and there, sunlight sparked fire from their armaments, blinking as they slowly moved downhill, winding their way towards her.

The sight of their helmets and plate removed all doubt that the approaching riders were soldiers. Jessamyn turned Merlin around. Best to get back inside the protective castle walls. Though these sol-diers would likely bypass Curlew, there was no point in taking any chances. Today, she had not bothered to disguise her sex, merely throwing a cloak over her wool gown. She did not fancy becoming a morning sport for King Henry's levies.

Jessamyn had been back inside Curlew an hour before Simon, the captain of the guard, came into the Great Hall to confer with Walter. She took little notice of them, being more concerned with warming herself before the hearth whilst she sipped a comforting cup of mulled ale.

Suddenly she noticed that Walter's demeanor had changed; his face was animated, his movements excited. Simon saluted and strode from the Hall.

All smiles, Walter hurried toward her, his face aglow.

"What now? Are those soldiers I saw coming here?" she asked grimly, wondering at her brother's excitement.

"Soldiers, yes, but . . . Oh, Jessamyn, they're not just any soldiers. *He's* here."

"He?"

"Sir Ralph of Cater's Hill asks permission to enter Curlew," he declaimed in ringing tones. "We must go out to greet him."

Jessamyn's heart sank. Grimly she stood and put down her cup.

"All right, let's get this over with."

"What do you mean, 'get it over with'?"

"Let's go meet our noble relative and learn the worst. God grant that we both have a roof over our heads by nightfall. If this is the column I watched, it stretches from here to Holly Ridge."

"Don't start that!" Walter snarled, stepping forward as there came a flurry of movement at the door. "I want you to put forth your best, for Christ's sake. At least pretend you're not a sour spinster."

Jessamyn pulled a face at him. "Why, do you

intend to marry me off to this one?"

The sickly smile Walter turned on her, the guilt flushing his face, revealed the worst. Her oath was lost in the ensuing noise of booted feet entering the Hall.

They stood aside as a procession of men-at-arms trooped inside the Hall, forming orderly groups as they awaited the arrival of their lord. Eyeing them warily, Curlew's own soldiers stayed apart from these strangers. Though the castle kept only a small garrison, Simon had already dispatched a dozen men to the Great Hall to guard Lord Walter and his sister, just in case these friends proved not so friendly.

At last, a buzz of expectancy amongst the ranks revealed Sir Ralph's approach. Jessamyn clasped her hands tightly, aware of her sweating palms as she awaited her first glimpse of their possible conqueror—or worse still, her prospective husband! She shuddered, finding the latter even more objectionable than the former.

Hurrying forward, Walter held out his hand in greeting as a stocky man of medium height, clad in light plate armor, entered the Great Hall. In this dim light, Jessamyn was only aware of his build and dress; she could not assess his age. Her brother and Sir Ralph embraced as kinsmen. They both turned, scanning the gloomy room for Jessamyn. She had purposely retreated to the shadows and stood before an arras on the north wall, not anxious to be part of the welcoming homage.

As he spotted her standing there, consciously deepening his voice, Walter called, "Come, sister, be not so bashful."

She could have hit him. Forcing a smile to her mouth, Jessamyn reluctantly moved forward to greet their guest. When she reached Sir Ralph, eyes still downcast, she sank in a billowing curtsy, aware of Walter's surprised gasp of approval.

"Welcome to Curlew, Sir Ralph. I trust your journey was pleasant," she mouthed sweetly, staring at his pointed solerets, winking and glittering in the light. The exaggerated points on his foot armor made his feet appear exceedingly long and narrow. Then she felt a hand on her brow as her face was gently tilted up to gaze full upon Sir Ralph Warren of Cater's Hill.

"My journey was indeed pleasant, yet not nearly as pleasant as my arrival has been. I didn't expect to be greeted by such a beautiful lady," he said gallantly, his voice somewhat gruff.

Jessamyn smiled sweetly at Sir Ralph's compliment whilst she quickly assessed his appearance. His jaw was square, his face smooth-skinned and handsome in an unremarkable way. His deepset eyes were slate blue, and the hair matted against his brow by the pressure from his helmet was golden brown and abundant. Though he appeared youthful, she doubted that he was quite as young as the dim light suggested. Jessamyn was forced to admit that she was pleasantly surprised by both his manner and appearance. She had expected a pompous, corpulent old windbag of a knight, raddled by a life of dissipation.

Sir Ralph wore a white surcoat over his elaborately engraved mail; the helmet he carried was topped by a silver plume. Most knights reserved such decorative gear for tourneys. Sir Ralph Warren chose to wear this fine suit of German armor on a daily basis, proclaiming his wealth and position.

Jessamyn rose, finding that she was nearly as tall as he. Sir Ralph smiled at her and she gave him a guarded smile in reply. Her attention was fixed on the insignia emblazoned on his surcoat: a shield quartered in blue and silver surmounted by a coiled serpent. After a moment's study, she translated the Latin motto beneath—*Bruise Not the Heel*. This unusual motto had probably been derived from the biblical passage wherein the serpent is condemned to bruise the heel of the son of man.

"Jessamyn, are you asleep?" Walter hissed, giving her a shove to get her attention.

She blinked, realizing that she had been so busy studying Sir Ralph's coat of arms, she had not heard what was said. Aware of the need to appear obliging, she simply smiled apologetically and waited.

"She's overcome by your magnificent presence," Walter explained swiftly.

Under cover of her skirts, Jessamyn kicked his shin. Walter winced, but maintained his smile.

"And I am overcome by your beauty, Lady Jessamyn. This could prove to be the most pleasant three days of my life."

She continued to smile like an idiot, mentally rejoicing in his words. Three days. Thank God! At least they would not have to endure him for weeks on end.

"I was suggesting that you order refreshment for our guest," Walter added sharply, his fingers gouging her forearm. "Sir Ralph must be hungry and thirsty."

Dropping a slight curtsy, Jessamyn moved away to do as she was bidden. She did not know how long she could affect simpering obedience. On consideration, she decided that she might just be able to manage the act for three whole days to please Walter—*if* she decided to please him. That decision depended on how hard he pressed his hateful intention to interest Sir Ralph in matrimony. It was probable Sir Ralph already had a wife, or so she fervently hoped. When he learned the bad news,

Walter's face would be a yard long.

Jessamyn remained absent from the men's company as long as she dared. Finally, she was forced to go down to sup, for she knew they would be impatiently awaiting her.

She had ordered a feast to be prepared for the main meal. They were eating later than usual to allow the cooks sufficient time to roast capons, to prepare jellied sturgeon and to bake pigeon pies. The guests' immediate hunger and thirst had been easily satisfied with bread, meat and ale.

Knowing it would be expected, Jessamyn changed her dress and carefully arranged her hair in thickly coiled plaits over her small ears. Though she supposed Walter would be annoyed, she did not wear her best gown, settling instead for second best. The reminder of the last time she had worn that silver-trimmed blue gown was still too fresh. In fact, when Mary pulled the gown out of the clothes chest, a painful lump rose in her throat and her heart hammered uncomfortably as memories too precious to bear were awakened. She had spoken sharply to the girl and hurt her feelings, an unkindness for which she later apologized.

Jessamyn smoothed her hand over the rose silk. This gown, with its wine-embroidered surcoat trimmed with rabbit fur, was almost as grand as her blue one. No doubt, Sir Ralph would find her attractive, best gown or not. Her mouth curled distastefully at the idea. It was not her intention to dress attractively in order to woo him. She was tempted to change back into her everyday wool but, for Walter's sake and Curlew's honor, Jessamyn resolved to dress as befitted the lady of the castle.

She made her way down to the Great Hall, the roar of voices growing louder as she drew closer. After making sure her plaited pink ribbon chaplet

was set straight on her hair, Jessamyn stepped boldly inside the noisy, candlelit Hall.

All eyes were immediately fixed on this beautiful
vision. Though respectful, the soldiers' glances were
vastly appreciative. Head high, Jessamyn bypassed
the lower tables, crowded close together to accommodate this unexpectedly large party of soldiers.

Candlegrease and pine resin from the firelogs
mingled with delectable kitchen aromas inside the
dark-beamed Hall. Much of her life had been played
out beneath this hammer-beamed roof, Jessamyn
realized as she crossed the rush-strewn flagstones.
Hopefully this latest incident concerning Sir Ralph
would not end unhappily.

Aware of the stir of interest amongst the men-at-
arms, Sir Ralph looked up to see her approaching
the High Table. Mary was walking at a respectful
distance behind Jessamyn, playing lady-in-waiting.
Though, in truth, she was but a maid, Jessamyn
had thought the introduction of her own waiting
woman would be an added nicety that would be
greatly appreciated by Walter. After all, she did not
want to be totally outdone by their rich relation.

"My dear Lady Jessamyn, what a vision you are,"
Sir Ralph complimented, stepping down from the
dais to greet her. He raised her hand to his lips,
pressing his warm mouth against her skin.

"About time," Walter hissed as she passed him on
the way to her chair at their guest's left hand. "What
took so long?"

"Your dinner," she swiftly retorted. Then, she sat
in her chair, hands meekly folded, and refused to
enter into further discussion with him.

Her arrival was the signal for the start of the
procession of dishes from the kitchen. Most of the
castle's servants had been pressed into action to
bring out the feast. As Sir Ralph had brought food

and provisions for them, Jessamyn reasoned that they could now afford to feed him well.

First came platters of roast capon swimming in purple wine sauce, their golden brown skins crackling hot from the oven, followed by spiced sturgeon afloat in an amber jellied sea, edged with sprigs of parsley; Smoked fish paste, and meat pounded soft with spices and wine. Floury circles of Welsh cakes and round loaves of barley and wheat bread were accompanied by wooden bowls of fresh-churned butter, and dishes of sweet rosehip jelly. Pink, foamy almond whip and spicy, fragrant gingerbread complemented steaming bowls of spiced apples. To wash down the meal, Jessamyn had ordered their best Gascon wine to be tapped in honor of Sir Ralph's visit.

Walter's eyes rounded in surprise as he beheld the feast, and a slow smile of anticipation spread across his face. Not only would the food be pleasurable, the fact that he was able to entertain Sir Ralph in so splendid a fashion fulfilled his dearest wish.

While they ate, the men discussed the garrison, provisions, and the current unsettled state of the country. Eager to impress Sir Ralph, Walter actually listened to him and took an active part in the discussion.

Jessamyn ate in silence, knowing that a woman was not expected to take part in the discussion. She doubted that Walter would retain much of Sir Ralph's fact-laden talk. She had been surprised to hear that King Henry was hard-pressed to quash Glyndwr's Welsh troops. She also noted with satisfaction that Walter had wisely not revealed that their father had been King Richard's man. It was clear that Sir Ralph supported Henry of Bolingbroke. It was better not to give him the slightest cause for distrust. Fortunately, he had not questioned them about where their own loyalties lay. Jessamyn found this fact unsettling. From such a man as he, she would have expected that question to have been asked at the start. To tell him that they had chosen no side in the struggle simply would not be acceptable to a king's man. Sir Ralph had already told them about the royal court, and about fighting the king's battles. This reminder of his exalted status did not surprise her, for his retainers' mounts and accoutrements proclaimed his wealth. Wealthy noblemen generally curried favor with kings in order to amass even greater wealth.

Turning to her, Sir Ralph laid down his knife.

"My dear Lady Jessamyn, we must be boring you with our talk of war and strife. Tell me what you lack in provisions and you shall have all you need," Sir Ralph said pleasantly. "You are to be commended for your splendid management of the castle's kitchen."

"Thank you, Sir Ralph, your offer is most kind. I'll give you a list in the morning."

He continued to eat a dish of spiced apples, accompanying his dessert with heavy sweet wine.

Sir Ralph's splendid doublet of peacock blue velvet was parti-colored in purple and red; his matching tights were also red and purple. His soft-soled, crimson velvet shoes were embroidered with gold thread and had elongated toes adorned by gold bells. Jessamyn supposed that such a color combination was fashionable at court, yet she found it garishly reminiscent of a jester's costume and not to her taste. His perfumed hair was brushed back from his face, softening his appearance. Yet, in the bright candlelight of the banquet table, the style revealed age lines on his brow. Beneath his eyes was a veritable nest of crow's feet, and twin furrows framed his mouth, suggesting that Sir Ralph was more advanced in age than his lithe looks betrayed. The candlelight made his blue eyes almost black. While he ate, Jessamyn was conscious of his appraising glances, which traveled unsettlingly from her waist to the top of her chaplet and back again. Her stomach lurched as she interpreted the lustful expression on his face. From then on, she intended to give Sir Ralph a wide berth, for he took no pains to conceal the fact he was highly interested in her.

Though, so far, he had treated her with politeness and gallantry, Jessamyn did not trust him. All the while, as he smiled and spoke so kindly, his eyes never changed. Jessamyn fancied that she saw a cunning, acquisitive gleam whenever he looked about the Hall. He had generously complimented Walter on the sturdy attractiveness of his small fortress, and on its splendid vantage point. Uneasily, Jessamyn wondered if her worst fears were to be founded.

Poor Walt, chatting away, all smiles, vastly impressed with their rich kinsman, was totally unaware of any undercurrent of deceit. It would be up to her to keep a sharp eye and ear out for any slip Sir Ralph might make to betray himself.

Chapter Eight

To her aggravation, Jessamyn found after three days at Curlew, Sir Ralph had yet to betray any hidden motive behind his generosity. She might even have begun to be swayed by Walter's overwhelming acceptance of him, had not William Rhees shared her unease. In this, at least, the castle steward was her ally.

Walter exploded with rage when, together, they confronted him, warning him to take care.

"Of all the ridiculous nonsense! May I remind you both, I am lord here. You, Rhees, can get out! Castle steward you may be, but you've no right to tell me who I should trust and not trust."

"Hush. Would you have him hear?" Jessamyn cautioned, glancing about as Walter's voice became shrill with indignation.

"He can't hear us. He's out riding. See, down there. Look at that splendid hawk."

"Walter, listen," Jessamyn cried, taking her brother's shoulder and turning him away from the broad window, where he smiled indulgently upon Sir Ralph and a couple of his men exercising their horses.

Walter pulled a face. "What now?" he asked, thoroughly put out by the suspicious attitudes of his sister and their steward. "If he can hear from this distance, it will truly be a miracle."

"He has men below, so keep your voice down," Jessamyn cautioned him. "All we're asking is that you don't trust him too wholeheartedly."

"He's given us provisions and he's promised more. He's even leaving some of his men to help defend the castle."

"That, my lord, is our main concern," William Rhees interjected, his face lined with worry. "Sir Ralph Warren travels with a large force, far too many soldiers for a mere friendly visit."

"How was he to know what he might encounter, the way the Welsh have been raiding everywhere? That's his reason for bringing so many men."

"He told you that?"

"Of course. Much to your surprise, I'm sure, but I'm not the complete fool you two take me for. I already asked him why he brought so many troops. His answer satisfied me."

But not me, Jessamyn thought silently as she nodded to William Rhees to leave them. "Did he say anything about when he's going to return?"

"Sometime in the spring, when we all know a little better how these confounded Welsh are going to behave. And he'll bring us more provisions then, if we need them. Oh, I tell you, Jessamyn, this is one time you are dead wrong."

"And he's still leaving in the morning, as planned?"

Walter smiled and shook his head in disbelief. "You suspicious woman, of course he's leaving. His wagons are being packed as we speak. Now, aren't you sorry you said all those cruel things to me?"

She smiled. "Walter dear, you shall have your answer to that question in the spring."

He scowled in displeasure. "You still won't admit it, will you? And I haven't discussed betrothing you to him, in case that's your next question."

"Thank you. So far I've pretended to be all meek and mild to please you, so that's the least consideration you can show me."

"He'd be a good husband. You couldn't do better, Jessamyn. He's a champion in the lists. He's handsome, too. And his clothes—he dresses like a king! You know, we could mention it to him, jog his memory about father's idea. He'll be gone tomorrow . . ."

"No. Walt!" she warned, her face tightening. "If you want me malleable, you'll do nothing of the sort. But, if you want me ten times more independant than usual, just try it."

Walter swallowed, his face flushed. He did not want to press his sister to carry out her threats. The past three days had proved even more satisfactory than he had dreamed. He had established such a good rapport with their kinsman, they had become friends. Ralph had promised that even after he left, they would continue to share this special close relationship. If she set her mind to it, Jessamyn could spoil everything.

"I'm making no promises," Walter said at last.

"Neither am I."

Jessamyn stood in the shelter of the tower and watched Sir Ralph riding back towards the castle. Unease still tugged at her mind. Though the nobleman and his captain had supposedly been training their hawks and exercising their horses in the water meadows beyond the walls, she could not help wondering what else they had done. Far too often, their heads had been close together, their faces stern, as if they discussed some secret maneuver. If they had hatched a plot, they had been clever enough to wait until they were outside the castle walls. That way they eliminated any chance of being overheard.

She sighed, shielding her eyes from the sun. It was possible that Walter was right. Maybe she had misjudged their rich kinsman. It was possible, but highly unlikely.

Glancing up as he drew close to the castle walls, sharp-eyed Sir Ralph glimpsed her bright-colored gown fluttering in the wind. His face broke into a charming smile of greeting and he waved to her.

Jessamyn waved back, then turned to go indoors.

"Hold, Lady Jessamyn, I would speak with you," he shouted, his resonant voice blowing across the battlements.

Though she had little desire for this meeting, Jessamyn knew it was polite to comply.

They met in the screen passage behind the Great Hall. Sir Ralph was pulling off his cloak and gauntlets, which he handed to his squire.

"How fortunate that I saw you, Lady Jessamyn. Is it my imagination, or have you been avoiding me?" he asked smoothly, his gaze never wavering from her face.

Jessamyn swallowed, knowing that she was found out.

"Walter's monopolized much of your time these past days. Besides, I've been needed elsewhere. I've patients to attend in the infirmary."

They were striding through the Hall, heading for the chairs beside the blazing hearth. "Patients? ah, yes, an old woman, and a Welshman! I saw them yesterday when your brother took me on a tour of the castle."

Thanks, Walt, Jessamyn thought in annoyance. That specific visit could have been left off the intinerary. Hastening to explain away Alun's presence, Jessamyn tried to appear nonchalant. "There was a fire in the village. The man's comrades helped put it out. Naturally, I offered them a couple of night's hospitality in return. Unfortunately, this man was injured when they were loading their wagons. There was little I could do but offer him board until he's well enough to travel."

"Naturally, being the kind soul that you are. But I do warn you, Lady Jessamyn, these Welsh are treacherous. It's wisest not to allow them within a mile of the castle."

Wine and cakes appeared on the table, as if by magic. Jessamyn had not ordered them and she looked askance at their guest, realizing that he must be responsible for the order.

"I took the liberty of ordering refreshment for my return. Come, share it with me."

Sir Ralph poured her a goblet of heavy malmsey.

Jessamyn sipped the sweet wine, watching him uneasily over the rim of her cup. He was already acting as if Curlew were his home. "You wanted to speak to me about something important," she prompted. She did not enjoy his company and she wished wholeheartedly that Walter would appear to distract them. As the minutes passed, Jessamyn had a growing premonition about the probable subject for discussion.

Sir Ralph stretched out his hands to her. On his stubby fingers she saw several gold rings set with jewels the size of bird eggs. His square, sunburned hands were not what she had expected of a nobleman; their hands were usually soft and white. But then, she reminded herself uneasily, Sir Ralph was not merely a decorative courtier. He had fought battles for his king, had quite probably seized castles as well.

When his fingers touched hers, Jessamyn shivered, but it was not in pleasure.

"Jessamyn—I can call you that, can't I?"

She nodded, swallowing nervously. This discussion had all the makings of her worst nightmare. The knowledge that he was going to ask her to marry him flashed through her mind so clearly, that when he actually spoke the words, she had an unsettling feeling of déjà vu.

"My dear lady, will you consent to be my wife?"

Jessamyn's eyes rounded in shock as she looked at him wordlessly.

"I know it's sudden. After all, I must leave tomorrow and we've not the luxury of time." He paused and gently stroked her fingers clasped in his own. "You're the loveliest woman I've ever seen," he complimented softly. "I need not remind you that I'm not growing any younger. If only you'll say yes, you can make me the happiest man in England. And, if not that, then at least say you'll consider my suit."

"Is Walter behind this?" Jessamyn demanded sharply, surprising him with her angry question.

"Your brother? Nay, I took it upon myself to speak to you. As you're a grown woman, I thought there was no need. Oh, I realize we must eventually consult your brother. As lord of Curlew, it's his right. But . . . no, this is all my own idea. Surely we're both old enough to know exactly what we want."

A sigh of relief slowly escaped her lips. Chalk one up to Walter on that score. At first Jessamyn thought that when he denied matchmaking, he had lied to her. If that had been the case, she would have given Sir Ralph a parting to remember. As he gazed eagerly at her, awaiting her answer, Jessamyn grew uneasy. His face had turned soft and youthful, like a lad in love. To her surprise, she saw longing and passion in his eyes. Jessamyn swallowed, wondering how best to extricate herself from this situation. If she were wrong and this nobleman was a genuine friend, it was wise not to offend him. She must bear that in mind, or she could easily have put an end to their discussion.

"I've no desire to marry, Sir Ralph," she began, keeping her eyes modestly downcast. "As you already know about my work in the infirmary, my next statement shouldn't surprise you. I intend to devote my life to healing the sick. Never to marry, to remain . . . chaste." She swallowed, hoping the Lord God would not strike her dead for lying. "I've vowed to devote my days to prayer and healing."

There was a long, uncomfortable silence. Sir Ralph was visibly stunned by her answer; Jessamyn was rather stunned by it herself. She felt that she should have been applauded for such brilliance at so short a notice. After a few minutes of silence, she chanced a look at him from under her long lashes. His face was stony with disappointment.

"Such an idea's sacrilege," he rasped at last. "Can you not pray and tend the sick as my wife? I promise not to make great demands on you. In my manor at Cater's Hill, I can provide for you in great comfort. You shall have trained women to assist you with the care of the sick. Jessamyn, dearest, we could establish a charity hospital. That way, you could satisfy your vow and the dearest wish of my heart, all at the same time."

His startling counterproposal was so unexpected that, at first, Jessamyn could think of nothing to say. "You overwhelm me," she whispered, whilst her mind whirled, searching for a plausible objection to the plan.

When he smiled, she knew that she had said the right thing.

"Think on it, sweet lady. Years ago, Sir Hugh suggested a betrothal between us. There, I see you remember."

Gulping at his reminder, she nodded. She remembered all right, and the memory was not filled with pleasure.

"Had I known then what beauty awaited me, I'd never have let the matter lapse. Eventually, I married another, who, God rest her soul, died several winters past. Strange how fate has directed me to complete your late father's wish. It's never too late, dearest Jessamyn. Can I dare hope to have your answer before I leave?"

Her heart thumped uncomfortably as she realized he was going to be persistent. "At such short notice," she murmured sweetly, "and with marriage being the furthest thought from my mind, I'm afraid, Sir Ralph, that today, my answer must be no."

"But there's always tomorrow, dear heart. I won't accept such an answer. Don't make me unhappy, Jessamyn. At least give me hope. Say you'll consider it."

He was determined to woo her. Jessamyn's stomach lurched uneasily as she wondered how best to extricate herself from this situation.

"If you insist, I'll think on it. Say—until spring."

"Though you've disappointed me greatly, you have my word. Spring, it shall be." His voice took on a warning tone as he added, "Dear Lady Jessamyn, by spring my heart could be so inflamed, I mightn't take no for an answer."

Then Sir Ralph rose, the discussion at an end. Bowing over her hand, he lightly pressed his mouth against her fingers.

Jessamyn watched him walk purposfully towards

a group of his men, who were waiting beside the door. Her heart chilled as she reviewed their discussion. Her chances of avoiding the match were slim. Walter would be overjoyed at the offer. As far as he was concerned, her dislike for Sir Ralph presented little impediment to marriage. She detected a veiled threat in Sir Ralph's parting words. Did he intend to abduct her, carrying her off against her will to Shrewsbury to be his bride? The thought was so chilling, she could scarcely wait for him to be gone. The sooner he left Curlew, the safer she would feel.

As night approached, the wind rose. Uneasily, Jessamyn wondered if they were in for a storm. She hoped Sir Ralph's departure was not to be delayed by bad weather.

To her dismay, Jessamyn discovered that their kinsman intended to leave behind forty of his soldiers and their captain to strengthen Curlew's defenses against a possible attack by the Welsh. Though she tried to dissuade Walter from the plan, her brother was adamant. This proposal was a dream come true, as was the budding friendship he shared with Ralph Warren. How could his sister be so dense? Ralph was their friend and relation, merely interested in their safety and well-being. This fact he repeated to her time and again, but to no avail. A burst of derisive laughter met Jessamyn's suggestion that Sir Ralph had a far more sinister reason for the morning's outing beyond the walls. Walter would listen to nothing which cast his new friend in a suspicious light.

Still seething over Walter's stubborn trust, Jessamyn was unable to sleep. By now it had stopped raining and the wind had grown calm. She was hungry and thirsty. Though she had rung for Mary earlier, the noise of the wind must have drowned out the bell. Now, for want of something better to do, and still being unable to sleep, Jessamyn decided she would go downstairs in search of refreshment.

Carefully she descended the stairs, shielding her candle against the draughts blowing through the arrow slits. Sir Ralph was yet another man who threatened to complicate her life. There was no way to compare the way she felt about Rhys to her feelings for Sir Ralph. Her anger with Rhys caused a deep pain in her heart, while Sir Ralph elicited a different form of anger. Despite Walter's angry protests to the contrary, she was plagued by thoughts of his possible deceit. At times Walter could be amazingly dense. Unless they were secretly plotting, why else would Sir Ralph and his captain be so deep in discussion outside the walls, where they could not be overheard?

Except for a scullion sleeping in the rushes beside the hearth, the kitchen was deserted. A couple of small white dogs, used by the cook to turn the spit, came running to her. When working, these dogs ran inside a wheel, turning the spit beside the hearth. Speaking softly to the animals, Jessamyn swiftly reassured them, and they ran back to their straw.

Jessamyn broke off a hunk of bread and spread it with honey. Next, she poured herself a cup of cider.

Carrying her food, she left the kitchen. As a child she had been afraid of the ghost purported to walk the passages at night. As an adult, she knew that there were flesh and blood creatures far more dangerous than shadowy wraiths from the past.

The castle seemed unnaturally quiet, especially considering they had so many guests. Was she being too suspicious, as Walter had suggested? He had hurt her feelings by telling her that she had truly become an old maid, with all her silly notions of treachery at every turn.

The cold wind gusted through the window opening and, shielding her candle, she peered outside into the darkness. Once the storm had passed, the moon was visible in the cloud-filled sky, casting its fitful light over the castle ward. On the battlements she could see sentries walking guard, though she did not know if the soldiers belonged to Sir Ralph, or to Curlew.

Life was so unfair, Jessamyn mused, as she resolutely turned and headed back to her bedchamber. Here was Sir Ralph, for whom she had no trace of affection, begging her to marry him, while the man she loved was already promised to another.

A man's laughter, then the hum of lowered voices, made her stop. She shivered in the cold, gloomy passage. The draughts made her candleflame dance wildly, casting grotesque images across the masonry. The voices were coming from the storeroom off the kitchens. Who could be stirring at this hour? Were there thieves at work? Or were the castle servants pilfering the new supplies unloaded from Sir Ralph's wagons?

Filled with indignation, Jessamyn marched forth to do battle. If they thought to evade detection by skulking about in the night, she would soon deflate their plans.

She stopped outside the closed door, her blood chilling. The voice she heard inside the room did not belong to a rough servant. Sir Ralph's clipped speech was unmistakable. She did not recognize the voice of the other man, who was hushed several times by his lord, for fear he would be overheard. The man must have been Sir Ralph's captain, the one who was to stay behind to oversee the men guarding Curlew.

"How long, my lord? This is a right hole to be stuck in," the man grumbled, and was promptly hushed again by his master.

"By all that's holy, Jackson, would you have them on top of us? These very walls have ears. Suffice it to say you won't have to stay here any longer than necessary."

His master's gruff reply did little to mollify the captain. "How long's that, Sir Ralph? Betsy's near her time, and I've a mind to see the little beggar before it's growed."

"Rest assured, you'll be home long before then. I've some unfinished business for the king. After that, we'll strike. If it takes too long, I'll send the wench and her brat here to you."

This suggestion obviously met with approval, for there was no dissenting voice. Sir Ralph continued, "Just do as you're bidden. There's no haste—they trust us implicitly. Spring, early summer, will be time enough. By then, you'll know this place inside out. First, I've got to placate Bolingbroke. Surely you realize the king's got first claim on me?"

"Aye, it's just that I don't want to be biding time here when I could be fighting alongside you."

"If I have my way, there'll be little fight to it. I'm no fool. All we have to do is make Bolingbroke *think* we're fighting on his behalf. A few skirmishes here and there should be sufficient."

Though she bore no love for King Henry, Jessamyn's mouth tightened as she listened; the revelation cast Sir Ralph Warren in an even blacker light. Not only did he intend to deceive them, he was not beyond deceiving his master, the king. She pressed her ear against the door, wishing the wood were not so sturdy, for the men had lowered their voices. The door stood slightly ajar and she pushed the heavy wood, quietly opening the door a little wider so that she might hear more clearly.

" . . . When I return, there will be time enough to move. You'll have no trouble out of them, Jack. The lad's a fool! We'll snatch the castle from under his nose, and he'll still be sniveling about imagined wrongs."

"What about her?"

"She's a woman—what else is there to say?"

Jessamyn seethed over his easy dismissal of her as no threat. How dare he dismiss her so lightly, as if she had no brain in her head? She would soon see about that! If only they were a little more informative, she could learn how and when they intended to overthrow Curlew. She had no idea how she could prevent their executing their plans, but she would think of something. Sir Ralph would not get away with stealing Curlew.

The sound of heavy steps heading for the door sent Jessamyn running. She hid behind the kitchen door, her heart thumping so loudly that she was sure it could be heard in the passage, barely a foot away.

"You'll be well rewarded, Jack. I promise. You can be castellan here, if you wish. Bess might like the place. It could benefit from a woman's touch."

Jessamyn barely contained her snort of indignation over his words. Not only was Sir Ralph a traitor, he dared to criticize her housekeeping capabilities to boot. She could have cheerfully wrung his neck.

"I'll send word back regular, Sir Ralph. Noddy's a good, steady lad. He can slip out without being noticed."

"Once a week—sooner if needed. We never know what might happen. Though they appear to have no allies, we could be surprised."

The two men walked away, leaving Jessamyn seething with rage and betrayal. She could hardly walk to Walter's chamber quickly enough, bursting to reveal what she had overheard.

"By all that's holy, what do you want at this hour?" Walter grumbled sleepily. His valet had admitted Jessamyn to his room. "Have you any idea what time it is?"

Jessamyn pulled her blue wool bedrobe tighter about her body to cover her shift. She nodded to the servant to leave.

"For once just shut up and listen to me," she hissed without preamble, barely giving the valet time to close the door. "Everything I've warned you about Sir Ralph is true."

"Oh, really, Jessamyn, you mean you woke me up in the middle of the night just to start this again," Walter dismissed in exasperation. Struggling out of his mountain of bedcovers, he suggested, "Why not have a cup of wine, then go back to bed."

He went to the chest beside the bed and poured two cups of wine from a pewter flagon. The floor was cold to his bare feet and he returned to the warmth of his bed, patting the coverlet beside him, indicating that his sister come inside the covers with him. The fire in the hearth had died down hours ago and the room was freezing.

"All right, now drink your wine, warm up, then out, Jessamyn, and let me get some sleep."

"First hear me out, Walter, *then* tell me I'm wrong."

Walter listened while he sipped his malmsey, though he did not believe what she was telling him. "Oh, come on, Jessamyn, you were dreaming, having a nightmare. That's all."

"No. Walt, I was wide awake, standing downstairs in the passage, listening at the door," she cried, her fingers biting sharply into his arm.

"Then you must have misunderstood what they

were saying. I think you're unhinged, skulking about the passages at this time of night, in this weather. What's the matter with you? Have you completely lost your mind?"

"I'm not the one who's mind's lost. It's you, Walt."

"Stop calling me Walt!"

"Walter, for heaven's sake, give me some credit. I have excellent hearing, agreed?"

Reluctantly he nodded. "You must have mistaken what was said. Ralph's our friend. True, he's leaving his men and returning in the spring, but as a friend, nothing else. From what you tell me, there really wasn't anything revealing . . ."

"Nothing revealing," she cried, hitting his arm and almost upsetting his cup. " 'We'll snatch the castle from under his nose?' Tell me that's not revealing."

Jessamyn was too kind to repeat the rest of the sentence. Her heart had sunk when she discovered Walter's cherished friendship with Ralph was non–existent. The older man had merely used him to further his own cause.

"You don't know that they meant Curlew," Walter argued stubbornly, loath to accept her story. "Did they ever say Curlew?"

Jessamyn had to admit they had not. "No, but they didn't need to. It was understood."

"By you, maybe. Look, Jessamyn, you've had this bee in your bonnet ever since you found out I'd written to Ralph. I knew you wouldn't rest until you'd uncovered something you could blame him for."

Jessamyn rocked back on her heels, crouching under the covers. "Walter, if you weren't my brother . . . What must I do to convince you?"

"There's nothing you can do. Now, go back to bed like a good girl and let me get back to sleep. This will all seem better in the morning. We'll discuss it then."

Patricia Phillips

"Walter, you're a fool!"
"And you're a bitch. Now go back to bed."
Seething, Jessamyn leaped from the bed and stormed back to her own room. She could not believe that Walter was so stubborn. The man held him in thrall. Were she to bring Ralph and his captain to Walter's chamber and extract a confession from them, she doubted that her brother would accept it. There was nowhere else to turn for help in solving their dilemma. She would have to work out a solution alone.

Chapter Nine

Sir Ralph and his soldiers rode out of Curlew in the chill dawn light. Their orderly ranks made a splendid sight with banners waving, the gold threads in their lord's serpent insignia glinting in the light from the smoking torches.

Walter waved farewell like an eager child as the troops rode over the causeway and on to the road. His wave was answered by Sir Ralph, whose smile was friendly to cover his black, treacherous heart.

Huddled in her thickest cloak, Jessamyn watched until the troops were mere specks in the distance. The sky glowed rose above a mountain of clouds, gilded by the rising sun. Had she not known better, she might have believed she had dreamed that damning conversation. Solicitous to the last, Sir Ralph had taken pains to point out to Walter how they might better their defenses. He even took lists of provisions which they would likely need by spring. He was also swift to point out that he had left an extra wagon of goods to help feed his men, who were to stay to bolster Curlew's defences. Even Jessamyn had not been forgotten. In a quiet moment, before he mounted his silvery charger, Sir Ralph took Jessamyn's hand and pressed it to his mouth.

"Remember, you have until spring," he had reminded her softly, his eyes devouring her beauty. "I longingly await your answer."

And I long to tell you that I know about your treachery, she had thought. All sincerity on the surface, all deception beneath. Sir Ralph Warren would take some outwitting. Jessamyn's most valuable asset in the battle to come was that she was forewarned of his treachery.

During the following days, she made it her business to identify Noddy. Hod, one of the older Curlew soldiers, who owed her much for saving the lives of his wife and child, agreed to watch Noddy for her. When the lad planned a journey, Hod would report it to Jessamyn.

Jackson, Sir Ralph's captain of the guard, quickly ingratiated himself with Walter. To Jessamyn's disgust, the man proved to be an avid chess player, which made her task of discrediting him even harder. Walter could be such a child over his *supposed* friends, angrily forbidding her to say another word to blacken Jackson's character. The captain spent more time at the high table than she, engaged in a perpetual game of chess with his young lord.

Disturbingly, now that the immediate danger was past, Jessamyn found her thoughts straying more often to Rhys. For a while, Sir Ralph's visit had helped fill her mind. Their impending doom seemed merely to heighten her emotions, leaving her painfully vulnerable to the heartache of lost love.

In two weeks' time, Christmas would be upon them. Jessamyn tried to concentrate on preparations for the upcoming festive season. She directed their men to cut boughs of bay, holly and fir. An agile lad climbed high in an elm to cut down mistletoe to be fashioned into a kissing bough. Though Jessamyn herself had no lover to kiss, she knew the servants and soldiers would welcome this seasonal excuse for flirtation.

She sat at the trestle in the Hall, cutting, stripping, and binding boughs of evergreens to form wreaths and garlands. Two women helped her. They all laughed and sang carols as they worked, cheered by thoughts of the coming festival.

Jessamyn looked through the window at the steel-gray sky. Frost whitened the stone battlements, and below the walls, the river flowed gray and choppy. And then she noticed Hod, the guard who was her lookout, beckoning to her from the doorway.

Quickly Jessamyn excused herself, leaving the chatting maids to their work.

"He's to leave before noon, my lady," Hod said, glancing about to make sure he had not been overheard.

Jessamyn's heart jumped at the news. She must steal the report Jackson had written to his master. When he saw the plain written truth before his eyes, Walter would have to believe her.

"Bring some trustworthy men with you and accompany me into the woods. First, I want you to block the path with fallen limbs, then we'll cut more evergreens while we wait for Noddy."

"Which direction be he taking, my lady?"

"South to Shrewsbury."

Trying to hide her excitement, Jessamyn quickly donned her boy's wool jerkin and tights. She pulled a heavy cloak over her clothing and accompanied the party to the woods. Two servants came with them to help chop down branches for decoration.

Patricia Phillips

Walter had grumbled, saying that they had more than enough greenery already. Jackson, the enemy captain, had stared curiously at her, but seemed to suspect nothing. Fortunately, Walter's objections to her proposal were quickly forgotten once he resumed his chess game.

The sun-sparkled grass gleamed white with frost. The sight served as an unpleasant reminder of another time when she had ridden to these woods. That wonderful day seemed to have happened in another lifetime. Jessamyn's heart ached at the memory of Rhys, and she drove her heels into Merlin's flanks, moving faster in an effort to outride her painful thoughts.

Quickly, the men set about cutting brush to form a barrier on the southern bridle path. Jessamyn watched the highway, alerting them when she saw a lone rider slip out of the postern gate and wind his way along the lane leading south. The lad was taking a circuitous route. For a panicky moment, Jessamyn wondered if she had lost him. Did he intend to cross the river, then double back downstream, to throw any curious watcher off the scent? But to her vast relief, he came at last, plodding along with his head down, hunched inside his thick cloak to guard against the morning chill.

A mound of fallen branches blocked his path. Glancing about for access, Noddy turned his horse into the nearby undergrowth, making his way through a sparse brush thicket where the tree branches hung low and the light was dim.

Jessamyn signaled to her man, who lay along a branch directly above the path where it veered back onto the main trail. As Noddy slowly approached, his horse floundering and snorting as it made its way back up to the path, a tree branch came down

162

with a resounding crash about his head and shoulders. Knocked from the saddle, and with a startled cry, Noddy landed in a gorse thicket.

Like lightning, Jessamyn sped toward the riderless horse as it plunged and whinnied in fright. Quickly she grabbed the loose reins, calming the animal. The letters must have been in the saddlebag, for she saw that Noddy carried no pouch at his waist. He was spreadeagled in the brush, his cloak caught in the branches above him.

There would be more than one piece of mail, for Walter, still gushing with praise for their kinsman's generosity, had insisted on writing his own letter to Sir Ralph. Jessamyn's fingers were clumsy with cold, for she had discarded her mittens to unfasten the leather straps. Afraid that the lad would be back to his horse before she opened the bag, she struggled with the buckles until finally she had them undone. There was a linen cloth containing Noddy's meal, and a flask of ale. She rummaged through the contents of the leather bag, finally extracting an oiled silk pouch. With trembling fingers she pulled out three letters, all sealed with wax. Walter's childish handwriting was easy to spot. Eliminating that letter, she put it back in the pouch. The other two folded parchments were written in the same hand. One was thick and she read through its end for a clue as to which one held Sir Ralph's report. To her relief, she spotted the words *love*, and *missing you*, and concluded that it was for Jackson's wife. In triumph, she grabbed the thin crisp parchment, folded and sealed carefully. The care over the letter's preparation should have told her the difference. In contrast, the love letter was not folded evenly and its wax seal ran in blobs on the parchment.

Jessamyn hid the report inside her shirt, before hastily returning the rest of the items to the saddle bag. And none too soon. She heard crunching steps behind her; Noddy was back on his feet and ready to reclaim his mount.

With a smile, Jessamyn turned about. Her men glanced at her and she nodded imperceptibly, focusing her attention on Noddy.

"I hope you're not hurt. This is a treacherous spot."

"Nay, a knot on the head won't stop me. I'm just fortunate you were here to help." The young man laughed good-naturedly. He was fair and proportioned like a ploughman with huge hands and a bland, ingenuous face. Jessamyn sighed with relief. This one would probably never suspect a thing.

"Here's your horse. He was frightened, but I've calmed him. I'm good with beasts."

"Thank you, Lady Jessamyn."

"In the future, it would be best not to stray from the path," she warned him solicitously, holding the animal's reins whilst young Noddy leaped in the saddle.

He sat smiling down at her, drinking in her beauty.

" 'Twas worth a spill to have you play groom, my lady," he said, blushing in his effort at gallantry. "I only came this way because there were branches blocking the road."

When she had first hatched her grand scheme to unseat the rider just long enough to steal the letter, she had never thought that he might simply leap over the obstacle and continue his journey. When she thought of how easily her plan could have gone astray, sweat broke out on her upper lip.

"I'm on me way to Shrewsbury," Noddy informed her, seeming in no hurry to leave. "Got important letters for his lordship."

"Then hadn't you best get going? It's a long ride to Shrewsbury," she reminded him, stepping back to clear his path. As she moved, the parchment scratched her chest; Jessamyn hoped she had hidden the letter well enough.

Noddy grinned at her and saluted before wheeling his horse back on the main path. Shouting his thanks to the soldiers who had pulled him from the thicket, he clattered south along the path on his way to Shrewsbury.

"Let's go back," Jessamyn said, watching until the lad was safely down the road. "I've got what I came for."

The small party proceeded back over the causeway, bearing fir branches and holly. Telling the men to take the greenery to decorate their quarters, Jessamyn went inside the Great Hall in search of Walter. As she had expected, he and Jackson were still engrossed in their game. She slipped unnoticed up the stairs and into the curtained room.

Jessamyn took out the parchment and went to the light streaming brightly through the unpaned window. As she broke the seal, her hands shook. For an instant, she was afraid that she had chosen the wrong letter. What if she held Jackson's love letter while the condemning report jogged south to Shrewsbury?

The writing was difficult to decipher, but she knew she had the right letter when she saw a highly detailed sketch of the castle's guardroom at the bottom of the sheet. All accesses were clearly marked. "We would best take the castle from the south," he had written, "the best time being when the guards are changed. So poorly run is the place, there's much chaos then."

Jessamyn's cheeks flushed as she read the damning statement. That oversight would be remedied immediately. That sentence alone was surely condemning enough, even for Walter.

Grimly, she refolded the missive and replaced it inside her shirt. She would wait for the right opportunity to present her evidence.

Her wait was long, for the chess game lasted until Jackson was finally forced go about his duties. Walter sat sulking beside the hearth, wondering what he would do to fill his time.

"Walter, I want a word with you. Up there."

Jessamyn had slipped up behind him without his knowledge. She had changed her boy's clothing for a blue wool gown and patterned surcoat. Her hair was braided tightly about her head giving her a severe look.

"What now? Have you found another clue to Ralph's deceit? I'm tired, Jessamyn, and I'm about to sup."

"Supper will wait. I've something important to show you."

She led the way, growing impatient while he slowly limped up the narrow stairs, grumbling all the while about having to leave the comfort of the hearth. A charcoal brazier glowed in the small room and Walter immediately went to it, holding his hands over the glowing embers.

"Are the guards still gone?"

Scowling, Walter lifted the edge of the curtain and looked into the Hall below. The tables were virtually deserted. The guard would be changing soon, and most of the men were already in the guard room.

"Yes. Why do you ask?"

"I want you to read this."

Walter accepted the parchment and unfolded it. First he studied the sketch, then read the two paragraphs. Jessamyn had the satisfaction of seeing his face blanch.

"Where did you get this?"

"I stole it out of a messenger's saddlebag."

"Going where?"

"Oh, don't be so dense—to Sir Ralph of course. This report's from Jackson to his master, noting conditions here and pointing out how best to overrun us."

"Are you sure?"

Walter sank unsteadily to the closest bench, reluctant to accept the fact that so treacherous a letter could have come from a friend—and be traveling to yet another friend!

"Walter, love, accept it. Surely this is proof enough of what I've been trying to tell you."

"I can't believe it. Ralph's my best friend—Jackson's my friend too. How could they . . ." he stopped, running his hand across his clammy brow.

"Because they aren't really your friends. They only pretended friendship so they could capture the castle."

Jessamyn put her arms around her brother. She did not point out it was his own stupidity which had placed them in this situation.

"He's my friend. He wouldn't do this," Walter said tearfully. The years seemed to slip away until, once again, he was a small crippled boy in need of comfort.

"Listen to me, Walter, he's never been your friend. Because you trusted him, we're betrayed. But we have the jump on them. They don't know we've found out about their treachery. Jackson can't possibly suspect, not until the lad gets to Shrewsbury and comes back. And maybe, even then, he won't guess what happened."

"What can we do? He's left forty men here. We've not that many soldiers to defend us, even if they'd fight, which I doubt. We could all be killed!" Aghast

167

at the thought, he turned frightened, tear-filled eyes toward his sister. Jessamyn's heart tugged at the sight of his pathetic face. She patted his arm.

"Hush, all's not lost yet." A daring plan had begun to form in her mind. "I'll go for help."

"To whom? We've no one to help us."

"Rhys of Trevaron will aid us."

"The Welshman!"

"Aye, far better to be rescued by a Welshman than to be imprisoned by your English relative, eh, Walter?"

"How do you even know he'd help? Besides, we don't have any idea where he is. Chester's a big city."

"The man in the infirmary probably knows. We'll ask him."

"Oh, wonderful plan—all he speaks is Welsh gibberish. Who's going to understand him, even if he can give us directions? Talk sense, Jessamyn."

Her eyes flashed in anger. "I am talking sense. Have you a better plan, or any plan at all?"

Disconsolately, Walter shook his head.

"All right then, that's what I thought. I speak some Welsh. And there are maids who can help."

"But who can we send without being found out? Jackson would suspect if we sent one of the guards."

"I'll go."

"You! Are you out of your mind? A woman can't go by herself to Chester. You'd never find your way, and you would be risking your life."

"As you've no better plan, mine's the best we've got. I'll travel to Chester, find him, and tell him what's happened. I'll bring him back with me."

"No!"

Turning decisive, Walter stood, his voice firm, his face set.

"It's our only chance."

"We'll have to think of some other way. It's too dangerous. I just can't let you go to Chester by yourself. Besides, everyone will know you're gone. There's no way to hide that. They'll start asking questions—they'd be after you in a flash. They'd ride you down in no time and drag you back."

"Not if we pretend I've been taken ill with a fever. I doubt that Jackson would insist on going to my room to see for himself. Anyway, I won't be alone. I'll travel with Jack the Drover, when he leaves for the Christmas Market."

"Travel with a drover!"

"He'll take care of me. He's loyal to us. Dressed like a lad, I'll be safe. Passersby will assume I'm his son."

Walter's eyes narrowed in suspicion as he surveyed his sister's face, which was all flushed with excitement. "This is just a plan to see that Welshman again, isn't it?"

"No. Walt, don't be absurd. It's a plan to save our hide."

"You think I'm such a fool I don't see through you scheme. You can forget it, Jessamyn. I'm not going along with such a harebrained plan, devised simply so you can be alone with him."

As her anger brimmed over, Jessamyn struck her brother across the face. "Walter Dacre, you're an ungrateful fool. You've no plan, yet you won't accept mine, just because you're convinced I'm going to Chester to see the Welshman. I've already told you, Rhys of Trevaron is betrothed to another. I've no romantic designs on him, or any other man, for that matter. I can manage well enough by myself. I've no need of a man to look after me."

"If that's true, why are you running to the Welshman?"

She stared angrily at him, lacking a comeback. Why indeed? "Because I need his soldiers, that's why. He said that if ever we were in need of help . . ."

"He was just being polite."

"Polite or not, I'm going to find him."

"We could send a message with the drover," Walter suggested brightly. "That would be far safer."

"What if it doesn't reach him in time . . . or at all? Jack's not the most brilliant of men. No, Walter, the best and surest way is for me to go."

"You may never reach Chester," he suggested darkly. "There are thieves roaming the highways. They'd soon see through your disguise. Besides, some of them prefer young boys, or so I've heard. You're sunk either way."

"We can sit here until doomsday, dreaming up obstacles. I'm going to Chester and that's that."

They glared at each other.

"You've still not convinced me you're not pining for the Welshman," he pointed out sourly. "And talk about obstacles . . . there's nothing wrong with sending a message. In fact, it's a sensible idea. We've got until spring to reach him."

"No we don't. Once he leaves Chester, we've no idea how to contact him. We've got two weeks until Christmas. There's no time for a mistake. I don't know where the Llys valley is, and neither do you. When he's gone home . . ."

"He has to come for his man, or had you forgotten?"

Jessamyn had forgotten. She swallowed uneasily. Could they wait that long? What if he delayed coming for Alun until well into the spring? "No, we can't take the chance. I'm going to Chester with Jack. And I'd best get down to the village to find out when he'll be leaving. I just pray God that he hasn't already left."

Walter knew that he had lost. When he saw the steely gleam in her eyes, he knew that he might as well give up.

"Very well," he finally agreed, with great reluctance. "Do be careful. I don't know what I'd do if anything ever happened to you."

His sincere words softened her heart. Jessamyn smiled at him. "I promise to be careful. Now, I want you to promise me you'll take your potions regularly. I don't want anything to happen to you while I'm gone."

Walter agreed. He disliked relying on medication, though he had to admit that since his sister had developed the current remedy, his life had become far sweeter.

"It's going to be hard pretending that nothing's wrong when I'm with Jackson," he said, as they walked to the stairs. "I don't think I can do it."

"You *will* do it. If you don't, we've no hope of coming through this," she reminded him, gritting her teeth. "Don't back out on me now, Walt. I'm taking a big risk."

"By that, I suppose you mean you're taking the risk I ought to be taking," he countered, stopping on the top step.

"It doesn't matter who takes the risk, just so long as the plan works. As you aren't able to ride to Chester, that leaves me, doesn't it? Now go on downstairs and play chess with the treacherous bastard, as if nothing has changed."

Seething with emotion, Jessamyn watched her brother on his descent downstairs. Could she trust Walter to play his part? "And don't drink too much!" she added. "Or you're bound to give us away."

"I resent that!" Scowling, Walter turned to face her. "I can handle myself well enough. You just look to your own conduct."

His bristling indignation cheered Jessamyn. She had begun to wonder if Walter had the mettle to handle his end of the plan. Though later, when she went to speak to him, she discovered that he was well into his second flagon of ale. True to character, Walter was handling stress in his own way. She started to remind him of their discussion, then changed her mind. She prayed that God was watching over them. There was little more she could do, short of imprisoning Walter in his room until she returned. Even at that, she thought ruefully, he'd probably bribe one of the servants to supply his ale.

"Sunup tomorrow," she said in an undertone, trying to gain Walter's attention.

"What's at sunup?" he questioned, baffled at first. Then, as he understood, he shot a quick glance at Jackson, who was filling his trencher with sliced mutton. The man appeared not to have heard. "That's no time at all," Walter hissed in dismay.

"Good. This way there's less time for me to get nervous," Jessamyn added, as she slid in place next to her brother. Her head was in a whirl: the danger of her journey, the possibility that her plan might not work, were both eclipsed by the nerve-jangling thought that, in a few days, she would see Rhys.

Chapter Ten

The momentous journey to Chester was begun in the predawn hours of the following day.

Already up for hours, Jessamyn had dressed warmly in the boy's tunic and hose, topping them with her warmest cloak and hood. Mary, who, out of necessity, had been taken into her confidence, had packed a small chest with her lady's toilet articles, a change of clothing, and a silk gown for her meeting with Lord Rhys.

As arranged, Hod met Jessamyn at the postern with her saddled horse. He had volunteered to escort her into the village, using the pretext of visiting a sick relative as an excuse, if he were caught as he returned to the castle. To Jessamyn's dismay, as they trotted down the grassy hillock, old Ned began howling and whining, distressed because she was leaving without him. She hoped no one would find the dog's strange behavior cause for investigation. Too many people knew of her plan already. Walter, of course, and now Hod, Mary, and Alys from the infirmary, had all been sworn to secrecy. She had taken Alys into her confidence because she was needed to care for their patients. Alys suggested that she take potions to Jessamyn's room, reinforcing their story that her mistress was struck with a raging fever and could see no one.

Jessamyn's stomach churned with excitement at the prospect of her journey. Though she tried to dismiss the idea, thoughts of seeing Rhys again made her heart quicken, and she knew that her high state of nervous anticipation owed much to that future meeting.

Hod brought her quickly to Jack the Drover's thatched cottage at the far end of the village.

They dismounted in the chilly darkness. To Jessamyn's surprise, a loaded farm cart stacked high with holly, bay and mistletoe was standing outside the cottage door. When she knocked on the door, it was Margery who answered, all dressed for travel in a cloak and hood. She was to accompany them to Chester.

"You'll need another woman along," Margery insisted, hardly able to contain her own excitement over the upcoming journey.

Jessamyn was grateful for Margery's concern, and touched by her insistence that the Lady of Curlew could not travel the roads alone with a common drover.

"But today, I'm not the Lady of Curlew," Jessamyn pointed out, opening her cloak to reveal her peasant boy's jerkin and hose. "Maybe I can pretend to be your brother," she suggested with a chuckle.

At first Margery was taken back by the suggestion. She finally agreed to the pretense, though she continued to show her far more deference than she had ever displayed towards her own brother.

When it was time to leave, the women climbed atop the hay, pulling a wool blanket over themselves to keep out the December cold. Jack had suggested that traveling to Chester in the cart would be more comfortable for Jessamyn than riding on horseback. Margery could sell their load of Christmas evergreens in the market as an added boon. Hod could take Merlin back to the castle's stables. Jack had worried that the beast would be missed and the subsequent search would uncover Lady Jessamyn's plan. This way, no one would suspect that the lady of the castle was anywhere but in her sick bed.

Jessamyn was pleasantly surprised by Jack's forethought. She had to admit that it was a point she had overlooked. Though this meant that she would be afoot in Chester, it was a far safer plan.

It was still dark when their cart rumbled down the village street, following the herd of cattle. Jack drove the beasts with the assistance of a village lad. The swaying wagon was driven by Jack's young cousin. Jessamyn and Margery found the Christmas evergreens vastly uncomfortable. They pushed them to the front of the cart and covered them with damp sacking to contain the prickling branches. Then they were able to nestle snugly in the soft hay beneath the wool blanket, while slow, faithful Dobbin plodded along the familiar route. The sounds of the lowing cattle and the steady, rythmic clop of the horse's great hooves gradually lulled them to sleep.

What began as an exciting adventure soon became a trial to be endured. By the following day, Jessamyn ached in every limb from riding in the jolting cart. The inns where they stopped offered barely palatable food and lumpy, flea-ridden mattresses. Jessamyn alone enjoyed the luxury of a roof over her head. The village lad and Jack's cousin rolled themselves in blankets and slept with the herd, while Jack and Margery shared the wagon. The drover and his wife thought they did their lady a great favor by renting her a room in the inn. Jessamyn had not the heart to tell them she would have preferred sleeping beneath the stars to this questionable lodging.

When they began their journey, Jessamyn had not realized how slowly they would travel, nor how many nights they would spend on the way to Chester. They could only progress at the cattle's speed; the beasts ambled along the highway, frequently stopping to forage in the roadside grasses and weeds. They had been on the road a week when they made their final, predawn departure before arriving in Chester. Jessamyn was relieved to discover that this would be their last night outside the city.

A cacophony of ringing church bells heralded their approach to the great port of Chester. As they drew nearer to the city walls, towering above the silver-gray river, the road grew even more congested. They had to wait for an hour to cross the bridge over the Dee, vying for position with produce carts, wagons of cackling geese and hens, flocks of sheep, and grunting pigs.

Mighty stone walls girded the city. Jessamyn felt a pang of homesickness as she looked up at the battlements, sharply reminded of Curlew, which she missed more acutely with each passing day.

Jostled and pushed on every side, the cart finally forced its way into the milling throng, blending with the noisy stream of men and beasts entering the city through the Bridgegate.

Jessamyn was overwhelmed by the suffocating feeling she experienced in these narrow streets. Timber and stone inns, dwellings and shops crowded close on either side of the thoroughfare. These multi-storied buildings leaned toward one other, virtually meeting overhead, so that only a patch of gray morning cloud was visible between the tiled roofs and their corbelled upper stories. Underfoot, the narrow street was mired with mud, filth, and offal. Jessamyn's senses were assaulted by the sheer noise and smell of this great city. There was so much racket on either side, she could scarcely hear herself think, nor did she feel safe drawing breath as the cart churned through filth, releasing a noxious smell of mingled sewage and refuse which flowed sluggishly along a choked kennel in the middle of the street.

All the while, they had been toiling uphill, away from the river. When they approached the city gates, Jessamyn had noticed tall, masted vessels moored in the harbor to their left. Just inside the walls stood Chester's mighty castle, built on a bluff overlooking the Dee. Yet, once they entered this dark, noisy tunnel between the buildings, all of that was hidden from view. There was much to see here, yet packed as they were, cheek to jowl with this swarm of humanity thronging the narrow lanes and alleys, Jessamyn could not take in the sights. The sheer press of people astounded her. Never in her life had she seen so many people crowded into so small a space.

Margery was ecstatic over the exciting bustle of the city. Finding it all so wonderful, she quite forgot her station as she grasped Jessamyn's arm, enraptured over this and that, as they slowly made their way along the congested street.

Fortunately for Jessamyn, this main route to Wales, Lower Bridge Street, was her eventual destination. Alun had told her through a translator that Eluned Glynne's sister was married to a wealthy cloth merchant named Proctor Massey, whose premises stood in Lower Bridge Street. Such a wealthy man should be easy to find. Though, as she looked about at the jumble of overhanging upper stories, chimneypots and roofs, Jessamyn began to doubt if she would ever be able to find anything in the maze of buildings.

When they were temporarily stalled, Jack stopped several passersby to ask about Proctor Massey. His inquiries were to no avail. They were beginning to doubt that they would ever find the merchant's house, when Jack stopped a black–robed friar sampling food from a stall against the lower story of a nearby house. Yes, the friar knew of Proctor Massey. His was a large house further along the street, with a gilded upper story; so striking was the architecture of the house, there was no way they could miss it.

Reassured, Jack was still reluctant to leave Jessamyn until he had lodged her at a nearby inn. Only then would he agree to take his noisy, unruly charges to the cattle market. The Falcon was the chosen hostelry, an inn of good reputation. The cost of a room there was far above Jack's modest means, but he deemed it suitable lodging for the Lady of Curlew.

While they made their arrangements, Jessamyn kept her long cloak wrapped about her body to hide her boy's clothing. She had thrown back her hood to reveal her braided auburn hair. The innkeeper readily accepted her as Lady Jessamyn Dacre, bowing in welcome after he had surreptitiously counted the gold coins she gave him to establish her account. She asked the innkeeper for directions to Proctor Massey's home, just to satisfy herself that they were on the right track. She was reassured when his directions were the same as those received from the Dominican friar.

Though it had been her intention to bathe and wear her silk gown, when she saw the filthy city streets, Jessamyn had changed her mind. She was reluctant to soil her only gown. Besides, an anonymous lad asking for Lord Rhys at the Massey kitchen door might be better tolerated by Eluned Glynne than the appearance of the Lady of Curlew. Jessamyn wanted no unpleasantness to mar this trip. She intended to deliver her message, secure Rhys's promise of help, then leave—or so she fondly imagined.

It was early afternoon when Jessamyn finally ventured out of the inn. When she stepped down the stone steps into the cobbled street, she felt as if she were taking her life in her hands. Though she tried to stay close to the buildings, out of the stream of traffic, this became virtually impossible. The congested street thronged with citizens, carts and animals, who were still flooding into the city for the annual Christmas market. Vendors' stalls had been built against the lower stories of the houses, leaving no place to walk but the narrow street. Stallholders' apprentices shouted their wares, attempting to drown out the cries of their competitors. The cackling, lowing, and grunting, the slaughter beasts, neighing horses, clopping hooves and the rattling carts all blended into a discordant background accompaniment to the shrill inducements to buy. Cries of "Pies, hot from the oven," "Fine green rushes," "Long-burning tallow dips," and sundry other offerings assailed her from every side.

Jessamyn finally reached the imposing double-fronted residence of Proctor Massey. No stall leaned against this house. The deep, upper story was heavily embellished in gold, its decorative, carved figures splendidly gilded. Jessamyn stared up in wonder at the broad expanse of diamond-paned glass windows fronting the street. Proctor Massey was wealthy indeed to be able to afford so many windows.

She had not expected it to be difficult to find the back entrance to the kitchens. The house leaned against its neighbor, giving no access to the rear. Jessamyn wondered if she should find the nearest alley and hope it would bring her to the back of the house, when she saw a painted panel open to reveal a long, narrow passage leading off the street. A young serving lad skipped into the street and quickly disappeared in the crowd.

Glancing about to see if she was observed, Jessamyn boldly pushed open the concealed door and entered the dark, narrow passage. The cobblestones were so uneven that she turned her ankle several times before she reached the side door. At the inn, Jessamyn had the forethought to write down her message, so that if she were denied entrance, she could at least leave a note for Rhys and pray that it reached him.

She lifted the gargoyle door knocker, banging loudly to overcome the noise from the street. Though it was far quieter here, she still wondered if anyone would hear her over the noises drifting from Lower Bridge Street.

The door finally opened and a serving girl stood looking her up and down. Jessamyn had hidden her hair under her hood and she consciously hunched her shoulders as she had seen peasant lads do when overawed by their surroundings.

"What do you want?"

"I bring a message for Lord Rhys of Trevaron. He's a guest of your master."

The girl hesitated, then turning about, called to someone inside. The door opened a crack wider, giving Jessamyn a wedge-shaped view of the large flagstone kitchen. Several steps led down to the smoky room, abustle with servants plucking fowl, kneading bread, rolling pastry, scrubbing, mopping . . .

Her view was suddenly eclipsed by a burly man in a leather apron. His face was kindly and Jessamyn felt more confident.

"What do you want, lad? You say you've a message for one of the master's guests?"

"A message for Lord Rhys of Trevaron, your honor."

"Give it here, then. Come in, get yourself a sup of something warm before you leave."

"I'm supposed to give it into his hands only," she ventured boldly. The man scowled at the news, but he did not argue with her.

"Just sit over there and wait, then. Get a pasty from the cook."

Jessamyn stepped down to the flagstones of the warm kitchen. Several young scullery maids smiled at her and someone handed her a crumbly, misshapen pasty. It was still warm from the oven. She nodded her thanks and bit into the tasty offering, surely a reject from the master's table. Another wench offered her a mug of ale to rinse down her food, then pointed to a stone bench beside the hearth, where the kitchen cat was lounging. The tomcat reluctantly shared its seat with her.

For what seemed a long time, Jessamyn observed the bustling Massey household preparing the Christmas feast. Finally, the man in the leather apron returned.

"Show me the message first."

Nervously Jessamyn produced the folded parchment, holding it tightly in case he tried to snatch it away. As it happened, the man merely wanted to reassure himself that there actually was a message.

He turned the parchment, as if to read the address. Then, Jessamyn saw that he held the note upside down; she wanted to laugh out loud when she realized the servant could not read.

"This way . . . and mind your manners, lad. No thieving, or the master'll have you in the stocks," he warned sternly as he led the way up a short flight of stairs.

They entered a dim hallway and walked in silence to the end of the hall. Here the man stopped and opened a door. Inside the room a bright fire burned in the corner grate, and dim shafts of daylight struggled through a green-tinged glass window overlooking the street.

"Wait here. Lord Rhys will see you presently."

Alone now, Jessamyn tried to compose herself for the ordeal ahead. That it would be joyous made it no less an ordeal. She debated whether to play the boy, or throw back her hood and let him see her clearly. The former seemed the wisest choice. She could assess the depth of her feelings for him before she revealed her true identity. It was possible she had little emotional attachment left for the handsome Welshman.

Pacing before the window, barely glancing at the slow-moving stream of traffic below, Jessamyn struggled to put her thoughts in order. Already her heart had begun to leap like a frightened bird and her knees were shaking. How foolish, she sternly admonished herself. This man had deceived her. She had little reason to be so excited. In a few minutes they would be face to face. The past weeks had shown her that she could survive well enough without him.

Then, she heard his step outside the door and she clasped her hands together, trying to stop their trembling. The door opened. And there he stood.

Despite her inner resolve, Jessamyn was still not prepared for her reaction at the sight of him. She had even begun to believe her own lies when she tried hard to convince herself that he no longer mattered to her. She swallowed, attempting to dislodge the lump in her throat.

"Well, lad, what's this message?" Rhys asked gruffly as he strode into the room.

She peered up at him from under the woolen folds of her hood. And her heart was beating wildly. It was disconcerting to learn he had the same disturbing effect on her emotions as before. He wore a fine mulberry cloth doublet, with a narrow gold belt slung low on his slim hips; his tights were sky blue, the fabric scintillating in this murky light.

"Have you no tongue?" he asked irritably, taking a step towards her.

Wordlessly Jessamyn held out the paper to him.

Rhys took the folded square from her fingers and strode to the window to read it. He held the parchment up to the light. A frown creased his brow as he read the brief message:

"Lord Rhys, you are desperately needed to help save the Curlew garrison from being overthrown."

"Who sent this, lad? 'Tis not signed," he said sternly, moving away from the window. "Come on, speak up, damn you. Are you mute?"

Suddenly finding her voice, Jessamyn raised her head and, as she spoke, tossed back her wool hood.

"No, Lord Rhys, I'm not mute, as well you know."

"Jessamyn!"

His voice had turned throaty and warmly seductive. She could have struck him for it.

"By all that's holy . . . you . . . here!"

"Aye, it's me. I'm not some apparition from the dead."

"What are you doing in Chester?"

"Delivering this note to you."

He grinned at her sharp retort. "You've not changed any. Is this true . . . you face overthrow? From whom?"

"Do you think I'd travel this distance for a jest? Of course it's true! Our wonderful kinsman, Sir Ralph Warren, has left forty men under our roof on the pretext of helping us defend ourselves. I overheard him plotting his treachery. So safe does he feel, thinking that we don't suspect a thing, he'll bide his time until spring."

"Good God! And how did this happen?"

Shamefaced, she had to admit that they had welcomed him into the castle as a kinsman.

"Where is he now?"

"Gone home to Shrewsbury to do the king's bidding."

Rhys considered her news for a moment. "Is your brother with you?"

"No. I came here with the village drover and his wife. Hardly anyone at the garrison even knows I'm gone. You're our only hope."

"You came to Chester alone," he repeated in surprise, "dressed like that?"

"What's wrong with this?" she demanded, bristling indignantly as he looked her up and down, his gaze lingering over her slim, hose-covered legs. "It's wiser by far than dressing as a woman. You said so yourself."

Rhys grinned. "You have a very good memory, Lady Jessamyn, very good indeed."

She swallowed as she looked into his dark eyes and saw the warmth kindled there, correctly interpreting his expression. "Yes, I also remember how you deceived me into thinking you loved me."

"There was no deceit to it," he said evenly. "We quarreled when last we met, let's not resume the

184

hostilities. What is it you want with me?"

The way his voice softened when he spoke, coupled with the smile playing about his mouth, suggested that Rhys was not speaking about the defenses of Curlew. Deliberately misinterpreting his words, she blurted, "The letter's plain enough. We need the strength of your men to overthrow Sir Ralph's soldiers. If you don't help us, we're as good as defeated."

He moved towards her, hands outstretched. How Jessamyn longed to accept his handclasp, to feel the warm strength of his fingers in hers. Valiantly, she resisted the impulse.

"Naturally I intend to help you."

She exhaled in a sigh of relief, unaware until then that she had been holding her breath, awaiting his reply. Her heart was beating rapidly, and her legs went weak as he softly touched her cheek, his hand so warmly comforting that she jumped in alarm at the caress.

"Nay, don't be so skittish, pretty lad."

Almost before she knew it, his arm was around her, his face close. Desperate to be free of the power he held over her, Jessamyn quickly stepped sideways, breaking his embrace.

"First let me thank you for your generous offer of help," she said stiffly, her voice sounding tight and unnatural. "What would Lady Eluned think if she were to walk in here and find you embracing me?"

He shrugged as if it did not concern him, but by the tightening of his mouth, she knew he was irritated.

"She'd probably think I'd developed unnatural tastes for young lads," he answered, attempting a weak jest. "What does it matter if she sees? She doesn't own me, Jessamyn. I've told you that before."

"Yes, I know that's what you said. I also happen to know men and women share different views about lovemaking. I'm not interested in you as long as you are hers."

He sighed in exasperation and strode to the window. "You're such a damnably hard-headed woman. I've told you that our betrothal is merely a formality; it took place long before I ever laid eyes on you."

She smiled thinly. "Ah, but I also know what deceivers men can be . . . Still, no matter, I didn't come here to revive our quarrel. Are you promising me your help?"

"That's right."

"When will you leave? We could travel tomorrow . . ."

He spun away from the window. Rhys looked at Jessamyn, still wanting to sweep her in his arms and swiftly dispose of her objections. She expected him to follow her home to do her bidding, whilst witholding what he most desired. Short of voicing his need outright, he could not make it any plainer. Pride kept her coldly aloof. Well, two could play at that game.

Stubbornly, Rhys set his jaw. Taking a step towards her, he said gruffly, "Nay, lady, you'll have to change those plans. I can't leave tomorrow."

"Well, the next day, then."

"I can't leave Chester till after Christmastide."

"What! That's next week, at the earliest."

"You're right, providing we don't count all twelve days of Christmas."

"Our lives are at stake and you insist on keeping Christmas!"

"Stop shouting or you'll have all the household in here. I'm a guest in this house. Arrangements for the festivities have already been made. It would be rude to leave before they're over. Besides," he added with a glimmer of a smile, "you have until spring before the evil Sir Ralph returns."

Fury surged hotly through her veins. He was delaying on purpose, making a flimsy excuse to pay her back for challenging his deceit. Eyes blazing, she stepped towards him, fists raised to strike his fine mulberry doublet. Jessamyn only succeeded in grazing her hands against the garment's jet buttons before he grabbed her wrists.

"No . . . we'll have none of that, Jessamyn. Take my offer, or leave it. It's the best I can make."

"How dare you mock me . . . as if . . . as if our danger's merely a jest! Don't you care more for my safety than . . . than . . . your lady's revels?"

"If you stay we can spend time together," Rhys suggested, his grasp slackening.

A quiver of hope shot through her and she quickly squelched the emotion. Fighting free of his grasp, she said, "So, you expect to continue your dalliance with me, under her nose! How dare you think of amusement when my very existence is threatened."

"Stop it!" He shook her, ending her tirade. "Don't be so dramatic. You, yourself, said we have until spring. I can be at Curlew's door in a week. Chester's a fine city. You shouldn't dismiss my idea so quickly. A quarrel can soon be mended. Besides, I've already agreed to help you. What more do you want?"

What more? She looked up at him through a hot haze of angry tears. Rhys mocked and humiliated her in payment for her discovery of his deception. He had cleverly concocted a way to keep both women for his amusement.

"Damn you! What a fool I've been to think you'd overlook what's gone between us to save Curlew. What a fool!"

He looked down at her; seeing tears trickling down her flushed cheeks, his anger softened. "What did you expect of me?" Rhys asked simply, resisting the urge to comfort her, to wipe away her tears.

"I don't know . . . Nothing . . . absolutely nothing."

Her vision still blurred by tears, Jessamyn turned away from him. "I'll suffer your whim because I need your help. But you'll have to turn elsewhere for a plaything. When this is over, I never intend to set eyes on you again."

"Jessamyn, wait." He came after her, but made no attempt to touch her. "You will stay in Chester then?"

"What choice have I? The journey's too long to go back to Curlew then return when you're done reveling. Besides, I'm not letting you out of my sight. There's a better chance of your keeping your word if I stay in Chester."

Was it her imagination, or did he sigh with relief? Gritting her teeth, Jessamyn glared at him. Stiffening, she drew away as his fingers caressed her arm.

"How triumphant you must feel, making me dance to your tune, keeping me dangling here whilst you make merry with her. Remember, Rhys of Trevaron, I'm staying only for Curlew's sake, no other reason."

"Tell me where you're lodging, so I can get word to you when my men are ready for travel."

"I'm lodged at the Falcon here in Lower Bridge Street."

"I know the place. Tell me, Lady Jessamyn, are you to spend Christmas with friends?"

She gave him a withering look and did not answer.

"I spoke to you."

"I heard. You know I've no friends in Chester, yet, out of spite and revenge, you keep me dangling to await your pleasure."

"You could come here to the feast. Eluned would not . . ."

"You must be mad! I'd sooner starve than eat at your table."

Jessamyn spun about, her heart thundering and the blood pounding through her temples. All she could think about was escape—from this house, this city, but most of all, from him. She had just bought herself a week of boredom, cooling her heels whilst he made merry with Eluned Glynne. She supposed Walter and the maids could prolong the lie about her illness. The garrison would be only too pleased to return to their slovenly ways, and might wish her permanently confined to her bed. The Christmas Fair would be over in a couple of days. Jack and Margery would return to Morfa Bach, leaving her alone in this strange city . . . with him!

"Take care, the streets can be dangerous, especially after dark," Rhys said, walking a pace behind her. "I'll show you to the door."

"I doubt that I'll be attending any festivities after dark, my lord," she snapped, alarmed by the quick surge of emotion her discovery had caused. Alone in Chester with Rhys a stone's throw away in Proctor Massey's gilded townhouse. Determined not to weaken, Jessamyn thrust her chin at a stubborn slant as she marched ahead of him down the gloomy corridor.

The only exit she knew was through the kitchens and, to her annoyance, she had to stand aside, waiting for him to direct her elsewhere. He opened a side door leading to the street beneath the stable arch.

"Remember, Jessamyn, be careful," Rhys said, his hand sliding beneath her elbow for a fleeting embrace before she shook free of him. "I'll get in touch with you at the inn when we're ready to travel."

"Thank you," she replied stiffly. "Goodbye, Lord Rhys."

When she rounded the corner, Jessamyn glanced back and could have kicked herself for doing so. He had seen her look back. He would think she still loved him—still wanted him.

Angrily, Jessamyn marched into the street, steeling herself not to look back again. What was the matter with her? Even after this final humiliating meeting, she still wanted him. Oh, how she hated to admit that weakness. She also hated to admit that her decision to stay in Chester through Christmas was not wholly selfless. A glimmer of hope made her wonder if Rhys would renounce Eluned and come, cap in hand, to beg her forgiveness. A bitter smile tugged at her mouth. If she were ever to witness that scene, it would be a miracle.

While she pushed her way back through the crowds, heading for the Falcon, a few snowflakes fluttered against her face, melting as they settled. How handsome Rhys had looked standing in the doorway. There, the light had been brighter and she had seen him plainly. The narrow frill of his shirt had shown above the collar of his doublet, his smooth, freshly shaved chin resting against the white cloth. His springy hair appeared jet black in the gloom. How perfectly the mulberry doublet had fit his body, emphasizing his broad shoulders and narrow waist. Those light blue tights with the silken sheen had displayed the muscles in his strong legs.

Damn him! He still exerted a hold over her. Rhys was so annoying, stubborn, and so devastatingly attractive that now, after all that had happened between them, she still had to steel herself not to give in to him. It would have been so easy to succumb to his comforting caresses. She had wanted to give in to him. Yes, she might as well admit that as well, though she hated to do so. How she ached to be held and kissed. All that and more could have been hers. Even in Proctor Massey's fine house, he would have made love to her, had she allowed it, beneath Eluned Glynne's nose, possibly in defiance of Eluned's hold over him, and certainly to spite her.

Jessamyn reached the studded, black oak door of the Falcon Inn. She stepped into the hostelry's dim, ale-scented interior, longing for the isolation of her small room beneath the eaves. Once there, she intended to do some soul-searching. Despite all to the contrary, she was so despicably weak that she was still madly in love with him.

Chapter Eleven

For the next two days, Jessamyn smarted in indignation over Rhys's casual response to Curlew's danger. Even when Margery came to fetch her to go to the market, prattling all the while about the wonders of Chester, part of Jessamyn's mind remained with her former lover. Anger, pain and disappointment curdled inside her, turning Jessamyn decidedly joyless in this festive season. The color and laughter of the open market, the frivolity of the brightly garbed acrobats and jugglers, failed to lift her spirits. When Jack and Margery eagerly asked if she had seen the Welsh lord and if he was going to help defend the castle, she mustered a grudging smile. She was very careful to speak in civil tones about him, not wanting them to know how deeply their savior had wounded her.

Though Jack and Margery were disappointed that she had to stay in Chester to await the soldiers, they readily accepted their lady's decision, knowing that it was not for the likes of them to question the ways of the gentry.

It always seemed cold in the city.

In an effort to throughly warm herself, Jessamyn frivolously ordered a scented bath to be brought to her room. Endless, steaming jugs of water were carried upstairs to fill the metal bath, at the cost of a pretty penny, but just this once, she felt low enough to need the indulgence. Jessamyn shivered in pleasure as the steaming water inched over her breasts. Sliding down, she allowed the scented water to come up to her chin. The maid helped Jessamyn wash her abundant hair, soaping, rinsing and toweling it. Gradually, the bath water grew too cool for comfort and Jessamyn dried her glowing body while the maids carried away the bath.

She sat before the blazing hearth, toweling dry her thick hair. After the warm bath, she felt more peaceful and relaxed. Rhys's indifference to Curlew's plight seemed not to hurt as acutely—after all, he had given his word that he would come to her aid. In this matter, at least, she had no reason to doubt his sincerity. Her mouth tightened and she quickly thrust away the disturbing memory of broken promises.

Though well-shuttered, with an adequate hearth, this room still seemed to be cold, even after her hot bath. Jessamyn wrapped her cloak around her bed robe. The extra covering kept out the chill draughts inching around the windowframe and beneath the door.

There came a sharp knock on the door and, shaking back her damp hair, Jessamyn went to answer it. Thinking that perhaps the maid had returned to bring her fresh towels, she pulled open the door without any thought of danger. A man was standing outside in the gloomy corridor. He wore a long dark traveling cloak and carried a bundle under his arm. Mindful of Rhys's warning of the city's danger, Jessamyn swallowed nervously as she kept her hand on the latch. Though, in truth, if this stranger meant to harm her, she had little chance of defending herself. The small dagger, which she usually carried in her sleeve, was far out of reach.

"Yes?" she tentatively asked. It was impossible to see his face because he kept it shielded by the hood.

"Lady Jessamyn Dacre?"

"I am she."

"This was brought to the inn for you."

Thinking that perhaps the bundle contained some provisions sent by Margery, she held out her hands for it.

"It's heavy. I'll carry it inside."

She gasped in alarm as he pushed aside the door and strode into the room. It had all happened so fast, she had no time to protest.

This man was tall with broad shoulders; in fact his dark bulk seemed to fill the small, firelit room. It was still daylight, but the oiled parchment covers over the windows let in little light. Jessamyn became increasingly uneasy.

"Thank you. Put the bundle down there." She pointed to the chair.

Then a frightening, even more startling thing happened. Instead of going outside when he had deposited the bundle, the man shut the door and shot the bolt.

"Now we won't be disturbed," he said.

Alarmed by his action, Jessamyn stared at him in dismay, wondering what he was going to do next. She was conscious of the frightened thundering of her heart.

Suddenly the man threw back his hood. It was Rhys!

"I should have known," she cried, as anger replaced her fear. "Get out of my room!" She was furious at having been so easily duped. "Disguising your voice like that, pretending to be delivering a package just to get inside here. How dare you!"

"I thought it a fair exchange, seeing how you came to visit me dressed like a lad," he replied evenly, glancing around the room as he spoke, quick to note its sparse furnishing.

"Have you come to tell me you're ready to leave?" she asked hopefully, swallowing her anger as the idea suddenly occurred to her.

"Not yet. We still have Christmas to celebrate."

"Then we have nothing to say to each other."

Determined to be shut of him, Jessamyn walked to the door. Shaking back her damp hair, she peered at the latch, trying to see well enough to draw back the bolts.

"Leave it."

Catching her arm, Rhys spun her away from the door. Bemused, he stared at her, fascinated by her appearance.

"I've never seen you like this before," he said, indicating her bedrobe and damp hair.

"You'd best look well, because you won't see it again," she snapped, pulling her bedrobe tighter about herself in a primitive, defensive gesture.

"Damn it, Jessamyn, why does your every word have to come out like vinegar?"

"If you find me so sour, then I suggest you leave."

While she spoke, Jessamyn pulled back her hair and attempted to braid it into one thick plait.

"Oh, I'm in no hurry," he replied casually. Then he unlooped the fastening of his cloak and slipped it off to reveal a dark green doublet and hose. Rhys crossed to the hearth, where he threw on a couple of logs, sending a burst of sparks up the sooty chimney.

Her heart was pounding and she swallowed uneasily. Inside this small room Rhys appeared massive and threatening. His head almost touched the low plastered ceiling and she had noticed he was forced to duck when he came through the door. He loomed very menacing in this confined space and she could not wait to be rid of him.

"Why are you here?" Jessamyn asked at last, when he made no move to leave, but merely stretched out his hands to the welcome blaze.

"I wanted to talk to you, to clear up any hard feelings you might be harboring towards me."

At first she did not reply; she looked at his strong hands extended to the blaze, his slender fingers, remembering how they had felt on her body. The memory made her shudder. Quickly Jessamyn pushed aside such dangerous thoughts.

"The hard feelings I have for you are all your own doing. If you hadn't deceived me . . ."

"I didn't deceive you. When I said I love you, I meant it."

"You can't love two women at once."

"Agreed. And I don't. Only you."

Now he left the hearth and stepped toward her. Jessamyn put out her arms, warning him to keep his distance. He made no effort to encroach on her barrier. Rhys just stood there, looking at her.

"Don't come any closer," she warned, swallowing as she tried to keep a tight rein on her surging emotions. Damn him! Why had he come here? It was all because she had been caught looking back at him in the doorway. That stupid slip gave him false hope. He probably thought that she still pined for him.

"You must think I'm a heartless bastard, keeping you here in this place through Christmas."

For once, he was absolutely right. She nodded in agreement.

"Jessamyn, I didn't intend it, but you came girded for battle, all accusations and injured pride. I came to say I'm sorry."

"Sorry . . . for what? Because I found you out in your deceit?"

"I'd be a fool to pretend that didn't concern me, but, no . . . that's not what I meant. I'm sorry for saying what I'm sure you interpreted as an ultimatum—if you want my help, you must wait until after Christmas. I never meant to say that, but you caught me by surprise."

Jessamyn swallowed, not expecting his apparent remorse. Was this just another clever trick? No, she did not think so. This time he seemed to be sincere.

"Your apologies are accepted. Does this mean we're leaving sooner than you said?"

"Yes . . . right after Christmas Day, if you want."

Her face fell. "That's four days from now," she blurted in disappointment. "What do you intend for me to do until then?"

The slow smile which curved his generous mouth made her catch her breath. What a foolish question to have asked. Jessamyn's heart pounded as she felt a bolt of excitement shoot between them.

"No," she warned, knowing that he felt it too. She stepped back. "I told you, I'll not be your plaything. There must be willing servant girls who are only too glad to entertain you . . . when you tire of Eluned."

His smile vanished, and he sighed in aggravation.

"This may come as a surprise to you, but I've never lain with Eluned Glynne, nor do I expect to."

197

Was he telling the truth? Jessamyn tried to overcome the choking lump in her throat. If he would just leave now. This meeting was becoming increasingly difficult.

"That information's of no interest to me."

"Liar!"

She gasped indignantly at his derisive chuckle.

"I won't be insulted in my own room! You weren't invited here and you're not welcome—so leave!"

"Very well, my love, if you insist. But before I go, will you at least look at what I brought. It's a Christmas peace offering."

She stood stiffly whilst he took the bundle and opened it on the bed, spreading out some bright-colored fabric on the gray wool blanket.

Slowly Jessamyn walked to the bed, still keeping a safe distance between them.

"What is it?"

Rhys stood aside to reveal a rippling satin gown the color of sunshine. The long sleeves fastened to the elbow with carved amber buttons. A broad, marten-trimmed collar framed the scooped neckline. There was also a matching headdress of padded, gold cloth, also trimmed with amber and edged with marten fur. Two separate, funnel-shaped hanging sleeves cuffed in marten could be tied to the shoulders of the splendid gown with glittering gold ribbons.

"I thought you needed a gown to show off your beauty. There's no need to look like a peasant lad all your days."

The gift of this beautiful gown was so unexpected that her anger softened towards him; her eyes misted with tears. Then common sense suddenly intervened and she blinked back the moisture.

"Thank you, but I brought a silk gown with me," she said, clearing her throat.

"But not as rich as this, I'll be bound."

"No . . . 'tis much plainer. Where did you get this?" she asked, a note of suspicion creeping into her voice. Surely he was not giving her one of Eluned's castoffs.

"Suspicious? Did you think I robbed a wench and stripped her naked? Proctor Massey's a cloth merchant and his brother owns a tailor shop with a crew of sewing women."

"As you didn't know I'd be coming to Chester, this could not have been made for me. The most skilled seamstress in the world couldn't have made so fine a garment in two days."

"Ah, I see I'm no match for your sharp wits, lady."

Jessamyn's anger began to rise at his mocking tone. She had almost been ready to accept the gown as a peace offering, until good sense overcame her emotions.

"You are right. It was not made for you. The gown was ordered for the daughter of an alderman who has since changed her mind about the color. I knew the gown would be a perfect choice for you and I couldn't see it go to waste. Accept the gift, Jessamyn, in the spirit in which it's given."

"It won't make any difference to my decision," she reminded him as she stroked the cool, smooth satin. Her hand strayed to the soft brown fur. It was such a beautiful gown, far more luxurious than anything she owned. The gown must have cost a fortune. Amber was a semi-precious stone, marten fur a noblewoman's trimming.

"I didn't bring the gown as a bribe. Wear it in good health."

Unguarded, Jessamyn picked up the lovely gown, surprised by the sheer weight of the yards of shimmering fabric. She had taken her eyes off him as she held the gown against her body, wishing that she could see her reflection. Her small room had not even a polished metal disk in which to admire herself.

Jessamyn stiffened as she felt the warmth of his hand on her shoulder. It all happened so quickly, her protests died in her throat. His arms went around her, drawing her close, successfully stifling her resistance. Jessamyn opened her mouth, angry words of denouncement on her lips.

"No, sweetheart, don't . . . love me instead," he urged, before his mouth came down on hers.

Rocked by fierce emotions, Jessamyn stood there, her head spinning. His mouth covered hers, devoured her lips in a deeply passionate kiss. The heat of his kiss melted the last of her reserve. With a sigh akin to a sob, she finally relinquished her strength against him. What joy to let him take her weight against his strong body, to abandon the burden of injured pride, jealousy and hurt. Blood was roaring in her ears like a mighty ocean. At last, unable to stand, they fell together on the feather mattress.

At the last moment, Rhys had the presence of mind to push aside the grand golden gown, and the satin slid unnoticed to the rushes. Yearning for love so long denied, they pressed close, their hearts pulsing as one. To Jessamyn, the firelit room seemed to spin in a heated whirl of passion.

"Tell me you still love me," he urged, whispering hoarsely into her ear.

"You know I do . . . I've never stopped. Oh, I wanted to hate you. I almost believed all the lies I told myself, but it didn't work. You're the only man I'll ever want," she confessed softly.

Her mouth hungry for his, Jessamyn sought his hot, fragrant lips. Desire made his mouth hot as a furnace. Deliriously, she pressed against his hard body, her lips swollen with passion, forever seeking more, desperate to assuage the empty loneliness of the past weeks.

"Tell me again how much you love me," Rhys urged huskily, his hand sweeping slowly across her shoulders and inside her blue bedgown, which gaped provocatively to reveal her full white breasts.

Shuddering in delight at his longed-for caresses, Jessamyn thrust her breasts into his eager hands, wanting to feel the delicious arousal of his touch, wanting to arouse him in turn. He needed little encouragement to delight in her flesh. Rhys lovingly fondled her smooth, white globes, gently tracing with his thumbs the erect nipples.

"I love you more than any man has ever been loved," she vowed, drinking in the hot fragrance of his neck. Burying her face in the smooth, tanned warmth, she found a safe haven against all her loneliness and pain.

Rhys caught his breath in a sob of passion as he heard her ardent confession. He held her close, showering her with kisses. Jessamyn's breasts throbbed with passion, the heat spreading in waves to the very core of her being. She pressed against his chest, wanting the intimate contact of flesh against flesh. Fumbling with the buttons on his doublet, her fingers shook so that she could not unfasten the garment.

Smiling at her clumsiness, Rhys unfastened his dark doublet and shirt. Eagerly pressing her full breasts against his bare chest, Jessamyn thrilled to the feel of his hot flesh, his matted black hair crinkling against her skin. Rhys shuddered at the contact and emitted a deep groan of desire. His mouth left a hot trail of kisses down her neck, across her breasts, nuzzling and caressing, until she was out of her mind with passion.

With shaking hands, Jessamyn held his head

fast against her breasts, delighting in his arousing mouth, in the stabs of flame as he gently took her nipple in his mouth, teasing, drawing out the pleasure until she cried out in passion.

"I've dreamed of this these past two days," Rhys revealed huskily, tracing his fingers along the fastening of her velvet bedrobe, parting the garment. Impatiently, he thrust her shift above her waist. He lay against her, kissing her, letting his mouth renew its acquaintance with her creamy flesh, relishing her scent and arousing warmth. His fingers meshed in her damp hair, which spread like a coverlet across the bed, all curling and springy in his hands.

Rhys fought the constriction of his clothing with clumsy fingers, trembling as he divested himself of the restraint of doublet, shirt and hose. At last, he lay against her, flesh to flesh, their throbbing hearts beating as one.

"You are magnificent, my wonderful Welsh stallion." Jessamyn gasped in delight at the strong pulsing wonder of his muscular body. Chuckling throatily, she eagerly claimed the firehot strength of his manhood. Rhys was more aroused than he had been before, ever more eager to possess her. The unexpected discovery thrilled her beyond measure.

Shuddering at the exquisite thought of being impaled on that firehot brand, of his caressing every delicate nerve ending of her innermost self, she pressed his throbbing heat between her thighs. Slowly she allowed the velvet textured flesh to touch the most intimate part of her body, before finally drawing away, the more to prolong their pleasure.

Rhys parted the silky auburn web which guarded the secret place between her legs, his knowing caresses inflaming her all the more. Rhys exerted every ounce of restraint he possessed, waiting until she was ready, holding back the hot flood of passion that he ached to release.

"Oh, Jessamyn, sweetheart, I love you, love you, love you," he whispered, his muscles taut, with tremors coursing along his arms and legs.

Then, he had no need to ask, nor she to acquiesce. An unspoken command passed between them. Automatically, her legs opened to him and her arms wrapped about him as she urged him in one swift, smooth action, to take her past the point of no return.

Showering her with kisses, Rhys rolled her on her back and lay above her, fitting his body into hers, joyously sliding deep inside her with a shuddering groan of passion.

Jessamyn cried out, striving to take him even deeper, to keep him inside her for all time. Together they began to move rhythmically, their love uniting them into one tumultuous embrace. Passion consumed their bodies, sweeping over them like the heat from a blast furnace, until no force on earth could have halted the course of their desire. His mouth fastened on hers, scalding and possessive, and she strived against him, desperate to share the ultimate explosion of senses.

Swiftly, and with intense sweetness, their desire erupted in a sweeping wave of ecstacy. Shuddering in the throes of passion, when the blackness exploded into light, Jessamyn cried out, clinging to him as she sank slowly into the deep, comforting well of fulfillment, lying in the protective strength of his arms.

Rhys breathed her name and she whispered his, still adrift, aware yet that he lay beside her to comfort and cherish her during the slow return to earth.

They must have dozed in each other's arms, for when they next became aware of their surroundings, the room had chilled. The fire burned low in the grate and no daylight penetrated the oiled parchment window covering.

When she turned slightly on the feather bed, aware of his presence beside her, Jessamyn's heart somersaulted in delight. For an instant, she thought she had dreamed one of those terrible, tormenting dreams, after which she would bury her face in the pillow and weep.

"It's real," she whispered dreamily, "you really are with me."

He smiled, stroking her smooth back. Feeling the chill of the room on their bare flesh, Rhys dragged the gray wool blanket over them. They nestled there in the warmth, bemused by their discovery.

"Did you sometimes dream of me?" he asked softly, hopefully.

"Not as much as I wanted, and far more than I could endure," she revealed, running her hand over his hard, muscular chest.

"I dreamed of you . . . oh, Jess, why did we part as enemies? I never wanted to hurt you. I love you."

He hugged her close and she sighed in pleasure as she relaxed against his hard body, finding it so smoothly hot and arousing; she shivered in delight.

"What shall we do now? It must already be night."

"Can you not guess, lady?" Rhys chuckled, slowly stroking the firmness of her buttocks, fondling and shaping the curving flesh.

"First we can eat, then make love . . . or we can make love, then eat . . ."

"Perchance we won't eat at all," she said. She reached for him and pulled his mouth to hers.

Chapter Twelve

Jessamyn stood at the murky window watching for Rhys. Whenever she thought about the past few hours, she wanted to pinch herself to make sure she wasn't dreaming. He had stayed with her until morning. During the night, they had dozed, then awakened to make love, unable to get enough of each other's arousing bodies.

In the half-light of early morning, Rhys had ordered a meal brought to the room. They dined beside the fire on baked fish in wine sauce, fresh bread, honey and butter, washed down with a flagon of hot spiced ale. Though the fare was simple, it might have been a fine banquet, so special would it always be in her memory.

Afterwards, they made love one last time, slowly savoring the pleasure of their lovemaking. Rhys had loved her so thoroughly that her body tingled just to think about it. Then, with the sun already up, he had reluctantly left her at the Falcon. Jessamyn had no idea how he intended to explain his absence to his host. The Masseys might not have found it unusual; perhaps Rhys often spent his nights elsewhere. No. Jessamyn thrust away the disturbing thoughts. Jealousy would not mar the pleasure of their reunion.

Determined to shut out the niggling doubt she felt about his faithfulness, Jessamyn forced her attention back to the street. The warmly dressed people milling about Lower Bridge Street reminded her of a colony of ants. Some men balanced boxes and bundles on their heads or shoulders, while young 'prentice boys struggled under great bales of cloth, trays of baked goods, or casks of wine. Again, the constant stream of traffic coming into Chester seemed to have no end.

There had been a light fall of snow overnight. Across the street, the windowsills and doorsteps gleamed unnaturally white. The rush seller's stall in front of the inn had bunches of holly, bay, and fir hanging from its wooden walls. Next to it was a poulterer's, where live geese and hens cackled inside makeshift wooden cages, their less fortunate brethren already plucked and hung by their feet. Other birds, ready for the oven, still bore white, brown or red feathers to cater to the housewife who preferred to pluck her own Christmas fowl. A steady stream of shoppers stopped to appraise the poultry, some buying, while others haggled unsuccessfully before moving away in disgust.

"Jessamyn."

Her heart leaped as she heard Rhys's voice behind her. Mindful that they were not alone, she did not run into his arms as she would have liked to do; she merely smiled and held out her hands to him.

"Oh, Rhys, I didn't see you. There are so many people in the street."

"Are you ready? The sun's struggling through the

clouds, so we'd best take advantage of it. If I'm not mistaken, there'll be more snow by nightfall."

He had suggested that they explore the city, then sup at an inn near the Watergate. The promise of his company for the next few hours was delight enough. Jessamyn would have been content just to sit talking to him, looking at him, but Rhys thought she needed entertainment, so entertainment she would have.

Though he had suggested that she might wear her new golden gown, Jessamyn had chosen instead her own rosy pink silk. She was saving the special gown to wear to Mass, for Rhys had promised to take her to the great cathedral on Christmas Day. She did not want to soil the gown in the streets.

Rhys wore a plain, dark green doublet under his fur-lined cloak. Solicitously, he tied the strings of Jessamyn's hood, warning her that despite the deceptive sunshine, the north wind blew cold.

They left the inn, threading their way through the busy streets, admiring the goods displayed in the open stalls as they passed. Everywhere they were assailed by apprentices, eagerly promoting their masters' wares. The bolder lads tugged at their cloaks with greasy fingers, trying to interest them in hot mutton pasties, or gingerbread figures, specially gilded for the Christmas season.

Jessamyn felt safe in Rhys's company. It was hard to believe that when she first entered Chester, she found these narrow streets threatening. Everything had seemed so alien after the windblown country-side around Curlew.

They strolled into the large open market. Jessamyn wished that she could have come the previous day, when Margery and Jack still kept their stall. The drover and his wife had already left Chester in the early morning, stopping by the inn to bid Jessamyn goodbye. They promised to get word to

Lord Walter that all had gone as planned, and help was on the way.

Quickly assessing the couple's noble station, a troupe of brightly dressed tumblers fell to the cobbles before them, twisting their seemingly boneless bodies into tortuous positions. Next, they balanced on their hands and climbed atop each other's shoulders before turning dizzying cartwheels, vaulting over each other's backs in a quick paced game of leapfrog. When the impromptu performance was over, Rhys threw the men a handful of coins. Doffing their red caps, the tumblers bowed solemnly before going in search of another audience.

Rhys and Jessamyn stopped at a haberdasher's stall where he bought her a bundle of gleaming satin ribbons to trim her gowns—deep purple, blue, red and green; the colors shimmered in the light. Jessamyn was delighted. Carefully, she rolled up the ribbons and put them inside the leather pouch which hung at her waist.

Next, Rhys stopped at a small goldsmith's shop in one of the two-tiered shopping streets known as the Rows. The goldsmith's was on the upper level, overlooking busy Eastgate Street. There they admired trays of jeweled belts, necklaces and brooches. Jessamyn had never seen such beautiful work. The white-haired goldsmith proudly explained that his artisans worked in the French manner, enameling gold and silver to create the unique designs. She admired an enameled gold heart-shaped brooch which could also be worn on a chain around the neck. Blue and white flowers were painted around the edge of the heart. At Rhys's insistence, Jessamyn chose instead a gold chain with an amber and pearl pendant set in an engraved gold setting. At intervals along the chain, amber beads alternated with small pearls. Jessamyn was sure it was too costly. Rhys insisted that she have the necklace to wear with her new gown. Jessamyn did not see how many gold coins exchanged hands, nor could she hear what Rhys was saying to the old goldsmith, but she was sure the necklace was far too valuable.

As they emerged from the dark little shop into the cold sunshine, Rhys kissed her lovingly, laughing at her protests.

"Stop worrying about the cost, sweetheart. I'm not a pauper. I want you to have the necklace to wear for my pleasure. I can already picture exactly where the pendant will rest."

Jessamyn smiled and hugged him in thanks, aware that he harbored lustful thoughts, and pleased to be the cause of them.

"You mustn't spend so much money on me," she added as they blended with the noisy crowd. He only grinned and squeezed her arm, well pleased with his transaction and considering the subject closed.

They walked past Chester's mighty stone-walled cathedral, its tall spires seemingly reaching to heaven itself. Outside the Abbey gates, Jessamyn was disturbed to see a line of beggars awaiting the distribution of alms. Here, Rhys told her, the famous mystery plays were performed at Whitsuntide and a great fair was held each summer on the feast of St. Werburgh.

All too soon, their two hours were spent. They walked down Greyfriars to the harbor, watching as several vessels unloaded their cargo to form a mountain of casks and bales on the wooden dock.

Outside the old Market Hall, they were serenaded by carol singers. Faces pink with cold, the group played lively tunes on pipe, sackbut, viol and tambor, singing ancient carols in both French and English. The boys' voices sounded sweet as angels, trilling the ages-old melodies. Jessamyn clapped her hands in delight. Rhys slipped her a handful of small coins to reward the singers for their efforts.

Finally, they reached the inn on Watergate Street. Tree of Jesse was the establishment's unusual name. A splendid biblical tree, painted in bright colors and bearing gilded leaves, adorned the inn's wooden facade.

Rhys had already ordered their meal to be served in a private dining room overlooking the busy street. A huge fire blazed in the stone hearth, soon thawing out their cold fingers and toes. A festive note was added to the small room by the intertwined boughs of bay and holly, tied with scarlet ribbon and hung on the walls. Their meal consisted of a steaming meat pudding, covered with a spicy purple sauce, a dish of honey-bronzed turnips, and crusty white loaves of bread. A flagon of spiced ale and porringers of savory gravy were left on the table so that they might serve themselves.

Jessamyn ate ravenously, finding the food delicious. She wondered why Rhys had become unusually quiet since they reached the inn. Was he regretting that their time together was over, or were his thoughts on obligations he must undertake with Eluned's family? She knew there must have been a reason why he could only spare her the early hours, but she steeled herself not to question him about it. Rhys had an aversion to a woman trying to own him; her cross-examination would not be well-received.

When they finished their meal, a serving lad brought in a pewter tray of spicy, gilded gingerbread figures. Jessamyn chose an elaborate church to remind her of Chester's great cathedral, yet it was gilded so prettily, she refused to eat it, whereupon Rhys ordered the boy back and made her choose another piece, one which would not be too pretty to eat.

Laughing at him, Jessamyn chose a figure of a woman carrying a bunch of flowers.

When they finally left the inn, they slowly walked back to the Falcon. Tomorrow was Christmas Eve. Rhys had said that he could not come to her until late in the day, but that when he finally arrived at the Falcon, he would stay the night. On the morrow, they would attend a Christmas Mass in Chester cathedral. Jessamyn knew that she must be content with this arrangment, though she jealously begrudged the Massey family so much of his time.

Rhys kissed her goodbye in the shadow of a stall. Jessamyn merely had to walk a few feet to the inn's side door; Rhys said that he would not leave until she was safely indoors. He also insisted that she accept a purse of coins to pay for her midday meal the following day, ignoring Jessamyn's protests that she had money enough for plain fare.

They parted reluctantly, their whispered goodbyes drowned by the noise in the street. Jessamyn stood in the inn doorway, watching as Rhys threaded his way through the crowd, heading in the direction of Proctor Massey's fine townhouse. She felt bereft when she considered how many hours she must wait for his return. Fat snowflakes had begun to fall and as Rhys hurried along the street, he pulled his hood over his head to keep out the snow.

With a sigh, Jessamyn turned and headed toward the stair.

The following morning, Jessamyn sat glumly beside the hearth, wondering what to do. On inspiration, she decided to go out by herself and walk through the open market near the cathedral. She was sure that she could easily find her way about if she kept to the main streets. It would be a pleasureable way to spend a few hours until Rhys could be with her again. She would also buy him a surprise gift.

While they had been in the goldsmith's shop in Eastgate Street, Rhys had admired an enameled hat badge. Providing that the price was not too high, Jessamyn intended to buy it for him. The enameled brooch had blue and yellow flowers growing out of a pool of water. For his own personal insignia, Rhys had chosen a daffodil surrounded by the tall flowers which grew in abundance in marshy areas each spring. He had told her that these were known as the Flowers of Llys. This brooch looked so much like his crest, it might have been made for him.

There was no cold north wind, and beneath the wintery sunlight, the snow-dusted streets seemed far more pleasant. The night's snowfall had merely settled into crevices and lodged between roof tiles, leaving little accumulation, for which Jessamyn was thankful. Though glistening snow was a delight to the eye, it made travel hazardous. Had the snow fallen heavily, these well-traveled streets would have become either a slushy mire, or scored by deep, frozen ruts, depending on the temperature.

Jessamyn easily found the goldsmith's shop again, perched behind the oak ballustrade on the upper row.

The goldsmith came from the rear of the shop to attend to her, blinking owlishly in surprise when he saw her.

"But 'tis not ready yet. I said late this afternoon," he protested shrilly as she stepped to the counter.

Surprised by his greeting, Jessamyn said that she had no idea what he was talking about.

After he peered shortsightedly into her face and saw her puzzled expression, the old man laughed and shook his head. "Nay, I'm mistaken. You're not the lady," he explained quickly. "Now, what can I do for you?"

"I saw a hat badge when I was here yesterday—a

crest with blue and yellow enameled flowers."

The old man nodded. He returned a few minutes later with the tray containing the enameled pieces. "Here, lady, very fine work indeed."

Jessamyn picked up the pretty piece, turning it over in her hand. On the back of the brooch was the Chester hallmark assuring its quality.

"It is very fine, maybe too fine for me. How much?" she asked him, aware that she had only five sovereigns in her purse. Now that she would not be staying after Christmas Day, Jessamyn felt that she could afford to squander some of the money she had been hoarding for board and lodging.

"For you . . ." he paused, eyes twinkling, "let's say two guineas, lady, and a bargain it is."

Two guineas. Jessamyn considered. She was sure the piece was worth that or more, yet could she afford to spend two of her precious guineas all at one time?

"I'll take it," she said quickly, before she talked herself out of it. The goldsmith nodded his approval and carefully wrapped the brooch in a scrap of purple linen. While she waited, Jessamyn scanned the tray for the heart-shaped brooch that she had admired. It was gone. Obviously someone else had also found the piece lovely. When she had set out that morning, feeling somewhat reckless, she had considered buying the heart, if it were modestly priced. Though she felt a pang of disappointment, perhaps it was just as well that the piece had already been sold. This way, she had enough money left to buy gifts for others.

The goldsmith smiled indulgently at her while she counted out the coins. He bit into the gold pieces to make sure they were not counterfeit.

Jessamyn carefully put Rhys's gift inside the pouch at her waist and, bidding the goldsmith good bye, she

213

walked back into the market.

She remembered seeing a vendor with a stall full of elaborate marchpane figures. Walter had always had a great weakness for the sweet almond confection. She would buy him a piece of marchpane. She had precious little else to give him. Then, Jessamyn smiled at her own foolishness. She had arranged a gift far surpassing any paltry marchpane favor—she brought him salvation in the form of thirty fighting men. Surely, that should be Christmas gift enough for anyone.

Still smiling, she made her way to the stall, where she spent some time admiring the small marchpane works of art before deciding on the most suitable one. Jessamyn finally chose a helmeted knight on a rearing charger. The figure stood on a pedestal, just like Walter's carved ivory chess pieces. She was sure he would be pleased with this gilded masterpiece.

At another stall, she saw a tooled, red leather dog collar, decorated with gold bells. The collar would be perfect for old Ned. He would look splendid in this wonderful new collar.

When Jessamyn finally retraced her steps to the Falcon, she had one and a half guineas left to her name, but her pouch overflowed with gifts. She had bought blue silk ribbons for Margery's golden hair and a plain leather pouch for Jack, small tokens of her appreciation of their kindness on the journey. Walter's marchpane chesspiece was wrapped in a scrap of red cloth, enclosed by Ned's splendid new collar. Best of all, and the most precious, was Rhys's enameled hat badge lying at the bottom of her black leather pouch.

Jessamyn felt generous and sinfully extravagant. At Curlew, she had never had the opportunity, or the money, to buy gifts for anyone. All Christmas gifts were painstakingly handmade. Waiting for Rhys would be pleasanter, filled as she was with the generous spirit of giving. Jessamyn smiled as she set out her splendid purchases to admire before she prepared for his arrival.

The clang of steel being hammered on an anvil, the rattle and clank of swords, and daggers being honed to razor sharpness brought Eluned to the window. To her surprise, she saw Rhys's men below, unusually busy with warlike tasks. The archers were even oiling their bows and fletching new arrows. It seemed odd to see such heightened activity right before Christmastide. They were not due in Wales for almost a month, for she knew the date Rhys was to meet with Owain Glyndwr.

Eluned pushed open the casement and leaned out. "You there? Why do you prepare for battle?"

The man glanced up and, seeing it was Lady Eluned, quickly doffed his cap. "We leave the day after tomorrow, my lady. Best to be prepared. Who can tell what will happen on the journey?"

"Leaving the day after tomorrow? That's utter nonsense."

Mouth tight in aggravation, she withdrew her head and slammed shut the window. Day after tomorrow! She had given no instructions to leave then. And certainly not before the Christmas festivities were over. The fools must have had their orders confused.

She swished angrily down the staircase, heading for the ground-floor solarium where she had last seen Rhys in deep discussion with his two lieutenants. Earlier, she had found their talk boring and quite beyond her comprehension. Now, she pondered their discussion about defenses and troop deployment. Could new orders have come from Wales? An important message had been delivered to Rhys. The servant girl had said that a lad had brought something so important, it could be delivered only into Rhys's hand. Though the girl should have reported this to her at once, the fool forgot to mention it, making her wait almost a week for the news.

"Rhys." Her voice sounded shrill, and she swallowed, forcing a smile. It was not wise to sound so irritated. Rhys was not at his most genial these days, and she must be careful not to rouse his temper.

He glanced up, then motioned to his lieutenants to leave them alone. Eluned crossed to the vast oak table where he sat, poring over some maps.

"Those fools in the courtyard are preparing for battle. How so? You've almost a month before you report to Glyndwr."

"We're leaving sooner than expected, right after Christmas Day, in fact. I was going to tell you tonight. Now, no arguments," he cautioned, as her eyes rounded in surprise and her face flushed. "I've made arrangements for you to be escorted home when you're ready. I've no intention of spoiling your pleasure, Eluned."

"Why are you leaving so soon? Is there to be a battle?"

He grinned. "I hope not, but one can never be sure. I'm going to a garrison's aid."

"A garrison? Which one?"

"Curlew. You remember, the place we stayed after that fire."

Twin spots of color burned high on her cheekbones at the unpleasant reminder.

"Ah, I see you do remember," Rhys commented, hiding a grin. "I thought you might, seeing as you allowed your temper to overrule your sense whilst we were there."

"What is so important that you're high tailing it back to Curlew before Christmas is over?" she demanded icily, ignoring his sarcasm. A picture of Curlew's beautiful lady flashed through her mind and her anger mounted.

"A relative of Dacre's has played him false. He left troops in the castle, the better to capture it, come spring. If we leave now, I hope we can thwart Sir Ralph's treachery."

"Why you?"

"Who else can they ask?"

"This Sir Ralph? What is his station? Is he important?"

"I don't know. Rich enough to support troops, for a start. He's their distant relative from Shrewsbury. Ralph of Cater's Hill is his title."

"Oh, I've heard of him. He has influence with Bolingbroke."

"What does that mean to me? I don't concern myself with King Henry's toadies."

"The lad who came to see you, he brought the message?"

Rhys nodded, glancing down at the map. "There'll be time to take care of this before we have to meet Glyndwr. You can travel with Proctor's cousin. He's going to Wales with a sizeable party, so there'll be plenty of protection. There, you see, you're well taken care of."

"But I wanted you to take care of me, Rhys," she said, blinking blue tear-filled eyes. "I won't feel safe unless I'm with you."

"I'm afraid you'll just have to force yourself to it, love. It can't be helped."

Eluned looked stonily at him, unsure whether to have a temper tantrum, or to let it pass. Wisely, she decided to let it pass. Her mind worked quickly, putting two and two together and not liking the conclusion she reached. Rhys's manner had undergone a subtle change these past few days. He had also been absent for long stretches without good cause. He had said that a lad had brought his message from Curlew. Stabbing pain shot through her chest. That was it! The messenger had been no lad! It must have been that bitch dressed like a boy, the easier to steal Rhys from her!

There he sat, pretending his flight to Curlew was merely a tactical move, and all the while he intended to be unfaithful with Jessamyn Dacre. She could have slapped him for his smug deceit.

Under the cover of her skirts, Eluned clenched and unclenched her fists, longing to tell him that she was on to his tricks. Instead, she forced a smile to her mouth and went to stand beside him, so close that their arms brushed.

A reminder of his commitment to her was needed to jar him back to reality. "Take care, Rhys dearest, I don't want my future husband coming to any harm," Eluned cooed, her voice like honey.

"I'm not your future husband, and I wish you wouldn't keep referring to me as such," he snapped, pushing back his chair and standing up.

"We're betrothed."

"Aye, and you took great delight in giving the Lady of Curlew that information, didn't you?"

"I thought she should know the truth, because you were obviously deceiving her into thinking you were available. That's all."

"It's not for you to decide what I should do and say. It so happens that I didn't tell the lady in question because I didn't think our betrothal significant. An infant contract can generally be broken if the man chooses."

Eyes blazing, she grasped his arm, digging her fingers in the sleeve of his doublet, wanting to hurt him.

"How dare you dismiss our betrothal so lightly?

We are still betrothed, whether you want to admit it or not. Your panting for some other woman doesn't alter that. A slut might warm your bed for a night, but I will be your wife!"

Angrily, Rhys shook off her hand. "I'll forget you said that, Eluned, because right now I'm far too busy to take issue with you."

Gripped by rage, she watched him stride from the room with nary a backward glance. He called to one of his men, who had been waiting outside. How dare he dismiss their betrothal so lightly? He didn't fool her—pretending that he was busy with military matters, while it was more likely he was off to keep a rendezvous with Jessamyn Dacre.

Eluned hurried to the doorway in time to see Rhys walking into the street. Damn him! He couldn't wait to see *her*.

A serving lad was carrying a tray downstairs and she spun round to face him.

"You—follow Lord Rhys. Tell me where he goes, and what he does. And don't let him see you, or I'll have you whipped. Go on. Be quick, or you'll miss him."

The lad put down the tray. He was concerned that the steward would have him whipped for leaving the tray, yet he was more worried about the wrath of the Lady Eluned, whose eyes burned like blue fire. She shoved him, then boxed his ear, forcing him to make a choice. He bolted through the door with a wail of pain.

For over an hour, Eluned stewed about the situation, concocting various forms of vengeance. She was helping her sister and the maids decorate the Hall with Christmas greenery for the night's revels. Gwen chatted away, oblivious to her distress, until Eluned could have throttled her into silence. Still, her sister had no idea that her heart was breaking. Eluned smiled tightly, considering the phrase. No, she was too angry to be called heart-broken. Besides, she was far too determined a woman to give in to such a pathetic emotion. Rhys must be made to come to heel.

She glanced up, holding aloft a kissing bough decorated with ribbon and strewn with bells and twined with mistletoe. At the door stood the serving lad, beckoning to her. Eluned's stomach lurched. Either Rhys had come back, or he was abed with that woman.

"Well, what did you learn?" she demanded of the boy, pushing him before her into an alcove off the tapestry-hung corridor. Just to make sure no eavesdropper lurked nearby, she lifted the wall hanging and reassured herself that they were alone.

"I followed him, just like you said."

"Yes, yes. Where did he go?"

"To a goldsmith's near the Eastgate."

"That's all?"

"No, lady, that's where he went first. Then he stopped at a haberdasher's in Bridge Street."

"And was he alone?"

"Oh, no, lady."

Her mouth tightened and the color drained from her face. Openly, brazenly, shopping for gifts with that slut! She couldn't believe it. Her bony fingers dug into the lad's arm, making him wince.

"Then where did he and the woman go?"

"Woman? What woman?" the puzzled lad asked. "There weren't no woman, just Lord Rhys and his man."

Eluned let out a sigh of relief. She had been wrong. He had not been racing out to meet that woman after all. He'd been hurrying to buy a gift for her to make amends for his churlish behavior that morning.

"Did you see what he bought?"

"Yes, lady. I listened at the goldsmith's door. They was talking about an expensive gold brooch, all special engraved for a lady."

"And at the haberdashers?"

"They give him a pair of blue gloves."

"You've done very well. Now, each time Lord Rhys leaves the house, I want you to follow him. I'll pay you well for it."

The lad's face lit up and he nodded eagerly. Following Lord Rhys and reporting on his movements was better than being at the steward's beck and call, and infinitely safer than being within his cruel reach.

For the next hour, as Eluned helped her sister string boughs of holly and twine ivy tendrils about the brackets of the wall sconces, she hummed Christmas carols.

She had been far too suspicious of Rhys. Fancy suspecting him of all manner of dalliance with that woman, while all the time he had been shopping for her gifts. When she asked him if he had bought her a present, he had laughed and said, not yet. It was quite possible he'd been innocent of wrongdoing since they'd left Curlew. That mysterious messenger may really have been a lad after all. But, just in case her suspicions were founded, it would be wise to have him watched. And she would make inquiries of her own to learn more about this Sir Ralph of Cater's Hill.

Chapter Thirteen

The Massey family and their guests were full of good cheer. The gaily decorated Hall of the Masseys' fine townhouse rang with music and laughter. Candles guttered and were replaced. On the walls, smoking sconces flickered in the draughts, casting the brightly colored scene in a ghostly, wavering light.

The Christmas Eve feast had been consumed and remained little more than a memory of spicy sauces, roasted fowl, burnt sugar custard, and fine Gascon wine.

Eluned sighed in contentment as she smoothed down the skirts of her pearl-encrusted ivory satin gown. Her gorgeous gown, with its matching marten-trimmed surcoat quilted with gold thread and pearls, was obviously the most expensive in the Hall. Smiling smugly at her achievement, she idly watched the dancers whirling past as the revels grew rowdier. Many male guests were already tipsy, for Proctor was renowned for his excellent wine cellar.

There was never a dearth of guests to attend his revels.

She scanned the crowd for that familiar, broad-shouldered figure, resplendent tonight in a holly-red doublet of silk, velvet, and white satin. The colors looked superb with Rhys's olive skin and black hair. The fine doublet had been her gift to him, and to please her, he was wearing it this night—the very reason she had given it to him before the banquet. Eluned wanted the other women to see how handsome he was, to pine for his attentions and to know that he belonged to her.

As yet, Rhys had not presented her with a gift. He must be delaying until they were alone. She smiled as she conjured a mental picture of that warmly loving scene. Naturally, he would apologize for his churlish behavior. At first she would pout and hesitate, but of course, she would eventually forgive him. Suddenly, she saw his dark head above a bevy of brightly dressed women, laughing at his humor. Her eyes narrowed as she failed to identify a pasty-faced woman who clung possessively to his arm. She must be the daughter of one of Proctor's merchant friends. How shamelessly she giggled and flirted with Rhys! Eluned's mouth set in a hard, thin line when she saw how little effort he put forth to rid himself of the forward baggage.

She walked toward them with a determined step. As she drew closer, Eluned seethed anew with rage. That hussy was provocatively pressing her breasts against his arm. The wench's leaf-green silk gown fit like a second skin, the bodice so snug, the protrusion of her erect nipples was apparent, even from a distance. That was the reason she brushed back and forth against his forearm, consciously arousing him. Her pink tongue darted to her soft lips like a cat contemplating a dish of cream!

"We've not danced all evening, dearest," Eluned reminded him sharply as she tugged his arm away from the temptation of that woman's bodice. No wonder he was making no move to rid himself of the hussy.

Rhys inclined his head to the woman in leaf-green silk, a teasing smile on his mouth. Eluned grew so angry as she watched him flirting with the slut that she could have slapped them both.

"Remember, you're welcome in our home all twelve days of Christmas, Lord Rhys," said the forward baggage in a husky, inviting voice. Then the wench dropped a low curtsy, allowing him a revealing view of her cleavage.

"Thank you for your kind invitation, Mistress Joan," Rhys acknowledged politely.

Eluned was positive that she saw him wink at the woman before she turned away, still giggling foolishly. Gripping his arm, Eluned steered him towards the dancers.

"You said you had a headache," Rhys reminded her as they joined the throng of finely garbed guests, who skipped and swayed to the music. Hidden from view behind the fretwork screen of the minstrel gallery at the far end of the Hall, a group of musicians played a lively melody.

"It's better now," Eluned answered through clenched teeth.

"Ah, miraculously healed when you thought Mistress Joan was about to seduce me," he suggested wickedly, noting how her cheeks reddened at his suggestion.

"You needn't jest about it. Why didn't you stop the wench from making such a spectacle of herself?" Eluned asked as they skipped beneath the arch formed by the other dancers' clasped hands.

"Few noticed, save you, dearest. What sharp eyes

you have." Rhys grinned at her discomfiture. He abandoned her to dance alone past the line of women dancers before joining his partner again at the end of the line. Eluned did not speak to him at first, so angry did she feel. Silently they joined the other dancers in the formation, moving about the perimeter of the smoky Hall.

"Christmas Eve's no time for teasing," she hissed, her eyes gleaming with mortified tears. "Stop it. Don't treat me so unkindly."

Rhys squeezed her hand, whispering a swift apology as they kept step with the other couples, who were already forming an arch at the other end of the room. When they had once again completed their pass beneath the tunnel of hands, Eluned tugged Rhys's arm, pulling him out of the formation.

"I'm thirsty."

"I'll get you some wine." Rhys motioned to a serving lad to bring them a cup of wine.

While Eluned sipped from the cup of sweet malmsey, she waited for Rhys to offer his special gift. Finally, unable to stand the suspense any longer she prompted:

"Did you forget to give me my Christmas gift? Or haven't you shopped for it yet?" She was trying to sound lighthearted, but after watching that woman shamelessly try to ensnare him, her humor had soured.

"Nay, I wouldn't forget your gift, Eluned. Wait here. I'll fetch it."

Smiling expectantly, she sat down to wait on a low bench against the wall, smoothing her skirts, aware that she was looking her best. All golden and white, her fair hair plaited in coils about her ears and bound with ribbons and pearls, she looked almost angelic. All she needed was a pair of gossamer wings to rival the two satin-clad angels mounted on either side of the blazing hearth, except that her face was far more beautiful than their painted plaster countenances, their cheeks all puffed out as they blew silent fanfares on golden trumpets.

Rhys approached her through the murky atmosphere. After a night of guttering candles and smoking torches, combined with billows of smoke from the hearth, the air inside the Hall had grown thick and full of soot particles. Eluned blinked to clear her vision, for the smoky atmosphere made her eyes burn.

"Come over here so we'll be alone. We needn't share this with the rest of the guests," Rhys suggested, motioning for her to move to a shadowy corner. He carried a small wooden chest under his arm.

Eluned's heart skipped a beat as she read an intimate meaning to his words. Obediently she followed him. She could afford to act meek and mild, she decided generously, smiling up at him, admiring his strong profile in the hazy yellow light. Rhys was the most handsome man she had ever seen. He was probably the most handsome man in the world, she thought romantically, reminding herself that he belonged to her. To know that other women admired him and envied her his attentions was the best part of all.

Like a child, Eluned clasped her hands in excitement as she awaited her gift. It might be worth a king's ransom, a jewel to eclipse all the jewels of Gwen's prosperous friends. After all, her sister was married to a mere cloth merchant. Her husband would be lord of the Llys valley. With a smile, Rhys handed Eluned the sandalwood box with its intricately carved lid.

Smiling prettily, she thanked him, pausing politely to admire the workmanship of the carved chest. It seemed rather large to hold jewelry, unless he was giving her a matching ensemble. She unfastened the small gold clasp with shaking fingers. Pearls probably, or rubies. The lid opened to reveal a pink satin-lined interior. A pair of embroidered blue kid gloves lay inside.

"Oh . . . how . . . lovely . . . a glove box," she whispered in surprise, lifting out the gloves. There was nothing else in the box.

"Try them on. Lloyd lent me a pair of your gloves to match the size," Rhys revealed, smiling indulgently as Eluned slipped her small white hands inside the soft gloves.

"Ah, they fit exactly."

She looked down at the gloves. The gauntlets had a design of birds and flowers worked in white silk. They were lovely, a work of art, but not what she had been expecting.

"Is this all?" she ventured at last, unable to conceal her disappointment.

Rhys laughed at her apparent greed. "By all that's holy, Eluned, did you expect the key to Chester? Indeed, these cost me a pretty penny, not to mention the sandalwood box."

"No . . . I didn't mean that," she stuttered, anxious to make amends. "I . . . I thought . . . perhaps some . . . jewelry, something more personal," she prompted, watching him closely. In the murky yellow light, Rhys's face lay in shadow and she could not accurately gauge his reaction to her statement.

"Well, there's no wedding ring hidden inside, if that's what you're expecting."

"Nay, Rhys . . . I didn't mean that." But he wasn't listening. He picked up her cup of malmsey and drained it.

"Your greed knows no bounds, lady. Now, I bid

you good night, for it appears I've caught your headache."

"Please, Rhys, don't go yet," Eluned cried, reaching for his hand, but he pulled it away.

"It's late and I've had enough revelry for one night, expecially since we must begin another round of yuletide cheer tomorrow."

He bowed formally over her hand, his face set, his emotions concealed from her. Eluned could have slapped him. So, he had not bought that piece of jewelry for her, after all! It surely wasn't a gift for that little slut with the pouting nipples!

Angrily, she glanced towards the hearth where she had last seen Mistress Leafgreen holding court. Two men stood talking and laughing with her, yet she was not behaving provocatively towards them. She barely glanced after them when they walked away. Was Rhys already her lover?

When Rhys walked from the Hall, he never looked at the wench, yet Eluned realized that he was clever enough to feign indifference. She shoved the blue gloves back inside the sandalwood box, longing to throw his paltry gift into the fire.

She crossed to the hearth where she scanned the woman's silk gown, looking for a brooch. Nothing. But, maybe he had not yet given it to her. Or could it be that she was too wily to wear it here?

"Mistress Joan, it's getting late. Many of the ladies have already retired," Eluned reminded her sharply. "Aren't you tired of all this frolicking?"

"Yes, it is getting late. Father's bringing my cloak," Joan agreed amiably. "We'll be back tomorrow. There's to be dancing and mummers and plum pudding," she recited, bubbling with excitement, her slanted green eyes noting the splendor of Eluned's gown. "Best of all, Lord Rhys promised to catch me under the kissing bow," she revealed throatily, aware of the angry glint in Eluned's eye and the tightening of her mouth.

"That will probably be the shortest pursuit in history," Eluned remarked spitefully, before turning on her heels and walking away. Mistress Joan's gale of laughter followed her, the sound grating on her nerves. It was pointless to try to insult the empty-headed ninny! If Joan was going home with her father, then Rhys could not be meeting *her*. Or were they cleverly going to elude the old duffer and keep their tryst behind his back? Rhys may not even have been interested in bedding giggly Joan. Clinging wenches were not his weakness. She had discovered that his tastes ran more to full-bodied, brown-eyed women like Jessamyn Dacre, who had more than their share of independence.

Eluned marched from the Hall, glad of the clean chilly air in the long passage connecting the house to the outbuildings. Might her original suspicions be founded? Was Jessamyn Dacre here in Chester?

Had he bought the brooch for her? Or was it for one of a dozen other probable lovers who had danced with him this evening? To Eluned's surprise, she felt the unmistakeable dampness of tears. Damn him! Surely she was not falling in love as these other foolish women professed to do? No—that was impossible. She had never allowed a man to rule her heart, and she was not starting now. Temporary weakness had overtaken her. The hour was late and the day had been stressful. Keeping reins on Rhys was proving more difficult than she had expected.

Was she even up to the task? Eluned asked herself miserably, as she leaned against the windowframe to peer into the dark courtyard below. He had no idea that she was having him followed, so she was ahead of him there. The kitchen lad who had spied for her this afternoon had been reminded anew that he was to follow Rhys if he left the house. All evening, Rhys had stayed put. This was the hour for him to step over the line.

Eluned strained to pierce the gloom as she saw lanterns winking in the darkness below. A groom led out a saddled horse. A lad moved forward, carrying a burning cresset to light a departing guest's way home. In the flickering light, two cloaked figures crossed the courtyard. Tensely, Eluned craned forward in an effort to identify the couple. Suddenly, Joan's innane laughter pealed out, audible even through the closed window. Joan and Rhys? No. The man turned, his face revealed in the glow from the torch, and she felt her heart jolt back into place. He was old enough to be the wench's father.

A slender figure slipped from the house. Eluned's stomach pitched when she saw that it was the lad she was paying to spy on Rhys. He was sprinting across the courtyard; he pushed open the outside door and disappeared into the street.

Rhys was going out!

Eluned turned away from the window. He was going to spend the night with a woman. Or he could possibly be delivering that piece of jewelry. Oh, damn him for his treachery!

She leaned against the wall, her hands clammy. From somewhere nearby came a shout of laughter, and several male voices raised in a melodious Christmas carol as passersby hastened home.

Christmas Eve—soon to be Christmas day. Guests would fill the house tomorrow and the next day and the next. How could she maintain her cool aloofness in light of her knowledge of his treachery? Rhys had no idea that she knew about his purchase. He had been trapped by his own stupidity.

Tomorrow she would learn the identity of the woman and confront him with the knowledge. She would see what lies he would invent to defend himself. Rhys would pay for deceiving and humiliating her—and God help the woman, for Eluned's jealousy knew no bounds.

Church bells pealed, their tones clear in the frosty air. It was probably the Abbey bell marking Matins or Lauds. Jessamyn was not sure what time the monastic offices were rung, but she knew it was already far into the winter night. In fact, it must be Christmas day. She had not expected to celebrate the holytide in a lonely upstairs room at the Falcon Inn.

Jessamyn pressed her face against the cold window, peering through the murky horn pane. Frost gleamed white on the shrubs flanking the inn door. Above the recessed doorway swung a lantern to light the way, casting its golden beams over the narrow cobbled street.

Morning. Rhys was not coming!

A tear slid down her cheek; a second dripped off her nose, splashing against her golden gown. She had been waiting for hours, hoping that the sound of each step, each voice heralded her lover's approach. And he had not come. Were the Christmas revels still in full swing at the Masseys' lordly house? Or was it more likely Rhys had other, more pressing obligations to his betrothed?

Angry with herself, she turned from the window, forcing away the hateful image of Rhys holding lovely Eluned. Even were he to give Eluned Glynne loving embraces, it would only be as expected. After all, the Welsh woman saw herself as his future wife. Jessamyn knew Rhys would not have forgotten that she waited for him.

Jessamyn threw another log on the hearth and slowly began to unfasten her golden gown. Her fingers brushed the pearl and amber pendant nestled against the hollow between her breasts and she clasped it like a drowning woman, drawing comfort, as if the jewelry were an amulet to ward off pain. The scene in the goldsmith's shop that frosty morning came vividly to mind. Rhys had placed this splendid piece about her neck, urging her to accept the gift to complement her new gown. He would not have taken such pains, or spent so much money on her, had he intended to discard her in favor of Eluned.

Tears dripped from her cheek to her hand and she gulped back her grief in a shuddering, painful sigh. She must have faith. Rhys must have a good reason for being late.

A few minutes later she heard steps below on the cobbles. Jessamyn darted to the window in time to see a dark, cloaked figure disappear beneath the inn doorway with its bright garland of holly. A traveler arriving so late without horse, or baggage? The man had to be Rhys.

Hands clasped, she waited before the hearth, watching the door, straining to hear his familiar tread on the stair. A few minutes passed before she was rewarded by the dull thud of footsteps. Then there came a tap on the door.

With a cry of delight Jessamyn ran to the door, lifting her voluminous skirts high so that she would not trip. For what seemed an eternity, she fumbled first with the bolt, then the latch, until at last she pulled open the door.

Moonlight slanted across the narrow corridor, splashing the wall with silver. A dark shape loomed in the doorway suddenly blocking the light; then she heard his voice and her heart turned over.

"Jessamyn, sweetheart, I'm so sorry to be late."

Now her tears were shed for joy. With a cry of delight, Jessamyn grasped his arms, drawing Rhys inside the room. He kicked the door shut behind him as he enfolded her in his arms, aching for the feel of her pressed against him, for the sweetness of her mouth.

Rhys kissed her tenderly, tasting the salt of tears. With a frown, he held her away from him, puzzled by her grief. "What . . . tears? You surely didn't think I wasn't coming. Oh, Jessamyn."

"It's so late. I thought maybe the revels were too pleasant to leave, or maybe you . . ."

"Was abed with another?" he suggested, frowning.

"Something like that," she admitted, shamefaced, hanging her head and gulping back tears.

"What must I do to show you there's no one else?" he whispered, holding her gently, his face buried against her sweet perfumed hair.

"I wore this gown specially for you," she ventured, trying to lighten the mood.

"And you're a vision in it. Come, let me look at you."

Rhys smiled as he held her at arm's length to admire the sleek, gold satin gown, the fabric gleaming as richly as royal robes. The fluffy marten fur settled light as swansdown against the creamy column of her neck and framed her swelling flesh. The arousing sight made him tingle with expectancy.

"Beautiful, but then, I never doubted you'd look like a queen. 'Tis almost a pity to take it off . . ."

He winked at her as he spoke, and Jessamyn laughed, her unease dissolving as if by magic. Now that he was with her, nothing else mattered.

"I don't mind the sacrifice . . . in fact, I'm going to insist on it," she whispered huskily, slipping her arms around his broad shoulders, reveling in the hot, hard substance of his body—no longer a dream lover, but a real man of sinew, blood and passion.

Carefully she unlooped his cloak and slid it off his

shoulders. Jessamyn gasped as his expensive doublet was revealed. She slipped her hand over the smooth white satin alternating with velvet, bright as holly berries, sewn in a dozen padded strips artfully designed to accentuate the breadth of his shoulders and slender waist. About his hips was slung a gold link belt. His dark hose and black kid boots were a stark contrast to his gaily colored doublet.

"You look like a prince in your fine new doublet."

"Thank you, sweet, it's a Christmas gift," Rhys said, reaching inside the black pouch at his belt. "And, speaking of gifts, I have one for you."

"Another gift!"

"Oh, love, I'd give you a gift every day of the year if it would make you happy," he vowed, taking her face in his hands to gaze lovingly at her beauty, shuddering at the emotion it awakened. "You're my darling Jessamyn, my own sweetheart."

His mouth came down on hers in a passionate kiss. Jessamyn eagerly kissed him back, shuddering at the bolt of emotion which shot through her body. She was gripped with such hot, sweet longing for him, her legs grew weak.

"Sit, Lady, before the hearth, if you please," he commanded, when he finally put her away from him, realizing that at this rate, they would get little accomplished. "It's a surprise, so you must close your eyes."

Obediently Jessamyn went to the bench beside the hearth where she sat, carefully arranging her golden skirts about her, anxious to look beautiful for him. She felt the warmth of his hand and she wanted to look down, but she squeezed her eyes shut. Cold metal was placed in her palm, and he gently folded her fingers around it.

"This is a gift from the bottom of my heart," he

whispered as he drew her to her feet. "A symbol to remind you always of how much I love you."

She opened her eyes and looked down. There, nestled in her palm, lay the golden enameled heart that she had so admired at the goldsmith's shop. Rhys had bought the trinket, not some stranger. The bright blue and soft white enameled flowers gleamed in the candlelight.

"Oh, Rhys . . . you bought it for me. Oh, thank you, it's lovely." She hugged him in delight, kissing his cheeks, his nose. "Thank you."

"Now, turn it over; see what it says. Here, hold it up to the light."

Jessamyn held her hand close to the candle, turning over the heart to read the engraved inscription. Fine script spiraled up from the base of the brooch where two engraved hearts held the initials *R* and *J*.

In a voice choked with emotion, she read, " 'Love makes two hearts beat as one.' Rhys, it's lovely. I'll always wear it, and when we're apart, it'll make you seem closer."

Once again, he enfolded her in his arms and Jessamyn rested her face in the warm hollow of his neck, feeling well loved. Their world was here in this room, isolated from reality and bound together by love.

At last, she raised her face, suddenly remembering the gift that she had bought for him.

"Now, 'tis your turn to sit beside the hearth and close your eyes," she cried, thrusting him toward the bench.

Jessamyn took the cap badge out of her purse and pressed the metal in the palm of his hand, shuddering as she held his slender fingers, recalling the pleasure of his caresses. Reliving the blissful arousal of his touch sent a warm flood of pleasure deep between her thighs.

"There, my gift to you."

Rhys looked down at the badge and his face lit up with pleasure. "You went back to the goldsmith's by yourself to buy this!" he said in surprise, turning the badge about in his hands, the gold winking in the firelight.

"Yes, aren't you proud of me? I knew you wanted it and the flowers look exactly like the Flowers of Llys."

"It could have been made for me. Oh, Jess, thank you, darling. But surely, you can't afford this."

"I think the goldsmith gave me a bargain. At first, he seemed to think I'd come to collect a specially ordered piece . . . now I understand. He thought I'd come for the heart and he wasn't finished engraving it. When I noticed it had gone, I never guessed you'd bought it for me. Instead I felt disappointed. I'd contemplated buying it myself. Then I decided it was just as well that I couldn't, because I wouldn't have had enough money to get gifts for the others."

Rhys smiled indulgently at her confession. "I'd no idea you would go back. Fortunately, the old fellow's made a lifetime of lying convincingly to his customers. He never mentioned it. He must have laughed to himself about this pair of silly lovers, each trying to surprise the other."

"We're not silly . . . and we did surprise each other. I'll always treasure this heart. Did you compose the inscription?"

"Of course," Rhys answered indignantly, as he pulled her onto his lap. "Surely you don't think the old man's blood runs warm enough to dream up these sentiments."

"Ah, but I thought after a lifetime of pleasing lovers, he might have suggested an appropriate phrase," she teased, running the tip of her tongue down his cheek, which was still cold from the night air.

"He had no part in it except to do the engraving. I still can't believe you were brave enough to venture out alone in the city. Thank God, you weren't harmed."

"It was broad daylight." She dismissed his words scornfully, pulling his ear, then nibbling the lobe. "I went to the market and bought Walter some marchpane and a lovely red collar for Ned. I even got some trifles to please the drover and his wife."

"Speaking of marchpane . . ." Rhys struggled to open his pouch, from which he produced a white linen bundle. Inside were two marchpane angels, brushed with honey glaze and colored pink with sandalwood. Though sticky, the sweetmeats were still edible.

Jessamyn was pleased by the unexpected treat—not only Walter was addicted to marchpane. She insisted that Rhys share the sweetmeats with her. Together they sat munching the sweet, almond confection before the fire.

Out of the darkness, the bells tolled again, announcing the passing hours.

"We're wasting the night. Mass comes early and I promised to take you."

"It's not my fault you spent half the night drinking and reveling at Proctor Massey's house. Had you come when I expected, we might already be asleep in our bed."

"It's likely I won't sleep a wink before Mass," he suggested wickedly as he stood and set her aside. "Now, let me have the pleasure of taking off your gown. And the necklace I so selfishly purchased."

She laughed as he glanced pointedly at the gold pendant nestled provocatively against the vee formed by the creamy tops of her breasts. Bending his head, Rhys kissed her flesh where the pendant rested, slipping his tongue between those warm

Patricia Phillips

mounds as he traced the delectable curves, making her shudder with pleasure.

"Oh, love, this is going to be my happiest Christmas," Jessamyn whispered, raising his head and pressing her mouth against his.

"Far better than I ever expected, and this is only the beginning. Have you forgotten? Tomorrow we set out for Curlew."

Jessamyn's heart leaped at his reminder. In the renewed joy of his company, she had forgotten their impending journey. Rhys's assurance of his love and the expectancy of his arousing lovemaking had sealed her pleasure.

Together they began to carefully remove their finery. Jessamyn's hands shook as she unfastened his doublet, eager to touch the smooth, hot flesh inside his shirt, caressing, stroking, until his arms began to tremble. As his rigid control was breached, it became harder for Rhys to negotiate the fastenings of her gown, to stay patient while the marten-edged neckline slid lower.

"Oh, Jessamyn, love me, love me," he groaned, pulling her against him, thrusting aside their clothing. Rhys fitted her soft breasts against his chest, delighting in the arousing pressure against his bare skin. He slid his hand between them to eagerly fondle the firm, silky delight, teasing her nipples until she gasped with mounting desire.

Hopping this way and that, balancing on one leg, Rhys struggled to remove his boots and hose until, laughing, they fell together on the bed. Jessamyn lay on top of him, pressing against his wonderful, thrusting heat, matching her thighs to his as she fitted his swelling body to hers and moved gently back and forth. The wonderful arousal of this intimate game became too strong, and Rhys tumbled her off him onto her back.

They kicked aside her gown. The billowing finery made a lake of brilliant color on the wool counterpane. Next, leather boots and shoes dropped on the floor with a thud. Together they rolled against the feather pillows, bodies locked, mouths fused. Rhys kissed Jessamyn so deeply—it was almost as if he sucked the life from her body. Limp, she lay against him, no longer able to control her shudders of passion.

"Oh, sweetheart, I love you more than I ever thought I could love a woman," he vowed sincerely, stroking her back, his hands warmly caressing her.

"Rhys . . . I love you so much," Jessamyn breathed, cast adrift in the pleasure of his lovemaking. "It's an eternity since you made love to me. I've longed to feel your arms round me."

He smiled down at her in purest love, finding her face little more than a pale blur where they lay, in the corner farthest from the candle.

Jessamyn eagerly sought the thrusting power of his manhood, shuddering in delight as she ran her fingers over the length and breadth of him, encircling the thickness. His smooth skin was velvety and soft; his flesh throbbed with desire.

He reciprocated, his fingers seeking and finding the moist sweetness between her thighs, stroking and rousing her to fiery desire. Tentatively, Rhys ventured deeper, until she finally clamped her thighs about his hand, warning him to be still. Rhys sought her mouth, her soft lips bruised from his kisses, yet still hungrily seeking him.

"Perchance I'll make love to you until it's time for Mass. Would you like that?" he whispered, his breath tantalizingly hot against her ear.

Jessamyn felt his tongue teasing her earlobe and she crushed him against her, violent in her passion. "Yes, oh, yes, I'd adore that," she answered, touching him, urging him home. With a shudder she could no longer control, she allowed Rhys to enter her, driving deep; she found his passion so hot and full that she could no longer think. He swept her up in his magnificent lovemaking. Their bodies took control, unfolding with sweetest desire, seeking, finding, asssuaging. Locked in each other's embrace, there, in the dark room beneath the eaves, their love was forged white-hot.

As his control neared breaking point, Rhys whispered endearments to her in his native Welsh. He laid bare the innermost yearnings of his soul, trusting her completely in the depth of his love. Together they soared to the heights of passion, mutually achieving that pinnacle in one long, tumultuous crescendo of joy.

Chapter Fourteen

In the frosty solitude of the December morn, Rhys saddled his horse. The family was still abed; he was grateful for that blessing. Though he was not sure why, the previous day, a distinctively chill attitude had prevailed within the household. Whenever he encountered Eluned, she looked daggers at him while her sister, Gwen, viewed him with a reproachful frown. It was almost as if they knew where he had spent Christmas night.

Rhys cinched the straps tighter, then glanced up at the window, fancying that he saw a movement there. It was possible that they'd had him followed to the Falcon. Eluned was not beyond such a devious act. If that were the case, then he knew exactly why he had fallen from favor. Still, it mattered little what they thought of him; he would shortly sever all ties with the Glynnes. Back home in Wales, he intended to dissolve the marriage bargain struck between his father and old Jasper Glynne. Though

241

it would be merely a formality, the act would assure Jessamyn of his good intent.

From upstairs in the chilly gallery, Eluned watched Rhys preparing for departure. Every time she thought about his treachery, she shook with anger. Unfortunately, she could not prevent his traveling to Curlew with the Dacre woman. She had wracked her brain for a means to stop them. There was simply not enough time. Short of hiring men to waylay them, she could think of nothing to delay their journey.

Mouth tight, she turned away, unable to look at Rhys. He was far too handsome. She had known that there would always be other women. In the past, she had not really minded. Only since Jessamyn Dacre came on the scene had her confidence been affected. This attachment seemed different from the rest. The Margeds and Betsis of the hills were only peasant girls—Jessamyn Dacre came from a noble family, or so she claimed. Eluned's mouth curled scornfully as she considered the primitive appointments of Curlew Castle. Nobility perhaps, but definitely of the most humble sort.

She would have to let Jessamyn Dacre have him for the next week. But their romantic idyll would not last, she had seen to that. Already, her messenger rode post haste to Shrewsbury, delivering an anonymous letter to Sir Ralph Warren, warning him that his intentions had been betrayed by the Lady of Curlew.

Her inquiries about the Warrens of Cater's Hill had proved fruitful. A friend of Proctor's lived near Shrewsbury and had been only too willing to reveal Sir Ralph's friendship with Henry Bolingbroke, his influence at court, and his military skill, his frequent competition in tourneys. Yet another snippet he had unthinkingly revealed could prove to be the most valuable information of all. Before his marriage to Eleanor Whitten, Sir Ralph had been considering betrothal to Jessamyn Dacre of Curlew Castle! Eluned could have hugged herself when she heard that news. Considering the woman's looks and Sir Ralph being a recent widower, she decided that he was interested in capturing far more than the Dacre castle. Likely, he also coveted the woman's body. So, in her letter, Eluned had casually mentioned that Rhys of Trevaron was Jessamyn Dacre's lover. To have to put it in writing had been painful, yet she had gritted her teeth and trusted that the information would inflame the Englishman sufficiently to hasten Curlew's downfall. Eluned also revealed the date on which Rhys was to meet with Glyndwr, hoping to assure his safety with that information. Were Sir Ralph half as clever a soldier as she supposed, he would strike when the castle's defenses were at their weakest.

Rhys waited impatiently at the crossroads, pulling his cloak around his chin to keep out the cold. Slitting his eyes against the wind, he scanned the highway for approaching riders. Two of his men had been sent to escort Jessamyn safely out of the city, yet they seemed to be taking their time about it. Surely nothing had gone astray. He swiftly dismissed that worrying thought, for Dan and Bronwy were two of his best men. The niggling worry that Eluned would seek revenge on him flitted through his mind. He no longer doubted that she knew he spent Christmas night with Jessamyn.

As he was about to ride out of the courtyard, Eluned had hurried outside to bring him a stirrup cup. Swathed in her best fur-lined cloak, yellow hair artfully disarrayed, she had smiled charmingly at him, though her eyes remained hard. He thanked her, returning the cup and kissing her hand in farewell.

"Enjoy her this next week, love, for I promise you it will be your last," Eluned said.

With that Eluned had turned on her heel and gone inside the house.

As he rode along Lower Bridge Street, dodging carts and cattle, Rhys had pondered her warning. In a week, he would reach Curlew. Eluned must have guessed Jessamyn was the messenger who asked for his help; she would also know that he was accompanying Jessamyn to Curlew. What devious plot was the little bitch hatching? Jealous and vindictive as she was, he doubted that Eluned would allow anyone, or anything, to stand in the way of what she wanted. And, for some unfathomable reason, she had set her heart on having him for her husband. This new development made him uneasy. Jessamyn was in greater danger and he must now be on guard to protect her. Fortunately, Eluned was not privy to the secrets of his head. Long before she went home to Wales, the contract binding them would be officially broken.

A small party of cloaked riders approached from the north, their heads down against the wind. They rode at a swift pace and Rhys's anxiety dissolved as he recognized the travelers.

"You took your time, boyo," he shouted to Bronwy, who spurred ahead to greet him.

"Aye, far too much traffic in the streets for my liking. I'll be glad to be shut of the place."

Rhys turned his attention to the slender form who rode astride a nag too tall for her, making her seem even smaller by contrast.

"Jess—thank God you're safe. I imagined all kinds of tragedies," Rhys revealed, his voice thickened with emotion. He took her hands in his, raising them to his lips. He would not embrace her before his men, though he suspected that they already knew where his heart lay.

"At last—oh, the hours seemed unending. I can't believe we're actually beginning the ride to Curlew," Jessamyn said, looking up at him, her heart lurching as she gazed full upon his lean, olive-skinned face. The cold had tightened his features, making Rhys appear older, or perhaps thoughts of the mission ahead had aged him. She had not stopped to consider the danger of the coming encounter with Sir Ralph's soldiers.

They fell into easy stride as they headed for open country, leaving the sprawling port of Chester far behind.

The grizzled Cheshire countryside was shrouded with mist as they rode over marshes and grazing land, taking a shortcut to the main highway. The horses gradually picked up speed and the party of armed men automatically closed ranks as they entered a narrow, sunken road. On either side, tangled brambles tinged purple and bronze hung low to the ground, with sodden leaves clinging along spiny branches. In the roadside ditches, stalks of grass sparkled, crystalline with dew and lacy spider's webs curtained the hedgerows.

At noon, they stopped to sup and rest the horses. Again, just before nightfall, they stopped to put in at a hostelry. This routine was to set the pattern of their days, though sometimes an inn was not available, forcing them to make arrangements to sleep in a farmer's barn.

The constant traveling was hard. Sitting long hours in the saddle made Jessamyn stiff and her hands roughened from holding the reins, yet she did not begrudge a minute of it, for she was riding beside Rhys. She posed as his young squire, clad in boy's homespun. As they rode the bleak miles to Curlew,

Patricia Phillips

he talked companionably to her, revealing much about himself, including some things she would rather not have known.

On the third day out, their conversation led inevitably to politics. Though she had hoped to keep their relationship non-partisan, she knew that it had been a vain hope.

"Then you are Glyndwr's man?" she said at last, mustering her courage. This issue had to be settled, though she already knew what his answer would be.

"Hadn't you guessed?" was all he said.

"Well, because you're a Welsh lord, I assumed it was so."

"And you, Jessamyn—where lies your loyalty?"

She shrugged, unsure of how to answer. "Curlew never took sides in the issue. We're neutral."

"Impossible. You must choose between Henry Bolingbroke or King Richard."

She stared at him in dismay, surprised by his statement.

"King Richard's dead."

"Or hiding, just waiting for his chance to reclaim his throne. Glyndwr believes that. He was his squire once. He tried to rescue the king when they took him under guard, but it wasn't possible."

"I know many of the Welsh believe he's still alive," Jessamyn began, placing her hand on his, feeling the warmth through his gauntlet. "The king's dead, Rhys. A minstrel told me that he saw them take Richard's body from Pontefract Castle. He knew the king—there was no mistake."

"Perhaps the man just wanted attention with the tale."

"No, I don't think he had any reason to lie."

For a few minutes Rhys was silent. At last he sighed and said, "For some time I've suspected as

246

much. Most Welshmen are still loyal to Richard. To learn he's gone would be a death blow . . . I think I'll keep the knowledge to myself. The legend gives them hope, you see."

"Does this make a difference to Glyndwr's cause?" Jessamyn asked hopefully.

Catching her hopeful tone, Rhys laughed and shook his head. "Nay, Glyndwr's quarrel's with Grey of Ruthin. He has much to pay back for the sack of Sychart."

"Glyndwr has already raided Ruthin. Doesn't that make them even?" Jessamyn asked, aware the Welsh had swooped down and burned the Marcher lord's town in September, during the annual fair.

"Pay back, love, that's what they call that. Burning Ruthin was only a minor payment for all the bad blood between them. You forget, Reggie Grey stole Glyndwr's land first. Croisau Common has long belonged to the Glyndwrs. It was Grey's claiming that which started their quarrel."

"Surely Glyndwr didn't have to make war over it."

"When the courts settled in favor of the English lord, what recourse did he have? We expected little else. That verdict's a foregone conclusion when the dispute involves a Welshman," he added bitterly.

Jessamyn did not know whether justice was as blind as the Welsh always claimed it to be. Apparently, Rhys believed it to be so.

"You still haven't told me who Curlew's for," he reminded sharply.

"The Dacre family."

"Who doesn't live on an island," Rhys reminded her tersely.

There came a sudden squall of sleet, and they had to pull their hoods lower in an attempt to shield their faces from the slashing cold.

"My father supported Richard."

"Then he would have been for us."

"He supported the crown."

"Even when a thief wears it?"

"He supported the crown," Jessamyn repeated stubbornly, anxious to get out of this uncomfortable discussion but not knowing how.

They had reached a narrow bridge across a stream and halted to allow the others to cross over.

"You do understand, Jessamyn, after I wrest Curlew from Sir Ralph's men, I'll fly the Welsh dragon from the ramparts."

Appalled, Jessamyn stared at him. "No, you can't! We don't support Glyndwr. You'll automatically lay us open for attack from any passing English force."

"If I command Curlew, I will fly the Welsh standard."

"Is that a threat?"

"Nay, lady, it's a promise."

For the next few miles, they rode in stony silence. Jessamyn seethed with anger over his stubborn insistence on advertising his loyalty to Owain Glyndwr. When she sought his aid, she had not bargained for this. It would be suicide to fly the Welsh Dragon. Once they'd declared for Glyndwr, they'd never be safe.

The sleet squalls increased in number and intensity, until Rhys was finally forced to put up for the night, though there was still another half-hour of daylight. The closest shelter was a farmstead with several outlying barns. Rhys sent several of his English-speaking men to ask the farmer for shelter and offer him gold for fodder for the horses and their own lodging.

Jessamyn huddled against the shelter of the barn wall, waiting out the storm. Rhys glanced at her, saw that she was well covered by her cloak, and left her. Their disagreement had left them both nursing injured pride, and he was not used to begging a woman's forgiveness.

Shelter was granted them and they thankfully unbolted the barn door and entered its darkened interior, smelling of fresh hay and the odor of long departed cattle.

Rhys parceled off the old, bare stalls. Men were dispatched to rub down the horses and feed them. He saw to his own mount; Jessamyn did likewise.

As she ministered to her long-legged nag, Jessamyn wondered if Rhys was going to speak to her, or if he intended to make the rest of the journey to Curlew in angry silence.

Later, she sat on a mound of hay munching bread and sipping ale purchased from the farmer's wife. There was also crumbly white cheese which was so strong, it made blisters on her tongue. Rhys had raked mounds of clean straw to make their bed and had thrown a blanket over it. When the work was finished and everyone settled down to sleep, Rhys took his cloak and, wrapping himself in it, rolled over against the wall, far away from Jessamyn. He had managed a gruff good night, though it appeared to cost him considerable effort. Their sleeping quarters were set apart from the rest, offering privacy, and she was disappointed when he made no overtures of love to her. She had hoped to mend their quarrel with kisses and passion. So angry and disappointed did she feel, she longed to punch him to vent her pent-up emotion. He was an arrogant, self-centered male. She fumed, glaring at the dark mound beneath his cloak.

For a long time, Jessamyn lay awake in the darkness, conscious of myriad rustlings in the hay. She hoped the rats would not creep out to investigate the travelers, for she had a healthy loathing of rodents.

Instinctively, she drew closer to the dark mound of Rhys's body as she heard loud rustling, followed by flapping wings in the rafters above.

Jessamyn stared up into the darkness and let out a startled cry. Two gleaming eyes peered down at her; she grabbed Rhys's arm in fright, shaking him.

"What is it?" he growled, pretending that he had been asleep. In truth, he, too, had been lying awake, wondering why they had quarreled and how best to mend it.

"Sorry to wake you," she hissed, highly aware of their strained relationship. "Look, up there. Someone's watching us."

Rhys raised up on his elbow to look where she pointed. Twin spots of light gleamed out of the pitch darkness, moving first to right, then left, still staring at them. He began to chuckle and pulled her back down beside him.

"Go back to sleep, Jessamyn. It's only a barn owl."

Jessamyn lay down, aware of her heart still pounding in fright. She was the victim of too many peasant tales of demons and witches. Soon she began to smile, chuckling softly at her own foolishness.

"Are you going to sleep, or laugh?" Rhys asked gruffly, rolling onto his back.

He surprised Jessamyn by suddenly reaching out and pulling her into his arms.

"I thought you were still angry with me," she whispered.

"I am. You were angry with me."

"It's silly for us to quarrel."

"Aye, and such a waste of energy."

They lay there silently, listening to the wind in the creaking old barn, and the sleet tinkling and pinging against the roof as a fresh shower assailed the winter countryside.

"Do you still love me?" Jessamyn asked shyly.

"Of course. Do you still love me?"

"You know I do."

"Let's not quarrel again, Jess, we've too short a time together for that."

"I promise, but you're still not going to fly the Welsh dragon over Curlew," she reminded him firmly. "I can't allow it."

For a few minutes, he was quiet. Her stomach turned over as she considered his probable anger. Then, she felt his body begin to shake with mirth.

"Damn you, woman, you must be the most stubborn female on the face of the earth."

"Curlew's my home and I have to protect it."

"Shall we compromise? We'll fly the Dacre standard above the dragon."

"No."

"Below it?"

"No. We're not going to fly the dragon at all. You're asking me to commit suicide. Once you leave, we're unprotected."

Rhys considered her argument for a few minutes. At last, he reluctantly agreed. "Very well, I see your point. Mayhap Glyndwr will never find out. No dragon. Are you happy now?"

Smiling, Jessamyn laid her head against his shoulder and stroked his face. "You could make me happier," she suggested, slowly sweeping her hand down his chest, his belly, until her fingers came to rest over that pulsing, steel-hard length beneath his clothes. She gasped in surprise at her discovery.

"A natural occurrence," Rhys said, dismissing her surprise easily, "having absolutely nothing to do with you. It happens quite often of a morning."

"Liar!" She playfully punched his chest. "It isn't morning. Why, we've barely had time to go to sleep. You wanted me all the while you were pretending not to."

"You never asked me to make love to you," he pointed out, pulling her to him until he pressed against her body. "Anyway, in your angry mood you'd probably have refused me . . . wouldn't you? Come on, tell the truth?"

She smiled and kissed his mouth, silencing his voice. After kissing him thoroughly and being rewarded by the answering leap beneath her hand as his desire mounted, Jessamyn reluctantly agreed.

"But you see, sweetheart, I'm not angry with you anymore. I'll never be angry with you again."

Rhys snorted in derision. "Now who's the liar?"

"Stop talking and start loving," she commanded, taking his unresisting hands and placing them on the swell of her breasts. Rhys did not move, allowing his hands to rest there in maddening inactivity. "Oh, you," she cried, biting his earlobe until he grunted in pain.

Grabbing her, Rhys rolled on top of Jessamyn, pushing her down in the soft, yielding hay.

"Very well, lady, you've tormented me once too often. You won't escape now. I'll make love to you until you beg for mercy."

"That sounds wonderful," she breathed in pleasure, slipping her hands inside his clothing, enjoying the hot, smooth touch of his bare flesh. She tangled her fingers in his thick chest hair and touched his nipples. "Oh, Rhys, I'm sorry we quarreled," she whispered, still teasing him with her tongue. "But you made me very angry."

He silenced her with his fiery mouth. His hands came to life as he fondled the soft prominence of her breasts. So sudden and intense was the fire in her veins as her passion soared, Jessamyn urged him to have done with the love play and take her without delay.

Eagerly Rhys obliged, his passion increased by

her mounting desire. Quickly, he stripped away their hampering clothes. Jessamyn opened to him, longing to feel his hot strength deep inside her. She shuddered and gasped as his burning flesh touched hers. Then, he entered her in a burst of heat, filling her body with fire. Jessamyn cried out softly, mindful of the others in the barn. She pulled him against her, wrapping her legs around his slim hips, locking her ankles. She arched her back to take him even deeper inside her body, striving to possess all of him.

Their mutual passion exploded in a fiery burst, like a dam giving way, so that Jessamyn cried out in surprise and delight as deep shudders of ecstacy overcame her. A tumultuous wave of passion swept her to a secret place where she drifted as if weightless, completely fulfilled.

Jessamyn lay heavy-limbed in Rhys's arms, gradually becoming aware of her surroundings, lying on a mound of hay inside an old barn, filled with the soft snores of sleeping men and the rustling of wild creatures.

Nuzzling Rhys's face, she whispered her thanks.

He smiled in the darkness, hugging her against him. "I assure you, it was my pleasure," Rhys whispered, kissing her face, and her lips, soft with spent passion.

Enfolded tenderly in each other's arms, they pulled Rhys's warm cloak over them and quickly drifted into a peaceful, dreamless sleep.

It was a cold, moonless winter night when they set up camp in the woods beyond Curlew. Had it not been so dark, Jessamyn could have seen the castle from there. Her heart pounded in excitement at the thought of being home, then her pleasure dimmed as she reviewed the danger of their position. What

if Rhys were wounded? It was too horrible to con-
template. What if the entire venture proved to be a
terrible disaster? Her stomach churned with unease
as she wondered what approach would work best.
As yet, Rhys had not revealed his plan, though she
knew he had one, for she had overheard snatches of
his discussions with his lieutenants.

The men lit campfires in several forest clearings,
some distance apart. Not until Rhys explained his
reasoning did Jessamyn understand the tactic.

"I want the garrison to think we're a larger force."

"You want them to know we're here?" she asked
incredulously, unsure if that were wise.

"That's part of our plan. You're sure the drover
could be trusted to pass the word to your brother,
so he'll be prepared for us?"

"Yes, Jack's always been trustworthy. Walter was
to tell the captain of the guard and the castle steward, but they won't know when to expect us."

"They'll have a good idea. The drover's been back
and forth to Chester often enough to gauge the distance. Now, I want you to pretend you'd been taking medicines to someone in the village, that you
left before dawn when no one was around. Tomas
and I will pose as village craftsmen—maybe smiths
needed to shoe the garrison horses—or some such
tale. We'll enter the castle with you."

Jessamyn swallowed nervously, hoping the plan
would work. "You're assuming Walter and Simon
will have covered for me."

"We must work on that assumption; we've no other choice. You're to tell Sir Ralph's captain that
many Welsh are camped in the woods. That won't
come as a big surprise—he'll already have seen our
fires. I'm hoping to draw the enemy out of the castle
to skirmish. If I don't miss my guess, after these
weeks of boredom, they'll be chomping at the bit.

He'll only be too glad of a little action. We'll engage them, hit and run several times, always pulling back into the woods. I'll leave a couple of men behind, while the main body doubles back across the river. We'll enter the castle by the postern. Can we cross the moat on horseback?"

"Yes, I'll show you where on a sketch. It's been fairly dry, so the water will be low by the postern. I'll give you a map to give them. The postern's hidden. We don't want to delay while they search for the right spot."

"Good idea. Now, while Sir Ralph's troops are debating whether to chase us down in the woods, we'll slip inside the castle and pull up the bridge."

"What will you do then? Do you think they'll attack?"

"No. They'll chase down Sir Ralph with some cock-and-bull story about a huge Welsh force. Just as long as they leave us in peace, I'll be happy. What do you think?"

Jessamyn shrugged, not as taken with the plan as Rhys appeared to be. So much hinged on the participation of certain men who might not be wholly reliable.

"We'll be all right if everyone plays his part." She hoped that Jack had done as she had told him, and that Walter had not revealed Rhys's coming during a boozy moment, or that a disloyal servant had not betrayed their secret.

"Stop worrying. Nothing ventured, nothing gained," Rhys reminded, squeezing her shoulder in reassurance. "If this doesn't work, we'll have to try something else. You surely weren't expecting them to open the doors and let us in, were you?"

She smiled and shook her head, realizing that she had not really thought about how Rhys intended to liberate Curlew. She had just been thankful that he had agreed to help her without questioning his methods.

It was cold, sleeping in the dank woods, and Jessamyn was not sorry when it was time to saddle their horses and be on the move.

Before dawn they were riding toward Morfa Bach.

Jack and Margery were astonished to find their lady standing on their doorstep. Baffled at first over the purpose of her visit, when they came fully awake and noticed two strange men riding with her, they understood.

Rhys explained his plan several times before Jack saw the wisdom of it. He assured Jessamyn that he had done as she asked by notifying Lord Walter to expect the rescuing party of Welshmen. Walter, in turn, had agreed to alert the castle's steward and captain of the guard.

Jack decided that it might be wise if he accompanied them to Curlew, taking a wagon load of hay. Instead of Rhys and Tomas riding their own horses, which Jack deemed far too fine for common men to own, he suggested that they ride on the wagon. With a grin, Jack could not help pointing out that most laborers he knew could not afford any mount at all. Only gentlemen rode fine horses.

Rhys and Jessamyn were glad of Jack's reminder; they could have given themselves away by this oversight. Jack found an old hessian smock and a worn wool cloak for Rhys. Tomas wore a wool tunic and leather apron. Jack assured them that if they were to play craftsmen, these peasant garments would make their ruse more convincing. He also suggested that they pose as carpenters instead of smiths, for inside Curlew's walls, a building was being built and more workmen would mean swifter completion of the job.

There was not time for Jack to smuggle out

Jessamyn's own horse. She decided to ride Tomas's gelding instead of the leggy mount she had ridden from Chester. The gelding was an unremarkable roan, and she guessed Captain Jackson would not be so familiar with Curlew's stables that the roan would arouse his suspicions. Jessamyn would pretend that she had ridden out before dawn to visit Margery, who was supposedly suffering from a fever.

They went over the plan several times, until Jack became confident in his part. At first light, they set out, Rhys and Tomas perched atop Jack's wagon on the load of hay. Jessamyn rode alongside them on her borrowed horse.

The sky was tinged pink and gold as they made their way along the deserted village street, then crossed the churning gray river. Though it was frosty, Jessamyn knew that her chattering teeth owed more to nerves than to the elements. Aware that the lady of Curlew was not on an equal footing with itinerant workmen, she ignored Rhys. She hoped he need not identify himself, for she was sure his pronounced Welsh accent would give him away.

Jack, however, was far ahead of Jessamyn on this score. Becoming part of this intrigue had given the drover an added sense of importance. Living up to his role made him surprisingly inventive. As they approached the castle causeway, he waved and hailed the sentries who were known to him. As they drew closer, Jack told a long, drawn-out tale of meeting two itinerant Welsh carpenters on the highway. Knowing that the castle was in need of more craftsmen, he had brought them with him.

Jessamyn was amazed how easily his story was accepted. Within minutes, they were slowly rumbling over the lowered drawbridge. With her head high, she smiled and greeted Simon as if she had left only that morning, mentally concocting the tale she would tell of taking a potion to cure Margery's chill.

When Sir Ralph's captain asked her why she was abroad so early, Jack quickly substantiated her story, looking suitably concerned about his young bride's health. Captain Jackson had eyed Jessamyn suspiciously as she rode slowly inside the ward. When she stopped, he paced around her horse, looking the animal up and down.

"Let me say, lady, you appear miraculously restored to health," he commented with a frown. "Riding a new mount, too, I see."

Jessamyn swallowed nervously, hearing the suspicion in his voice. Trying to appear calm, despite her shaking knees, she slowly dismounted.

"Yes, Merlin seemed to be going lame, probably because I haven't ridden him lately. I took this old nag instead. It's only a stone's throw to Morfa Bach."

"Aye, you must have been ill indeed to have stayed so close to your room these past weeks. Missing all the Christmas festivities, not once coming down to wish us well," Jackson said, looking closely at her face. She was pale, he observed, her eyes large and dark-shadowed.

"I thought I was likely to die. Pray you don't come down with the same malady, Jackson," she said, looking him straight in the eye. "I'm better, so you'd best be prepared. There'll be no slacking now."

He had the good grace to look sheepish and Jessamyn realized she had unwittingly chosen a sore spot. Walter would have no idea whether the men slacked off, having had little to do with running the castle since their father died. She had not been making her daily inspections of the guard room and armory, and because of that, she assumed garrison discipline had grown lax.

"We're soldiers, lady. We don't slack off. We always do our duty," Jackson blustered, his face coloring.

"Aye, that's what they all say," she said sharply. "Well, you'd best be right. The Welsh are camped in the woods. That's why we were abroad so early while they're still asleep. We didn't fancy having our throats slit."

"I saw their campfires. How many do you think there are?"

"Oh, I don't know, maybe hundreds—far too many for you to fight."

Jackson laughed scornfully. "You'd be surprised how many we can take on. If they stay long enough, we'll be only too glad to show them a taste of English justice."

"They're probably waiting for reinforcements before attacking the castle. Do you think that's why they're here?" she asked innocently.

"That's probably why they're camped in the woods."

Jackson frowned, rubbing his chin thoughtfully.

"What will we do?"

"If that's the case we'd be wise to stamp out the vermin before they multiply." And he laughed heartily at his own witticism.

"I won't give permission for my men to go out of the castle," Jessamyn said sharply. "I don't want anyone killed or wounded, and there are far too many Welsh already camped out there for you to handle alone."

"Don't you know that an English soldier's worth five Welsh? We'll fight them without any help from Curlew's wet-eared boys and old windbags." He looked pointedly at Simon, who drew himself up indignantly, simmering with resentment over the younger man's insult. "We're all seasoned troops in service to King Henry, God bless him." As he boasted, Jackson puffed out his chest. "Besides, lady, let me remind you, securing your permission's not necessary before I act. Sir Ralph put me in charge— that is, in charge of your defense, Lady Jessamyn," he added hastily, almost forgetting himself. "You go inside and rest. Leave everything to me."

With that the burly captain strode away.

Jessamyn caught Rhys's eye and he winked at her, nodding in approval for the clever way she had led Jackson into their trap.

Now all they had to do was wait.

Chapter Fifteen

Being back amidst the old familiar sights and smells of home brought tears to Jessamyn's eyes. How wonderful it was to be inside Curlew again. Every servant she met expressed pleasure at seeing her miraculously restored to health, their concern so genuine, she felt guilty for having deceived them.

She nervously approached Walter, who sat before the hearth whittling a piece of wood with his hunting knife. Would he remember to keep up the pretense?

When he heard her steps Walter glanced up, and for an unguarded moment, started to voice his surprise at seeing her, before he remembered that his sister had only supposedly been confined to her room. He quickly resumed his usual, surly expression.

"Well, you must be feeling better today. Couldn't you at least look like a woman once in a while? Wear a gown like other women?"

While his sentiments were quite in character, his voice, purposely raised for the servants' benefit, was not.

"Walter, I was ill with the ague; I wasn't struck deaf," she reminded him sharply.

Her brother gulped and lowered his voice. "Have some food," he suggested, gesturing toward a platter of fried sweet cakes on the table.

Jessamyn scooped up three of the small golden cakes and hungrily began to eat them, savoring the cinnamon-flavored sweetness of the unexpected treat. It had been days since she had tasted anything so delicious. She debated taking some of the cakes to Rhys, but decided against it. Just as the Lady of Curlew did not engage workmen in friendly chatter, neither did she take them sweets.

"Jack the Drover brought in a couple of extra carpenters," she said, hoping that Walter was sharp enough to guess the true identity of the workmen. It was a vain hope.

"More carpenters!" he exclaimed, his lip curling. "There's already an army of them scurrying about. Sir Ralph even sent some of his own men to help with the project."

Jessamyn gulped, wondering if they were truly carpenters, or merely soldiers in disguise. "What are you building?"

"Me? Nothing! Extra quarters for the defense force. And without consulting me in the matter, I might add."

"I'd better go look at their progress," she said, squeezing her brother's arm affectionately as she passed. Jessamyn handed him the wrapped marchpane chesspiece. "Here, a belated Christmas gift," she whispered as she walked around the table on her way out to the ward.

Uneasily, Jessamyn wondered if the carpenters

were building additional quarters, or reinforcing their defenses. As soon as she stepped outdoors, the deafening sound of hammering made her ears ring. The workmen must have been asleep when she had ridden inside the castle precincts that morning, for all had been peaceful then. So intent had she been on getting back inside the ward without rousing suspicion, she had never noticed the new construction.

It was easy to pick out Rhys from the rest; his bearing and height set him apart from the other workmen. Though they tried to appear busy, she was afraid he and Tomas would soon be spotted as frauds. When she drew closer, she heard them both speaking in Welsh, feigning little knowledge of English in the hope that the language barrier would explain their poor comprehension of the foreman's instructions. They had cleverly pretended that they were robbed, their tools stolen, to explain why they traveled without carpenter's tools. The other workmen had grudgingly loaned them hammers.

Jessamyn stood for a few minutes watching Rhys and Tomas work. She hoped Rhys's plan would be put in action soon, before their work came under scrutiny. Even she could spot their section from the rest, if for no other reason than its crooked boards and bent nails.

Rhys glanced up and saw her, but wisely showed no recognition, aware that he might be observed. Jessamyn walked on, heading for the infirmary to check on the progress of her patients, whom she had not seen since before Christmas. Alys and Mary could now abandon their charade of nursing their ill mistress.

Around noon, there came a sudden commotion from the ward. Shouts of "Fire," followed by the clang of the castle bell, alerted the fortress to danger.

Jessamyn raced into the ward and saw several bales of hay ablaze. Men were beating out the flames with rags and shovels. The hay bales were pierced by flaming arrows, which had been lobbed over the battlements from the nearby woods. Jessamyn knew that Rhys had many skilled archers amongst his men, but she was amazed that they had found their marks from so far away.

Over the commotion, Captain Jackson's voice could be heard bellowing orders to his men. Though he had blustered heartily enough that morning, he had been reluctant to actually ride outside the walls to engage the Welsh. Now this opening enemy volley had galvanized him into action. He struggled with his helmet, cursing his squire for his laggard ways, cursing anyone who came into earshot, so enraged was he that the rabble Welsh dared attack a castle under his command.

"Get indoors, Lady Jessamyn, there could be more arrows," he shouted, noticing her in the doorway. "Have no fear, we'll soon have them routed."

To Jessamyn's surprise, Jackson next began rounding up the carpenters, dividing them into groups of men who could ride, use weapons, or both. The rest of the men formed a bucket brigade to put out the blaze which had spread to the thatch on the blacksmith's smithy. With the addition of several dozen workmen, Jackson's troops swelled to a respectable size.

"Do you see, lady, I'm not using one of your precious Curlew men," he snarled as he rode past her, on the way to the keep.

The party of workmen hurried after the departing soldiers, some bouncing ungainly in the saddle, wielding pikes or pitchforks; others were armed merely with hammers. All were shouting enthusiastically, eager to be part of this exciting event.

Rhys, who had professed to have no skill in either field, was left in charge of the fire squad. Under his direction, the fires were quickly brought under control. A second flaming arrow had landed on the stable's thatched roof, and a group of men were sent to extinguish the blaze before it took hold.

Jessamyn wondered how many more flaming arrows they intended to shoot from the woods. Though she saw how well the ruse was working, she did not want Curlew burned down in the process.

The winch creaked as the drawbridge was lowered. Barely waiting for the bridge to be let completely down, the first horsemen thundered across, leaping the gap of several feet to the ground, eager to be at the enemy. The rowdy workmen ran after them, shouting and cheering as they tried to keep up.

Jessamyn raced up to the battlements for a better view, hoping that she would be safe up there. Now that the desired effect had been achieved, she hoped that instead of lobbing burning arrows over the walls, Rhys's men would engage the soldiers who streamed over the meadowland, their pennants fluttering and war horses snorting in excitement.

"What's happening? Are we already rid of them?" Walter asked eagerly. He stood at her elbow, panting, very much out of breath from hurrying up the tower stairs. He shielded his eyes from the unexpected glare of the winter sun, glancing off lances and harnesses.

"Not yet. Sir Ralph's soldiers have gone out to fight the Welsh." Seeing his brows raise in concern, Jessamyn smiled and shook her head. "Nothing serious," she said in an undertone, "all's going as planned."

Walter smiled in relief, for he had thought that perhaps the coming attack was a plan gone awry. He settled in comfortably to watch the spectacle unfolding before them on the water meadows below.

The English soldiers rode full pelt for the trees. When faced by the wood's impenetrable barrier and no waiting Welshmen, they had to disperse and regroup. Their elusive enemy had disappeared in the tangled woods. From the far right came a sudden hail of arrows. They quickly found their marks, falling from the sky like rain. Wounded men cried out in pain and toppled from their saddles.

A second small party of archers appeared on the left, taking aim and getting off a couple of volleys before retreating to cover. The arrows were shot high, for the Welsh soldiers' intention was to harry more than decimate Sir Ralph's troops. Three swift horsemen, seemingly coming from nowhere, rode close to the mounted ranks. Hanging from their saddles, they slashed girth straps, unhorsing several unsuspecting riders. In the ensuing commotion, the riders disappeared into the forest just as swiftly as they had come.

The English soldiers' angry frustration erupted in shouts of protest and rumbles of dissent. Comrades crouched over the fallen to see if they were badly hurt. Those unable to remount were carried back to the castle. Several of the sturdier workmen had been earmarked as bearers, and they struggled across the marshy ground with their groaning burdens.

This was a highly unusual battle. The enemy seemed never to be in the same place twice, making their capture impossible. Jessamyn leaned forward, resting her elbows on the crenellated stonework as she watched in amazement the Welshmen's swift strikes and lightning disappearances. Well-known for their ability to harry their enemies, the Welshmen made up with guile what they lacked in number. Though Jessamyn was aware how few men Rhys commanded, by their different tactics and diverse routes, even she wondered if they had been reinforced. She could have sworn there were many more than thirty men hiding in the trees. She had also heard that when the Welsh tired of their sport, entire armies had the ability to melt into the woods. Some said Glyndwr was a wizard, able to control the elements and to spirit his forces away by magic from under their enemies' noses.

"Do you suppose it's time to change our tactics?" Rhys asked. Jessamyn spun about, surprised to find him standing beside her on the battlements.

"Are the fires out?"

"One still smolders. Don't be concerned, there'll be no more burning arrows. We just wanted to roust the captain from the castle. How are we doing?"

Walter turned to him with a smile of admiration.

"Superb! It's like a giant game. Your men are fearless. Just look at that!" Walter pointed to a man riding a sure-footed mountain pony, making for the center ranks, which stumbled about in disarray, wondering what to do next. The Welshman hung from his saddle as he thundered past, cleverly avoiding random sword slashes while he neatly sliced through girth straps, then disembowelled a horse from under its rider in the same sweep.

Jessamyn cried out in protest, aware that such tactics were employed in battle, yet full of sympathy for the defenseless animal. The screaming war horse galloped about the field in a frenzy, his entrails dragging in the dirt.

Rhys's face remained impassive when she looked at him in dismay, questioning the action and pleading with him to stop the senseless mutilation.

"As you can now see, Lord Walter, this is no game. It often proves most deadly," Rhys said sharply as he turned away. "I'm going below to see how the land lies."

Jessamyn had turned her back on the bloody spectacle below, rapidly losing her appetite for the spectacle.

White-faced, Walter gripped the stone coping before him, forcing himself to watch—he was lord of Curlew, and a little blood should not distress him. Yet his squeamish stomach rebelled at the sight, and he had to quickly swallow the bile which rose bitterly in his throat.

Ned had run on to the battlements and was barking at the shouting men and clashing armaments. Hushing him, Jessamyn fondled his rough head, noticing the milkiness in his old eyes, and experienced a stab of pity for her friend's increasing affliction.

"Come on down, Ned, love, and see the present I brought you." Firmly Jessamyn grasped the brindled ruff at his neck, turning him about, guiding him toward the tower door. "Are you coming down, Walter?"

Though he had valiantly tried to be manly, Walter was finally forced to abandon the battle. Several more men had been wounded. Directly below, a group of carpenters approached, bearing their grisly bundles, all bloody and bruised. His stomach rebelled, and he bit his tongue in an effort to control his weakness. Now the salty taste of blood was in his mouth.

"Aye, I might as well join you," he said, his enthusiasm squelched by the gore. "We'll go below and share a cup of ale."

They went to the stairs, aware that Curlew sentries were hurrying to new positions on the battlements. Suddenly, Jessamyn noticed that Sir Ralph's blue and silver standard of a coiled serpent had been struck. The plan had entered its second stage, which was to have the men, by prearranged signal, double back to the river and slip unnoticed into the castle.

For the moment, the clash outside the walls seemed to have quietened, until a fresh shout went up, and the sharp clang of steel against steel told her that a final foray was being made. This was not the type of engagement Captain Jackson had been anticipating; he had thought more in terms of a pitched battle. Having never fought the Welsh before, his woeful inexperience became plain. His plans had been swiftly revised, yet the enemy proved far too elusive for victory.

For the next hour, Walter sat before the hearth, nursing an alecup. Jessamyn produced Ned's splendid new collar and, though she doubted the old dog understood much about his gift, he wagged his tail and barked in joy when she told him how beautiful he looked.

A sudden commotion at the entrance to the Hall made her glance up. Jessamyn jumped to her feet in surprise as three of Rhys's men entered the room. They had already doubled back and crossed the moat, their leader admitting them through the unguarded postern. She could hardly believe the speed with which they had completed their maneuver. As the men were all speaking Welsh, she decided not to try to question them. Instead, Jessamyn headed for the postern to learn the news firsthand.

As she approached the small entrance, four more riders slipped through in single file, heading for the ward. On the other side of the castle, she could still hear shouts and the clang of arms. Jessamyn went inside the south tower. Gulping for breath, she raced up the narrow, twisting stairs. Even as she stepped out into the cold air, she heard fresh shouts and the hiss of many arrows. Captain Jackson's men were firing blindly into the woods. They had divided their troops into three sections: one held the center; the other two rode east and west to encircle the woodland. Her heart lurched in dismay. Surely this tactic would cut off Rhys's men! Arrows still flew out of the trees, so she knew that not all his men were safely inside Curlew.

Back down to the postern she went, anxious to tell Rhys about this latest development. Even as she sighted the gate, he was admitting the last rider and securing the postern.

"Are they all inside?" she asked Rhys in surprise as he strode towards her.

"Aye, except the last two. They'll be all right. They know how to stay under cover. We're going to raise the bridge. It looks as if Sir Ralph's captain is still busy with bigger and cleverer strategies to flush us out."

Jessamyn had to skip and jog to keep pace with his hurried stride. Simon, captain of Curlew's guard, was already at his post. When he saw Rhys approaching he acted on a pre-arranged signal, telling his men to raise the drawbridge.

In the beginning, the creaking winch was masked by the blowing wind and thundering hooves. Captain Jackson maneuvered his men into a wedge before charging the trees to enter a clearing where they had spotted what they thought to be the fleeing Welsh. No one noticed the raising bridge. Only when it was one-third of the way up did one of the carpenters glance back and sound the alarm.

Aware that they had been spotted, the men in the gatehouse's upper room winched faster and faster, desperate to raise the bridge high enough to keep the soldiers from re-entering Curlew. Jessamyn shrieked an alarm as one rider, his mount speedier than the rest, pelted toward the slowly rising bridge.

At his command, the horse leaped high and, to her horror, Jessamyn saw the man land on the end of the rising bridge. The extra weight jerked the chain, making it slip a few notches. The winding became even more frenzied as the men tried to make up for lost time. It was too difficult for the mounted man to keep his balance as the bridge angled higher. His terrified horse reared, screaming in fright, and with a cry of alarm, horse and rider toppled backwards from the great height, splashing down in the moat.

By now the bridge was too high for anyone else to try to breach it. A dozen galloping soldiers had already skidded to a halt at the edge of the moat, perplexed by this unexpected development.

Red-faced, Captain Jackson thundered to the head of his troops, his pursuit of the elusive Welsh momentarily abandoned.

"What are you doing, you fools!" he bellowed in anger. "Lower this bridge. I've not given permission to raise it. Lower it at once, I say, or you'll pay for this, you treacherous dogs."

His angry voice drifted across the moat and echoed back off the castle walls. In the ensuing silence his men glanced uneasily at each other. Finally, Rhys strode to the front of the gatehouse battlements. The blue, yellow and silver pennant of Trevaron fluttered before him, bright against the graystone. Simon, Curlew's captain of the guard, walked proudly beside their liberator, his chest puffed out as he scornfully looked down upon the boastful Captain Jackson.

"I'm giving the orders today, Jackson," Simon shouted over the battlements. "And I say the bridge stays up. We're not the fools you took us for—we know of Sir Ralph's intentions."

Rhys raised his hand and Simon stepped back.

"What do you mean . . . in charge?" Captain Jackson bellowed indignantly. "I'm still in charge here. Where's young Lord Walter? Bring him out."

"Lord Walter can tell you nothing new, Jackson. He's down below under guard," Rhys shouted, moving to the edge of the battlements where Jackson could see him clearly. "I'm claiming this castle for Owain Glyndwr, Prince of Wales. You've been out-maneuvered. Now you'd best run home to your master like a whipped cur with your tail between your legs, and tell him how you were defeated by thirty Welshmen who each appear to be worth quite a few Englishmen, wouldn't you say?"

Captain Jackson stood in his stirrups, his face purple. Shaking his mailed fist at Rhys, he was clearly enraged to have been duped. It was all so clear to him; he winced when he saw his own stupidity. He had always heard tell that the Welsh were treacherous bastards, and today's action proved the claim was well-founded.

"Lower the bridge and I'll parole you, Welshman," he bellowed in a final effort to save face. "You haven't a chance. When Sir Ralph returns you'll all be killed."

Rhys threw back his head and his derisive laughter echoed around the battlements.

"You surely don't think I'd be such a fool as to believe *your* assurances of mercy. Besides, with Glyndwr's army at my back, our chances of winning seem mighty healthy. You're going to find it cold sleeping out tonight. My advice is that you go in search of your lord—and when you find him, tell him Rhys of Trevaron sent you."

With this Rhys turned about, not anxious to give them such an easy target. His sharp eyes had already seen an archer unslinging his bow while Captain Jackson tried to engage him in further conversation.

Rhys had barely entered the tower door when an arrow whistled harmlessly past him and struck the stonework.

Jessamyn found it hard to believe their plan had worked so well. Patrols were sent to watch the postern, in case Captain Jackson tried to copy the Welsh soldiers' method of entry. He was surely aware of the postern gate's location, though he might not know where the moat was shallowest, or where the access channel led to the entrance. Fortunately, Sir Ralph's troops had no Curlew men amongst them whom they could torture to reveal such secrets. Men were often tortured to reveal water sources, so that an enemy could poison a garrison's wells, or to reveal a secret entrance whereby attackers could gain control of the fortress.

The men who were not stationed on the battlements had assembled in the Great Hall. One glance at Walter told Jessamyn that he was going to be of no further use to them. Her brother was slumped awkwardly in his chair, threatening to fall forward. When she spoke to him, he looked at her with a foolish grin.

"All's well, I take it, sister?" he said, his voice thick, his face flushed with wine.

"For the moment. Why don't you go up to your chamber, Walter. The excitement's over."

"Trying to get rid of me?"

"You'll feel much better in the morning."

"Better? I couldn't feel any better and still be alive." He tried to stand, steadying himself against the table. Bleary-eyed, he made an effort to focus on the tall presence standing behind his sister. "Good work, Lord Rhys. You've been a good ally."

"Thank you, Walter," Rhys replied gravely, aware that Jessamyn's brother was deep in his cups. "Sleep on it. We'll talk policy tomorrow."

"Nay, the night's still young. We can play a game," Walter suggested, lurching forward as he tried a second time to stand. "I'm feeling lucky . . . get out the board. We'll play a victory game."

Rhys shook his head. "Not tonight. It's been a long day. I've built sheds, fought fires . . . we'll have a rousing game tomorrow. Will you settle for that?"

Walter started to grumble then, in the midst of his complaints, he smiled and fell back in his chair.

"Very well. Tomorrow it is."

Without warning he pitched forward, falling face down on the rushes. Rhys called a couple of servants to carry their master to his chamber.

Jessamyn was humiliated by her brother's behavior.

"I must apologize for Walter. He's never been able to stand the sight of blood, so I should have expected this. He really isn't much help to me, as you can see."

Suddenly she felt very tired, her legs seeming too weak to support her. Jessamyn dropped wearily into her brother's vacated chair and leaned back against its carved wooden back.

"You're not his keeper," Rhys said, patting her glossy head in affection before he left to address the assembled men.

Rhys assigned each man to his duty, explaining what was expected. Simon had learned great respect for the Welshman and his force, and he knew his men shared his feelings. There was not a peep of dissent amongst them over the assignment of Rhys's own troops to serve alongside the castle soldiers.

At last, Rhys came to sit with Jessamyn before the fire and eat the light meal the servants had carried in. All day they had been too busy to give much thought to food. The thick, steaming vegetable soup and fresh baked bread spread with meat paste tasted like a banquet. They were both weary and triumphant. Jessamyn could hardly believe that the day's events had run so smoothly according to plan, as if everyone had been following a script written by a guardian angel. Perhaps things had gone too smoothly for comfort, she thought, as a wave of unease passed over her. Was this merely the lull before the storm?

"Do you think we're out of danger yet?" she asked Rhys presently, finishing the last of her soup.

He sighed heavily, reluctant to destroy her newfound security. "Jessamyn, I won't lie to you. In all probability, you're safe, but I can't promise they won't be back. Let's hope Curlew's of so little importance to Sir Ralph, he'll let matters rest. They won't know whether we've been reinforced, or even when I leave, unless they post spies."

"When must you leave?"

"I can stay about ten days, and that's stretching it, especially if the weather turns bad. If I don't meet with Glyndwr as arranged, he'll consider me disloyal. As it is, I'll be late, but when I explain the reason, I'm sure he'll understand."

Ten days. The words clanged like a bell inside her head. For the next ten days Curlew was promised respite from worry but, best of all, for the next ten days, she had this wonderful man to herself. Rhys would be beside her every day and every night.

"Ten days is going to seem a lifetime," Jessamyn whispered, taking his hand in hers, noticing fresh nicks and cuts marring his smooth flesh. "I'll pretend you're my husband and lord of the castle." She smiled and, making a great concession, added, "You have my permission to run up the Flowers of Llys above the Dacre standard, if that will please you."

Rhys grinned at her generous offer. "Aha, trying to appease me. What about the Welsh dragon?"

Patricia Phillips

"No dragon," Jessamyn declared emphatically. "We already discussed that. My answer's still the same."

"Argued would be more apt."

"And we said we wouldn't argue again," she gently reminded him, not wanting to rouse his temper. "Will you accept my generous offer?"

"I accept. Now, lady, will you hear and accept my generous offer?"

Jessamyn correctly interpreted the slow smile which lit his face and her heart leaped with love. The flame of passion ignited inside her veins and she grew warm from head to toe.

"Oh, sweetheart, you know your offers are always dearest to my heart," she whispered, leaning against his hard shoulder, feeling safe and greatly loved.

"Then come, let's go up to bed. I've a feeling these next ten days and nights will pass like the blinking of an eye."

"Or the sweetness of a lover's kiss," she offered, turning her soft pink mouth up to his. "Will I never have enough of your kisses?"

"I hope not . . . I couldn't endure such failure," he whispered, groaning as he pulled her into his arms.

Jessamyn smiled, realizing this would be the first time they had shared a room at Curlew. Wondering what the servants would think of their lady's loose morals made her a little uneasy. Then she thrust aside her worry. What did she care if they condemned her? Rhys would be hers for ten blissful nights, and she was not going to allow another's disapproval to spoil the wonder of that gift.

Their bliss was to last less than a week.

One sparkling January morning, when chunks of ice floated on the river, and the grass was white with hoar frost, a challenge rang out over the battlements, breaking their slumber.

Rhys jumped from the covers, already reaching for his leather jack and boots which lay on the floor beside the bed.

"What is it?" Jessamyn cried, awakened from a deep sleep. Clutching the wool blankets about her chin to ward off the morning chill, she was alarmed to see Rhys already girding for battle.

"Your peace has just run out, sweetheart. If I don't miss my guess, it's Ralph Warren come to pay us a call. Stay inside. I don't want you hurt."

Jessamyn protested his order, but to no avail. Rhys was adamant. The enemy would surely have archers and she could be hit by a stray arrow. From her window, Jessamyn looked out over the silent meadows, seeing nothing out of the ordinary to mar the sparkling, pristine winter view.

Dressing quickly, she wrapped her thickest cloak around her and hurried to the west tower, aware of the noisy clangor of their garrison leaping to action. She drew in her breath in shock at what she saw below. With banners waving, and armanents sparkling in the sun, the treacherous serpent of Cater's Hill defied them in the winter morn. Sir Ralph had, indeed, come to pay them a call, bringing with him several columns of men. They appeared to have no siege equipment, so she presumed that laying siege to Curlew was not to be their strategy.

Rhys found her shivering in the unheated turret room. His face was grave as he said, "Jessamyn, love, I've a favor to ask of you. I know this goes against your principles, but this one time I'm asking you to forget your convictions. It may be our best hope of turning Sir Ralph away. I want permission to run up the Welsh dragon above Glyndwr's own standard."

Jessamyn drew in her breath in shock. Appalled, she stared at him, knowing that he proposed a dangerous gamble.

"We talked about that—you agreed."

"I know." Sheepishly, he grinned, taking her hand. "Because of my own bravado, it's a gamble I must take. Like a fool, I told Jackson he'd been bested by thirty Welshmen. No doubt Sir Ralph's aware of our small force, so he's come to drive us out. On the other hand, if he think's we've been reinforced by Glyndwr's men, he may change his mind."

Jessamyn considered his words, wondering if there was another way around their dilemma. Sir Ralph's superior numbers spelled defeat. Even if they had no battering rams or war machines, they only need put up enough scaling ladders, or gradually pick off Curlew sentries at their posts, ensuring easy access for his troops. With barely enough men to man the battlements, they would be no match for Sir Ralph's superior strength. Yet, Jessamyn knew that once they openly flew the Welsh dragon, Curlew would be an acknowledged supporter of Glyndwr; by this declaration of allegiance, they challenged any opposing force. There was so little time to weigh her decision, for already Rhys stood impatiently, his hand on the door latch.

At last, with a heavy heart, she agreed. "If you think it's our best chance, do it." Jessamyn knew that she should have consulted Walter in the matter; yet, at the best of times he was not a decisive man, and awaiting the slow process of his drunken mind might prove their undoing.

"Good. I hoped that's what you'd say. I've already ordered it done."

With that Rhys was gone, leaving Jessamyn feeling as if she had been tricked. The old independent Jessamyn resurfaced as she stalked across the room.

She stood fuming at the window. There she saw the huge, flapping white flag with its ferocious red beast, its standard edged with green, flying from the flagpole.

Turning away, Jessamyn whispered a prayer of forgiveness from her father's shade, who no doubt lurked in the corridors with a disapproving frown. He would consider that she had betrayed Curlew and England's crown. The guilt of this knowledge weighed heavily on her as she went out on to the battlements in defiance of Rhys's orders, staying close to the tower, out of the line of fire. She was still lady of Curlew, and she'd be damned if she was going to be confined to quarters like some naughty child.

Three men separated themselves from the main body of enemy troops and slowly rode forward, a standard bearer riding before them. She immediately recognized Sir Ralph, resplendent in a tall plumed helm, his engraved armor scintillating in the sunlight.

"Surrender this castle, Rhys of Trevaron," Sir Ralph bellowed, his voice echoing around the stonework.

"Never. I hold Curlew for my liege lord," came back Rhys's defiant answer.

Ralph Warren and his captains conferred, heads lowered in discussion. For a few minutes there was silence, then Sir Ralph rode forward alone.

"I already hold Curlew for *my* liege lord, Welshman—Henry, King of England."

Rhys stepped to the edge of the battlements, covered by his three best archers. "You can't best me, Warren. I, too, hold this castle on charter from a king—only my liege lord is Owain, King of Wales." Here Rhys had taken some license, for Glyndwr had merely styled himself as Prince of Wales. But as this was a contest of bravado, he was not going to allow Ralph Warren to best him.

Sir Ralph gestured towards the Welsh standard, flapping in the brisk wind. "You fly his standard—that's treason."

"Nay, it merely means Glyndwr's troops are quartered inside the castle."

The stony silence which followed this statement revealed Sir Ralph's unease. He had not expected to face a force of any size. In fact, he had been expecting thirty Welshmen who would crumble without a fight in the face of his superior force.

"If Glyndwr's men hold Curlew, why aren't they out here facing me?" challenged Sir Ralph loudly.

"Because they're below breaking their fast, my lord, and they didn't think the matter of enough importance to interrupt their meal," Rhys shouted back. Behind him his men roared with laughter.

Ralph Warren's face flushed crimson with rage inside his fancy helm. Turning, he moved back a pace to again confer with his men.

"Then I would speak with the lord of the castle. Let's see whom he chooses to garrison Curlew."

"Not possible. He's under guard."

After some discussion, Sir Ralph finally rode to the edge of the moat, his face set. His visor up, he stood in the stirrups to shout, "Listen well, Welshman, we, too, intend to break our fast. You've one hour to come to your senses and surrender the castle."

With this, Sir Ralph turned about and very slowly rode toward the rear of his troops, almost as if he dared them to loose a volley of arrows at his back.

"What now?" Jessamyn asked uneasily, glancing up at the fierce dragon, her stomach turning as she considered the danger.

"We'll do the same. I'm hungry." Rhys entered the

tower and descended the stairs with Jessamyn on his heels.

The meal was tense. Jessamyn barely ate anything. At any minute she expected to hear the alarm warning them that they were under attack.

The hour passed uneventfully.

Back up to the battlements they went to await the next move. They had not long to wait. Within minutes there came a sudden burst of flame from the edge of the forest as Sir Ralph's supply wagons were set alight. A teasing hail of arrows greeted the men who galloped to put out the fire. They found their unconscious cook sprawled across a wagon, his arm pinned to the vehicle by an arrow to which a note was attached. As the note was written in Welsh, none of Sir Ralph's men could understand it, and their ignorance further enraged them.

Watching the scene with satisfaction, Rhys saw his enemy ride this way and that, drawn first to the left, then to the right, following down each teasing burst of fire from the woods. While Sir Ralph and his troops ate, Rhys had sent a handful of his men, via the postern gate, to wreak havoc on the English knight, hoping that he would be discouraged from setting up camp outside the walls.

Several armored men slipped clumsily from their mounts, arms waving as they tried to find a handhold before crashing to the ground, unaware that their saddle girths had been slit. Stealthily, and with much skill, Ivor had crept amongst the beasts while they were standing at the edge of the trees.

From the right came an unexpected clash of steel, followed by cries of triumph from the enemy ranks. His face tense, Rhys looked toward the sounds, to find that one of his men had been taken. He could not indentify the man. He knew that by now the others would be pelting along the forest trails, taking a circuitous route, hoping to reach the castle later, under cover of darkness. Only when they were safely home would he know who had fallen.

Some time later, Sir Ralph again rode close to the castle, stopping at the edge of the moat.

"Welshman," he shouted, and Rhys walked to the edge of the battlements. "We've captured one of your men."

At a signal, a soldier rode forward carrying an inert form across his saddle bow. He rode slowly back and forth, making sure Curlew's defenders could see, taking pleasure in exhibiting this trophy.

"Unless you surrender Curlew, we'll torture the prisoner. He should provide us with much valuable information. You have a choice. Surrender now and save him, or wait—and bury him!"

Rhys pondered the situation, aware of the ripple of discussion passing between his men. He had quickly identified the limp body—Daffydd, a young shepherd from a neighboring valley. Pain stabbed in his heart when Rhys considered how best to tell the lad's widowed mother that her son was dead. Ignoring his men's hoarse comments, Rhys gambled, praying he was right.

"You must take me for a fool, Warren. Anyone can see the lad's already dead!"

"Nay, he's got plenty of life in him. He's merely bound and gagged."

"If he had a breath of life left, you'd already have tortured him. You wouldn't have waited this long. We're back where we started, though you're now lacking your supply wagons."

His face dark with anger, Sir Ralph motioned to the soldier to take the body away. "You're too clever by far for your own good, Welshman," he shouted at last, silently cursing the outcome. Damn the Welshman! He had not expected him to be so shrewd. There was one remaining ploy by which they could outwit him, yet contemplating that move made Ralph grit his teeth in anger.

"What, struck dumb, Sir Ralph?" Rhys taunted, casually planting his booted foot on the parapet and leaning forward, resting on his knee. "I'm disappointed. I'd thought you'd have a dozen new tricks to confound me."

"I've a mind to spit you and leave you for the crows to eat," Ralph snarled, aware that the archers behind the Welshman had tautened their fingers on their bow strings, tensing at his threat. "I've a mind to it, but you can thank your Maker I haven't more time to waste on you. For the moment, you can enjoy your hollow victory. Today you've won—tomorrow's another story."

To Rhys's amazement, Sir Ralph rode quickly back to his troops. He raised his hand for them to form up for travel. Hardly able to believe his eyes, Rhys saw them dump Daffydd's body in the meadow, leaving him where they could go out to retrieve him. Now the soldiers turned and rode towards the river. He was expecting more men to ride out of the forest and take up positions, but there was nothing more menacing than the dark trees against the pale winter sky.

"I don't believe it!" Walter gasped. He stood at his elbow, leaning from the parapet for a better view. He had finally found both the courage and the equilibrium to master the tower stairs. "The great Sir Ralph's leaving without more fight than this? He's a fraud! War hero, indeed!"

"Don't speak too soon. He's gone—for today. No doubt he has some trick up his sleeve."

Rhys watched the party of soldiers slowly splashing across the river. They took the wrong direction for Shrewsbury. Though Sir Ralph had not come prepared for a siege, to meekly withdraw, offering no more resistance, was exceeding strange. And Rhys liked it not.

Sir Ralph did not return at nightfall, nor at dawn. The scouts Rhys sent out reported finding no sign of the English lord's force. It was too good to be true.

"Oh, Rhys, you've done it," Jessamyn gasped, when the last report had been made. "He's gone. He's gone." Triumphant, she danced about him, taking his arms, making Rhys join her in a victory dance.

Rhys suddenly stopped the movement and pulled her into his arms, kissing her, outwardly sharing her delight, yet inwardly experiencing cold, gripping fear. All was not as it seemed. He had so little time left to defend Curlew. Torn between his deep love for Jessamyn and the allegiance he had sworn to Glyndwr, Rhys fought an inner battle with his conscience. Though he longed to stay with her, he knew that he would have to join Glyndwr at the appointed time. There was a chance that Ralph Warren had lost interest in capturing Curlew. His obligations to Bolingbroke might keep him from doing as he wished. For whatever reason, he had chosen to leave. A man as powerful as Warren would not suffer defeat at the hands of the Welsh without retaliating. It was trying to guess the form that retaliation would take which stole his peace of mind.

Chapter Sixteen

Jessamyn lay drowsily in Rhys's arms. At the moment of waking she felt blissfully happy. It hardly seemed possible to have had such joy as she had known during the past week, their days and nights filled with shared happiness. Then she remembered that this was the day he must leave to join Glyndwr at his mountain stronghold!

Jessamyn's heart plunged. Desperately she tried to go back to sleep in the childish hope that when she woke, this day of parting would be no more than a bad dream, and the pleasure of having him always beside her would be the reality.

With a ragged sigh, she turned to look at Rhys. Beside the bed, a candle still sputtered in its dish. In the night they had not bothered to blow it out, lapsing into blissful sleep in each other's arms after several fulfilling hours of love. They were more attuned to each other's needs, and there was not as much urgency to their lovemaking. Her lover's kisses and skillful caresses brought Jessamyn even deeper pleasure. Sadly she realized that there would be no more waking to find him at her side. No more early morning caressing, nor kissing, nor lovemaking . . .

A tear trickled down her cheek, and Jessamyn reached up to brush the moisture from her lashes. She had always known Rhys would leave. As it was, he had stayed as long as he dared. He would have to ride hard to keep his rendezvous. Rhys had chanced displeasing Glyndwr to be with her—and also to protect Curlew—but mostly to be with her.

Jessamyn turned to smile at him in the feeble candlelight. His dark lashes were curved against his cheek, his face relaxed in sleep. Rhys had turned his head to the side and she studied the gleaming black hair curling against his strong neck, forming an inky shadow on the white linen pillow. The sight of his square, muscular chest and shoulders evoked such delightful memories that she shuddered with pleasure. During the night Rhys had flung aside the covers, one muscular arm across his chest, the other spread out to cradle her.

Jessamyn gently kissed his firm mouth. How much she would miss him. Since leaving Chester, their love had deepened until she could not imagine life without him. Rhys had promised to return. He had also assured her that he intended to break his betrothal contract with Eluned Glynne. He had promised, and Jessamyn trusted him to keep his word, yet she could not prevent a fresh surge of jealousy when she thought about perfect Eluned with her fine clothes and dainty ways, comparing herself to the noblewoman and finding herself wanting.

"Why so sad?" Rhys whispered, reaching up to stroke her cheek and finding it damp with tears.

"You needn't ask that question. You already know. Because you're leaving today."

Rhys smiled as he gently stroked her back. "I'll be back before long, I promise. You know I can't stay away from you."

A sharp rap at the door made them both start in alarm.

Rhys asked who was there, and received an answer in Welsh from one of his men. All was ready for their departure; the sun had been up over an hour.

Surprised, Rhys went to the window and threw back the shutters to see feeble light filtering through the clouds.

"Not much of a sun, but probably all we're going to get in January," he said, hugging Jessamyn against his side as she stood barefoot on the rushes looking out. "You mustn't be so sad, sweetheart. I'll come back as soon as I can. And then I'll make you mine, whether Walter likes it or not."

"Why should he object? Though I know he entertained thoughts of betrothing me to that serpent, Walter's disenchanted with Sir Ralph, thank God."

A pang of unease speared Rhys's heart. Could Ralph Warren be interested in capturing more than the castle? Jessamyn was so lovely; any man would covet her. Crushing her in his arms tighter than he intended, Rhys made her gasp as he vowed intently, "Don't be afraid of Sir Ralph. If the bastard as much as touches you, I swear, I'll kill him."

There was such intensity in his voice that Jessamyn shivered uneasily. The introduction of this vengeful element to their parting shrouded it in even deeper gloom. If Rhys went into battle, he could be wounded—or even killed, she thought in shock. How could she endure such pain? In the short time they had been lovers she had grown to expect his love and support, relying heavily on him for many things. Gone was that old, defiant Jessamyn, leaving in her stead a softer person. She was truly a woman, for Rhys had made her whole. Never again need she wonder what it was like to love and be loved, for he had shown her the deep bond of two hearts beating as one.

When he was finally dressed and ready for travel, she could delay the inevitable no longer. "God keep you safe," Jessamyn whispered, her voice breaking with emotion.

"And you."

Gravely Rhys looked at her, drinking in her beauty. These few minutes would have to last him for a long time. He had not told Jessamyn that Glyndwr would likely fight come spring, nor that he might enter an organized campaign during the summer. He had not told her because he did not want her worrying about his safety. But the omission caused him pangs of guilt as she gazed up at him, her lovely face open and trusting.

Together they walked from her small tower room with its shared memories, down the winding stairs and out into the ward. His men were already mounted, their restless horses puffing great clouds of steam in the chill morning air. The sky was heavy, as if full of unshed tears, Jessamyn thought fancifully, looking out on the gray morning. The sun had already disappeared behind gathering clouds.

Rhys cast a wary eye at the heavens, hoping that it was not going to turn stormy, or they would have a rough journey into the mountainous country to the north. He had already pushed his time to the limit and now would have to press hard to keep this rendezvous with Glyndwr. Every mile he galloped would take him one mile further away from helping her, should a crisis occur. Though the scouts he sent out saw no sign of Sir Ralph's soldiers, Rhys could not believe they had simply turned tail and abandoned their quest. There was something strangely worrisome about the English knight's swift departure.

As he paused beside his horse, already saddled for the journey, all he said to Jessamyn was: "You mustn't trust anyone, sweetheart. Mayhap Sir Ralph has some trick up his sleeve. Be careful."

"I will. No more open gate welcomes for our generous relative." She laughed, but her heart was not in it.

Jessamyn would not cry in his presence. Their women's grief was an added burden for departing soldiers to endure. Father had taught her always to smile and wave as he rode away. Later, when Rhys had gone, there would be time to indulge her grief. This morning, it took a far greater effort than she had expected to keep her vow. Though Jessamyn managed it, her wan smile was forced as Rhys mounted his tall black horse. As he swung into the saddle, his silver rowel spurs gleamed in a sudden burst of sunlight. Finding a hole in the clouds, the winter sun shone fitfully over the troops gathered in the castle ward.

"Let's hope that's an omen of better things to come," Rhys said, glancing up at the brightening sky. With all his heart, he longed to stay at Curlew. Bending down to her, he whispered goodbye.

Jessamyn reached up, straining to touch his mouth.

"Goodbye, love. Come back safely," she whispered, blinking rapidly as unwanted tears filled her eyes.

"I'll ride like a thousand devils are after me," he vowed, with a grin, finding the comparison not quite as far-fetched as it sounded. No one could know what lay ahead in the summer campaign. Rhys hoped that his words were not prophetic, and that he would not be riding hell for leather to seek shelter from the enemy in this border fortress, but rather galloping like the wind to be with Jessamyn and make her his wife.

Hands locked, they gazed silently into each other's eyes, then Jessamyn finally stepped clear of the horses. Rhys put on his helmet and gauntlets, then signaled to the column to form up. From the serving women who had formed attachments amongst his men, a gale of weeping was loud in the background as the horses' hooves thudded over the open ground, heading for the drawbridge. The wooden bridge was already down and the soldiers clattered across it without stopping.

Jessamyn ran up the stair leading to the battlements and out into the chilly air. She leaned over the parapet, waving her kerchief from atop the gatehouse.

Stopping on the road, Rhys reined in, allowing his men and wagons to come across before he rode to the head of the column. He waved to Jessamyn and turned to wave again when they were stopped at the river crossing.

Now it was safe to weep and her tears spilled down her cheeks, dripping on her gown, staining the silk. The cold wind whipped her skirts, but Jessamyn did not notice as she stared into the distance as the riders grew ever smaller. Now she could no longer tell if he waved, but she tirelessly fluttered her kerchief in case he could still see her. The standard bearing the Flowers of Llys and its accompanying bright colored pennants was hidden behind the trees. The squeak and groan of the rising drawbridge formed a constant accompaniment to her tears. Simon had received instructions from Rhys on how best to deploy his small force of soldiers. Keeping the bridge raised was one of the most important factors in their continued safety.

"Now he's gone, perhaps we can take down that damned flag," Walter growled beside her.

Surprised, Jessamyn turned, wiping away her tears. Her brother also stood upon the battlements, yet she had been so grief-stricken, she had not noticed him.

"Can't you at least wait until he's out of Morfa Bach?"

"Don't get snippy with me. I never agreed to fly the thing in the first place. As I remember, you didn't choose to ask me."

Angered by his ungrateful attitude after all that Rhys had done for them, Jessamyn snapped, "Probably because I thought you too drunk for reason, the way you've been every night since I got back. There was no time to debate the point. The flag flew and achieved its purpose. Order it struck if you want."

"I do want."

Walter turned, limping away as quickly as he could. A few minutes later, she heard his gruff command. Immediately the red and white Welsh dragon began a slow, fluttering descent down the pole. And though Jessamyn knew the flag must come down for safety's sake, part of her was saddened because this last remaining link with Rhys was gone. It was as if Rhys and his soldiers had never been part of Curlew's life.

Rhys had been gone two days and it seemed like a month. Without him the tower room was cold and lonely. Those happy winter nights when they had held each other beneath the wool blankets, confiding dreams and fragments of their pasts, kissing and loving, belonged to another time.

Jessamyn sat before the hearth in the darkness of early morning. During the night Walter had had a seizure and she had been up half the night supervising his care. To her dismay she discovered that he had not taken the medicine she had brewed for him, and she sharply admonished his servants for not making sure he took his regular dose. The most trusted of his servants promised he would follow her instructions and insist that Lord Walter do as he was told. Jessamyn wondered if her lecture would make much difference to her brother's behavior. Walter was becoming more difficult to handle. Far from being grateful for Rhys's intervention, now he loudly proclaimed to all who would listen how glad he was to be rid of the Welshmen. Once the danger had passed, Walter again entertained ideas of running the castle by himself—until the next crisis.

Whenever Jessamyn pointed out to him that were it not for the Welshmen, they would be Sir Ralph's prisoners, Walter dismissed her reminder with a sneer. He accused her of manufacturing the crisis, because she wanted to have the handsome Welshman back at Curlew. Jessamyn could hardly believe her ears. He had conveniently forgotten Sir Ralph's treachery, even going so far as to accuse her of misinterpreting the captain's message to further her own purpose—the conquest of Rhys of Trevaron.

From the servants, Walter learned that Rhys had shared her bed, and though Jessamyn tried to ignore Walter's angry outburst about her lack of morals, his words hurt her nonetheless. He was acting as if Sir Ralph's threatened takeover of Curlew had existed only in her imagination, that the whole point of their recent struggle to hold on to Curlew was a ruse to get Rhys in her bed. Sometimes Jessamyn seriously wondered if Walter was losing his reason.

Jessamyn glanced up as there came a rap on the door and the latch was lifted. Beside her Ned raised his head, sniffed the air, listened, then lay back down, assured there was no danger.

"My lady."

Mary stood in the doorway, wringing her hands in her apron. "Oh, lady, a messenger's come from the top farm. Can you go see Meggy? Her baby's not coming right."

"What about the midwife?" Jessamyn asked, childbirth not being her specialty. She had assisted on several occasions, but usually left birthings to the skilled hands of old Bet, the midwife from Holly Ridge.

"Slipped on the ice down by the stream. She's laid up. 'Tis her what suggested they send for you, my lady."

Jessamyn sighed. It didn't matter; she had not been sleeping anyway. Perhaps she could help poor Meggy Hughes.

"All right, Mary. Pack my basket. I'll go."

Mary smiled in relief, for Meggy was a relative of hers. "Thank you, my lady. I'll tell the lad you're coming."

After Mary had left, Jessamyn sighed as she considered the absolute faith the surrounding families placed in her. If only she had half as much faith in her healing abilities, she thought ruefully, pulling out her thick woolen petticoat and fur-lined cloak. The top farm was close to Holly Ridge. The exposed farmland would be searing cold in these predawn hours. She chose her warmest fur-lined hood and gloves.

Carrying a candle, Jessamyn slowly made her way down the stairs. The flame cast wavering shadows on the stone wall, grotesquely shaped and endlessly changing. Sometimes, in the stillness of a winter morn, Jessamyn dwelled on the legend of the castle ghost. This was such a time. Swiftly she dismissed her disturbing thoughts before she allowed her mind to run away with itself and transform the shadows into ghastly apparitions. In this world, there was far more to fear from flesh and blood creatures than from disembodied spirits from the past.

Jessamyn made her way to the infirmary. There she looked inside the basket Mary had packed for her, glad that she had included the new pain-killing mixture Jessamyn had developed, one which relied heavily on marjoram and sallow willow. She had used this tea to good effect to ease the pains of the soldiers wounded in the recent skirmish with Rhys's troops. Six of Sir Ralph's men were being treated in Curlew's infirmary. They needed her care, yet Jessamyn was uneasy at the thought of nursing the enemy back to health.

At last she was ready. She had packed the top of her basket with clean cloths to wrap up the newborn baby and to staunch the flow of blood should the mother hemorrhage. In her past experience, peasants had no clean cloth for bandages, so she had started bringing her own.

There was still no glimmer of light in the black sky when Jessamyn mounted her horse. The young groom attending her shivered as he handed up her basket. Ben, the husband of Alys from the infirmary, was to ride with her. The servants had been drilled by Rhys not to let their lady ride out alone. Though Jessamyn doubted Rhys would consider Ben sufficient protection, she did not want to wait for others to get dressed for the journey.

They left the castle by the postern gate. They were soon traveling the rough track winding uphill to the top farm. Had she not already been awake, Jessamyn knew that the stinging cold wind would have blown away the last vestiges of sleep. She shivered and hunched down inside her warm cloak. This had been a cold winter. She could hardly wait for spring, when the breezes softened and flowers bloomed in the woods.

As she struggled up the last hundred yards of track to the bleak hill farm, Jessamyn wondered wistfully if Rhys would come back in the spring. At the wonderful promise of his return, a shiver of anticipation went over her, and she smiled at her very private thoughts as she swung from the saddle. For Rhys, she would wait a dozen springs.

Beside her Ned nuzzled her hand, panting heavily, despite the cold, for the journey was hard on the old dog. Jessamyn had given up trying to discourage Ned from accompanying her. The morning that she left for Chester without him had been such a shock that Ned refused to let her out of his sight.

"Go on, love, inside, to the fire," she urged the dog as the farm door was opened to them. Not needing a second urging, Ned shot towards the glowing hearth where he received a growled greeting from the other dogs already resting there.

"My lady." Alden Hughes bowed to her, his weather-beaten face seamed with worry. "Meggy's been at it over two days. Old Bet said they was twins, but neither babe'll come out. She's over there."

Jessamyn blanched at this ominous news. Swiftly she went toward the sleeping end of the old wooden farmstead. At one end of the building, cattle lowed and Alden excused himself, saying that he had to milk the cows.

Pungent with the smell of animals, straw and cooking, the Hughes' hilltop farmstead was larger than most. Sturdily built, with a sound thatched roof and dry, whitewashed walls, it was considered an excellent property. Alden Hughes was a prosperous yeoman farmer and well-respected in the district.

Close-fitting wooden shutters over the windows kept out the winter wind. On a chest in the corner, a candle glowed, shedding a pale circle of light across a writhing heap of blankets. Deep moans came from the huddled form under the blankets and Jessamyn knew that she had found her patient.

At her command, Ben put down the basket and stood diffidently in the shadows, awaiting further instructions.

Jessamyn pulled up a cricket and squatted beside the low, rope-mattressed bed.

"Meggy . . . it's Lady Jessamyn. Alden says you've been in labor two days."

The woman on the bed turned her waxen, sweat-beaded face toward her. Jessamyn was appalled at the change in the young third wife of Farmer Hughes. In the past Meggy had appeared to be a strapping, sandy-haired bundle of energy, the perfect candidate for childbirth.

"Lady Jessamyn . . . I'm . . . that pleased . . . to see you," Meggy croaked, taking the comforting hand extended to her. "Can you give . . . something . . . for pain?"

"Yes, but first let's see how things are doing."

Jessamyn was alarmed by the large amount of blood Meggy had lost. The stench of it hung in the air; the bedding was dark with it. Two babes, old Bet had said. Gently Jessamyn felt Meggy's huge, mounded abdomen, discerning several little legs and arms and two distinct nobs of skulls. What felt like a tiny knee blocked the birth canal; it felt cold to the touch. There was no movement.

Jessamyn was alarmed by her findings and she wondered if the long ordeal had been too much for Meggy's twins. In terse, pain-dazed words, Meggy told her what had happened so far, how much she had suffered, and that no matter how hard she pushed she had not been able to birth the babies. While she spoke, Jessamyn mixed and brewed a pain-killing potion over the open hearth.

"Lady, likely they be breached," Ben whispered to her as she turned from the hearth. "I seen it before. Sometimes mares suffer like this over a breach."

Jessamyn's stomach turned over. A breach birth of twins. She had no experience with that. "What shall I do?" she asked Ben in an undertone.

"Firstly give her the drink. The way I sees it, pushing's not going to get the job done, so we don't need her. We just has to reach in and turn the babes. Sometimes it works and sometimes it don't."

With these less than encouraging words, Jessamyn pushed up her sleeves and prepared to do what Ben suggested. After several hours of struggling, during which the men both helped, for Arden was back at his wife's bedside, Jessamyn managed to turn the babies. The first child they pulled out was dead; his lifeless body had prevented the birth of his twin. Slowly they worked the small limp baby out of the birth canal. Then Arden held the tiny red face and blew air into the child's mouth. This technique had not worked with the first baby, but the second child responded with a feeble wail.

Tears of relief gushed from Jessamyn's eyes as she heard the cry. She hugged Arden and Ben out of sheer joy. A serving woman came forward to care for the tiny mite, swaddling him in woolen bands and giving him linen rags soaked in milk to encourage him to suck.

Jessamyn turned her attention back to the mother. Here, she was less sure of success. Though the sedative had soothed Meggy's pain so that she had lapsed into fitful sleep, she now seemed as lifeless as her dead infant.

Motioning to Arden, Jessamyn told him to remove the dead baby, not wanting Meggy to see it when she regained consciousness. Jessamyn washed Meggy and changed the sheet with the help of the servant. She tried to sew together the jagged tear Meggy's flesh had sustained during her futile efforts to give birth. Jessamyn did all she could for the new mother.

Meggy awakened and smiled feebly in thanks, patting Jessamyn's hand. She was weak, exhausted, but still alive and aware enough of her surroundings to ask about her child. Jessamyn told her she had a healthy boy as she soothingly brushed back Meggy's lank hair from her eyes. Then, as Meggy drifted back to sleep, Jessamyn sank down on the rushes, suddenly aware of her own exhaustion.

"I've done all I can for her," she told Arden when he voiced his concern about her weariness. "I'll be all right. I'm just tired."

"You're a saint, Lady Jessamyn," he said in awe, repeating the praise Jessamyn had heard many times before. "Anything. . . . anything I can do to repay you . . . just ask."

Jessamyn smiled and patted his hand, thanking him for his offer and promising she would remember it. By nightfall, she hoped that Arden Hughes would still be as admiring of her efforts. Murmuring a prayer, all three stood with bowed heads, then Jessamyn made the sign of the cross on Meggy's sweaty brow with holy water from a vial she had brought with her.

"She's in God's hands now, Arden," Jessamyn said wearily as the farmer seized her hand and covered it with kisses, repeating his vow to repay her however she chose. From the far end of the house, she could hear the baby's cry, stronger now. A wave of relief washed over her. Perhaps this child was going to live.

Calling to Ned, Jessamyn left the Hughes' farmhouse. She was surprised to see wan sunlight washing the wintery brown grass with gold and sparkling jewels from the tangled hedgerows as they slowly plodded downhill. She had expected it still to be dark. It had taken far longer than she realized to attend to Meggy Hughes.

Jessamyn discovered that her hands were shaking with fatigue as she gripped the reins. The past hours had taken their toll. She knew it was a miracle that she had brought poor Meggy through her ordeal. Ben had been a great help to her and she had told him so, bringing a beam of delight to his square face at the unexpected praise.

In the distance, the castle lay in dark shadow beneath passing clouds. Something made Jessamyn lift her head, some instinct stirring inside her, for she had heard nothing unusual. In fact, all appeared placid and still in the winter morn. Ned had also pricked up his ears and his fur ruffled along the back of his neck. Uneasily, Jessamyn shielded her eyes with her hand to survey the castle. All was serene. Now that the clouds had passed overhead, the castle walls glowed with light, the curving moat sparkling like a necklace about the stonework. Ben plodded along beside her, smiling proudly over his achievement, oblivious to her uneasiness.

As they grew closer to Curlew, Jessamyn's sense of foreboding heightened. Her apprehension was probably in part because of sheer nervous exhaustion. The past weeks had not been easy, and the morning's ordeal had merely stretched her nerves a little tauter. Jessamyn whispered a prayer for Meggy and for her sons, both alive and dead. Hopefully

Arden would not have cause to regret that she and not old Bet had attended his wife's delivery. At the moment, Jessamyn felt too bone-weary to dwell on the probable dire consequences of the twins' births. All she wanted now was a bath, clean clothes, and to be able to slip inside the warm comfort of her own bed. After she had luxuriated in a hot bath, she would eat a light meal in bed. Surely she had earned that luxury.

The drawbridge was down!

Jessamyn reined in her horse. Beside her Ben frowned, glancing at her, puzzled by this unexpected discovery.

"The bridge was up this morning, wasn't it?"

"Oh, yes, lady. Mayhap a delivery," Ben suggested uneasily, glancing about for wagons, but seeing nothing out of the ordinary.

"Well, delivery or no—they should be quicker than this about drawing it up. Come on, we'll ride in this way. I've a few well-chosen words to say to Simon!" Jessamyn declared, urging Merlin forwards.

The horse picked up the pace and they were soon cantering across the wooden bridge, the horse's hooves ringing and echoing off the stone walls. Ned ran along beside her on his long legs, struggling to keep pace.

To Jessamyn's surprise, no one seemed to notice that she was coming across the bridge, nor did anyone even glance out to see who was riding into the castle. Gritting her teeth, Jessamyn's fury mounted. Surely Walter had not already countermanded Rhys's orders. It would be just like him to do something this dangerous and stupid, once her back was turned, just to prove *he* was the lord of Curlew.

They came through the open gate into the ward. Suddenly an unexpected flutter of blue against the stone tower caught her eye and she glanced up.

Jessamyn gasped in shock. Two flags flew from the mast: the one below was the white on gold Dacre standard; above that flapped the silver and blue coiled serpent of Sir Ralph Warren!

Chapter Seventeen

With a cry of alarm, Jessamyn maneuvered her mount about. She shouted a warning to Ben, who had followed her, but it was far too late. Armed men materialized from nowhere and they were quickly surrounded by Sir Ralph's soldiers.

"Welcome home, Lady Jessamyn."

She need not turn to identify the speaker. Sir Ralph's gruff voice was unmistakable.

"What are you doing here?"

"That's a long story. Won't you dismount?"

Ben had refused a similar invitation and was dragged from the saddle. Rather than suffer that indignity, Jessamyn dismounted unaided, forcing herself to move slowly, gracefully—she would not give them a spectacle to jeer at.

With thundering heart, she looked round, alarmed by the large number of soldiers she saw standing around the perimeter of the ward. What had happened? How had Sir Ralph tricked them this time?"

Beside her Ned gave a low, warning growl, sensing danger. Jessamyn patted his brindled head, reassuring him. Sir Ralph faced her now, his distinctive coat of arms displayed on a white silk surcoat covering his engraved armor. He eyed her, sniffed distastefully and curled his lip.

"Dear God, Lady Jessamyn, were you rooting with pigs?"

Incensed, she clenched her fists, longing to strike his supercilious face. "I've just assisted at a difficult birth, you arrogant b . . ." She stopped short of speaking that word, but he had already guessed what she had been about to say. He stepped closer; his eyes narrowed menacingly.

"You'd be advised to curb your tongue."

"By what trickery did you take Curlew?"

"No trickery. The gates stood open for me."

Jessamyn gasped in dismay, hardly able to believe what she heard. "How can that be?"

"A cooperative farmer, a few carts of hay . . . so simple when one is dealing with fools," he sneered, a scornful smile curving his thin lips. "It does not matter how, lady, just accept that it's done."

"Where's Walter?"

"I assure you, nothing's happened to your poor brother. He's safe in his room. You might be advised to save your concern for yourself. I understand it was you who betrayed me. Though your face is beautiful, your heart is black."

Ned growled again in warning as Sir Ralph reached out to touch her face. Angrily Jessamyn struck away his hand.

"Keep your hands off me!"

"Off you, you betraying bitch . . . I've a mind to whip you senseless for your treachery. Acting so saintly with me. Dedicating your life to prayer and

303

healing, indeed, and does that include taking that damned upstart Welshman to your bed—this Rhys of Trevaron? Isn't that his name?"

Jessamyn did not reply. Her heart began a thundering shudder as she grew afraid of the rage in Sir Ralph's face.

"Answer me—is Rhys of Trevaron your lover?"

Still Jessamyn said nothing, wondering if he actually knew the truth, or if he merely assumed that she and Rhys were lovers. Surely Walter had not unthinkingly revealed their secret . . .

"Knowing how uncouth the Welsh can be, I assume he forced you to his bed," Sir Ralph continued, his voice softer, coaxing. "Is that how it happened, my dear?"

For an instant Jessamyn wondered if she should agree with him to give herself a margin of safety, but she discarded the idea. If she neither agreed nor disagreed, Ralph Warren would continue to speculate.

"Damn you! Answer me!" he snarled at last, when she still refused to answer. A flush darkened his square face and his slate blue eyes were menacing beneath his thick brows.

"I've nothing to add. You're making all the accusations," she said at last, daring to face him down without flinching.

"First you stole my messenger's letters. Then you and that damned Welsh rebel tricked my captain. Still not content, he challenges me for control of Curlew, sneaking like a thief from the trees to set fire to my wagons," he growled, his face hard as stone. "Now, as if that's not crime enough, I find you've welcomed the bastard to your bed. So much for your piety and dedication to the sick! Do you think I shouldn't punish you for all you've made me suffer?"

Jessamyn did not answer. Across the ward, a horse

whickered and men shifted their feet, their armaments clinking in the ensuing silence. A fresh wave
of hatred for Ralph Warren stirred in her breast.
He was punishing her further by broadcasting the
details of her private life to these soldiers' eager ears,
deliberately humiliating her before their combined
troops. He had stripped away her dignity as Lady
of Curlew and publicly accused her, like a common
harlot.

" 'Bruise not the heel,' " she quoted, staring at his
splendid surcoat. "You seem rather fond of biblical
themes, Sir Ralph. Am I now to expect that 'He who
is without sin,' is to cast the first stone?" she asked
sarcastically, raising her voice for all to hear. "As I
am aware that person cannot be you, who is left
to punish me?" she asked, glancing around at the
stunned faces ringing the ward.

Ralph Warren sharply drew in his breath, his eyes
glittering with rage. His hand was raised to strike
her, but he changed his mind and bellowed for a
soldier to take her away.

Ned suddenly lunged at him. The old dog leaped
high, catching Sir Ralph's outstretched arm and
sinking his teeth into the padded sleeve of his
jambeson. The force of the dog's unexpected attack
staggered the knight and he lost his balance. Sensing victory, Ned leaped on the fallen man's chest,
pinning him down, growling loudly as he sought to
protect his beloved mistress.

It all happened so fast that Jessamyn had not
the presence of mind to call Ned off; she merely
stared uncomprehendingly at the spectacle unfolding before her. Ned continued to growl, clamping
his teeth harder about the man's arm. There was
a sudden flash of steel as Ralph Warren drew his
dagger, the long-bladed knife clenched in his free
hand. Without hesitation, he plunged the dagger

deep in the dog's exposed throat and twisted. A strangled, unearthly cry issued from Ned's bloody jaws as he reared back. Then Ned fell, a torrent of blood gushing from his torn throat.

The horror of what she saw momentarily paralyzed Jessamyn. She suddenly came back to life, giving a blood-curdling shriek as she leaped forward to save Ned. His huge brindled body was red with gore and though his heart still fluttered, his eyes were already glazing. As she bent over him, Ned's tail thumped feebly, and then lay still.

Jessamyn screamed again and again, her control snapping at this cruel, senseless act. All the love she had felt for her dog drove her to vent insane fury on his killer. Jessamyn carried a small dagger in her sleeve; never before had she drawn it in anger, but she drew it now. Spinning about, the only moving object in a frozen sea of faces, she leaped at Sir Ralph. With a cry like a banshee, she bore the startled man back to the ground from which he had risen. Repeatedly Jessamyn plunged her small dagger in his arm, ripping the padded cloth to shreds as she struck flesh. She would have stabbed his black heart had not his steel breastplate protected him. Blood spurted out. Jessamyn tried to stab him again, her anguished fury lending strength to her assault. He caught her wrist, trying to wrest the dagger from her hand. Clenching her other fist, Jessamyn drove it hard into his face, rejoicing in the pain as she contacted bone and soft yielding flesh. Her hatred for what he had done to her old near-blind dog boiling over, she cursed him with the last of her strength as they grappled on the ground.

Finally gaining control, Sir Ralph grasped her arms in his struggle to subdue her. Others came to his assistance and soon pinioned Jessamyn's arms behind her, cruelly twisting her wrist until, with a cry of pain, she was forced to drop the dagger or have her wrist snapped.

Clutching his bleeding arm, Sir Ralph stood before her. So enraged and humiliated was he over her attack, his taut features were a mask of hatred. When he spoke, his voice rasped, as if each word threatened to choke him.

"Take the bitch and throw her in a safe place so I don't have to look at her. I'll teach her a lesson she won't soon forget," he finally ground out through clenched teeth.

When several of his men came to examine his wounds, voicing their concern, he thrust them aside with a curse. Then, striding over the ward towards the infirmary, he left them standing outside.

Tears poured from Jessamyn's eyes; though she tried, she could not stop crying. Tormenting herself, she kept looking at Ned's lifeless body. Somehow, he looked much smaller in death. The splendid red collar she had bought him in Chester market was still about his neck, unrecognizable now, all covered in gore.

"Come on, lady, don't make this any harder for me," muttered the soldier who was trying to bind her wrists.

Suddenly all the fight left her. Jessamyn let her arms go limp. Standing there unresisting, she continued to sob, not caring that the enemy soldiers saw her cry. Her grief was a terrible thing, her noisy sobs coming from deep in her chest. Now she was a prisoner in her own home, degraded like a common criminal as they dragged her away with bound wrists. All she lacked were fetters about her ankles. Doubtless, Sir Ralph would add that refinement later.

Stumbling, Jessamyn was pushed and dragged toward the main tower. Strangers though they were, these soldiers already knew the location of Curlew's dungeons. Appalled to discover where she was headed, Jessamyn refused to plead with them. She had too much pride for that; besides, condemned as she was by her own actions, her pleas would have been useless. She would pay dearly for Sir Ralph's public humiliation at the hands of a woman, this final indignity heaped upon a long line of blows to his masculine pride. A man like Ralph Warren would exact a high price for such an insult. Likely, imprisonment would be just the beginning.

Fear quivered through her as she stumbled down the narrow stairs, so roughly pushed and pulled. She lost her balance and slid down the last three treads, bruising her back and thigh.

Jessamyn soon lost count of the long hours of darkness. At first, she had marked the days by the passage of light across the barred opening high in the wall. Soon she abandoned even that device. February was too dark and rainy a month for an accurate count; here, in the bowels of the earth, day and night looked too much alike. Miraculously, the cell where she was housed was dry, and for that she gave daily thanks as she heard rain sluicing down the castle's stone walls. On the beaten earth floor they had spread fresh straw and given her a blanket for sleeping. They had even allowed her to keep her fur-lined cloak, hood and gloves, all of which she wore in a futile effort to keep out the penetrating winter cold. The stone walls emitted such cold dankness, she doubted that this place was warm even in summer.

Her regular jailer was one of Curlew's old soldiers, and he wept, tears trickling into his grizzled beard, at the plight of his lady. Jem brought her a cross plaited from bullrushes gathered on the eve of St. Bride's day, January 31. Locally, Saint Bride's crosses were used to keep away evil spirits and Jem considered such protection a necessity in this god-forsaken hole.

The old soldier became Jessamyn's eyes and ears. He reported that he had seen the first pinkish brown tassels on the hazels, a sure sign of approaching spring. He wept with her when he related how Ben, the groom, had retrieved Ned's body from the moat where it had been flung, and daring Sir Ralph's reprisals, buried the old dog outside the walls beneath the willows. Jem brought Jessamyn a small bouquet of the first primroses, picked from under a hazel thicket at the edge of the wood. He wondered why she wept over his gift.

Jessamyn had no wish to endanger Jem, but she grew desperate to get word to Rhys about Sir Ralph's capture of Curlew. Her jailer was her sole contact with the outside world, and her only hope. At first she expected Sir Ralph to keep her there only a couple of days. But that hope soon died. Her imprisonment showed no sign of ending. She had not seen Ralph Warren since that fateful day in the ward when she had dared to challenge him.

February was by no means warm, but as the month passed, the temperature inside her cell seemed to rise. Jessamyn no longer shuddered beneath her blanket while cold rain pelted against the walls. Jem managed to bring her writing materials, smuggling them inside his clothing. Jessamyn wrote a brief note to Rhys telling him of her plight. She had no idea where he could be found, merely that his stronghold was at Trevaron in the Llys valley.

"I can't take this, lady." Jem gasped after she explained what she had written and to whom. "They never let me out of their sight that long."

"Are you still allowed to visit your daughter on the hill?"

"Sometimes they lets me," he agreed with a toothless smile. "She's just birthed a babe."

Perfect. Jessamyn swallowed, wondering how best to route her plea for help. "Listen carefully, Jem. When next you visit Bron, take my letter to the Top Farm. Tell Arden Hughes that Lady Jessamyn wishes to collect on his offer." An uneasy thought crossed her mind: What if Meggy or the baby had died? "You do know Arden?" she asked him.

"Oh, aye, everyone knows Arden. He's besotted with his new little lad, swears he'll be a champion farmer . . ."

"And Meggy? How's she?"

"Middling. Last time I sees them, they both says to thank you, my lady, for all you done for 'em."

That was all she had wanted to know.

"Don't give this to anyone but Arden. Tell him I'm Sir Ralph's prisoner and need to send this message to Lord Rhys. I must trust Arden to find a way."

Jem turned over the folded parchment in his hand, a worried frown on his brow. "How's Arden to send this to the Welshman? Do he know him?"

"Just tell him Lord Rhys lives at Trevaron in the Llys valley. Or he might find him at Glyndwr's camp in Snowden."

Jessamyn made Jem repeat the message until he had memorized it accurately. She doubted that either Arden or Meggy could read, and unless told, they would not know where to send her letter. Jessamyn hoped that the Hughes' farm had a trusted hand with enough wits to find his way through Wales. Getting word to Rhys by this route was a slim hope, but it was all the hope she had.

Several days later, Jessamyn was startled to hear a different step coming along the stone passage to her cell. This was not the shuffling, uncertain gait to which she had grown accustomed. In fact, there appeared to be several pairs of steps.

Stiffening, she braced herself for the worst. Sir Ralph must have intercepted her letter. What fresh punishment would he inflict on her?

The door creaked open and a lighted lantern dazzled her eyes. She shut her lids, finding the light too painful.

"Jessamyn . . . it's me."

Her eyes popped open as she recognized her brother's voice, but all she could see were twin halos of light burned into her pupils.

"Walter . . . you're here to join me?" she gasped.

"Nay, I'm not that much of a fool," he dismissed, coming toward her with outstretched arms. Appalled by the smell of her clothing, he stopped several feet away. "God, you smell like a sewer."

"Thank you, brother dear. You'd probably smell the same way had you been down here as long as I have . . . How long has it been?"

"Only a month," he replied cheerfully.

She gritted her teeth, infuriated that he should dismiss her miserable confinement with such good cheer.

"You wouldn't say it like that if you were the one living in this hellhole. Down here, a month seems like years."

"I know, and it pains me to keep you here, but there's nothing I can do. Had you not been so damned vicious toward him, Ralph wouldn't have had to do it."

"Ralph," Jessamyn repeated angrily, her eyes narrowing. "Don't tell me we're best of friends again."

Walter stepped back, injured by her accusing tone.

"Someone had to at least *pretend* to be his friend,"

he defended himself in an undertone, glancing behind him to make sure he was not being overheard.

"I can't believe this! After all he's done, all he's put us through, not even considering what he did to poor Ned . . ."

"I know how much you loved the old dog. I loved him too. But he *did* attack Ralph. How was he to know his life wasn't being threatened. Come on, Jessamyn, be reasonable."

"Reasonable! That's another thing you can suggest because you're upstairs with a fire, good food, your own bed and water to wash yourself. Damn you, Walter, I thought you'd more sense than this."

They glared at each other in the dim light.

"You're still an ungrateful bitch! After I've spent weeks softening him up in the hope he'd let you back in your own room, this is all the thanks I get."

"Back in my room," she repeated, swallowing her anger. "Then I'm to be allowed out of here?"

Walter smiled and held out his hand. "Yes, my love, you can go back to your own bed tonight. Now, what do you think about that?"

"It's wonderful news . . . I'm very grateful for your efforts, but I wish you hadn't had to bow and scrape to Ralph Warren to gain it."

"I'm not bowing and scraping—I am a Dacre, after all. It's just that I thought maybe we could think up a plan. If he's not on guard against us, it'll be far easier. When you come upstairs, Jessamyn, at least try to be civil to him."

She seethed at his suggestion. All the injuries Ralph Warren had inflicted upon them were too fresh for civility.

"If I'm forced to speak to him, I'll try," Jessamyn grudgingly agreed.

Walter was not pleased by her decision. "Look,

you're going to have to bend further than that, or you'll never get out of your room."

Something about his statement alerted her. "Get out of my room. You mean this glorious freedom I'm promised hinges on my being charming to Ralph Warren? Am I to be held under guard in my room? Is this what you've been bargaining for?"

Walter frowned at her seeming ungratefulness. "Surely it's a start. At least try to sound grateful for that. You can sleep in a real bed . . . take a bath— good God, Jessamyn, you need that worst of all."

Jessamyn sighed with pleasure as she stretched in the luxurious comfort of her own bed. She had spent the past hour soaking in a hot, fragrant bath. Her hands and arms had been coated with grime and dried blood; stiffened blood fouled her clothing. Jessamyn's gown was ruined; Mary had taken her cloak to try and clean it.

The luxury of being in her own room at last was so wonderful that Jessamyn felt reborn. Cleanliness, warmth and comfort were all blessed gifts that she had previously taken for granted. Guiltily she realized how miserable was the lot of forgotten prisoners in dungeons. She had endured imprisonment for only a month. Many a poor soul spent a lifetime in prison. She resolved to remember these unfortunates more frequently in her prayers in the future.

There was a tap on the door and Walter pushed it open carrying a loaded tray. He had very carefully negotiated the twisting stairs; still concentrating intently, he crossed the room without spilling a drop.

Jessamyn was touched by his unexpected thoughtfulness. Though she was still angry with her brother, she saw that he was trying to make amends for her unpleasant experience.

"Meat pasties, fresh from the oven. A cup of good malmsey to celebrate the occasion. And, for the sweet tooth." Walter held up a small marchpane-covered cake the cook had baked specially as a treat for Lady Jessamyn.

She smiled in pleasure. "Oh, Walter, what a pleasant surprise! Now do you find me more fragrant company?"

He grinned, looking her up and down with approval.

"A great improvement. You're quite like your old self." Then, with a grin, he added, "On consideration, that's probably a mixed blessing."

He brought the tray to the bedside.

"If you expect me to forgive and forget this easily, you can think again."

"Have you seen the soldiers on the stair?"

"I saw them."

"We might be able to do away with them, if you give me your word that you'll be nice to Ralph."

Jessamyn snorted. "I've no intention of being *nice*, whatever that entails. Ralph Warren is going to have a piece of my mind before he's done."

"It won't bring Ned back," Walter reminded her quietly, sitting atop her mounded bedcovers to eat.

She sighed. "I know . . . I only wish it could. How did the bastard get inside the castle this time? They had orders to keep the bridge up at all times."

"Ssh." Walter glanced behind him. "They might be listening at the door." Trying to be stealthy, he crept to the door and quickly yanked it open. A cold draught entered the room. The stairs were empty.

"They forced a carter to hide soldiers inside a hay wagon; then, when he was safe inside the castle, they jumped out and overpowered the guards at the gate. The rest of them galloped out of the trees and followed their friends over the lowered bridge. End of story."

So simple. Jessamyn could hardly believe her ears.

"Why did he turn so bold? What if Rhys and his men had still been here?"

Walter shrugged, sipping the heavy malmsey in his goblet. "Ralph seemed to know they'd gone. He must have had spies in the countryside."

Jessamyn nodded in agreement, yet she could not help wondering if they had been betrayed. To her knowledge, no one had left the castle to deliver such a message, yet she supposed a spy would not advertise his departure.

"By the way," Walter said cheerfully, finishing up the crumbs of his cake, "Ralph thinks you brought the Welshman here by yourself—that I didn't know about it."

"Walt!"

"He's already angry with you, what did it hurt to let him think that . . . *Jess*?"

She flashed him a rueful smile. "Nothing I suppose, except that he would have known we're united against him."

"I told him that you were so madly in love with the Welshman, you'd have done anything to get him here."

Jessamyn quailed at the news. "That was most kind of you, Walter. Now he hates me twofold. When he was here before, he proposed marriage. He was to come back in the spring for his answer."

"Damn!" Walter frowned at the unexpected news. Then he shrugged. "It's your own fault for not telling me."

"I was afraid you'd go after him and beg him to come back if you thought there was a chance of our marrying. I can't trust you on that score, brother."

"It might have been preferable to your galloping after the Welshman."

She scowled at him and finished her meal in silence.

Walter got off the bed and crossed to the window. A cold moon and stars lit the black sky. He sighed. "I might as well tell you, Jessamyn. Ralph's claimed the castle by conquest for Bolingbroke. We're seized as rebel property."

"What! He knows we're not rebels."

"Thanks to you, we did fly the Welsh flag. He has a hundred men who'll attest to that. It doesn't take much to be condemned."

Jessamyn digested this alarming piece of news. Sir Ralph's actions would be sanctioned as a necessary act of war. She would have no redress before the courts if she tried to have him ousted from Curlew.

"I don't suppose it matters. So hand in glove is he with Bolingbroke, the king would have given him Curlew anyway, if he wanted it."

"Aye, you're probably right . . . Jessamyn, you can save us, if you choose."

"How?"

"By telling Ralph that you accept his marriage proposal. Then, if you hate him as much as you profess, pray that he goes away campaigning and leaves you in peace."

Appalled, she stared at Walter, infuriated by the unfailing cheerfulness of his tone now that he imagined a solution to their problem.

"I'd sooner marry a swineherd than Ralph Warren. Besides, you surely don't think he'd have me now."

"Oh, some men can be fools where a pretty face is concerned. If you pretend to like him, he'll probably forgive you," Walter suggested.

Incensed by his lack of sensitivity to her feelings, Jessamyn pitched an empty pewter goblet at him. She missed, and the goblet harmlessly struck the door.

"Well, you can be sure it'll be one of those proverbial cold days, before I beg Ralph Warren's forgiveness!" she shouted in anger. "And if those are all the bright suggestions you can offer, you'd better leave."

Thoroughly annoyed, Walter headed for the door.

"Very well, Lady High and Mighty, but when the year passes, and you're still holed up in here, we'll see where your pride gets you then."

With that, Walter was gone, deliberately slamming the door behind him. Jessamyn picked up a silk pillow from the bed and hurled it after him to vent her anger. How could her own brother expect her to feign affection for their conqueror? Jessamyn clasped her hands over her heart in a futile effort to calm its pounding, shuddering beat. She felt such impotent rage. There was no one she could turn to. Even Walter suggested something so odious that she could hardly believe her own ears. He would sell her to Ralph Warren in exchange for the castle. Pretend to like him indeed! She'd have to be desperate to employ such a ruse with their avowed enemy.

Angrily she pushed aside the tray of empty dishes, resisting the urge to send it after the pillow. If Rhys would come to their aid, she need never face odious Ralph Warren again.

But Rhys did not come to their aid. The weeks crawled by and still she had no message from him. Jessamyn stared out over the countryside, straining to see pennants bobbing in the distance, waiting in vain for their liberator to come.

It was the seductive lure of spring which finally forced her to swallow a measure of her pride.

Day after day, she watched through the window of her tower prison, longing to be free, to walk and ride about the awakening countryside. Beneath the woodland trees nestled sweet violets and primroses. The river banks were green with new willow fronds, and the crimson flowers of the wych elms glowed in the spring sun. The air coming through the window, so heavily fragrant with the scent of growing things, made her heart ache with loneliness.

At dusk she could hear the cries of the tawny owls in the woods, and saw them fly out on dark wings to capture their prey. Nest-building rooks squabbled noisily in the wind-wracked elms to the north, and bright yellowhammers darted about the gold-dusted gorse ringing the heath. Buffeting easterly winds brought sudden showers which soon gave way to sunshine. Above all, she could hear the constant, mournful chorus of gulls and curlews circling the battlements. The countryside was throbbing with life while she was held captive inside stone walls, a prisoner in her own home. Jessamyn could endure the unnatural state no longer.

Her mind made up, she dressed in her green and violet silk gown, the shimmering fabric soft as a rain-drenched violet. Her burnished hair hung loose beneath a circlet of plaited ribbon. When she studied her reflection, Jessamyn felt despicable for what she was about to do. Yet, she could no longer endure the terrible loneliness and boredom of her days. After their last squabble, even Walter stayed away from her room. She saw only Mary and the guards on the stairs.

Jessamyn headed for the door with determined steps. She flung open the door and called down to the guard at the bend of the stairs.

The man was understandably wary of her. A half

dozen times during the first week of her confinement, Jessamyn had tried to storm the stairs, only to be turned back by force. Lately, she had made no attempt to come down.

The guard stood up straight and moved up the stairs. He had grown used to lounging beside his favorite arrow slit, passing his lonely watch surveying the changing countryside, and the peasants working the fields.

"You want something, my lady?"

"I want to speak to your master."

"He's conferring with his captains."

"Then send someone to tell him, or escort me downstairs to wait for him. I care not which. I intend to see him today."

The determination in her tone dissuaded the guard from dismissing her request and sending her back to her room. He nodded and went around a bend in the stair, telling someone there to take the message to Sir Ralph that Lady Jessamyn wished to see him.

She waited on the stone steps, her hands shaking with excitement. She waited a long time, refusing to go back inside her room. The guard did not know what to do; he had not been prepared for this eventuality.

"I'm still waiting," she reminded him. "Are you going to take me to him?"

The man swallowed nervously and nodded.

Jessamyn came farther down the stair. Her legs felt weak after long disuse and she took slow steps, not wanting to stumble on the winding stairs. A feeling of great joy filled her heart as she moved freely down the tower stairs and along the passage leading to the Great Hall. Nothing within the household appeared to have changed in her absence, she noted with satisfaction.

Several servants looked up in surprise as she

passed, whispering their greetings. So swift and vicious were their new master's punishments, though all were indignant over their lady's imprisonment, none dared cross Ralph Warren.

The soldier led Jessamyn inside the Great Hall.

Golden March sunshine slanting through the arrow slits formed pale, crossed daggers on the rushes. A fire blazed in the hearth and there, in Walter's chair, sat Sir Ralph.

As Jessamyn approached, Ralph Warren glanced up. Several other men were with him, and he waved them away to a lower table, farther down the Hall.

Jessamyn fought to suppress the rage she felt when she looked at Sir Ralph, and remembered that terrible scene in the ward. Whenever she thought about Ned's death, her heart ached afresh and she could not prevent tears misting her eyes.

"Lady Jessamyn, to what do I owe this honor? A change of heart?"

She faced him, wondering what she really had to lose by telling the truth. "No, Sir Ralph, you can attribute it to sheer boredom. What do you want from me? Am I to stay a prisoner for the rest of my days?"

His lids flickered in surprise at the directness of her questions, for he had not expected them. Jessamyn looked so lovely with her hair falling loose in a bright cloud about her face. Her features were sharper than he remembered, but he attributed the change to her recent tribulations. She was still so beautiful, she took away his breath. The anger he had expected to feel toward her, that he had intended to express in no uncertain terms, dissolved like magic. At this moment, all he wanted was her goodwill. Well, not all, he thought, his lips twitching in amusement—the rest would come later.

"Had you dealt more kindly with me, you need not have been a prisoner in the first place," he said evenly, motioning for a servant to bring refreshment. "Come, will you share a cup of wine while we resolve our disagreement?"

Jessamyn stiffly mounted the steps to the dais, finding the warmth of the hearth welcome, for the high-raftered room was chill. Sir Ralph wore a fur-trimmed houpelande of russet velvet, the color freshening his complexion and making him appear younger. He smiled at her as she sat beside him, and held out his hand in friendship. Reluctantly, Jessamyn took his hand, suppressing the shudder she felt at his touch.

"Even after all these past tribulations, you're still the most lovely woman in the world," he complimented her sincerely.

"Thank you."

Jessamyn sat stiffly, her back ramrod straight. She had the feeling that she must not relax her guard when dealing with her treacherous kinsman. His choice of a serpent on his personal crest was apt indeed. She waited uncomfortably while he poured a cup of Bordeaux and handed her a platter of fried bread spread with salted venison paste.

"I intend to forgive you your outburst in the ward," he said at length, his expression guarded. "I understand your anger, as I hope you can understand mine."

"How badly were you wounded?" Jessamyn forced herself to ask, though she knew he had not been wounded near badly enough, or he could not now be sitting so smugly in the lord's chair.

Without answering, Ralph undid the long row of pearl buttons on his velvet sleeve. He stripped back his sleeve to reveal a half dozen crisscrossed scars still purplish-pink with newly healed skin.

"There, between you and your hound, I'll carry this memento for the rest of my days," he said ruefully.

A pity the wounds were not on his throat, Jessamyn thought vindictively, trying to thrust aside the mental picture of old Ned all covered in blood.

"Why did you kill him?" she blurted suddenly, surprising even herself, for she had not meant to say it.

"Self-defense."

"Not so! You had no need to kill him, damn you! He was old and almost blind."

Jessamyn had half-risen from her chair as she spoke, itching to strike the man beside her. His mouth twitched with humor at her passionate speech, and she felt a deep surge of loathing for Ralph Warren.

Pressing her arm, he indicated that she should sit back in her chair.

"Strange how the loss of that mangy cur seems more important to you than losing the castle," he observed smoothly.

"Ned is gone—the castle's still here."

Ralph nodded in agreement. "So it is. I suppose Walter told you I've repossessed Curlew for King Henry."

"He said you claimed it as a rebel holding."

"Are you denying you're Glyndwr's supporter?"

"You know I'm no supporter of the Welsh prince!"

"What about that upstart Welshman who stood on the battlements and defied me? What of the Welsh dragon flying so brazenly from yon tower? You have all the appearances of being Glyndwr's ally."

She glared at him and said nothing.

"That's evidence enough for me."

Sir Ralph leaned closer, his eyes slitted angrily in his stern face. Jessamyn drew back as far as the high-backed chair would allow.

"While pretending to consider my suit, you dallied with him, lady. What does the Welshman have that other men do not? Your brother tells me you were so desperate to bed him, you chased him all the way to Chester."

Jessamyn's cheeks grew hot as she listened to his smooth, sneering accusation. "Walter doesn't know what he's talking about. I went after the Welshman to seek his aid, not his bed."

"But from what I hear, your plans soon changed."

"I've told you, Walter's not a reliable source."

With his blunt forefinger Sir Ralph gently traced the soft curve of her cheek. Longing to smash away his hand, Jessamyn forced herself to endure his caress.

"So lovely to have been despoiled by a Welsh peasant," he murmured thoughtfully, touching her glowing hair, her smooth brow. "Walter may not be reliable, but there are others who are. Your brother's not the one who condemned you, but no matter who points the finger, I want to hear it from your own lips. Is Rhys of Trevaron your lover?"

Jessamyn looked him square in the face, surprised to see a flicker of hope in his eyes. He wanted the truth to be different. Shattering all his hope, she said clearly, "Yes, Rhys of Trevaron is my lover."

In anger, Sir Ralph smote the table, setting the pewter goblets dancing noisily. "Damn you for your honesty!" he snarled.

"Would you take comfort from a lie?"

Shamefaced, he fell silent. "Nay," he said at length, "the truth cannot be altered."

"I didn't come here to discuss my lover. I want to know what I have to do to be free?"

Ralph stood, his russet velvet houpelande falling into myriad pleats about his sturdy legs. He stared silently into the fire, then at last he turned to face her, his expression soft.

"Jessamyn, I've caused you grief—it wasn't my intention. Even you must realize your brother's not capable of ruling Curlew. Someone with the strength and fighting ability of your late father is needed to maintain a castle. I am such a man. Unfortunately, neither you, nor your brother, could see that. I regret having to wrest the castle from you by guile."

Jessamyn stared at him in shock, never expecting such an honest, even-handed assessment from Sir Ralph Warren.

He smiled slightly as he saw her shocked expression.

"You see, I'm not evil incarnate, as you seem to believe. I'm a soldier who demands to be obeyed. Nothing more. Walter can continue to ape the lord, yet it is I who will wield the sword."

"And me . . . where do I fit into your plan?"

"Oh, Jessamyn, surely you're not that simple-minded—you'll be my wife. You must have realized that's the obvious solution to your imprisonment."

Her mouth dropped open in shock. "You mean—unless I agree to marry you, I'll never be free?"

"There, I knew you were a clever woman. You've just answered your own question. I must admit, when you came at me like a savage, when you cursed me to high heaven, I was tempted to plunge the dagger in your treacherous little heart. But I'm a fair man and on consideration, I understood your rage. I'll get you another dog—they're easily replaced."

"No!"

He shrugged. "As you wish."

"I want freedom to move about my home. Even if I can't go outside the walls, at least don't make me stay in the tower . . ."

"It's *my* home now. You've heard my terms. I won't bargain."

"And what about Walter?"

"What about him?"

"He needs a potion I mix to control his seizures. If you keep me in the tower, I can't do that."

"You stay in the tower until you meet my terms."

His face was hard, his eyes pitiless. Jessamyn's alarm mounted as she realized that he was not going to bend.

"Then let the women mix the potion. I'll instruct them."

"No. It's a lot of mollycoddling. That's young Lord Walter's problem now. He'll be all the better for a bit of discipline. He's an overgrown child with an unhealthy fondness for the winekeg. Stop me if I'm wrong." By the dull flush spreading over her cheeks, he knew he had come uncomfortably close to the truth. "As long as it suits me, Walter can pretend to be lord . . . that's if he causes no problems. He's not part of our bargain. When you change your mind and agree to wed me, then you'll gain your freedom. Until then, I hope you enjoy your room."

Anger bubbled inside her. Jessamyn could sit silently no longer, listening to his rules and orders.

"And I hope you enjoy Curlew, Sir Ralph, because you'll grow old here waiting for me to marry you."

His face tightened and he clenched his fist around the chair arm. "That's your choice, lady," he said thickly, fighting to control his temper.

"Exactly . . . and I'd sooner die than marry you!"

Jessamyn picked up the half-full wine goblet before her and threw its contents in his face.

With an angry oath, Ralph leaped up, the crimson wine spilling down his fine russet gown. He yelled for the guards who sprinted forward to seize Jessamyn's arms.

"Take Lady Jessamyn back to her room. She's not yet learned to behave." He ground out the words, using immense control, for he would dearly have loved to thrash her himself.

Chapter Eighteen

March was well advanced when next Jessamyn was brought from her room. In less than thirty minutes she had been returned to the tower, banished for not agreeing to Sir Ralph's proposal.

She leaned on the windowsill, gazing out at the greening land. Was this to be the pattern of her days? Brought out once a month like some ancient heirloom for dusting, then returned to safekeeping? If she had given Ralph Warren the answer he wanted, she could have enjoyed her freedom today. The tantalizing prospect brought tears to her eyes. If she promised to marry him, she could be free. That was the only condition she must meet—the one she could not accept.

Not only did he keep her imprisoned, Sir Ralph punished her further by withholding all outside contact. At first it was only Walter who was forbidden access to her; soon, even the maids had to leave her food outside the door and likewise collect the previous day's slops and empty dishes. Solitary confinement for the rest of her days, or marriage to Ralph Warren: for loathesomeness there was little to choose between the two.

Surely by now, Rhys would have received her letter. Or had Alden Hughes' messenger failed to find him? She had asked Mary for news, but so far, her efforts had not been successful.

During the next couple of weeks, Jessamyn began to notice increased activity in the garrison. Wagons frequently came and went; parties of soldiers rode out of the castle, possibly to practice maneuvers on the water meadows beside the river.

Her heart beat frantically as she examined the possibilities behind this unusual activity. Had Rhys's men been seen close by? Or were Sir Ralph's men practicing for a possible engagement with the Welsh?

That night Jessamyn could hardly sleep for excitement. When she contemplated seeing Rhys again, she trembled expectantly, longing to feel his arms around her. Out of sheer loneliness she concentrated on him so deeply, she half expected to conjure Rhys out of the gloom of her tower prison. The exciting prospect made her smile. If only such a thing were possible.

Slipping from her bed, Jessamyn crossed the cold floor to the window where she stood gazing out at the moonlit night. Somewhere in the Welsh mountains, Rhys looked at this same moon. Was there a chance he did not know about her danger? Had the message never reached him? Rhys might even have been injured in battle . . . or worse!

Jessamyn turned from the window when she heard the latch click on the door. "Mary?" she whispered hoarsely, wondering if the maid had bribed the guards to let her bring news.

"Not Mary."

Jessamyn's blood ran cold as she saw Ralph Warren carrying a candle in a dish. He pushed open the door and came inside the room.

"Why are you here?"

Jessamyn stood at the far side of the room, though in truth, it was such a small room, that did not place them very far apart. Her hands grew clammy with nervousness as she awaited his answer. He looked searchingly at her. She had not bothered to put on her bedgown and her white linen nightrail clung revealingly to her curves. Defensively, Jessamyn crossed her arms across her full breasts, uncomfortable beneath his burning gaze, aware that he could see through her thin garment.

"I asked you why you're here?" she repeated, her voice sounding more shrill than before.

"I came to try to talk some sense into you."

He put the lighted candle on the narrow stone mantel and relit her own candle by the bed. Then he turned to face her, his smile speculative. He motioned for her to sit on the bench before the hearth.

Jessamyn declined, preferring to stay where she was.

"Say what you came to say, and be quick."

"Very well, I'll be brief. You've had ample time to make up your mind, Lady Jessamyn. Apparently, you find imprisonment preferable to marriage. Would you be as hesitant if I sent you back to the dungeon?"

She swallowed fearfully, stifling the gasp of shock his words produced. The horror of being shut down there for the rest of her days was unthinkable. Trying to keep the quaver from her voice, she said, "If that's what you choose to do, I can't stop you."

"Exactly . . . in fact, my dear, you can't stop me

doing anything I want, can you?"

Tremors of fear shook her knees as she looked at him. He loomed large and menacing in her small room, his elongated black shadow splashed across wall and ceiling, greatly magnified.

"Do you still refuse my offer? Or have you had a change of heart these past few minutes?"

Stubbornly refusing to budge, Jessamyn said clearly, "No change."

She forced her voice to stay calm, though now her heart fluttered so wildly and her throat choked; speech became difficult. A terrible feeling of foreboding washed over her. Glancing about the room, she sought a weapon with which to defend herself but saw none.

"We leave tomorrow for Shrewsbury. And you're coming with me. Don't take too much comfort in that. We have dungeons at Cater's Hill to accommodate you."

"I'm not leaving Curlew."

"You're coming to Shrewsbury if I have to bind and gag you, though I'd much prefer to take you home with honor—as my bride."

"Ralph, can't you understand I don't love you," she whispered, trying a different approach, for now he seemed to have softened; his voice was less harsh. "You have much to offer. You'll make some woman a good husband . . . only it's not me."

"You're the woman I want."

To her horror, Jessamyn watched him bolt the door from the inside. Her heart beat so loudly, she was sure that he could hear it.

"No," she cried, holding up her arms defensively as he turned to face her.

"Make this easy on yourself. Get on the bed."

Jessamyn backed against the wall, the stone striking a chill through her thin nightrail.

Angry at her stubborn refusal to cooperate, Ralph grasped her arm. "We can do it against the wall if that's your fancy," he growled.

"Leave me alone!"

Jessamyn kicked his legs with her bare feet. Desperately she pummeled his face and neck with her fists, striking his Adam's apple and making him cough.

Enraged by her resistance, his face red from coughing, Ralph hit her. Jessamyn yelped with pain, nursing her cheek with her free hand. So deeply did it throb, she wondered if her cheekbone was shattered.

"Enough of that, you bitch. I've humored you, tried to be patient . . . no more! Likely the Welshman didn't have to endure this pathetic performance. You probably leaped on the bed and opened your legs right eagerly . . ."

Jessamyn struck him as hard as she could across the face with the flat of her hand. With an oath, he bore her backwards across the bed, slamming her into the feather mattress, knocking the breath from her body.

Both her arms were imprisoned as he pinned her down with his weight. Jessamyn gasped, fighting to speak. At long last, when she found her voice, she screamed for Walter.

Ralph hit her across the mouth, cutting her lip against her teeth. "Be quiet. There's no point yelling for that inept fool . . . besides, he's helpless as a babe in his bed."

"What do you mean, helpless . . . what have you done to him?"

Struggling to free herself as she spoke, Jessamyn found that she was no match for his superior strength. Perhaps if she could keep him talking, he might relax his guard, or maybe she could find a weapon. The lighted candle lay almost within reach.

Ralph tightened his grip on her arms, as if he sensed her intention. "I didn't do anything to him. He fell downstairs—probably drunk."

"He might have had a seizure . . . please, send someone to him. Let them give him the medicine . . ."

"No one's giving him anything. Now, shut up. I didn't come here to talk about Walter. I've far more important things on my mind."

"Don't do this. You'll live to regret it."

"Oh, really? You frighten me with your threats. And what do you propose to do? I'm going to take what you refuse to give me. And you *will* come to Shrewsbury as my wife. If you choose to be imprisoned for the rest of your days, that's your choice. You will be brought to me when I feel the need to use you. Who knows? You might decide staying with me's the best way after all. A dungeon can be very cold and damp."

He smiled cruelly at the absolute shock on her face. Ralph was glad the candles were lit, for he could watch the expressions on her lovely face, discover the treasures of the body which she had always kept from him.

Slowly, deliberately, Ralph Warren forced Jessamyn's arms up. Fighting him and finally losing the battle, Jessamyn sobbed deep in her throat as her arms were pinioned above her head. He imprisoned her wrists with one strong hand, crushing so tightly she thought her bones would break.

"If you'd yielded to me, this would have been much pleasanter for you," he said, ripping her nightrail from neck to hem with his free hand.

In self-defense, Jessamyn tried to draw up her legs and knee him in the groin, but he was too heavy to budge. Sir Ralph fought to control her as she writhed this way and that, struggling desperately to be free. He pulled aside her torn nightrail and gazed greedily at her body. He admired her firm white breasts, generously curved and pink-tipped. Licking his lips in anticipation, he roughly slid his hand over her breasts, kneading her flesh with such force as his desire mounted that Jessamyn yelped in pain.

The heat of his body engulfed her in a sickening wave as Sir Ralph pressed her deeper in the mattress. His mouth covered hers in a suffocating kiss and Jessamyn grew painfully aware of her cut lip, stinging beneath the pressure. His hot, smothering kisses made her gag.

"You're so lovely, even more beautiful than I dreamed," he whispered hoarsely, moving slightly aside to admire the voluptuous curves of her body. "A pity you let the Welshman spoil you. For his mistake, he'll die."

His ominous threat struck like a blow. Jessamyn's heart began such a heavy, shuddering beat, she was almost unable to draw breath. "You don't know where he is."

"I'll find him, even if I have to go to the ends of the earth. And when I do, I'm going to kill him in front of you. That'll make my pleasure so much greater," he threatened cruelly.

"I hate you!" she cried, still fighting him, though her strength was ebbing.

Ralph chuckled. Thrusting his hand clumsily between her legs, he drew it up so sharply that she gasped as he bruised her tender flesh. "Open to me," he commanded, his voice rasping with desire.

At first Jessamyn had fought his inept overtures, but she finally gave up the effort. Even if she had managed to throw him off, he would have called in the guards to tie her to the bed. It was pointless to fight any longer. Unresisting, she went limp, trying to imagine herself miles away, walking in the sunlit meadow . . .

He slapped her across the face. "Wake up, damn you. I don't want to mount a wildcat, but neither do I want to bed a corpse."

Tears of mingled pain and hopelessness trickled from Jessamyn's eyes, running into her hair and behind her ears. She shuddered with revulsion, for he had unfastened his clothing and she felt the moist, hot pressure of his naked organ against her thighs. Probing, jabbing, bruising, he fought to enter her. Jessamyn clenched her thighs tightly in self-defense. Ralph Warren was making her pay for her resistance. Tears of pain and loathing poured into her hair as he grunted atop her, trying to violate that which she held dear for the man she loved.

Something was happening. Ralph Warren's struggle lessened and with a groan he rolled off her, yet still he imprisoned her arms above her head. Casually he fingered her breasts, damp from his sweat; he flicked her nipples and made her gasp.

"Cold as brook water," he sneered, his mouth curling in derision. "Why would any man fight to keep you?"

"If you feel that way, then let me go."

A smile twitched his lips. "Thought you had me then, didn't you, little bitch? I'll warrant you weren't cold to the Welshman. Well, we've got time on our side. Mayhap someday you'll come to your senses. Played me too long tonight and you lost your chance. No matter. There'll be plenty other nights for me to show you what it's like with a real man."

Chuckling, he pulled away from her. A surge of relief passed over Jessamyn as she saw that his organ grew flaccid; she felt the wetness against her thighs. Her resistance had saved her. Sir Ralph's pleasure had been premature. She doubted a man of his age would renew the assault. This conclusion was joyfully affirmed as she saw him fastening his clothing.

Picking up his candle, Sir Ralph said, "Be ready to travel in the morning. I'll send a woman to you. We leave at first light."

Then he was gone.

Jessamyn lay stunned, her tears trickling into the pillow. She felt filthy and violated by his touch. And her heart ached for the helpless futility of what her life had become. Then another thought, more powerful than her own hurt, overcame her self-pity. Was Walter badly injured? The tower steps were steep and narrow. He might have struck his head on the masonry; he might even die from his injuries. Ralph Warren was so callous that he had refused help for her brother, not taking seriously Walter's history of seizures. She must get help for him.

Jessamyn started to get up and go in search of Walter, then fell back against the soiled bedcovers. What was the use? If she started downstairs, they would soon turn her back. It had happened a dozen times before. Perhaps tomorrow, when they were occupied with preparations for the journey, she could escape in the early morning darkness. If she could slip away, she might hide at one of the nearby farms. She might even take Walter there and hide him where he would be safe . . .

These thoughts swirled around in her mind for hours, half-formed plans, swiftly discarded as Jessamyn slowly grew drowsy. She wanted to wash away the loathesome smell of Ralph Warren's body, the horrid wetness on her thighs, but she had been given neither basin nor water. He had dared to blame his violation on her and, in a minor way, she supposed he was right. Had she pretended affection for him, he would not have tried to rape her. Several times he had softened toward her, reaching out for a crumb of affection, praising her beauty, offering to replace her dog. She had scorned all his attempts at a truce.

Before dawn Jessamyn was dressed and waiting. Mary hugged her tearfully, crying at the thought of her lady being taken away to a strange place. She was not to accompany Jessamyn on the journey, Sir Ralph deeming it too dangerous to have someone loyal to Curlew in their party. Jessamyn would have to fend for herself on the way to Shrewsbury.

Several times Jessamyn had asked about Walter. Mary had said that no one in the castle had seen him since he fell on the tower stairs.

Down to the Great Hall Jessamyn marched, all hope of escape dimming as two armed guards followed her every move. It felt strange to be seeing Curlew for the last time. All her memories, her very life itself, was bound inside the tall stone walls.

The Great Hall was filled with soldiers. Holding her head high, Jessamyn walked the length of the room, not anxious to meet their curious stares. They were probably aware of what had taken place the previous night. The sentry on the stair could not have mistaken the sounds coming from her room. Ralph Warren might even have boasted of his conquest to his men.

Stonily she looked at him seated at the High Table, dressed for traveling, his armor glinting in the firelight. He was not wearing his distinctive surcoat with the coiled serpent.

"Good morning, Lady Jessamyn. I trust you slept well?" he said, smiling slightly as she walked past him to take her place. "I'm surprised to see your disposition unchanged this morning," he added with a grin.

336

Beside him, Captain Jackson snickered, assuring Jessamyn that he, at least, was privy to what had taken place behind her locked door. A dull flush of shame mounted in her cheeks as she looked down at her hands, refusing to meet his gaze.

A platter of bread and meat was pushed before her. Her lips were stiff and when she moved them the healing wound, edged with dried blood, hurt. She ate only a little of the bread. The mixture formed an unappetizing lump in her throat and she found it difficult to swallow. While she sat there, Jessamyn glanced around the packed Hall, wondering how best she might escape.

She soon realized that her fledgling plans were doomed to failure when, after she had eaten her fill, two soldiers came to bind her wrists.

"Just in case you get any ideas about leaving us," Sir Ralph explained in an undertone, leaning close, his hot breath playing across her face. His inquisitive gaze roved over her curving cheek, her slender neck, finally resting on the delectable swelling inside her bodice. He smiled suggestively, making no secret of his interest. His bold, insulting stare made Jessamyn flush with shame. With his forefinger he tapped her cut lip, making her wince in pain.

"Where's Walter?" she asked later, when her brother had still not come down to the Hall to sup.

Sir Ralph's face hardened. "I've already told you, Walter has nothing to do with our bargain. Anyone would think him a babe in arms, the way you fuss over him. He's up in his room abed, where he should be, sleeping it off. Now, I don't want to hear any more about him."

"I at least want to say goodbye; surely that's not too much to ask."

"We'll see," Sir Ralph dismissed, turning his attention to more pressing matters.

When they were ready to leave, Jessamyn was marched outside under guard into the chilly, gray dawn. After she mounted Merlin, her hands were tied to the reins and soldiers positioned themselves on either side of her. She was to ride a few paces behind Sir Ralph himself. The scene made her think of stories she had heard of captive women being moved across country, tied to their conquerors' horses, but when she voiced her thoughts to Sir Ralph, he looked sourly at her and told her to hold her tongue.

"What about Walter?" she asked again, her alarm mounting as the column formed up in preparation for departure.

William Rhees watched from the shadows, and Jessamyn called to him when no one else would listen.

"Will you make sure Walter's well?" she asked him, as the lead soldiers trotted across the ward, heading for the lowered bridge.

Almost as soon as the words were out of her mouth, one of her guards rode closer and wrenched her bridle about.

"You're forbidden to talk to anyone," he growled.

"I'm just asking William Rhees to take care of my brother," she repeated, refusing to be quiet, even though he yelled at her.

Sir Ralph himself came cantering back to her side.

"What's going on?" he asked sternly, scowling at those responsible for the disturbance.

"She's trying to talk to the steward."

Sir Ralph smiled and waved his hand. "My dear lady, speak with the man, if you wish, though he's steward no longer. One of my men has assumed his duties."

Jessamyn gasped in surprise at the news, not

338

aware until then how complete had been Sir Ralph's takeover of Curlew.

"I want Walter brought down."

"No!"

"Then at least let me get William Rhees's word he'll make sure he's well cared for."

Sir Ralph nodded his assent. The steward had been standing by uncomfortably, silent during their exchange. He assured Jessamyn that he would see Lord Walter got the care he needed.

"Now, any more last words or instructions for your retainers, my lady?" Sir Ralph asked sarcastically. "No orders for the cooks, or the scullions . . . or your faithful Captain of the guard?"

Simon was waiting in the shadows by the gate to say goodbye to her. Jessamyn gulped, her voice shaking with emotion. She saw tears pouring down the old soldier's unabashed face as he bid her goodbye.

Angry at this display of emotion, Sir Ralph motioned him to step aside. "She's going to be married, not executed, damn you," he snarled, urging his horse forward and carrying Jessamyn along with him.

In a matter of minutes they were over the causeway and out on the road.

Tears poured down Jessamyn's face as she turned in the saddle for a final look at her home. Dear old Curlew stood solid against the brightening sky. Her teeth gritted when she noticed the serpent flying boldly from the tower, high above the Dacre standard. Anyone who saw that flag would know that Curlew had fallen. Rhys would know at once that Sir Ralph Warren had captured the castle, but he would not know where she had been taken, she thought in dismay. Surely he would guess that Sir Ralph had carried her off to Shrewsbury—to be his bride!

Her stomach pitched as she recalled the second part of his threat. They would be man and wife! Though she would never agree to marry him, she supposed that her consent was not needed. Fathers often negotiated marriages without their daughters' knowledge, so she had no reason to believe Ralph Warren could not do the same. Her signature might not be necessary to finalize the agreement. It was likely that Sir Ralph would choose to marry her by proxy before a priest, making their marriage binding in the eyes of the church. She was a helpless pawn in his powerful hands. And though he would never have any joy in their marriage bed, she would legally be his to do with as he wished.

Rhys would think she had betrayed their love, that she had agreed to become Ralph Warren's wife. The pain of that realization made her weep.

Miserably, Jessamyn headed towards the south, blinded by tears, seeing only the narrow view between her horse's ears.

She was disturbed in her misery only when Sir Ralph dropped back to ride beside her, motioning for the soldiers to ride a short distance away so they could be alone.

"Tears, my dear? Surely you don't weep because you're afraid your lover won't be able to find you."

She refused to answer. Her efforts to dry her tears met with little success. They continued to drip on her cloak, marking the fabric.

"You need have no fear on that score," Sir Ralph said presently. "I've sent him a letter to tell him about our joyful news. Lord Rhys will be the first to know about our marriage."

With that, he motioned the soldiers back and spurred his mount to the front of the column, leaving Jessamyn to ponder his startling news. She quailed when she considered the probable contents of his letter. Rhys would be enraged to think she had betrayed him, that she had cast aside their love to sell herself to the enemy.

Her tears flowed nonstop to Carshalton.

Ralph stood watching her come into the inn, her face puffy, her eyes red-rimmed. He felt a pang of remorse at being responsible for her grief, at having destroyed, even if it was only temporary, her striking beauty. Telling her about the letter he had sent to the Welshman had given him much pleasure. Even he had been unprepared for the absolute shock and pain on her face. On reflection, however, he grew angry when he realized her shock and pain arose out of love for that Welsh bastard. And this conclusion did not please him. Scowling, Ralph called for wine and stamped to the hearth to warm himself.

He hoped the Welshman would not be able to contain himself until he had sought him out, and challenged him to a fight to the death. Then he would kill him. It would be easy. He was a trained knight. At best, the Welshman could only be a guerilla fighter, brave but undisciplined. He would win hands down, and the thought cheered him. Perhaps, when the bastard was dead, Jessamyn would abandon all her romantic notions about her dashing lover and decide to become his obedient wife. Beautiful Lady Jessamyn would be his most valued asset, a jewel amidst the many treasures of Cater's Hill.

Chapter Nineteen

Sir Ralph's army moved slowly through the English countryside as the early May sunshine bathed the land in gold. The sunken lanes were adrift with blackthorn blossom, while blue speedwell, dandelions and white stars of stitchwort sprinkled the roadside grass. Overhead was the constant, twittering cacaphony accompanying nest building in trees and hedgerows. Deep in the woods, the first cuckoo called, and bees buzzed lazily about the spring flowers.

Showers, interspersed with sunshine, marked the lazy days as they meandered about meadow and wood. Often they stopped for shelter from the rain, traveling only when the sun reappeared. At night, Jessamyn was given her own room. When they stopped, be it at inn or manor house, she was kept constantly under guard. It was purely for her own protection, Sir Ralph explained to the curious gentry they visited, hinting about some love-smitten Welsh supporter of Glyndwr who had threatened poor Lady Jessamyn's life.

When she got wind of this tale, Jessamyn tried to dispel the notion. To her amazement, she got nowhere. Ralph's friends seemed not to hear, or believe, what she tried to tell them. They refused to be shaken in their belief that Ralph Warren was her loving husband-to-be. Eventually, she gave up, shifting her energies to watching every day for an opportunity to escape. Her hopes dwindled more, the deeper they moved into England. She did not know her way home, but she was determined not to let that stop her if she ever had a chance to leave. Her constant, armed companions thwarted all attempts she made to slip away. She could not blame them for their vigilance, for she knew that if she escaped, both men would lose their lives. She had heard Sir Ralph threaten them with this punishment.

Mayblossom frothed alongside the lanes and the heady fragrance of new-mown hay blew on the breeze. The pale candles of the horse chestnut were in full-bloom and the trees dotting the countryside were heavy with leaves. Though she had lost count of the days and weeks, Jessamyn realized that they could not have been bound for Cater's Hill. Even she knew that by now, they had had time enough to travel to Shrewsbury and back three times over.

The still, damp dawns were noisy with birdsong. The distinctive song of the skylark began the symphony, closely followed by the sweet voices of thrush and blackbird. The sunny days seemed to increase the intensity of the birds' song, and this told Jessamyn that the month was well-advanced. There were too many heralds of summer for her to be deceived into thinking they had only been on the road a couple of weeks.

The proportion of Welsh-speaking people in the surrounding countryside increased, making her wonder if the hilly terrain they meandered through was even in England. By observing the placement of the sun, she saw that they were heading west. Yet, whenever she asked questions, or voiced her observations, Sir Ralph scoffingly dismissed them, suggesting that the sun had overheated her brain. He only laughed scornfully when she told him she thought they were back in Wales.

"When are we to reach Shrewsbury?" she asked him one morning, finding him seated at the table ahead of her. She took her place beside Sir Ralph, and her guards stood behind her chair. The guards never left her side, even waiting outside the privy door until she emerged. She had grown used to their presence. The men hardly spoke to her, being distinctly unpersonable. Lately, she had begun to regard them as casually as pieces of furniture.

Sir Ralph shrugged and handed her a platter of freshly cut rye bread.

"I'm about the King's business," he answered, his mouth full. "We'll get there when I'm ready."

"We're not even in England, are we? We're back in Wales. I'm not the fool you take me for. All your tales of too much sun don't deceive me. I've been right all along."

"What if you are? Surely to you, one place is as good as another."

"How much longer am I to be kept prisoner?"

"We can marry at any parish church we pass," he suggested with a half-smile. "Are you growing eager for me again, my love? Is that the reason behind all these questions?"

Jessamyn shuddered at the idea. To her great relief, during the journey he had not approached her sexually. The memory of that hateful night was still fresh, all the degradation she had felt, the touch of his hands and mouth, so hateful that she had scrubbed her skin almost raw in an effort to eradicate the lingering feel of him. The guilt. The shame. Ralph Warren could never make amends for these past weeks, whatever he tried to do. In fact, he had made considerable effort to befriend her. So lonely had she grown, she was ashamed to admit she had relinquished a little hatred towards him. They had even played a quiet game of chess one rainy night at Harrows Hall, presenting a picture of domestic bliss to the Hall's curious owners.

"You already know the answer to that."

He smiled at her swift retort, but his expression was humorless. "Ever charming, ever kind Lady Jessamyn," he said, an edge to his voice. "If you must know, my curious one, we're going to join Mortimer in the fight against your champion—Glyndwr."

Jessamyn gasped, her hand flying to her mouth. "When?"

"Whenever we find him. True to form, the slippery devil hides in the forests. He's been sighted here and there, but he always stays one step ahead of us. We'll find him soon. He's in the region."

She fell silent. So that was why they had been backtracking over the same countryside. Though Sir Ralph always denied it when questioned, she was positive they had traveled over the same terrain on several occasions. He had been deliberately hanging back on the off chance of meeting the Welsh troops. Not for one minute did she suppose he was really anxious to fight Glyndwr. He was looking for Rhys.

"And me?"

"You'll stay with me."

"In battle?"

"There are always droves of wives and camp followers traveling with an army. No one will think it strange. If there's a decent lodging when we choose the battlesite, you'll be billeted there. Now, no more questions. Eat your meal. We have to leave."

It was June before they finally got within range of the Welsh forces. The English troops had been skirting the vast Clun forest, riding slowly over the rough countryside, making a few miles progress each day.

At Ludlow, Sir Ralph engaged a woman to care for Jessamyn's needs during their journey. The unexpected company of this middle-aged companion brightened her days.

Tansy was a jolly, apple-cheeked woman, the widow of a farmer who had been dispossessed. She was only too glad to have a position, especially since Sir Ralph assured her that if she were acceptable to Lady Jessamyn, she would be retained when they finally went home to Cater's Hill. Tansy was soon made aware of the true relationship between Jessamyn and Ralph Warren and she was quick to sympathize with Jessamyn. Yet when questioned by Sir Ralph, who had intended to pay her to spy on Jessamyn, Tansy feigned ignorance of all except a few harmless snippets of information which she revealed to pacify her master.

Sir Ralph's troops had joined up with the much larger English force commanded by Edmund Mortimer, an uncle of the young Earl of March. Jessamyn was introduced to Mortimer as Sir Ralph's future bride who had been unavoidably caught up in the hostilities. Ralph failed to tell Mortimer that they had been wandering back and forth since April, killing time, circling far to the south of Shrewsbury in the hope of encountering the Welsh.

The land where they were camped was a combination of heavily forested hills and marshy valleys. They first stopped at Whitton, northwest of

Presteigne, before traveling further north to Pileth, where a motte and bailey castle had been built by the Normans several centuries before to guard the valley. Mortimer chose to defend the hillside rather than the marshy valley, afraid that his troops would get bogged down in the mud. The top part of the hill was covered with rough gorse, while the lower slopes were green with new bracken.

There were so many troops assembled that Jessamyn began to grow uneasy. She had no desire to be trapped in the middle of a battle. Sir Ralph usually kept her heavily protected at the rear. When a fight seemed imminent, following continued reports of scouts seeing the Welsh, he sent half a dozen extra men to guard her. She slept with Tansy inside a wagon, finding it a pleasant accommodation during the cool June nights. As yet, no one had seen the bulk of the enemy troops, but all were positive that Glyndwr was close by. Sir Ralph reinforced her guards to be on the safe side, jealously guarding his treasure in case Rhys of Trevaron got wind of her presence amongst the English ranks.

"When this is over, we're bound for Cater's Hill," Sir Ralph announced one morning over a meager camp breakfast of gruel and stale bread.

Jessamyn's heart pitched at the news. That meant he knew Rhys was traveling with Glyndwr. By now she knew Ralph Warren well enough not to be taken in by his apparent loyalty to Bolingbroke. His first loyalty was to himself, his own desires always taking precedence over those of his king. Once they actually engaged the Welsh forces, she knew that he would seek out Rhys to kill him.

Jessamyn was desperate to warn Rhys of the impending danger but she, like Mortimer, had no idea where to find him.

The surrounding countryside was peaceful under

the soft summer sun. Yellow flags and purple comfrey grew in the marshy valley where narrow brooks trickled placidly into reedy shallows brightened by king cups and forget-me-nots. It seemed unthinkable that thousands of men gathered, itching for battle. The dense woods were alive with the song of woodwarblers and flycatchers, nesting in the towering oaks. Some of the men reported seeing wild goats on the hillsides and had spent fruitless hours trying to catch them.

The soft, golden dawn blossomed into a perfect June day. They broke camp early and moved higher up the hillside. No recent activity had been reported by the scouts sent out to find Glyndwr's troops. Jessamyn was sure that the Welsh were hiding in the dense woodland, waiting for their opportunity to strike. They were probably watching this slow pilgrimage up the steep hillside with interest.

Jessamyn found it hard to believe that Rhys was close by, unaware that she, too, was near, or even that Ralph Warren had vowed to kill him. The latter thought brought with it a chilling dose of reality. Pleasant though the countryside appeared, their purpose there was deadly. Before the day was done, the two armies could have engaged, inflicting massive casualties. She prayed that Rhys saw his attacker first and got the upper hand, for there was no way she could forewarn him of his danger.

With gaudy banners flying, the mass of horses and men labored up the steep incline. At the head of their contingent of troops the Warren serpent gleamed in the sun, the flag flapping overhead in the cool breeze sweeping down from the hills. Sir Ralph's force was still in the center of the mass of advancing troops.

When the English troops were halfway up the hill, toiling slowly over the rough terrain, a man in the forefront shouted a warning as movement was spotted in the trees. General confusion reigned as the army halted amidst thickets of tangled gorse. Suddenly the sky darkened, giving them only a moment's warning before a hail of arrows struck the frontline troops.

As Jessamyn had suspected, Glyndwr's army was entrenched at the top of the hill, watching their advance. Pandemonium broke out. As arrows rained from the trees, Sir Ralph grabbed Jessamyn's reins and galloped with her through a break in the ranks, taking her to the cover of a grove of trees on the far right flank. Tansy and some other women camp followers rode after them. Screaming women ran toward the cover on foot, falling, scrambling up, running again over the rough terrain as they fled for their lives from the devastating fire.

Jessamyn nervously waited and watched from under the cover of the dense oaks, hoping they were safe. Before them men and horses maneuvered into position on the hillside, shouting orders, their voices drowned by screams and whinnies of fright as volleys of arrows found their marks and men and horses went down. Beside her, Tansy began to pray, with several other women joining in the familiar pleas for God's mercy.

Down the slope came a rush of men as the Welsh descended on their enemies with shouts of triumph. Mortimer's troops tried to push their tired men and horses back up the slope to engage the Welsh, slipping and falling on the rough terrain, pitched as steep as the roof of a house. All the while, the Welsh were raining arrows on them. When, at last, the two opposing sides met, Glyndwr's troops fell upon the English army with whoops and shrieks. Amongst the jostling throng of banners and pennants, Jessamyn temporarily lost sight of the Warren insignia, though she was sure it still bobbed with the rest. The women with her cried, wringing their hands in fright, convinced that they would be raped by the Welsh. While the fierce battle raged up and down the hillside, the women huddled under cover of the trees, guarded by half a dozen surly soldiers who were annoyed to have missed the excitement of battle just to protect a handful of screaming females.

The Welsh were lightly armed, giving them an advantage in the treacherous terrain. The heavily armed English soldiers, their war horses struggling up the incline, were repeatedly driven back by the entrenched Welsh. Dead bodies were hurled back amongst the living; men fell at the top of the hill and came tumbling down. Some of the wounded were trampled to death by their advancing comrades. Too late, Mortimer realized his mistake. No wonder they had not seen the Welsh; they had been hiding in the forest all the time, aware of their every move.

Ralph Warren fought like a madman, pushing his way deep into the Welsh forces. Men fell back in awe of him, wondering at his sanity. He was driven by a deadly purpose. As he fought, he watched for a specific pennant of blue and yellow flowers—those damnable Flowers of Llys! He knew that when he saw that banner, he had found his enemy.

Blood trickled into his gauntlet from a scratch on his forearm, but he ignored it and fought on, still searching for that banner. Arrows plinked against his helm, but failed to penetrate it. He had pushed up his visor to wipe sweat from his eyes when, looking to the east into the sun, he spotted the flowered insignia shimmering in the distance. With a cry of triumph, he slammed down his visor and motioned for his men to follow.

"By God, we've finally found our man!"

* * *

Rhys and his followers stood apart from their body of archers, his men occupied in hurling back the English attackers, delighting in sending men flailing down the hill to crash into their companions. The wounded were fortunate if they suffered no worse an encounter than a spiny gorse thicket on their way downhill.

Fighting on foot, he had already dispatched a goodly number of invaders. His sword ran red; his hands, his arms, likewise. Sweat stung his eyes and burned his lips, and he wiped his sleeve across his brow. Like many others on this ridge, he had set aside his helm, as the warm sun turned helmets into ovens.

As he glanced over the teeming mass of men advancing uphill toward him, he noticed a large party of horsemen suddenly veer to the right, into an open space. His breath rasped as he recognized the pennant fluttering at their head, for it bore a glittering coiled serpent on a blue ground. A wave of loathing washed over him as he looked upon the treacherous serpent of Cater's Hill.

Jamming his helmet back on his head, Rhys motioned to his men to mount up and follow him. Rhys leaped into the saddle and careened madly through gorse thickets, seeking a path amid acres of spiny vegetation. When he found his way, he rode straight for Ralph Warren, eager to avenge all the wrongs that the English knight had inflicted on Jessamyn.

His horse drew in its stride as the track steepened. Rhys continued to wind about gorse thickets as he kept veering to the left. The two men identified each other's banners and they shouted in unison, ordering back their followers who would have rushed forward to do battle.

Into a barren patch of heath forming a flat plateau, they galloped, two adversaries bent on destruction.

"Damn you, Welshman, for all the grief you've caused me," bellowed Ralph Warren, swinging his sword in a wide arc over his head.

"And damn you, Warren, for your treacherous heart. This is for Jessamyn Dacre," Rhys shouted, circling Sir Ralph and slashing his arm. Their mounts virtually jostled each other as their riders engaged at close quarters, clashing and banging swords, neither man gaining the upper hand. Rhys was thankful he had the presence of mind to wear his helm as the flat of Sir Ralph's sword struck him broadside, setting his head clanging like a church bell.

Sir Ralph unhooked the mace which hung from his saddle and tried to batter Rhys from his horse. Ducking, maneuvering his beast, Rhys fought to keep his seat. He cut again at Sir Ralph with his broadsword, puncturing his jambeson at the armpit and severing the leather strap which buckled his breastplate.

Cursing the Welshman, Ralph Warren pulled back and roundly cursed himself, too, for not being fully accoutered. He had thought they were merely climbing the hill to take a stand, and had worn only his helm and breastplate.

His men, finally convinced that their lord was getting the worst of the fight, decided to wait no longer. With bellows of fury and yelling, "A Warren, A Warren," they came to his rescue.

Rhys heard the battlecries and saw a wave of horsemen heading toward him. His own men turned and dug in, prepared to battle their foes. With a great clash, the opposing sides met, fiercely hacking each other with sword and lance. Many men were unseated and wounded horses went down. Scores of other Welshmen dropped out of the main body of troops to come to their aid, and the battle intensified.

Suddenly seeing an opening in the fray, Ralph Warren put his head down and plunged through the gap. Aware of this unexpected move, Rhys maneuvered about, his horse rearing as he pulled the reins up short. Swiftly he managed to change directions, and galloped after the fleeing knight. His men, who had dispatched a goodly number of their opponents, hacked out a path to follow him, shouting in their excitement as the promise of a chase quickened their blood.

Ralph Warren headed for the grove of trees where Jessamyn was sheltered, desperate to get her and take her with him before the Welshman found her. To his alarm, he found the Welsh horsemen almost on his tail, riding more skillfully than he had anticipated, easily maneuvering about the rough terrain, jumping gorse thickets to lessen the gap between them. There was no way he could outride them. He turned sharply, changing direction, riding away from the trees to save his own hide. He headed downhill, praying that his horse could keep its footing on this steep hillside.

Rhys suddenly found his way blocked by a challenging band of soldiers carrying Mortimer banners. They were forced to engage the hostile newcomers, squandering precious time before their way was again clear. By then, Sir Ralph Warren had disappeared from sight.

With an oath, Rhys charged in the direction his enemy had gone, riding downhill, his surefooted mount mastering the rough terrain. Behind him rode his men, but though they went to the bottom of the hill, they saw no sign of Ralph Warren. Their enemy had run to ground.

Rhys finally called off the pursuit, laboring back uphill to rejoin the battle. Why had Warren been riding so hard towards the trees, before changing direction? His first thought, that the English knight's followers were hiding there, proved false when they went out of their way to surround the grove of trees. As they slowly advanced, tightening the noose, they met not arrows and armed resistance, but the loud wails of frightened women. A score of women knelt in prayer on the loamy ground, fearfully beseeching them to spare their lives. Though the rape of captive women was considered one of the spoils of war, Rhys generally kept a tight rein on his men. Many Welsh leaders allowed their men to rampage through captured towns, taking whatever they wanted. Rhys knew that his men were often tempted to join in the savagery, yet his severe punishment of those who disobeyed orders, deterred them from testing him too often.

They skirted the weeping captives. When he came close enough to be heard, Rhys assured the women in English they would not be harmed. The half dozen soldiers who guarded them put up feeble resistance which was soon quelled.

Jessamyn watched the soldiers advance from under the shelter of a massive oak, set slightly apart from the rest. She refused to beg for her life. She could tell the soldiers were Welsh by their light arms and surefooted ponies. Harrowing tales were told of Welsh battlefield justice, for they generally took no prisoners; yet, she had heard just as many horror stories about English knights. Head held high, proud to the last, she steeled herself not to weep, though a lump choked her throat and her eyes burned. When the Welsh drew close she would ask them to take her to Rhys. Perhaps when they realized she was under his protection, they would treat her with respect. These men carried no banner, having just galloped from the thick of battle in pursuit of a fleeing man. She had watched the action from her vantage point, but was too far away to identify any of the chase's participants.

One man drew apart from the rest, and she assumed that he must have been their leader. He sat straight in the saddle, moving slowly toward her, for he had spotted her standing under the tree. As his black horse drew closer, her heart began a frenzied beat, for she suddenly knew who this man was—Rhys had come to rescue her!

With a cry of joy, Jessamyn ran toward him, picking up her skirts as she stumbled on the loamy ground. As he came closer, Rhys recognized her and spurred forward. Reining in, he leaped from the saddle and ran the last few feet, scooping her in his arms with a shout of joy.

"Jessamyn . . . oh, sweetheart . . . why are you here?"

Now he knew why Ralph Warren had been riding like the wind for this grove of trees. He had been going after Jessamyn. So the story he had heard, that Warren was bound for Shrewsbury, had been right. When he rode into Morfa Bach on his way south, he had learned from the villagers that their lady had been taken away against her will.

"Rhys . . . Rhys, I can't believe it's really you," she cried through tears of joy. "At last my prayers have been answered."

"Come, love, let me take you where it's safe."

Jessamyn unlooped Merlin's reins from a nearby tree branch and Rhys helped her to mount. Tansy stood hesitantly in the background, wondering if this Welsh knight could be the wonderful lover Lady Jessamyn had told her about.

"Tansy's with me . . . may she come too?" Jessamyn asked.

Rhys agreed to take the maid as well, but he told his men to let the other women go, cautioning them not to harm their captives. He had no use for a gaggle of weeping females on the road; they would only slow him down. Now that he had found Jessamyn unharmed, he intended to take her to Trevaron for safekeeping.

Taking only a handful of men with him, Rhys sent the others back to the fight. They rode through the stand of trees, plunging out on the other side on a ferny mountain path. Slowly they headed along the narrow track, winding uphill on the backside of the mountain. Sporadic fighting still went on, but the bulk of the English force had fled downhill, spreading over the bracken-clad slope with the Welsh in hot pursuit. The hillside was littered with dead and wounded. The higher up they rode, the fainter grew the din of battle. Here the birds sang in the trees as if nothing out of the ordinary had taken place.

They finally came to a low stone farmhouse where Rhys dismounted and took Jessamyn inside. A peasant woman and her daughter greeted him, wondering why Lord Rhys brought them a captive. When he quickly explained who the lady was and why he wanted her safe, they both nodded and smiled, agreeing to watch over her.

"Liddy Owen will care for you," Rhys assured her, as he handed Jessamyn over to the older woman for safekeeping. "I'll be back for you before dusk. There might be a lot left to do, so I must get back. Will you be all right? You're not . . . hurt?" he asked, stopping short of voicing the actual question on his mind.

Jessamyn knew what Rhys was so reluctant to ask and she shook her head. She had not been raped, though she dreaded telling him about her hateful ordeal at Curlew. That Sir Ralph had stopped short of penetration was a fact that Rhys might not overlook. For that unpleasant recital, there would be a far better time and place. Affectionately pressing his hand, she tried to ignore his gore-streaked clothing, rank with the stench of battle. The sight of Rhys besmirched in this manner was an unpleasant reminder of how hard and bloody the fighting had been.

"Now that we've found each other again, nothing can hurt me," she whispered sincerely, her eyes filled with tears of joy and gratitude.

He smiled softly, and stooping, gently kissed her mouth. "God keep you, my love," Rhys whispered, before he turned and strode outside.

Chapter Twenty

It was full light before Jessamyn saw Rhys again. When he did not come by dusk, she agonized throughout the long night, picturing all manner of tragedies. When she finally heard horses' hooves outside in the yard, she sobbed with relief as she raced to the window. There, in the bare yard, she saw Rhys and four of his men. He dismounted and came to the farmhouse door.

Possessing only what she had on her back, Jessamyn did not need to pack for the journey to Trevaron: she was already prepared for travel. Rhys had rounded up his men during the night and they were assembled for the ride back to Trevaron. The bulk of his force was waiting for him at the foot of the hill. Rhys seemed to be in a hurry to leave as he quickly embraced her, apologizing for making her worry over his safety. It had taken longer than he expected to take care of his troops in the aftermath of battle.

They mounted up and headed downhill. When they reached the waiting men, Jessamyn saw blanket wrapped bundles slung across a half dozen riderless ponies—Welshmen going home to their beloved valley for the last time.

It seemed strange that Rhys should be leaving for home within hours of fighting the battle of Bryn Glas. Rhys explained to her this was common practice amongst Glyndwr's forces. Many of his men were farmers and had pressing needs at home. As they were largely a guerilla force, there was no reason to maintain the army in the field throughout the year. Men came and went at will, so that the army's strength fluctuated from month to month. Between raids the Welshmen had farms to tend and crops to plant. When there came a call to arms, it took only a matter of days to round them up from the surrounding valleys.

Rhys still wore his battle-stained clothing and he apologized for his dirty, disheveled appearance. He had not shaved for days, and a stubby black beard covered the lower half of his face. This was a totally different man from the Rhys she was used to seeing, and Jessamyn studied him curiously, aware that if she was to become his wife, she would have to get used to his battlefield appearance. As long as the hostilities between the Welsh and the English continued, they would never know when Owain Glyndwr would recall his men to battle.

They rode hard for the north, the gruelling pace making conversation difficult. Rhys was familiar with the hilly terrain and knew many shortcuts. Jessamyn sensed a mounting barrier growing between them. Their conversation had become strained and this stern, gruff man was more like a stranger than ever. She puzzled over this unwelcome change in Rhys, not understanding its source, and was made uneasy by it.

Fortunately, they had met no further enemy resistance on the road. From the others, Jessamyn learned Glyndwr's camp followers had mutilated many English corpses, castrating them in revenge for the mass rapings which often accompanied the soldiers' retaliation on Welsh villagers for Glyndwr's rebellion.

In less than a week, they were riding through the high country to the north. Each passing day made Rhys seem even more of a stranger. Jessamyn puzzled over the reason for this estrangement between them. It had come after a messenger met them on the road, riding from Trevaron with a pouch of letters for Rhys. The man caught up with them on the road from Pileth, the second day out. After Rhys had finished reading the letters, his brows had drawn together in anger. From that day, their relationship had cooled.

Though this high country was spectacularly beautiful, in her present despondency, Jessamyn could not fully appreciate its beauty. Bluebells, wild pansies, foxgloves and cuckoo flowers tangled amongst the grasses. Narrow streams dropped in white, frothing ribbons down the steep gray mountain sides. The woods were carpeted with flowers, and the towering oaks were alive with birdsong. They were never far from the coast, and the cool air was sharp with the salty tang of the sea. They were surrounded by mountains; before them towered great Snowdon, its snowcapped peak covered by clouds. Sir Ralph had told her that Owain Glyndwr's camp was there in the Snowdonian Range, beside a mountain lake. Fortunately, he had not known the way to that mountain hide-out, or they might have meandered through the Welsh mountains in their search for Rhys.

That first night, when she told Rhys that Sir Ralph had vowed to kill him in revenge for becoming her lover, Rhys had laughed. He told her Sir Ralph had already had his chance to kill him at Pileth and failed. Apparently, Rhys considered the matter closed: Jessamyn was not as optimistic. Ralph Warren was a proud man. In his eyes, Rhys had despoiled that which he coveted most. She knew that his quest for vengeance would not be given up so easily.

Rain spattered against their faces as they put up for the night in a small hostel. The wind was heavily salt-laden. When Jessamyn licked her lips, they tasted of dried tears—a melancholy comparison which did little to lift her spirits. If Rhys was not going to discuss the content of those letters and clear the tension between them, she would.

A hearty fire glowed in the inn's small, oak-paneled common room, jammed to the rafters with soldiers. The food was plain, the ale flat, but the fire's pleasant warmth and a dry roof over their heads made up for the inn's shortcomings. The landlord told them it would rain until the tide had gone out, for the squalls generally came in with the tide and went back out to sea with the departing tide.

As usual, the only room for rent was assigned to Jessamyn and Tansy. Though Jessamyn was grateful for the comfort of a bed instead of sleeping on straw in the stables, this arrangement allowed no time to speak to Rhys in private. In the inn's noisy common room there was no opportunity to discuss the reason for his ill humor. If he would not come to her room to sleep with her, the least he could do was to come to talk.

When their meal was finished, Jessamyn caught his arm.

"Rhys, come upstairs with me. I must talk to you."

He looked down at her, his face impassive. "I don't think you'll fancy a man who stinks of battle in your bed," he dismissed gruffly.

"I said *talk*," she repeated, her temper stirring. "What else you choose to do is up to you."

A faint smile tugged the corners of his mouth. He nodded. "All right," he finally agreed, pushing back the bench.

The small sleeping room was directly under the slate roof. The sloping eaves made the ceiling so low that Rhys had to stoop in all but the center of the room.

No sooner had he shut the door and set down the candle, than Jessamyn confronted him.

"What's happened between us?" she demanded, her heart jumping erratically as she faced him.

"I just fought a hard and bloody battle, lady, I don't feel much like playing the courtier," he snarled.

"It's more than that. Something's gone terribly wrong between us. We're never alone. Every night you sleep with your men in the stables . . ."

"I assure you, because I don't sleep with you, it's not from lack of wanting to," he countered angrily.

"Sleep with me. You barely even speak to me!" she cried, her eyes flashing as her temper mounted. "At least have the courage to tell me why you're so angry. You owe me that much."

So determined was she, Rhys knew he could no longer evade the issue. "All right—I shouldn't have put it off this long. Sit down."

Uneasily Jessamyn perched on the edge of the feather bed, nervously winding the wool coverlet between her fingers whilst she waited.

Rhys picked up the candle and handed it to her. Then he reached inside his leather jack and took out several folded sheets of parchment. Just as she had guessed, the letters were to blame. Though he had not been overly communicative before he received them, whatever those letters contained had succeeded in destroying the remainder of his good will.

"How do you explain this? Here, read it."

Rhys handed her a stiff, folded paper with a broken red wax seal. Jessamyn's stomach pitched when she saw the insignia of the coiled serpent of Cater's Hill stamped in the wax. Just as she had supposed, the root of the trouble between them was Ralph Warren's announcement of their impending marriage. Quickly she scanned the concise note, hardly blaming Rhys for his angry reaction. From the wording, anyone would have thought that she and Sir Ralph had been sweethearts. His challenging postscript boldly invited Rhys to attend the nuptials— if he dared!

Rhys contained his anger until she had finished reading, then he burst out: "Hardly news of the sort to lift my heart, beloved."

"I knew he was writing to you. What can I say?"

"Tell me if it's true, damn it!"

"It's true, Ralph Warren wanted to marry me. And when I didn't agree, he took me captive. I'd little choice in the matter."

"That's all you've got to say?"

"What do you want me to tell you? That I was delighted by his offer, for God's sake," she cried, wounded to find him so lacking in understanding. "You know how much I hate the man."

"Hate him—you agreed to marry him, woman!"

"I never agreed. But, as you're aware, my consent isn't needed to make it legal."

Aghast, Rhys stared at her in shock. Through gritted teeth he finally asked the question he had dreaded asking. "So now . . . you're . . . man and wife?"

"No, there wasn't time for that."

"But I thought . . . after all these weeks you'd be wed."

"Why haven't you asked me before?"

He glanced away. "I was a coward. I was afraid of hearing your answer," he admitted.

"All that time on the road Sir Ralph was looking for you. We rode back and forth halfway across England and Wales. We would have been in Shrewsbury months ago were it not for that. Just once his injured pride served me well."

"You were with him all those weeks on the road?"

Though his question was simple enough, Jessamyn's annoyance mounted. His implication was plain enough. Had Rhys that little faith in her? "Yes, but I didn't sleep with him if that's what you're thinking."

By the visible relaxing of his tense jaw muscles, she knew her suspicions were right. Uneasily, she also knew that she deceived Rhys. It was true, she had not slept with Ralph Warren on the road to Shrewsbury, but she did not tell him about that hateful night at Curlew, when Sir Ralph forced himself upon her. The outward scars of that assault had long since healed; only the inner ones remained.

"Then, you're still mine, Jess?" he said as he came to her and knelt on the rushes at her feet. Taking her hands in his, Rhys raised them to his lips.

"I'll always be yours."

In the shadowy candlelight their eyes met and held, and Jessamyn saw his remorse for all the bitter thoughts he had harbored.

"I'm sorry, sweetheart. Jealousy robbed me of sense," he finally admitted. "I should have known you wouldn't agree to marry Warren, even to save Curlew."

Jessamyn smiled and gently stroked his stubbled

cheek. "Yes, you should have known, but I'm willing to forgive you. Oh, Rhys, darling, I've missed you so."

At first he smiled in pleasure at her touch, then his expression changed, his smile dimming as if a shutter had been closed over it. He took her hands from his face and stood up.

"Jessamyn . . . there's something else you have to know."

Eyes widening in alarm, she knew the stern gravity of his face foretold bad news. She wound her hands together in agitation as she asked, "Tell me . . . what is it?"

Rhys picked up the rest of the letters he had laid on the bed. The first two were reports from his stewards, which he stuffed back inside his jack. The third letter, and the one he had most dreaded giving her, was still in his hand.

"This came from Curlew," he said gruffly as he handed the letter to her.

With shaking hands, Jessamyn unfolded the stiff, crumpled parchment. The note was brief and she held it close to the candle's flame to read. She immediately recognized the small, neat handwriting of William Rhees, Curlew's steward.

To Lord Rhys of Trevaron:
Greetings, my lord. I am writing to inform you that Lord Walter Dacre has died of injuries received in a fall. We now have no lord of our own and are under Sir Ralph Warren's dominance. He has carried off Lady Jessamyn . . .

There was more, but Jessamyn could no longer see. A building wave of grief pounded her body as she considered the shocking news. The words contained such finality. Her brother was dead! Walter could even have been dead the morning she left Curlew. Was that why Sir Ralph would not let her say goodbye to him? She groaned as she pictured poor Walter lying injured and unattended.

Jessamyn sat with her head bowed, the tears flowing down her face. Rhys sat beside her to offer comfort, his arm about her shoulders. Jessamyn barely noticed his blood-stiffened clothing smelling of horses and travel; she knew only the warm comfort of the man she loved. For a long time she wept: deep, heart-wrenching sobs for her dead brother. She wept not as much for the man he had become, but for the child he had been.

When at last her sobs lessened, Jessamyn realized in her heart that she had already faced the possibility. The steward's letter had been a shocking confirmation of her worst fears.

"Ralph wouldn't even let me nurse him, or send medicine," she whispered brokenly, the reminder producing a fresh gale of tears.

Rhys rocked her and held her close for a long time, while the candle burned low in its dish. Finally he laid her across the bed and pulled the covers over her.

"I must get back downstairs, love. I'll send your woman up to you. Cry it out, sweetheart. You'll feel better."

Only at the moment of waking did she forget Walter was dead; then, as she came fully awake and remembered, Jessamyn began to weep again. She allowed herself the indulgence of tears, then drying her eyes, she steeled herself to put her grief behind her. All her anxiety about her brother's welfare could be laid to rest. Walter had gone to a safe place, free from pain. She prayed that Walter Rhees had seen to it that he was laid to rest, if not with honors, then at least with decency.

Her mouth tightened as she remembered what they had done with old Ned's body. Surely even Sir Ralph's mercenaries would afford the lord of Curlew more ceremony than that. At least she prayed that it was so.

Chapter Twenty-One

The sun hung low in the blue sky as they rode inside Trevaron's courtyard. The gates of Rhys's stronghold stood open to receive them, for their approaching party had been sighted hours earlier. The sun was partially hidden by thick woodlands as it slid over the far side of the mountain, its lingering, mellow gold rays burnishing the manorhouse's graystone walls.

Square and sturdy, the house's thick walls were built with masonry from an ancient castle, for Trevaron stood on the former site of the fortress of a warrior prince of Gwynedd. Trevaron commanded a splendid view of the green Llys valley, washed softly in sunlight. Glittering streams trickled down the hillsides to form a narrow, sluggish river which meandered over mossy wetlands abloom with yellow and blue flowers, growing so abundantly that they choked the shallows of the river itself.

All day, as they had ridden through the surrounding countryside, Rhys had been greeted joyously. Word that the men were home spread like wildfire through the hills and valleys. At the crossroads, and on mountain tracks, people came from their homes to greet them, weeping either in joy or sorrow as their men were returned to them.

During their travel through his remote country, Jessamyn had looked at everything with great interest, because anything which concerned Rhys was of interest to her. The unspoiled land was even wilder than the borderland surrounding Curlew. Wild mountain goats came down to the streams to drink; foxes, otters and pine martens abounded. Hawks and buzzards circled overhead in the blue sky searching for game. Underfoot, the lush grassland was brightly carpeted with wild flowers. Jessamyn had not anticipated the soft, summer welcome from this northern land, its climate tempered by a soft, westerly wind. Nor had she been expecting such joyful greetings from Rhys's tenants, their open affection telling her how well-loved and respected he was. In a way she felt as if she, too, were coming home. Her mother had grown up amidst these misty mountains, gathering herbs and accumulating the lore which had made her famous for miles around. Jessamyn felt that Gwyneth would have been pleased with her daughter's choice.

A half dozen dogs raced from the manor house to greet Rhys, turning somersaults of joy as their master spoke to them. Hounds and mastiffs became as tame as lap dogs in his presence. Laughing as he was continuously asaulted by the leaping, wagging, barking tumult, Rhys finally made his way to Jessamyn's side to help her dismount.

He held up his arms and she gratefully fell into them, letting him take the weight of her body against his. The tension had gone from his face. Being home again had acted like a tonic to smooth out lines and frowns. Standing in the soft light, Rhys looked younger and more vulnerable than she had ever seen him.

"Welcome to Trevaron, sweetheart. Bringing you home is something I've dreamed about ever since I first laid eyes on you," he whispered tenderly, resting his face against hers.

"I've dreamed about it, too. And everything's just as wonderful as I expected," she said with a sigh of pleasure. She stood with his arm around her, surveying his land. The sun had disappeared behind the trees, and shadows darkened the grounds surrounding the house. On the lawn stood a sundial, its elongated, purple shadow spreading across the grass. A semicircle of flowering shrubs framed the house and beyond that stretched a tangled woodland. The blackthorn hedges were hidden beneath pink briar rose and fragrant honeysuckle. Over their heads, homebound birds called as they swooped toward the trees, and in the distant valley, cattle lowed and spring lambs bleated for their mothers.

As Jessamyn looked around her at the land belonging to Trevaron, a shiver of pleasure went through her. Highly aware of the warm strength of her lover's arm about her waist, she smiled at Rhys. It was all like a magical dream, and she hoped her wonderful dream would not dissolve with the dawn.

"Come inside, love, you must be weary from traveling," he said softly.

Rhys led her through a heavy, nail-studded oak door. The house appeared smaller inside than she had expected, though the gatehouse of the original castle had been incorporated within. Walls of timber and graystone had grown up around the forbidding defensive fortress, softening its outward appearance with a deceptive air of domesticity. The manor's vaulted ceilings and sweet rush-strewn slate floors, reminded Jessamyn of Curlew. She wondered sadly if she would ever see her home again.

Trevaron's sparse furniture was carved from native wood. Armaments and hunting trophies covered the walls. Over the vast stone hearth was the head of a bristly wild boar with great, curving yellow tusks; a massive, evil-looking wolf with exposed fangs, glowered down at her from over the doorway.

"Did you kill those?" she asked Rhys in awe, as she surveyed the fierce creatures.

Rhys grinned. "You'd be surprised what lurks in these mountains . . . but no, those are from my father's day. When I hunt I don't save the spoils for posterity. Will you bathe and rest, or eat first?"

Jessamyn wanted to say neither, for she longed to finally be alone with him, yet she found herself bashful in the strange surroundings. As they moved about the house, Rhys's servants and retainers had eyed her with mingled curiosity and hostility. Obviously she was an Englishwoman, and it had not been explained to them if she was a spoil of the English campaign, or if she had come with their lord of her own will.

"Bathe, sup, and then . . ." Here she paused, smiling up at Rhys while she affectionately squeezed his hand.

The response in his dark eyes filled her with joy. There was no need to voice her desires, for his expression told her they were his, also.

Jessamyn was given the manor's best bedchamber and Rhys orderd a bath to be taken to the room.

Through the chamber window Jessamyn could see Snowdon's dark shadow in the distance, its cap of snow gleaming through the gathering dusk. Soon it became too dark to see anything more, and she turned back to admire her small, comfortable bed-chamber. The whitewashed walls were hung with red and blue tapestries depicting a biblical tale. A chest carved from ash and inlaid with holly in a tree of life design stood beneath the window. Soft, white, fleece-covered cushions made a padded window seat. The large carved oak bed had crimson wool hangings fringed in gold, and tied back with damask bands.

The maid who came upstairs to help her bathe spoke no English, but she chattered nonstop in her native Welsh. Jessamyn understood a little of her speech. Responding in stilted Welsh, she told the maid about Curlew and about the misfortunes which had recently befallen her. The woman seemed impressed that she had ridden such a distance, though she appeared to doubt that Jessamyn was truly the lady of an English castle.

When the metal bath was filled with steaming water, Jessamyn sank down thankfully in the heavenly, scented bath. She had not realized how filthy and travel-weary she was. Her hair hung heavy with grime and her skin was sticky with sweat.

As Jessamyn had no clean clothes of her own, the maid offered her freshly laundered linen undergarments and a Welsh wool gown of purple, trimmed in pine green. A soft green surcoat edged with rabbit fur was a welcome addition to the gown for, despite the fire struggling in the hearth, the room was chilly.

The garments fit her well enough and Jessamyn thanked the woman, wondering whose clothing she had borrowed. After drying her hair before the fire, she plaited it in a single thick braid which hung to her waist, and secured it with a purple ribbon.

After the maid left, and male servants had carried out her bath, Jessamyn wondered what she was expected to do. Would Rhys come up to her room, or should she go downstairs to join him?

When she opened the door, she found the corridor pitch dark. Two candles burned in a silver sconce beside the bed, and she went back to get them in anticipation of lighting her way downstairs to go in search of Rhys.

A tap on the door made her turn about, and her heart pitched in joy at the unexpected sight of him in the doorway. Rhys had also washed away the grime of travel and the stench of the battlefield. He stood with his jaw as smoothly shaved as when she had seen him that first day. He wore a dark wool jerkin and full-sleeved cambric shirt over black hose and boots. The simple dress made him look young and darkly handsome.

"Oh. Rhys. I was just coming downstairs to find you."

"There's no need of that, sweetheart. You surely didn't think I'd leave you to your own resources for long."

He motioned to someone in the corridor and a procession of servants entered the room, each with a special duty to perform. One woman carried in a heavy tray of food; another bore a flagon of wine and two cups. Behind them staggered a young lad burdened by an armload of logs, which he set in the hearth; he began to mend the fire. A second man carried a bedwarmer filled with live coals which he slid inside the covers of the big bed. In a matter of minutes, the servants completed their tasks and, each bowing in turn to their lord, they left the room.

Amazed by the speed and efficiency of the service, Jessamyn clapped her hands in delight. "Oh, how wonderful. We're to sup here, just the two of us."

Rhys grinned conspiratorially as he went to the door. Not sure what he had in store next, Jessamyn waited impatiently for his return. She could hear him speaking quietly to someone outside; there followed a strange squeaking, mewling noise; then he reappeared, carrying a large wicker hamper.

"Now, my lady, sit down while I present my gift. This is to make amends for my idiocy on the journey. I hope it suits you."

Smiling, and still not sure what to expect, Jessamyn waited expectantly as he knelt before her. Rhys looked so handsome in the fireglow, his dark hair crisply curling, his finely chiseled features made angular by the shadowy, dancing flames, she wanted to take him in her arms and cover him with kisses.

"What is it?"

"Open the basket and see."

Jessamyn undid the simple wicker latch. Aware that the hamper was moving, she half expected something to jump into her lap. Carefully she lifted the lid and peered inside, encountering two round, brown eyes gazing soulfully up at her. When she gasped in delight, the movement inside the hamper increased to such a degree that the hamper began to jump and slither about her lap.

"Oh, Rhys—a puppy!"

Jessamyn's eyes filled with tears of joy as she lifted out the furry black creature. The dog licked her face enthusiastically before it finally burrowed its head in the curve of her neck, nuzzling her warmth. When Jessamyn had confided to Rhys the story of Ned's terrible death, he had comforted her, knowing how deeply she loved her old dog. Aware of the empty space in her heart, he had given her this little black hound who was rapidly wiggling its way into the vacancy.

"Oh, thank you, love. He's beautiful."

Rhys knelt to take the dog from her, receiving his own share of licking and affection. "Betsi was due to whelp when I left. Luckily all went well, and I had a litter of six to choose from. He'll make a fine dog when he's grown. Not as big as old Ned, mind you, but large enough to guard you. Now, what are you going to name him—Ned?"

She shook her head. "No, that was his special name. This little boy deserves a name all his own. Maybe I'll call him Owain after your leader. Without him, we'd never have found each other again."

Rhys smiled affectionately at her. "That's right. If I hadn't been answering Glyndwr's call to arms, I'd never have gone in search of my fairy princess stolen from her tower."

Jessamyn smiled fondly at his foolishness.

The hamper held a soft red cushion and she laid the dog on his bed, and placed the hamper beside the hearth with the lid propped open for him to look out. The little dog made no move to climb out of the hamper, being content to gaze at the flickering fire as he dozed off to sleep.

"Thank you, Rhys. You know how much I loved Ned. This little dog will have an extra special place in my heart because you gave him to me."

Rhys stooped to kiss her mouth, his hand lingering on her hair. "You look like a proper Welsh woman in that dress," he remarked, admiring the sweep of the soft wool where it clung to her breast and thigh.

Smoothing her hand over the gown's skirts, Jessamyn said, "I don't know who to thank for the loan. All my clothes are somewhere in Sir Ralph's supply wagons, even the gorgeous dress you bought me in Chester. But I still have my brooch; luckily it was pinned to my gown."

"We'll get other dresses. All that matters is you're safe with me."

Rhys brought the trays of wine and food to the hearth where they ravenously set about their meal. Between them, they soon devoured a platter of roasted lamb in gravy, four Welsh cakes, leek soup, sliced fruitbread, spread thickly with freshly churned butter, and cherry and rhubarb flummery piled high with a froth of whipped cream.

Everything tasted so delicious, Jessamyn could not believe she had eaten so much. At first she thought the juniper–and–honey–flavored wine, tasted strange. However, partway through her second cup, she began to enjoy it, discovering the mixture to be far more intoxicating than she had expected.

Their meal was finished, the crumbs shared with the puppy who had fallen asleep, his head hanging over the basket. Jessamyn sat in the flickering firelight and did not remember ever feeling so content. Absently, she stroked the little dog's head smooth as silk beneath her fingers. She touched its plump body, finding it extremely muscular beneath the shining black coat. Though he appeared to be asleep, when she stroked the puppy, he affectionately nuzzled her hand.

"This is one of the happiest nights of my life," she whispered to Rhys, leaning back against his warm strength as they sat before the fire. The wind had risen and it moaned eerily down the chimney and rattled the shutters, making her draw instinctively closer to her lover.

"Tomorrow I'm going to introduce you to my people," he promised, stroking her back and shoulders as he spoke. "They'll be so proud of their lovely new lady."

"New lady?" Jessamyn questioned, her eyes widening in surprise. "Have you already broken off your betrothal with Eluned?"

"I said I would. After all, it was nothing more than a formality, despite your worries to the contrary."

"What did she say?"

He shrugged. "In public she was icily polite. What she said in private was probably unrepeatable. Anyway, it's done now, so let's not spoil tonight by talking about Eluned. Come, sweet, make love to me under my own roof. It's a pleasure I've long anticipated."

Jessamyn had not realized that Rhys's breaking his commitment to Eluned Glynne would be so easy. Now there was nothing in the way of their marriage. Thank the Lord, Ralph Warren was miles away in England.

Jessamyn smiled as she relaxed against him, while Rhys slowly aroused her, the heat of his hands penetrating her wool bodice and setting her breasts tingling with anticipation.

"We can be married then?"

"As soon as you wish. Next week if you want."

"Rhys, may I ask a favor of you?"

He kissed the top of her head. "Of course, ask away."

"That we wait to be married at Curlew?"

He whistled. "It might take some time until we can get rid of Warren. Must it be so?"

"Traditionally Dacre marriages always take place there. I'd like to uphold the tradition, seeing as I'm the last of the line. I don't mind waiting."

He kissed her brow, pleased by her faith in him. "As you wish, though we might get tired of waiting when our hair starts to turn gray."

"It won't be that long," she dismissed with a smile; she reached up to stroke his face. "Oh, sweetheart, I love you so," she whispered, trembling as his hands grew more possessive. "Now you're all mine . . . I can't believe it's true."

"Neither can I. Oh, Jess, you're all I've ever wanted in a woman," Rhys whispered, tilting back her head to kiss her soft, inviting lips. "Come to bed with me. Don't make me wait any longer for you."

They left the fire, arms around each other's waists, their desire fanned by the arousing thought of making love to each other. There was not the frenzied haste they had sometimes known in the past, because they knew they had all their lives ahead of them to love and kiss. That night was only the beginning.

With shaking hands they helped each other disrobe, laying their clothing aside on the wooden chest. The room's chill atmosphere brought goose bumps to Jessamyn's bare flesh and she leaped inside the bed, discovering it was comfortably warm, heated by the pan of coals. She allowed herself to sink into the goosefeather mattress, snuggling beneath a mountain of down and wool covers.

Rhys knelt beside the hearth, putting an armful of logs on the fire to keep the room warm whilst they slept. He had already taken off his jerkin and shirt and Jessamyn admired his broad shoulders and muscular back rippling in the golden firelight. She shuddered with anticipation, longing to feel his arms around her, to hold him against her in an intimate embrace. When she was running back and forth across England as Ralph Warren's captive, she had never dreamed such bliss could be hers again. All those miserable weeks were behind her, and she had the soft, summer sweetness of the Welsh valley to look forward to, shared with the man she loved.

When Rhys turned from the hearth Jessamyn held out her arms, eager to embrace him. With hammering heart, he quickly divested himself of his remaining clothing. Kicking aside his hose and black leather boots, he padded over the rushes to the big, curtained bed where she waited with outstretched arms. He found the prospect of his lovely woman eagerly awaiting him to be highly arousing.

Rhys slid inside the covers and Jessamyn pulled him into her arms. Tears of happiness trickled onto his bare shoulder as she held him close. This arousing embrace made their bodies throb with passion as their hearts pulsed as one.

"For ever and ever, I swear, you are my only love," Rhys vowed huskily, holding her face in his hands as he kissed her soft mouth. "Never think I'll forsake you, Jess."

Eagerly she answered his kiss, thrilling to the heat of his mouth. Throbbing with passion, she ran her hands over his smooth, muscular back, and down the broad, hard sweep of his shoulders. With trembling hands she reacquainted herself with the splendor of his virile body.

Rhys slipped his hand between them to cup her full breasts, shuddering with pleasure at her quivering response, gently fondling, cupping the weight of her flesh before he teased her nipples erect with his thumb.

"Oh, love, it's been far too long," he breathed, suddenly aroused to heights far beyond his expectations. "All these nights I've longed to make love to you."

"Why did we wait? It didn't really matter whether you were clean shaven or splendidly dressed," she whispered, her voice hoarse with longing. "That we love each other is all that matters."

His hand slid between her legs and she opened to his caress, excited by his knowing touch. Suddenly the unwanted memory of Ralph Warren's assault shot through her mind, of his hateful, demanding touch. Shocked, she tried to force the picture away. This man was her lover; the only man she had ever wanted. Forcing herself not to shrink from him as the heated, arousing probe of his flesh tingled between her legs, Jessamyn tried to dispel the memory which marred her pleasure. This was Rhys, whom she loved and trusted, whom she welcomed with open arms. She had longed for him in the darkness of the night. When Rhys slid inside her body, when the full pressure of his flesh expanded inside her own, the unpleasant memories dissolved. With joyous abandon, Jessamyn allowed Rhys to rekindle all the desire she felt for him. Gradually she was borne upwards on wings of passion, carried far away from conscious thought and unpleasant memory, feeding only on the white heat of his love.

Chapter Twenty-Two

Sunlight slanted through an arrow slit high in the wall, spearing the heavy laden banquet table with golden shafts of light. The central hall belonged to the crenelated old castle built by Meredudd, Prince of Gwynedd, who had once laid claim to all the Llys valley. The manor house had been constructed around the forbidding gatehouse, making that portion of Trevaron austere and forbidding. If Trevaron were attacked, it was there the family would make its final stand.

Such dismal thoughts cast a momentary damper over Jessamyn's pleasure. Shrugging her melancholy aside, she turned to smile at Rhys, her heart leaping with pleasure as she saw how handsome he looked. Rhys wore a red damask doublet edged with fur, with a heavy, gold medallion and chain bearing the likeness of Owain Glyndwr around his neck. The fluted design of his feast day doublet emphasized his broad shoulders and slim waist. His silk hose and soft leather boots were black.

Rhys looked as magnificent as a prince, Jessamyn mused, completely besotted with him. So deprived had they been of luxuries during their recent travels, she had almost forgotten how handsome he could look. In the dim light, the glint of the gold chain about his neck and the gold rings on his slender fingers made Rhys's olive skin appear dark as a gypsy. His black hair had been newly barbered and was layered to the base of his neck in crisp waves gleaming dark as a raven's wing.

Jessamyn's own gown was borrowed, though Rhys had assured her that they would soon attend to her wardrobe. That morning, sewing women had come to her room to measure her for new gowns. Though she did not expect they would be stylish like the gowns she had seen in Chester, Jessamyn was pleased by the prospect of new clothes. No choice of fabrics had been presented to her, so she assumed that she would have whatever the seamstresses had on hand. The other women wore finely woven Welsh wool, spun from the abundant sheep dotting the hillsides, and dyed soft shades of purple, blue, red, and green.

Jessamyn wore an ivory brocade gown with a red, quilted satin band around the hem. The gown had belonged to Rhys's mother; with its narrow skirt, high neck, and trumpet-shaped sleeves, it was very old-fashioned. But the girdle about her hips was gold, and the regal gown made her feel very grand. The previous day, one of the serving women had produced Lady Eirlys's feast day gown for her approval. Apprehensive, in case Rhys was annoyed that she was wearing his mother's gown, Jessamyn had gone downstairs nervously seeking his approval. He had smiled so fondly at her that her heart had leaped for joy. She was sure he must have recognized the gown, yet he did not remind her to whom it had belonged, merely telling her that she looked every inch the fairy princess.

As Jessamyn reviewed this incident, she smiled in pleasure, reliving his warm touch and the unconditional acceptance in his eyes. Rhys loved her without question. And she was still not used to the wonder of it.

Rhys stood, holding up his hand for silence. The diners paused amidst the remains of roast venison and stuffed capons, brownly crackling in great pewter dishes on the red covered tables.

"I want to introduce to you my future wife—Lady Jessamyn Dacre, the daughter of our own Gwyneth of Trevaron. She's come home at last to her ancestral land."

Jessamyn nervously wondered if she would see acceptance or hostility in the sea of faces at the trestle tables ranging the length of the Hall. All the soldiers and the tenants under Rhys's rule had been assembled at Trevaron to share the homecoming feast to welcome back their lord from the English war. Hair-raising tales had been passed around the Hall, retelling the heroic exploits of the men of Trevaron. Jessamyn was highly aware that she was an Englishwoman, and as such, considered one of the enemy.

Biting her lip, she smiled at those gathered there and said in her very best Welsh, "I'm very pleased to have come home to Wales."

Surprise, shock, then overwhelming pleasure transformed the sea of faces from strangers to friends as a roar of approval echoed around the high-raftered room.

Rhys laughingly hugged her against his side, discarding the former restraint he had always displayed before his men.

"Oh, *cariad*, you know just the right thing to say to make them accept you," he whispered, hugging her tightly. "They love you as one of their own."

Cups were raised and a toast was drunk to the new lady of Trevaron. Other toasts soon followed, to Lord Rhys for his safe return, and for the many valiant exploits of their soldiers.

Jessamyn sat down, growing light-headed as the non-stop round of toasts continued.

There came an unexpected commotion at the door and the celebrants, pausing in their hearty good fellowship, turned to see who was the late arrival.

A bright blue shaft of color appeared in the shadows. Then the blue took form and shape as a woman in a dazzling blue gown marched through the Hall to the High Table.

All heads turned and there was much commenting and whispering as Eluned Glynne headed to the lord's dais. She stopped directly before Rhys.

"Good day, Eluned," he said evenly. "Have you come to welcome us home?"

She glared at him, her eyes blazing points of blue fire. Her gaze shifted next to the woman at his side, and her face whitened in rage. Raising her hand, Eluned jabbed an accusing finger at Jessamyn.

"I see you're entertaining Ralph Warren's whore. I thought you had better taste than that, Rhys."

A startled gasp rippled around the Hall, followed by silence. Though Eluned had spoken in Welsh, Jessamyn understood enough of the language to translate her insult. Color blazed across her face, and she clenched her fists beneath the red table cover. How she longed to slap Eluned's haughty face, to make her apologize for what she had said, yet Jessamyn was too afraid of what the other woman knew to openly assault her.

His face dark with anger, Rhys leaped to his feet.

"If you've come to welcome us home, then take a seat. If, instead, you come to make trouble, Eluned, you're not welcome here."

"You've no need of me to make trouble. You're adept at making your own by bringing that strumpet home to Trevaron. Don't you know she belongs to Ralph Warren?"

Fists clenched, Rhys cried, "Go and leave us in peace. Or must I have you thrown out?"

"I'm not the one you should throw out. You only broke off our betrothal to whore with her. I won't let you go so easily. The contract's still binding to me."

Rhys motioned impatiently to several of his men who had been watching uneasily, unsure of how to handle the situation, for Lady Eluned's family was important in the district and they were careful not to insult her.

"We no longer have any ties between us. Show Lady Eluned to the door; she's not fit company for our celebration."

"And you think *her* fit company?" Eluned cried, jabbing her finger at Jessamyn. "I've brought you proof of her infidelity. Will you be fair enough to hear me out?"

Jessamyn had risen now, tugging at Rhys's arm, aware of his mounting anger. She had no idea what trick Eluned had up her sleeve, or who she might produce to validate her claim. A terrible sense of foreboding had gripped her, for she guessed that Eluned Glynne was not making empty threats.

"Please, Rhys, no," she pleaded, tugging at his red sleeve.

Angry beyond redemption, Rhys shook off her hand. And leaning forward, he growled, "You'd better substantiate your claim, Eluned. You have my attention."

Jessamyn dropped back in her chair, feeling as if all the life ebbed from her, leaving her body limp and worn. Like a slowly unfolding nightmare, Eluned turned to face her, a triumphant smile on her face.

"Just ask her if she ever slept with noble Sir Ralph. Go on, Rhys—or are you afraid of her answer. If she's innocent, she just has to say so." Eluned smiled in triumph, her eyes glittering as she beheld Jessamyn's horror. Her high cheekbones were bright with color as she urged, "Come now, tell the truth, Lady Jessamyn, for if you lie, I've someone here who'll prove you false."

"Jessamyn has no need to answer your outrageous charges. If you've nothing better to say than that, you'd best leave us," Rhys thundered, finally nodding for his men to remove Eluned from the room.

Miserably Jessamyn sat there, staring down at her trencher, wondering what she could possibly say to defend herself. All eyes were on her now, the spectators' attention switching back and forth from her, to Rhys, whose lean face was tense with anger, and then to Eluned, who was smiling sweetly as she pushed aside the detaining hands. She beckoned to someone in the shadows.

A woman emerged, walking apprehensively towards the High Table. And Jessamyn's last hope died. She recognized Bertha, one of the Curlew maids. The woman currently warmed Captain Jackson's bed and was no friend to her. On several occasions, Jessamyn had chastised her for slovenliness. Bertha was later caught stealing, yet she had a crippled mother to support and Jessamyn had hated to turn her away without a means of support. Her own kindness had proved her undoing.

"Tell Lord Rhys who you are and where you come from. Go on, don't be afraid," Eluned directed, giving the woman a nudge forward.

Nervously Bertha twisted her apron in her hands as she glanced about at the strangers.

"I'm Bertha Locket, my lord, a maid at Curlew Castle."

"Why are you here?"

"That lady sent for me last week," Bertha replied, turning toward Eluned.

"Do you know this woman, Jessamyn?" Rhys asked, seeing that her face was white as a sheet.

"Yes, she's a maid at Curlew," she agreed painfully. Why had Eluned sent for the woman the previous week? She could not have known in advance when she would arrive at Trevaron. In fact, how had Eluned even known about her involvement with Ralph Warren?

"Come, out with this so-called evidence—our meal goes cold," Rhys snapped.

"Go on, tell Lord Rhys what you told me."

"The lady—Lady Jessamyn—was going to marry the English knight what captured the castle."

"I know that much already," Rhys dismissed with a sigh of relief. "If this is your startling evidence, you'd best be gone, both of you."

"Wait!" Eluned stepped forward, grasping Bertha's shoulder; she shook her impatiently. "Don't be so dense, woman. Tell him what we talked about."

"That Lady Jessamyn had Sir Ralph in her bed chamber. 'Twas all over the castle the next day . . ."

"That's enough!"

Rhys turned to her, and Jessamyn thought she would die with shame. If only she had told him everything in the beginning, there would have been no need of this terrible scene. If Rhys had been forearmed, he wouldn't be looking at her now with that terrible accusation in his eyes, showing all his hurt and pain.

"Is what she says true?" Rhys demanded, his voice tight, a nerve in his jaw in spasm with the stress of the situation. "Did you and Warren spend the night together?"

"It's true that Ralph Warren tried to rape me . . . that's the only time he was in my bedchamber. Doubtless the guards and servants assumed I welcomed him . . ."

Jessamyn's voice faded as a collective gasp circled the room, the news being swiftly relayed to those too far away to hear her tearful admission. An excited buzz of conversation spread the length and breadth of the Hall. Jessamyn was so ashamed as she recalled the hated intimacies of that night, as she imagined the bawdy jokes and stories which must have made the rounds of Curlew the following day. All her pleasure and joy in the banquet had been destroyed.

"Rape, indeed. I ask you, Rhys, what did you expect her to say. There was never anything of rape mentioned to me."

"That's right, my lord, there weren't no rape to it," Bertha agreed indignantly. "I'll swear to that on the Bible if you wants."

"That's not necessary. Eluned, get out. You've already done your worst," Rhys growled, his face stormy.

"Worst? Oh, no, I've only just begun. You're too proud to want Ralph Warren's leavings. We'll be married yet, my love, despite her trickery."

Not waiting to be thrown out, Eluned pushed aside the guards' restraining hands and stalked through the Hall, her head held high.

Bertha was left alone before the High Table and, suddenly growing afraid of what might happen to her, she burst into tears and fled from the Hall, following Lady Eluned.

Though the silence was brief, it seemed to Jessamyn that it lasted for hours. She grew aware of her heart thundering so hard, she thought she could not draw breath. Her whole body ached, and she could not look Rhys in the eye and face the hurt and accusation she knew was there.

"Jessamyn, if you want to go to your room, we'll excuse you," Rhys said icily, making no move to escort her there.

Numb, she rose, her knees shaking, her legs feeling too weak to support her. A maid came out of the shadows, her eyes wide in alarm as she glanced from Jessamyn to her lord, wary of the anger on his face. Quickly she urged Lady Jessamyn from the room, not knowing what Lord Rhys might do next.

Stumbling, blinded by tears, Jessamyn managed to reach her room, repeatedly tripping over the hem of her gown, stumbling on the stairs, until the maid had to guide her. At last, in the privacy of her room, she gave in to a fit of weeping, throwing herself across the bed and crying as if her heart would break. It was so cruel to have this bitter truth come between them now that Rhys had finally pledged his undying love. She had brought terrible shame upon him. Surely Rhys would believe her side of the story, but even of that, she was no longer sure.

It was already dark when she heard his tread on the stairs. Twilight had come and gone, and she without a candle. She lay in the darkness feeling stunned, her emotions drained by hours of weeping. Had she lost the man she loved? Was there never to be an end to her trials?

Rhys pushed open the door. He was carrying a candle, the halo of light dancing across his face, revealing the stern set of his features, the hard line of his mouth and jaw.

Quietly he closed the door, and she jumped up, moving to the head of the bed. Defensively she shrank from him, half expecting him to lash out at her for the humiliation he had endured before his followers.

"Is what Eluned said true? Were you Ralph Warren's whore?" he asked her point blank.

"You know I wasn't," Jessamyn whispered miserably, her voice thick and hoarse from weeping.

"I thought I knew you. Now I'm no longer sure. If you'd nothing to hide, why did you keep this from me?"

"Nothing to hide? Dear God, only a man could see it that way," she groaned miserably, burying her face in her hands. "He mistreated me. He stripped and fondled me, made me feel filthy and used. Had not nature tricked him, he would have raped me, and I could not have stopped it. I never wanted *anyone* to know what had happened."

"Not even me?"

"I intended to tell you—when the time was right."

"Would it ever have been right?"

Miserably she shook her head. "I don't know."

"Well, by God, that's honesty for you."

"Do you believe me?"

For a moment he said nothing, then she felt his hand on her shoulder. "Yes, I believe you. Only I wish you'd told me all this in private. Then we needn't have endured a public scene."

"Oh, Rhys, I always meant to tell you, only I was too ashamed."

"Hush, don't cry," he whispered in comfort, staring at the dancing candle flame as he tried to quiet the turmoil in his heart. How would he explain this to his retainers? Would they be willing to accept

Jessamyn now, after Eluned's damning accusation?

"Why did she do it?" Jessamyn whispered through her tears, sobbing into his red doublet.

"Jealousy. When I dissolved our betrothal I wounded her pride. She imagines she's in love with me, though in the past, she always treated me like last year's cloak."

"How could she have known about Ralph Warren? Why would she even ask about him?"

Rhys shook his head. The same questions had been puzzling him, also. He knew how cunning Eluned could be, and the fear he had felt at Chester had surfaced again. He would not put it past Eluned to have contacted Warren and told him when Curlew would be left unprotected. She would use any means at her disposal to defeat a rival.

"It wasn't wholly a lie. You did spend time with him in your bedchamber."

"Only because he forced me to it. Surely you don't think I'd take pleasure in him?"

He pressed his face against her hair.

"When that serving woman stood there, bold as brass, and denounced you, I admit I had a niggling doubt . . ."

"Oh, Rhys!" she gasped, dashed that he should have so little faith in her. "Must I swear on the Bible, like she proposed? Will that convince you I'm telling the truth?"

"Nay, love. I'm already convinced," he said remorsefully, as he held her close. "We'll let our people think Eluned made trouble out of jealousy. They know this man kidnapped you and I rescued you from him."

"How can I face them again? It wasn't my fault that he tried to force me to bed him. Eluned made it all sound so sordid, as if I enjoyed him night and day."

"Come, love, don't cry anymore. We'll put this behind us. I won't let Eluned spoil things for us, however hard she tries."

Jessamyn buried her face in the warm fragrance of his neck, her tears still falling; she wanted to hide there from the world, far from jealousy and spite. Time would tell if Rhys's tenants and soldiers believed she had told the truth. Her heart ached for Rhys, almost as much as for herself. He had been shamed by having his lady's morals publicly questioned.

Eluned was walking in the garden of her manor at the other end of the valley. She still seethed with rage. When her spy, a maid from Trevaron, reported to her that Lord Rhys and Lady Jessamyn were happily together again, she bubbled over with fury.

This was unthinkable! How could a proud man like Rhys accept such public humiliation and still keep that woman at his side? The least she had expected from him was that he put the slut away. Knowing men's despicable cravings, she had been prepared for him to visit Jessamyn Dacre on the sly, at least until the fire cooled, but never to keep her openly at his table and in his bed. That woman enjoyed all the privileges of the Lady of Trevaron! The only thing missing was their marriage ceremony to complete this outrage.

When she had paid Simkin, the peddler, for any gossip he could learn from Curlew, she had not been expecting so juicy a reward as Jessamyn Dacre whoring with Ralph Warren. This had seemed the perfect weapon to turn Rhys away from that woman. And she had failed.

Eluned was so angry that her legs were too shaky to continue walking. She sat abruptly on a nearby rock wall, wrapping her cloak about her, for the wind blowing off the mountain was cold. She looked out over the green valley toward the dark blur of Trevaron at its southernmost tip, half hidden by woods. Damn the woman! Now she was openly enjoying Rhys both in and out of bed. What must she do to rid herself of the witch? She was a witch indeed, for how else could she withstand such obstacles? Mixing her brews and potions—likely Jessamyn Dacre had bewitched Rhys with black magic, or fed him daily potions to keep his interest alive. She could spread the rumor that Jessamyn was a witch. Yet, the results of that approach might take too long.

Ralph Warren had captured and lost her. That fool Rhys was well and truly under her spell. Even the revelation of her unfaithfulness had not dimmed his pathetic need for her. Black magic had to be the cause. After all, she was far more beautiful than Jessamyn Dacre, more splendidly dressed, better at everything, and men did not show *her* such devotion.

Viciously Eluned plucked the petals from a spray of dog rose which twined about the tumble-down wall. She would have liked to snatch Jessamyn Dacre's hair from her head, to tear her body limb from limb. Why, in God's name, had Ralph Warren proved to be such an inept soldier? Had he been half a man, he would have locked her in the deepest dungeon, where she could never escape. If Jessamyn Dacre were her prisoner, she'd make the witch pay dearly for stealing Rhys from her.

Eluned jumped up as an idea shot through her mind. It was not a new thought, and in the past even she had shrunk from so decisive a step, but if she were to triumph, the situation called for sterner measures. Her mistake had been in relying on men to carry out her plans—foolish, love-smitten men.

And they had both failed her. This time, she would rely only on herself. The pleasure and relief of her decision lightened her step and brought a smile to her face.

The black puppy chased a small wooden ball across the floor, finally losing his toy in the rushes. Desperately he began to dig, pieces flying everywhere as he searched for his plaything.

Jessamyn laughed at his foolishness. When he found the ball at last, Jessamyn tossed it in the air; leaping high to catch it, he turned an unexpected somersault and landed in a heap under the table.

Beside her Rhys laughed, also, glad that she took such pleasure in his gift. Since the unpleasant confrontation the night of their welcoming banquet, Jessamyn had been much quieter. Rhys had tried to show her patience and understanding, knowing it would take time for her to forget the scene and the assault which provoked it. They both wished that neither had taken place, but wishing did not make it so.

A servant came to speak to Rhys, his head bent low as he whispered a message to his lord.

Jessamyn glanced up, for Rhys swiftly looked in her direction as he spoke, and she wondered what was amiss.

When the servant had left, Rhys said, "Jess, sweet, will you humor me?"

"Humor you?"

"Aye, apparently Eluned and her brother have brought gifts to placate us."

"Oh, no, Rhys—not again."

"I promise, there'll be no denunciation tonight. Besides, what would be the point? There's no audience," he added, with an uncomfortable smile as he glanced about the virtually deserted Hall.

"I suppose, if it will please you," she agreed at last, though her stomach had begun to pitch. She wanted to vent her pain and anger on the other woman, but knew that hospitality precluded such displays. If this was a peace offering, she must accept it as such and hold her tongue.

Nervously Jessamyn waited for Eluned and her brother to come inside the Hall. She quickly brushed pieces of rushes from her wool skirt and patted her hair to make sure it was not loosened from its fastening. Doubtless, Eluned would be splendidly jeweled and dressed in the height of fashion, in contrast to her own simple gown. Could she not leave them alone? Why would a woman keep pursuing a man who didn't want her? Then, Jessamyn had to smile at her own naivete. When the man was Rhys, the answer was plain. She loved him so intently; she knew that if she were the spurned woman, she would not be able to accept the truth that he no longer wanted her, and would keep fighting for him with her last breath.

To her surprise, when she viewed Eluned Glynne in that same light, it helped to lift some of the hostility she felt towards her.

Eluned finally walked inside the Hall, looking ravishing, swathed to the eyes in a scarlet, fur-edged cloak. Jessamyn gasped at the sight of Eluned's elaborate hairdressing, all wound about with ribbons and pearls. Her gown, revealed as a servant took her scarlet cloak, was soft, sea green silk, billowing with silver tissue which lined the long hanging sleeves and trimmed the surcoat embroidered with lilies and roses. The gown must have been worth a fortune.

Rhys smiled as he stood to greet their guests. He exchanged a hearty handshake with young Bryn. As she watched, Jessamyn breathed a sigh of relief, for she had not known whether Eluned's brother shared her animosity. Apparently Bryn was accepting of Rhys's change of mind.

"Will you take a cup of wine?" Rhys asked, sending a servant for wine and cups before he ushered his guests to the fire.

The black puppy bounced up and raced towards them, excitedly tripping on the rushes and falling at their guests' feet. Eluned's eyes narrowed as she correctly guessed the animal was Rhys's gift to Jessamyn.

"Isn't he lovely?" Jessamyn asked fondly as she restrained the puppy from his boisterous welcome.

"Yes, so young." Eluned moved the dog with her satin shod foot and chose a cushioned chair before the hearth. "I've brought you a peace offering, Rhys," she said charmingly. "A skin of fine wine which Proctor gave me at Christmas. I've been saving it for a special occasion."

"Well, if you've come to apologize for causing that unpleasant scene, it's a special occasion indeed," Rhys remarked sarcastically.

Bryn laughed, delighted by his humor.

Eluned scowled at them both. "I said a peace offering," Eluned reminded them pointedly, her face tightening. "In the basket are honey cakes and marchpane for you, Jessamyn, all the way from Chester."

Jessamyn forced a smile. "Thank you, Eluned, that's most kind of you."

"The gifts are all her idea," Bryn explained, still not over his surprise that his sister should wish to make amends. Everyone in the surrounding valleys knew about that night. The story, much embroidered, with time had assumed legendary proportions.

"This is probably as close to saying she's sorry as Eluned will ever come. You'd best enjoy it while it's offered," Bryn added in an undertone to Jessamyn, as he sat beside her on the bench.

She smiled at Bryn, immediately liking him. He was probably no more than seventeen, blonde like his sister, with fine features and hazel eyes, in contrast to her blue ones. He was not as pretentiously dressed as she, wearing a plain brown, cloth doublet and hose, though the belt slung about his slim hips was made of gold links interspersed with pearls.

"Here, Rhys, you must eat some of this, too."

Eluned took out of the basket a plate of decorated marchpane figures. Taking one first, she bit into it, as if to demonstrate the food was not poisoned. Though Jessamyn knew that Eluned could have chosen a figure which she knew was safe to eat, when she handed one each to Rhys and Bryn, she decided the confections must have been harmless. Eluned hated her with such fury, Jessamyn would not have put anything past her.

While they ate the marchpane, a servant brought in wine cups. Bryn was telling Rhys an involved story about his new hunting dog, who was swifter than any hound he had ever seen. While the two women eyed each other warily, the men laughed and remained oblivious to the current of hostility generated between them.

"I didn't know the true story about that night," Eluned said at length, her face fixed in a simper. "You'll just have to forgive me."

"You should have made it your business to learn the truth before you created such a shameful scene."

"So, you still bear me malice," Eluned snapped, her eyes flashing.

"I bear no malice toward you. I'm merely reminding you of the truth," Jessamyn replied carefully.

"Rhys has accepted my account of the incident, so no lasting harm has been done—except to our pride."

Eluned's face tightened. "Ah, I know well enough how that feels. Don't you think I was humiliated beyond belief when Rhys broke our betrothal?"

"You cannot *make* a man love you," Jessamyn reminded her evenly, wishing that Rhys and Bryn would involve them in their conversation, and relieve her of the unpleasantness of entertaining Eluned alone.

"*You* seem to have managed that well enough," Eluned accused. She swept to her feet to place a skin of wine on the table. "Here's the special brew from the royal cellars, given to Proctor in consideration of his loyalty to the king," she remarked smugly, aware of Rhys's loyalty to Glyndwr.

Bryn had taken the puppy onto his lap and was playing with it, his hand in its mouth. The puppy growled in delight, gnawing his fingers, then fastening his teeth on Bryn's sleeve.

Eluned carefully poured out the wine, filling their cups half-full—small cups for the ladies, slightly larger ones for the men.

"Bryn, put the dog down! You'll spill the wine. And this is all there is," Eluned cried shrilly.

Bryn leaned down, the growling puppy still fastened to his cuff. Rhys and Jessamyn pulled the puppy's plump body in an effort to disengage him; the puppy held on even harder.

While the others were distracted, Eluned swiftly tipped a white powder into one of the smaller cups, stirring the wine with her finger until the powder disappeared. Then she set the cup at Jessamyn's elbow.

Suddenly the dog let go and Bryn sprawled over the bench, arms flailing. Rhys shouted a warning and quickly rescued the wine cups as the dog dived at Eluned and landed in her lap, yapping excitedly. She squealed in distress, trying to protect her face from being licked. Amidst much laughter, her brother managed to save her, pulling the wiggling dog off his sister's grand gown.

Rhys motioned to a servant to take the excited puppy from the Hall.

"I thought you liked dogs. He wouldn't hurt you."

"Not in my new gown," Eluned said stiffly. "He'd likely piddle all over it."

Bryn laughed. "I'd like to have seen that. Eluned would have screamed the place down, I'll be bound."

"If your clothes cost as much as this gown, you wouldn't be as easily amused, brother," Eluned snapped, quickly scanning the wine cups. To her horror she saw that in the uproar, they had been displaced from where she had set them. Perhaps a few inches, she decided, her heartbeat slowing. It looked as if someone had nudged the cups, for wine had spilt on the table and trickled in a fine red stream to the rushes. Damn that dog! If he hadn't been allowed to run riot, nothing would have happened. Still, there appeared to be enough wine left in the cup, so that all could proceed as planned.

"Now that the dog's gone, let's drink a toast to your future happiness," she proposed sweetly, smiling at Rhys, her eyes bright above the rim of her raised cup.

"Yes, let's be friends again," Rhys said, raising his own cup. Jessamyn and Bryn followed suit.

"Excellent wine," Rhys commented in surprise, savoring the unusually delicate taste. "You must thank Proctor for me."

"I thought it a trifle bitter," Eluned remarked peevishly, taking a second drink. "Mayhap it spoiled on the journey."

"Nay, it's good wine. Let's drink a second toast to Rhys and Lady Jessamyn. May their life together be happy," Bryn said, holding his cup high and clinking it with the others.

"Aye, happiness together—for as long as it lasts," Eluned added in an undertone. She drank a little more of the wine, finding that her throat had grown unusually dry. Typically, she was the only one with discerning taste; excellent wine, indeed—it was as raw as the cheapest tavern brew. Then a horrifying thought struck her—her wine had tasted bitter! Mayhap hers was the only cup to taste that way! Mayhap this was the poisoned cup! Her heart thundered in shock as she contemplated the possibility.

"Was your wine slightly bitter, Lady Jessamyn?" she asked sharply.

"A little—'tis likely the marchpane. We should have eaten the sweet afterwards." And Jessamyn wondered at the dawning smile of relief on Eluned's face.

"You women, with your bitter wine—too particular by far," Bryn dismissed. "I'm ready to compare the king's brew with some good Welsh ale. What say you to that, Rhys?"

"That's an idea after my own heart." Laughing, Rhys sent a waiting servant to bring them a jug of ale.

"I hear you're soon to be wed," Eluned said, when the men were temporarily distracted as they examined a sword Rhys had retrieved from Bryn Glas.

"Does it surprise you?"

"Nothing *you* do ever surprises me, Jessamyn Dacre. With your potions and cures, one might even suspect you of witchcraft, so quickly have you changed my love's heart."

Jessamyn gasped in shock. It did not bode well to bandy about the word *witchcraft* in this region.

She had learned that much in the short time she had been there. The Welsh had a great dread of witches. Many legends abounded about evil spirits, werewolves and ghosts inhabiting caves and forests. One might expect such superstitious fears from the peasants in a misty mountain land, but not from the ruling class.

"Surely you don't believe in witches. That's for peasants," Jessamyn retorted quickly. Had she thought long and hard about her answer, she could not have chosen better words to wound proud Eluned.

Drawing herself up to her full height, Eluned glared at her. "How dare you suggest I'm a peasant!" she cried.

"Not in your person, lady, only in your beliefs," Jessamyn corrected her, secretly glad that she had struck a blow to the other woman's pride. The damage had not been intentional, though Eluned usually put her on guard, sharpening both her wit and her tongue.

"Likely Rhys will think twice about marrying someone suspected of black magic," Eluned spat. She wiped her brow, finding her face unusually hot. The palms of her hands were clammy with sweat, and she could barely control her rage that a strumpet had chosen to match wits with her.

"We're going to be married at Curlew, so everyone will have ample time to see that my cures are only for the good."

"Oh, indeed," Eluned snapped, unable to think of any clever retort. Her mind was fuddled and her composure slipped with the imposition of having to deal with this creature on an equal footing. How could Rhys and Bryn put her in such a difficult position while they swilled ale and discussed the recent battle? It was an insult to leave her to entertain this

Patricia Phillips

Jezebel who had stolen her betrothed from under her nose.

Unsteadily, Eluned got to her feet. Drawing herself up to her full height, she announced icily, "Bryn, we must leave. The company bores me."

Her brother cocked an eyebrow at her insulting words. He shrugged by way of apology, for he understood that Rhys was privy to Eluned's ways and he need not explain.

"We'll be on the road then," Bryn said reluctantly. "Are you to invite us to your wedding, Rhys?"

"There's just to be a simple ceremony here. The actual marriage is taking place at Curlew. It's Jessamyn's wish, and I'll honor her request."

"Oh, good, so we can make a two-week revel out of it," Bryn suggested, finding the prospect most appealing. "I might even go on to Chester. I'm in need of some . . ."

"Are we to stand here gossiping all night? Say good night and let us go," Eluned interrupted. That woman had made her feel positively light-headed with rage. Well, the shoe would soon be on the other foot. She would grow light-headed, sick to her stomach, then very, very sleepy. But it would be a sleep from which Jessamyn Dacre would never waken. Once she was gone, Rhys would be hers again.

Dwelling on the pleasant prospect of Jessamyn's death was immensely satisfying. Eluned took her rival's hand; it was the least she could do for the wretch, considering that she would not live to see the dawn.

"Congratulations on your achievement," she whispered, her smile distinctly unpleasant. "May you long enjoy him."

Jessamyn murmured good night and was heartily glad to see the back of their unpleasant visitor.

"*Nos da*," Rhys called, as the couple disappeared into the shadows of the far end of the Hall.

"*Nos da*," Bryn called in reply, though Eluned chose not to speak.

"Oh, thank God, they're gone," Jessamyn sighed in relief, finding her tension slowly ebbing away. "We've made peace, now let us never entertain her again." Her limbs had stiffened as she had braced herself for Eluned's verbal assault. Now that the woman was gone, she could let go of all the built-up hostility and tension.

"Yes, you were wonderful, and I'm grateful for your generosity. I didn't want to drive any more wedges between her family and mine by refusing to let her in. Bryn's a good lad and bears us no malice. On the whole, I thought she behaved well under the circumstances—for Eluned at least."

Jessamyn smiled. Rhys had not heard Eluned's veiled threats and insults. She would not burden him by talebearing. She hoped this would be Eluned's final visit to Trevaron.

"Well, possibly—for Eluned," she conceded, slipping her arm around his compact waist.

Rhys smiled down at her. "Tomorrow I'm going to announce our coming marriage. Everyone will be given food and a measure of ale to drink to our health. Perhaps that'll make up for their missing the big event. You're still sure you want to wait until we can be married at Curlew before your priest?"

"Positive, unless you intend to desert me in the meantime."

"No. We'll already be man and wife by civil law. They practice handfasting in these parts—every bit as binding, if we choose, as a religious ceremony."

Shocked, Jessamyn looked up in alarm. "And what if you don't chose? What's the time limit to change your mind?"

"A year." He was laughing at her. Rhys hugged her, then swept her off her feet. The telltale beginnings of anger flashed in her hazel eyes as she pummeled his chest, anxious to iron out all the details of this strange arrangement whilst there was still time. "Please, lady, don't batter me to death. I swear, I won't change my mind. You have my word on it."

And beyond that he refused to say more.

Chapter Twenty-Three

On a fine July morning, when the trees were alive with birdsong and the air was fragrant with the scents of grass and foliage wet with dew, Rhys and Jessamyn were officially promised to each other in a brief outdoor ceremony beneath the towering oaks.

Bards in flowing white vestments praised their lord in song and fable. Then the chief bard sang an original composition of many verses in praise of his lady. The Welsh was flowery and Jessamyn understood little of it, but Rhys was visibly pleased by the tribute. Stirring songs of his ancestors' prowess in battle followed, with an extra few verses tacked on to the narrative to recount his own bravery at the battle of Bryn Glas. Accompanied by sweet harp music, these songs floated over the wooded hillsides, continuing the centuries-old tradition amongst his people.

This lengthy ceremony smacked of paganism, for the chief bard crowned them both with twisted mistletoe boughs tied with ribbon. Jessamyn recalled that mistletoe had been a sacred druid plant and the reminder made her uneasy. As the white-robed chief bard intoned a lengthy prayer, she nervously fingered the small gold cross around her neck, just to be on the safe side. She smiled at her own foolishness. Rhys was a well-traveled, educated man. These ancient rituals were more meaningful to his people than to him. Yet, when she looked sideways at him and saw the serious set of his features, the gleam in his dark eyes, she knew his ancient Welsh beliefs had not been eradicated by travel. In his veins ran the blood of the princes of Gwynedd. He shared his ancient heritage with warriors and bards, for his ancestors came down from the mists of time, when they had roamed the barren hillsides and called all Britain their own.

Following their handfasting, Rhys welcomed several young men into the sacred band of warriors. Solemnly the lads knelt before their lord and promised him fealty unto death. He took his great two-handed sword, passed down through many generations, and moving it over their heads, he rested its tip on each of their shoulders in turn. One by one, the lads stood and kissed their lord on the mouth to seal their bond.

So solemn, so silent were these budding warriors that shivers ran down Jessamyn's spine. She sensed such a feeling of continuity, of ancient times, gone but never forgotten. Rhys's ancestors were revered in song and story; his own exploits added to the saga to thrill many generations to come. Never before had Jessamyn realized the burden of lordship which rested on his broad shoulders. Rhys needed sons to continue his line. A thrill shot through her veins when she contemplated it was she who would provide that continuing link to his ancient Welsh lineage. The enormity of what she had heard and seen had given her a great feeling of pride.

At dusk that same day, word reached them that the Lady Eluned Glynne had fallen ill and died! Poison was suspected in her sudden death, but no one had suggested a murderer.

Jessamyn was stunned by this unexpected news—and relieved to such an extent that she could have wept. Eluned was gone where she could no longer revile and torment her. It was strange, for the previous night Eluned had appeared well and she had certainly been in voice with all her accusations and insults. How could she have sickened in the space of one night?

When she voiced this question to Rhys, she added in hushed tones that she hoped Eluned had not been the victim of plague, bringing the malady to Trevaron with her basket of goodwill offerings.

"Nay, I don't think you need fear that. They say she could have been poisoned," he said at last. He had been deep in thought, staring into the fire while he puzzled over some disturbing factors. "Jessamyn, remember how Eluned was so particular about placing the cups just so, pouring the wine herself, setting out small cups for the ladies, bigger for the men?"

Jessamyn shrugged. "What of it? Eluned always had to have things her own way."

He gripped her hand, and leaning forward, said intently, "I suspect it was done for a far more sinister reason."

"I don't understand. You think she intended to poison you?"

He smiled softly at her and stroked her cheek. "Not me, love—you!"

Eyes wide in shock, Jessamyn looked at him, seeing he was deadly serious. "And you think she drank the cup meant for me?"

"Remember when the dog was leaping about, I moved our wine out of harm's way. I may have exchanged the two smaller cups without thinking. Oh, sweetheart—it could have been you! She meant to kill you!"

Appalled, they looked at each other, their faces registering fear and shock. Rhys pulled Jessamyn into his arms, holding her tightly, his heart thudding uncomfortably as he reviewed his startling conclusions.

"If you died, Eluned thought she'd have me back."

"I remember her asking me if I thought the wine bitter," Jessamyn recalled, her hands starting to shake. She clasped them firmly to stop the tremors. "After eating the marchpane, everyone's wine probably tasted bitter."

"Why do you suppose she gave us the sweetmeats first? Eluned knew enough about wine not to serve it last. God, what a trusting fool I was. By thinking to patch up old ties, I endangered your life, sweet. I trusted that treacherous bitch!"

"No, shh," Jessamyn whispered, placing her fingers against his lips. "She's gone where she can't hurt me now."

They held each other tightly, weak with relief that Eluned had made a fatal mistake. Instead of a solemn handfasting ceremony beneath the oaks, Trevaron could have been preparing Jessamyn's funeral, laying her to rest on the hillside amongst Rhys's ancestors. This shocking and sobering thought was an uncomfortable reminder of their own vulnerability.

Out of respect, Rhys attended Eluned's funeral. Her maid had reported that her mistress had been mixing several potions, which she was told were love potions, for Lord Rhys and herself. Though

Rhys knew otherwise, he allowed Eluned's grief-stricken family to think that perhaps Eluned had accidentally poisoned herself with this home-brewed concoction.

As he rode back to Trevaron, his men riding silently beside him, Rhys wondered how the Glynnes would have reacted had he told them what he suspected was the truth behind Eluned's accident. Better that they not know Eluned's final act had been an attempt to murder her rival.

For Jessamyn, daily life at Trevaron evolved into a comforting, predictable pattern. A courier, returning from Curlew at Rhys's behest, brought her news of home and a smuggled bundle of Jessamyn's precious possessions; her herbal, which she needed to mix medicines to cure the ailments of Rhys's tenants, her set of silver engraved hair brushes; some sentimental keepsakes belonging to her mother; and her treasured French romance.

With a smile of pleasure, Jessamyn turned the book's stiff pages. She no longer needed to pretend she had a place in those pretty pictures, for now she had her own courtly lover who far surpassed the lovelorn gentlemen, both in looks and actions. Rhys had become her minstrel and courtier, her lover, her everything. Pray God he would never be taken from her.

The year of handfasting was almost over. Sometimes Jessamyn teased Rhys about his decision. It was the beginning of July and soon the official time limit to their agreement would expire. If there was no child, and regrettably Jessamyn's stomach was still flat, either party had the right to terminate the agreement. Though she did not doubt Rhys's love for her, Jessamyn could not wholly dispel a niggling fear that he might have grown tired of her. Lately they had settled into such comfortable domesticity: he, administering his lands and people, and regularly drilling his men in fighting skills; she, taking charge of the domestic details of the manor, and the establishment of an infirmary to treat people from the surrounding valleys. Following in her mother Gwyneth's footsteps, Jessamyn's reputation as a healer had spread far and wide. She was relieved that she heard no mention of witchcraft when people spoke about her cures, merely a healthy respect for her herbal remedies.

Just in case there should be any suspicions, Jessamyn was always careful to participate in all church ceremonies. This she did as a hedge against accusations, and also out of concern for her own soul. Though Rhys's people professed Christianity and kept priests in the district, Jessamyn found them alarmingly pagan in their customs and beliefs.

At the end of their full days, it was pleasant to be able to sit with Rhys and exchange the day's news over supper. Then, when it grew late and the fire burned low, she lay in his arms in the privacy of their bedchamber. Their passion for each other had not cooled and she still reveled in his skillful love-making. This peaceful, comforting existence was as close to paradise as she ever expected to find on earth.

Her blissfully uneventful existence was cut short one thunderous July day. The sky behind Llys mountain was black, the still air heavy with the impending storm. Jessamyn was gathering herbs from the small herb garden on the manor's south side, when a rider skidded to a halt before the gate, shouting for admittance. He carried a summons to arms—Owen Glyndwr was rallying his troops for battle!

This startling news shattered her well-being. When the storm finally broke, the rain slanting in sheets across the face of the mountain, pouring down the gulleys and battering the oak woods with its fury, the deluge mimicked her tears.

In a matter of hours, Rhys was prepared for the road. His men were assembled just as quickly, for the nature of their service to Glyndwr demanded that they maintain a constant state of readiness.

Gulping back her tears, with determined steps Jessamyn marched to the infirmary. There she hurriedly packed several bags and baskets with herbs. She could readily guess what would be most in demand—pain-killers, mixtures to stop bleeding, and poultices to draw out festering wounds. She had almost finished when Rhys strode into the room, already dressed for travel, wearing his metal-banded leather jack over a dark doublet, and carrying his helmet in his hand.

"There you are. I've been searching for you. Oh, good, you're sending a supply of medicines with us. Likely we'll be needing them. They say Glyndwr's allied himself with the Scots and the great northern lords. Harry Hotspur himself has come to our side. Now all we need is someone to tend to our scrapes and makes us good as new," he remarked cheerfully, forcing all apprehension from his voice for her sake.

"You've got someone."

"Oh, who are you sending?"

"Me."

"You! No, I'll not agree to that!" Rhys cried, grabbing her arm. "You must be out of your mind to think I'd let you come."

"Aye, and shortly to be out of our contract. You need someone to tend the wounded. And I need you. I'll not twiddle my thumbs here for years waiting for you to come back."

Taken back by her determined voice, Rhys slackened his hold on her arm. The steely glint in her eyes and her set face told him a battle royal was forthcoming if he tried to change her mind. Would it really be so bad? She could stay in the rear, well-protected, and they would certainly benefit from her skill.

"I've ridden with an army before, and I was in the midst of a battle," Jessamyn reminded him, seeing that he was weighing the situation carefully.

"That's right, I'd forgotten."

"So, I can do it again."

Still he stood fast, warring between his sense and his heart. They did not always engage the enemy on these forays. Sometimes a town or encampment was struck at night, allowing them to melt back into the forest under cover of darkness. Battle might almost be enjoyable with his spirited woman at his side. Though Rhys did not expect Jessamyn to wield a sword, he knew her well enough to have learned if the need arose, she could use a dagger as well as any man.

Finally he agreed. "Only if you promise to do exactly as I say."

Jessamyn pulled a face. "Only if you promise not to give me foolish orders I can't obey."

They grinned at each other and clasped hands.

"A bargain, lady. Dear Lord, help me, for I think I'm going soft in the head."

She grasped his arm, propelling him towards the packed baskets and bags. "That might well be, but before you get soft in the arms, carry these outside for me, there's a good lad."

"At once, my lady." Rhys gave a half bow and hefted a bag on his shoulder and picked up the wicker basket. He had not noticed before that Jessamyn wore her cloak and a serviceable gown. He wondered what she would have done had he refused to let her come with them. He grinned as he stepped outside into the warm, rain-sodden afternoon. If he did not miss his bet, Jessamyn would have saddled up and followed them.

Their journey to England almost took the form of a royal progress, as they stopped for the night at castles and manorhouses loyal to Glyndwr. They picked up many supporters along the way, until the men of Llys grew very optimistic about the success of their cause. This time, King Henry Bolingbroke would have to listen to Welsh demands for fair treatment under the law. They were not just a ragtag band of Welsh farmers, but an organized rebellion. Rumors abounded. Glyndwr had allied with the French. The Irish were soon to join them, their chieftains merely awaiting the word. The Scots had already thrown in with them, for it was rumored that Earl Douglas's army was riding through Cheshire recruiting men. Glyndwr's force was set to rendezvous with the other elements of their army at Shrewsbury and capture the city.

Jessamyn did not remind Rhys that Cater's Hill lay close to Shrewsbury, but in private, she dwelled on that unpleasant fact. It was too much to hope that Ralph Warren would forgo the excitement of battle, especially when it was so close to home. His old hatred of Rhys still smoldered and she anticipated that Warren would seek him out from amongst Glyndwr's troops with the intention of killing him.

Because Rhys carried the Flowers of Llys, a banner well known to Ralph Warren, he would be an easy mark. Jessamyn prayed the two would not meet again on the battlefield. At Bryn Glas, Rhys had been spared; the odds of that happening again were too unlikely for comfort.

On their journey south, they passed within a few miles of Curlew. From Arden Hughes, Jessamyn learned that Curlew's garrison was poorly manned, for Sir Ralph's men grew fat in their master's absence.

The farmer and his wife greeted her like a long-lost relation, thanking her again and again for helping them during the birth of Meggy's son. Meggy had grown plump and contented during the past year, and she embraced Jessamyn warmly before proudly introducing her sturdy son, who preferred toddling after chickens to bowing to Lady Jessamyn.

They spent the night at the farm. Rhys assured Arden that he and his men would return when the time was right and recapture Curlew for Jessamyn.

Meggy was thrilled to find Jessamyn so happy. When Meggy kept referring to Rhys as her new husband, Jessamyn's conscience pricked, for she knew in the eyes of the church they were not yet wed. She told Meggy that after they took back the castle, she and Rhys would repeat their vows before Father Paul in Curlew's Great Hall, in keeping with Dacre tradition. And she invited the Hughes family to the ceremony as her special guests. Meggy was delighted with the news.

When they prepared to leave the following morning, the farmer's wife pressed a plaited, corn fertility symbol into Jessamyn's hand.

"Here, my lady, this will do the job for you," she whispered conspiratorially, closing her lady's fingers around the object so the men couldn't see. "Your man's very fine, so likely 'tis you who needs the help, I used this to get my little lad."

Not wanting to hurt Meggy's feelings, Jessamyn did not point out that Father Paul denounced such pagan beliefs. She thanked the farmer's wife and slipped the corn symbol inside the chatelaine hanging from her waist.

Meggy beamed. "That's right, milady, keep it

always on you, especially at those times—under the pillow will work fine." She nudged Jessamyn's arm and went into a fit of giggles, and was still laughing when they waved the travelers on their way.

"What was that woman laughing about?" Rhys asked curiously, as they headed uphill to the highway.

"She gave me a fertility symbol because you haven't been doing your job properly," she teased, with a wicked grin.

"If I do it any better, I'll not have strength enough to fight," Rhys dismissed with a scowl.

"Well, you surely didn't expect me to tell her that."

He laughed and reached out to affectionately clasp her hand, then pulled away to direct their wagons around the bend in the narrow road.

July was exceptionally stormy. Heavy rains beset them all the way into England. To Rhys's surprise, they had not met any more troops heading toward the rendezvous at Shrewsbury. He had taken many shortcuts, possibly putting him out ahead of the others, but he still found it strange that there was no sign of Glyndwr's gathering army.

On the road he learned that Harry Hotspur had been in Cheshire since the ninth of the month, recruiting men to Glyndwr's cause. Hotspur now rode beside his traditional enemy, the Scottish Earl Douglas, both having united with Glyndwr because of their mutual dislike of King Henry Bolingbroke. The Great Percy still smarted over the king's unfair dealings. The powerful border lord had fought bravely in his battles against the Scots, who frequently harried the border country, taking captive many important nobles. The wily and financially embarrassed king had kept the massive ransom paid to free Earl Douglas, without giving Percy any of his rightful bounty. This was insult enough for the powerful border lord to decide King Henry had become too unreasonable to support. Joining with other enemies of the king, he hoped to oust Bolingbroke from England's throne and place there in his stead the young Earl of March, who was next in the line of rightful succession.

With these powerful allies on his side, Owain Glyndwr's army was bolstered, both in strength and spirit. A showdown with King Henry was expected to take place at Shrewsbury.

As they drew nearer to Shrewsbury, they met hordes of soldiers milling about the countryside, bloody and battered after fighting a battle outside the city. The rebel plans had gone completely awry. Glyndwr had failed to show with his army, leaving Douglas and Hotspur to defend themselves against the king's troops, who had taken the city and locked out the rebels. From these scattered troops, Rhys got confused accounts of a huge battle, the rebels greatly outnumbered by King Henry's men. The sky had rained arrows, the barrage constantly refueled by thousands of skilled archers gathered to the English cause. Bolingbroke's son, Prince Henry, had been shot in the face with an arrow. Following this battle, many powerful captives had been executed.

Now hundreds of fleeing soldiers choked the narrow roads leading from Shrewsbury, constantly harried by parties from the king's victorious army.

After hearing this devastating news, Rhys wisely chose a quick route across open country, hoping to lead his men safely away from the danger of these retaliatory troops. Jessamyn rode hard beside him, wondering why Glyndwr had not met with the others, as arranged. Many accusations of cowardice were leveled at the Welsh leader. Others laid blame for his delay on the recent heavy storms which had flooded some roads and made travel difficult.

They rode without stopping until they had passed Ludlow. Only then did Rhys think it safe to camp for the night. There was barely any daylight remaining when they camped inside a tumble-down barn to await the dawn.

The green Herefordshire countryside was misty in the early morning light as they headed southwest. Rhys had it on good authority that Glyndwr's troops were massed near Leominster, and he was heading for that city. Black and white Herefordshire cattle stood in the pastures, drenched by mist, watching their clattering flight. Soldiers from Bolingbroke's army had been spotted the previous evening and they had to keep on the move, or risk being caught in a disastrous rear action.

Still riding across open country, keeping clear of the highways and taking cover in woods when necessary, Rhys managed to stay out of the way of the king's harrying troops. A relative of his mother's lived in the vicinity, and Rhys asked directions from a nearby farm to the home of Lady Catherine Vere of Oxley Holden. He was gambling that the lady would shelter them for the night, helping them escape detection.

Some might term his actions cowardly, he mused, as he rode along, yet by this means, he hoped to survive to fight again. Lacking war machines and hundreds of heavily armed knights and warhorses, Glyndwr's army was forced to conquer by guile what they could never have hoped to win in a pitched battle.

Lady Catherine Vere was an old, white-haired lady who barely remembered her niece, Eirlys, Rhys's mother. Nevertheless, she willingly offered them hospitality, for she had no love of Bolingbroke, her family being loyal supporters of King Richard. She gave them sleeping space in the barn, food for the men, and fodder for the horses. To Jessamyn and Rhys, she offered her best room in the old stone manor house.

Jessamyn found unexpected pleasure in being able to sit before the fire, for the summer evenings were chilly, and in being able to sup without constantly looking over her shoulder for approaching troops. Through the broad windows, Jessamyn glimpsed banks of color amongst the trees. The grounds of the manor were laid out in bays of flowers bordered by clipped hedges and neat, flagged paths. There was a large sundial on the lawn, and statues of various saints enclosed in niches in a tall, ornamental bay laurel hedge.

"May I walk in your garden, Lady Catherine?" Jessamyn asked, when their meal was over.

"By all means. It's past its prime, I'm afraid, but still lovely," that lady replied, patting Jessamyn's arm affectionately. "You're a garden lover, too, I see."

Jessamyn did not tell her the only real gardens she had seen were pictures in a French romance.

Rhys walked beside her, enjoying the pleasant respite from danger. The evening sky was washed with gold, turning to milky turquoise in the west, where the dark outline of the Welsh hills was visible on the horizon.

They walked along the flagged paths, holding hands, relishing the abundant fragrances brought out by the recent rain. Flowers lay drenched in the grass, their blooms shattered by wind and rain.

As they rounded a corner, Jessamyn squealed with delight and began running. Wondering at her excitement, Rhys sprinted after her. There, at the end of the stone path, stood a wooden garden seat surrounded by masses of crimson roses huge as goblets

The Constant Flame

and so fragrant that the heady scent hung like a cloud in the air.

Hands clasped in rapture, Jessamyn stood there, hardly able to believe the beautiful sight was real. Rhys came up behind her and slipped his arm about her waist.

"Your rose trellis. They could have used this as a model," he said, recalling her favorite illustration in her French romance. "I said I'd show you a rose garden someday," he said, hugging her against his side. Slowly Rhys turned her about, pointing out the neat oval borders where rain-drenched shrub roses cascaded to the ground in showers of pink, white and red blossoms. Carefully pruned smaller bushes formed a cross of color—orange, yellow, pink, white and red. The spectacular garden was like nothing either of them had ever seen before.

"It's really true. They don't just exist in a book," Jessamyn marveled. "Can we pick a few of the roses to take with us?"

Rhys agreed, assuming that Lady Catherine would not miss a handful of blooms. They stood under the heavily perfumed arch, and Rhys swore as rose thorns tore his fingers. Jessamyn took his hand to kiss his wounds. He handed her a bouquet of roses and she buried her face in their heavenly scent, breathing deeply the intoxicating fragrance.

"Now I've seen everything," she sighed, looking around at the lovely garden. "Do you think we could take cuttings of some roses and grow our own?"

"I don't know why not, providing Lady Catherine will be so generous."

"I'll ask her tomorrow. To have a rose garden would give me so much pleasure."

"If it gives you pleasure, I'll move heaven and earth to give it to you," Rhys said softly.

The tender expression on his handsome face, the

419

softness of his dark eyes revealed his deep love for her. When she looked up at him, Jessamyn's heart pitched. She laid her bouquet of roses aside on the wet grass and eagerly slid inside his embrace.

"Thank you, Rhys, for loving me so well," she whispered, her voice husky with emotion.

"Oh, sweet, you're so easy to love," he answered, kissing her closed eyelids, her nose, her cheeks.

His warm mouth aroused deep emotion within her and Jessamyn pressed hard against the strength of his body. Rhys straddled his legs, so that their thighs met and the stirring heat of his arousal pressed against her, exciting her beyond measure.

"If we were both to die tomorrow, I'd thank God for having given us this time together . . . our year of happiness."

"Always love me, Jess, whatever happens, wherever we go."

"I will. I promise."

Rhys drew Jessamyn to the garden seat, pressing her close. The throbbing heat of his body, the exciting pressure against her thighs, aroused her to deep emotion. Rhys devoured her mouth, his kisses like fire. Jessamyn's limbs grew heavy with passion. She ached for his lovemaking, for their hurried flight had given them little time for romance.

Overhead, a twittering flock of homeward-bound birds made a passing shadow across their faces. Jessamyn shuddered, considering the black shadow an unlucky omen. Dismissing her morbid thoughts, she hugged Rhys closer, chiding herself for becoming far too Welsh of late, always seeing omens and magical signs.

"Love me, Rhys," she invited him huskily, pressing hard against his swollen heat burning into her thigh. "I've never made love under an arch of roses," she whispered, tantalizing him with the tip of her tongue, tracing his mouth and cheek.

"You're too eager by far," he teased, pulling slightly away from her, tormenting her in return.

With an indignant snort, she pulled him back against her, biting his earlobe in retaliation. Pressing hard against his exciting body, she began to move rhythmically against his wonderful swollen heat which promised so much delight. She shuddered with passion as he swelled even larger, freshly aroused by her actions.

Rhys slid his hands over her breasts, stealing inside her gown, tweaking open the lacings of her bodice to allow access. There, he buried his mouth in her soft white flesh, kissing her breasts, moving his tongue teasingly about her nipples until she gasped in pleasure.

The purple shadows lengthened in the rose garden at Oxley Holden, until only a glimmer of gold remained in the sky. Gray night clouds gathered beyond the trees. The breeze stirred the roses, and fragrant scarlet petals rained down upon them and formed a carpet around the bench.

Jessamyn opened her eyes to admire the fragrant beauty of the secluded garden, knowing that she would always remember this night as long as she lived. A little shiver of apprehension accompanied her thought, and again, she chided herself for her foolishness.

Pressing her mouth against his, she slipped her hand inside his clothing, shivering in delight as she clasped her fingers around the blazing heat of his organ. Jessamyn fondled his silky, smooth flesh.

Rhys had swept up her skirts to stroke her thighs, touching that silky, secret place. Jessamyn moved urgently against him, motioning for him to dally no longer. Smothering her with kisses, Rhys unfastened his clothing and in a burst of renewed passion, their flesh met. Deep shudders of desire beset them as the fiery heat of his manhood slipped between her thighs, her flesh chilled by the evening breeze. When Rhys slowly slid home, Jessamyn arched her back, trying to take him deeper. She did not notice the wooden garden seat ridging her back, or the showers of rose petals shaken down by the movement of the bench; she knew only the exquisite arousal of her lover's magnificent body and the satisfaction of his lovemaking.

Urging him on, Jessamyn delighted in his deep, hot thrusts of passion, touching every nerve ending of that most sensitive part of her body. She felt the delight searing deep, inside the very core of her being. Kissing him, grasping his muscular back, she matched her rhythm to his until they moved as one, swept along in a dark flood of passion as deeply consuming as death. Jessamyn soared high, before plunging down, holding Rhys tightly against her as tears coursed into her hair—not tears of sorrow, but tears of deepest fulfillment as they became one in heart, soul and body.

They rode toward Leominster through a morning shower. Jessamyn's precious rose cuttings were wrapped in wet sacking inside one of the wagons, packed round with wood chips and bearing written instructions on how to plant and care for the treasures. When she pictured the rose garden they would grow at Trevaron, Jessamyn virtually hugged herself with delight.

Rhys smiled as he watched her, pleased that she was so happy with this simple gift. It was strange that they should be happy, considering that they rode cross-country in an effort to ditch King Henry's troops, and to rendezvous with Glyndwr to prepare for yet another battle. They were together, despite all odds. And Jessamyn loved him. Besotted as he was, Rhys realized he must seem a bit of a fool to his men, yet on reflection, he recalled that some of them had sweethearts at home, lovely girls who made men's hearts and bodies sing. The only difference between the men and their lord was that he had brought his sweetheart with him.

The first group of Welsh soldiers were spoted at noon. They had stopped to shelter from a heavy shower, and suddenly saw dark shadows cresting the brow of a nearby hill. Hands on their swords, alerted to possible danger, the men waited. Then their lookout shouted in joy as he saw a pennant bearing a Welsh dragon carried at the head of the force.

From the newcomers, Rhys learned that an army of English knights were only a few miles away, riding in pursuit of the scattering rebels. There was little chance they could outride them, so Rhys looked over the surrounding countryside for a suitably defensive position. The other Welshmen came from Merioneth and rode with their lord, Griffith of Nels. Together, the two leaders dispatched their combined army to make the best of their small force.

Jessamyn tried to fight her fear that Rhys would be wounded. For the past few days, she had tried to ignore a mounting feeling of apprehension, dismissing it as an unhealthy preoccupation with omens and such. Her mother had possessed the Celtic gift for foretelling events, and Jessamyn shuddered to think that she, too, had inherited this gift and was now being forewarned of doom. Danger, within reason, was something she could handle—over doom she had no power at all.

"Take care, sweetheart. Don't be a hero," she whispered, as Rhys sent her to the rear of the troops with the guarded wagons. Men from both armies milled about, saluting her, aware that she was the wife of Lord Rhys, and not some camp follower. Their own women kept their distance. She was not one of them, and was despised for her elevated rank.

"What a warning—every man wants to be a hero," Rhys rebuked, before he kissed her goodbye. "Don't take any unnessary risks yourself. If these men are as well-armed as I'm told, we'll need your skills when we're done. Apparently, they're hot for Welsh blood."

Rhys put on his helmet and tested his sword and dagger. He checked his horse's girth and, when he was ready, raised his hand in farewell before riding toward the head of the troops.

They were ranged in an arc on a wooded hillside with a good view of the road. The coming conflict promised to be a miniature version of Bryn Glas, with the exception that the English knew they were there.

Lord Griffith formed the foremost rank, for he had few archers. Rhys had deployed his men at the edge of the trees, hoping they could get off enough volleys to make their presence felt. His archers were good enough to easily get off ten shots per minute, though they had not practiced much of late, being too often on the march.

Gritting his teeth, Rhys watched the enemy come. Fifty. A hundred. Two hundred. Dear God, there were more of them strung out along the highway. They were outnumbered by at least three to one. The English rode in formation, well-outfitted, highly trained soldiers. Their horses were armored, as were their archers on foot beside them. They had no more than thirty archers, at the most. This was the only encouraging thing about the odds—his archers outnumbered theirs.

Pennants fluttering, the armored troops slowly

wound their way up the muddy road. Beside a jagged piece of woodland they halted, looking up at the defenders. Rhys had held up his hand, making his men wait. He wanted the enemy to come closer, for the longbow was more deadly at shorter range. He hoped Griffith would not charge too soon, for he knew his men itched for conflict. The English began to move again, sending columns of men to the flanks, forming a triple advance. Perhaps they thought to outflank them and execute a pincer movement, unaware of the thickly forested slope to their rear.

When they were about two hundred yards away, Rhys raised his hand and volleys of arrows blackened the sky. Men fell screaming from their mounts, arrows finding chinks in their armor. Once these first few volleys were dispatched, Griffith waited no longer. Down the slope he charged, his men shouting their war cries, brandishing swords and pikes, whilst the archers let fly another volley. Opposing sides met now in hand-to-hand combat. The front rank of archers downed their bows and leaped into the fray to batter their steel–encased enemies with hammers and axes.

After the first deadly engagement, both sides fell back to regroup. The hillside was littered with the slain. Rhys had not time to count them, but he could see many holes in the Welsh ranks. Griffith was wounded in the arm, and his helmet dented so badly that he had to borrow a replacement from one of his men. At this rate, Rhys knew that they could not hold out. Griffith had sent a swift rider west to where he thought Glyndwr was camped, hoping their leader would send reinforcements.

The English kept coming. The roads below were choked with men and wagons, stretching as far as the eye could see. A heavily armored man on a large roan charger seemed to be in command of the opposing force, for he rode up and down the front ranks, his elaborate plate glinting in the sun.

Rhys slitted his eyes, suddenly alerted by the banner carried before this knight. He strained into the distance but the wind whipped the banner back about its staff, and he could no longer see the insignia.

The knight rode apart from the others, with three men following. The buffeting wind unfurled the standard and Rhys drew in his breath as his suspicions were confirmed. Dear Lord in heaven—Ralph Warren!

Griffith had alerted his troops for a possible trick when he saw the English leader riding toward them.

Rhys came to him. "Your men need have no fear. It's me he's after," he said, his voice echoing hollowly inside his helm. "I know him well—we're old enemies."

Surprised by the news, Griffith fell back, ordering his men to hold their fire.

Rhys unlooped his horse's reins from a nearby tree. Then, after a few words to his men, he mounted and slowly rode downhill toward the oncoming party. There was a plateau about halfway between the opposing sides and he headed for this. Warren must have seen his insignia from below, marking him from the start. He had to be right, or why else would such a superior force fall back after the first engagement.

"So, Welshman, it is you. I thought my eyes deceived me."

From her sheltered perch atop the slope, Jessamyn heard that distinctive, rasping voice and her blood ran cold. Over the murmurs of the men, the clank of arms, the whickering horses, his hated voice rang out loud and clear. Ralph Warren, the serpent of Cater's Hill, had come to repay a debt.

"What do you want with me today?" Rhys asked, standing in the stirrups. He lifted his visor and looked down at the advancing man. Splendidly accoutered in engraved armor, his foe was an impressive sight.

Ralph Warren likewise raised his visor, pausing thirty feet away. "I've come to finish our feat of arms."

"As I recall, you *ran* from the last field."

Laughter spread through the ranks behind Rhys and Ralph Warren's face turned purple in rage.

"Aye, and true to type, Welshman, you stole from me what I hold dear."

"Lady Jessamyn is my wife."

Stunned by this unexpected news, Sir Ralph said nothing. Finally mustering his wits, he rasped, "You are a knight in your own land. Is that not true?"

Wondering at this unexpected turn of speech, Rhys agreed. "Aye, though we don't set as much store by chivalric trappings as you. We fight bravely for control of our homeland, not for the entertainment of the crowds."

Ralph Warren's anger mounted, for he realized this Welshman mocked his prowess in the lists. He smiled, a pinched expression devoid of humor. "So you've heard of me then, even in that barbaric place. Well, have no fear, we don't come here to joust. Today, I propose a far more deadly game."

"Not to joust? You surprise me. Isn't that where you excel?" Rhys taunted, playing for time, hoping Glyndwr's troops would soon come to their aid.

"There are no lists, no crowds, no caparisons here. Lord Rhys of Trevaron, I propose that we alone decide the outcome of today's battle. You must agree; you are badly outnumbered. This way you'll have a fighting chance to keep your hides. We'll act as champions for our opposing sides. Do you agree? Do you accept my terms?"

Rhys considered the offer and realized it was the only thing which would give them precious time. If today's fight could be decided by this means, perhaps by tomorrow Glyndwr would have come to their aid.

"Very well."

"I propose we fight *à outrance*. Shall I translate that for you, Welshman, you not being of a chivalrous bent?"

"You have no need. I understand the French. You're offering me mortal combat—to the bitter end."

Ralph Warren nodded, the plumes on his helm waving with the movement. Taking off his gauntlet, he pitched it onto the empty ground between them.

"I, Ralph Warren of Cater's Hill, do challenge thee, Rhys of Trevaron, to mortal combat. The victor shall decide the outcome of today's engagement."

Silence had descended on the assembled troops during their exchange. Now an excited rumbling began in the ranks, swelling and spreading as the situation was relayed to the rear of the armies.

Jessamyn received the shattering news with dread. How could Rhys hope to win against Sir Ralph, who was a champion of the lists? She knew Rhys was a brave fighter—the battle of Bryn Glas had shown her that much—yet he was not a knight trained through life for formal combat. As she watched him ride forward and pick up the gauntlet, she wrung her hands in despair.

A murmur had begun to spread through the assembled ranks, followed by a resounding cheer once the challenge was accepted.

"I ask a favor. I'm told Lady Jessamyn is with you."

"She is."

"Then I beg a boon. Let her come closer. I want her to watch our contest."

Rhys shook his head, reluctant to inflict such misery on Jessamyn.

Ralph Warren curtly reminded Rhys that he had agreed to accept his terms, and that was one of them. Finally Rhys agreed.

"I have a boon to ask of you, in return. If I should lose the contest, promise me she'll be treated with honor."

"I always treat ladies with honor," Ralph Warren remarked smugly, licking his lips as he contemplated tasting again Jessamyn Dacre's delicious body.

"We both know that for a lie," Rhys ground out, longing to strike the English knight in payment for what he had done to Jessamyn. "But this is neither the time, nor the place for that discussion. Promise, on your honor as a knight of the realm and before these witnesses, that Lady Jessamyn will be treated with the honor befitting her rank as Lady of Curlew."

Ralph Warren hesitated a long time. He glanced about at the expectant audience, fidgeting now, growing impatient during the lull. And he knew he must agree or lose his honor.

"Very well," he said gruffly, "you have my word."

Rhys nodded. He turned and rode back to his own ranks. Several men came forward, eager to act as his squires; they handled his weapons with care, making sure that all were in readiness. Sir Ralph carried a lance with warhead intact. Rhys armed himself in a similar manner.

Now Rhys watched Sir Ralph strutting proudly,

unhurried in his preparations. He exchanged his elaborate plumed helm for a heavyweight jousting helm. This exchange ignited a spark of hope in Rhys's brain. The jousting helm would benefit Warren only in the charge. He would be virtually blind once that first course had been run.

No rules were set for their combat, as was the custom in organized tourneys. No number of prescribed blows was declared, nor weapons specified. This feat of arms was to be a struggle to the bitter end. Rhys had done all he could to assure safe passage for Jessamyn should he lose: the rest was up to God.

Grimly Rhys rode towards his opponent. They had chosen opposite ends of the plateau, which barely gave them room to charge. The contest was being fought open course.

Sir Ralph sat with his shoulders hunched, head bent in order to see through the eyeslit in his jousting helm, holding his lance in the proffering position as a herald from the English side completed a brief fanfare. At the signal, his lance dropped into strike position and the horses thundered towards each other, showering mud in their wakes. Sir Ralph's lance struck with such force that Rhys was toppled from his horse. The warhead, however, had not met him squarely, being deflected off his breastplate. It left behind a deep gash in the metal. His own lance had been carried too high and caught Sir Ralph on the helm, knocking him off his horse.

Stunned, the two warriors finally struggled to their feet. Both lances lay splintered on the ground. Gathering his wits, Rhys pulled free his two-handed sword, wielding the huge weapon as he approached Ralph Warren.

On his feet also, Sir Ralph soon realized his mistake. When he moved from the perfect position, he was virtually blind in his jousting helm. Cursing his own stupidity and lack of forethought, he staggered about, drawing his own two-handed sword and proceeding to hack at thin air. If he hunched his shoulders, he could see through the narrow eyeslits, and at those times, he delivered resounding blows to his opponent's armor.

Rhys was younger than Warren, but lacked the lifetime of formal training in arms which the older man possessed. He hoped one asset would offset the other. Through the grill of his visor he watched his opponent's staggering gait as he held his head down, shoulders hunched.

Rhys moved about the field with great agility. He wore only partial plate; what he had given up in protection, he gained in maneuverability. Repeatedly, he dodged the great swinging arc of his opponent's sword. Then Rhys slid in the mud, and the point of Sir Ralph's sword caught him in the upper arm, slicing through his padded jambeson. A resounding cheer came from the English ranks—the first blood had been drawn.

Again they squared off, each hacking and flailing. Rhys brought his sword crashing down on Sir Ralph's helm at point–blank range, driving the other man to his knees as the thundering blow reverberated through his steel helm.

Doggedly they fought on, the ground underfoot slowly reduced to a quagmire. They were both tiring as they slipped and fell, staggering to their feet with increasing difficulty. Rhys's armor was badly dented, for now Sir Ralph also wielded a mace and its deadly spikes penetrated weak spots in the plate. Again and again, Sir Ralph hit those vulnerable spots, having developed a new crouching technique which better enabled him to see his opponent. At every movement, blood spurted from Rhys's arm and he began to feel lightheaded.

Sir Ralph suddenly brought up his sword, catching Rhys off guard and sending his sword flying through the air to land upright in the mud, twenty feet away. A resounding cheer echoed from the English troops, while the Welsh groaned in dismay. Now the only weapon Rhys had left was his long dagger. Swiftly he drew this deadly sharp steel. And he waited.

The sight of blood flowing down his opponent's arm made Sir Ralph overconfident. All he had to do was to plunge his sword through a vulnerable place in the Welshman's armor, created by his repeated mace blows, and the victory was his!

Rhys maneuvered widely about the muddy area which had caused him trouble, knowing now where not to step. Sir Ralph came on in a running crouch. Raising his great sword, his voice muffled by his steel helm, Sir Ralph cried, "Prepare to die, Welshman."

Just as the great sword descended, Rhys sidestepped. The weight of the blade striking the earth threw Sir Ralph off balance, and he slid and fell. Sir Ralph grappled in the mud for the hilt of his sword, grasping it just as Rhys leaped on him. They rolled in the mud, struggling for possession of the sword; when it slipped out of reach, Sir Ralph tried to draw his short sword. Momentarily on top of his opponent, Rhys plunged the narrow dagger blade between a vital joint in Sir Ralph's armor, driving the blade in at an angle, slicing through padding, leather and flesh. A great gout of blood spurted out. Sir Ralph bellowed in pain and rage. He managed to grasp his short sword, fastened to his breastplate by a chain, and he stabbed hard beneath Rhys's arm, finding that vulnerable spot perfectly exposed.

Rhys reeled back in shock, giving Sir Ralph enough time to crawl to his feet. The English knight stood swaying, bellowing like an angry bull, for he had not anticipated such a fierce fight from his enemy.

Bone tired, and growing weak from loss of blood, the opponents staggered toward each other. Rhys held his dagger in readiness to strike again at that same opening. Sir Ralph raised his short sword above his head, yelling fiercely as he brought down the blade in a vicious swoop, intending to make short work of his opponent.

A haze swam before Rhys's eyes, and he blinked rapidly to clear his vision. He managed to jump away from the deadly stroke. As Sir Ralph drove down, Rhys simultaneously drove up; he could feel the other man's sword blade slicing down his back. Then Rhys had Sir Ralph's weight balanced on the point of his dagger, the force of impact staggering them both. The two men fell face down in the mud. This time neither man got up.

The cheering slowed, then stopped. A stunned silence greeted this unexpected development. Then the onlookers suddenly came to life as men from either side ran forward to minister to their champions.

Uttering a strangled cry, Jessamyn picked up her skirts and raced surefooted down the incline. Her heart thundered in fright and she gulped for breath as she ran. "Dear God, don't let him be dead," she prayed, over and over as she ran, beseeching the Lord and the Virgin Mary to spare her lover. By the time she reached them, the battered opponents had already been moved away from each other. One of Rhys's men tugged off his helm. Jessamyn crouched beside him, tears spilling down her face. Rhys was so white! His hair was matted to his brow with sweat and blood. Sharp fragments from his crushed helm had sliced his flesh, and a steady red trickle ran down his cheek and dripped off his chin.

"Oh, dear God, Rhys . . . Rhys . . . speak to me," she cried, holding him in her arms, pressing her tear-streaked face against his. Suddenly, against her cheek, she felt his lips move. Stunned, she drew back in time to see his eyes flutter open, and his blood–caked lips moved in a weak grin.

"Oh, blessed Mother, you're alive!" she cried in joy, holding him against her, rocking him as she tried to soothe away his pain.

"Did I win?" he croaked through cracked lips.

Jessamyn nodded, glancing toward the other party of men who crouched over their fallen champion. The battered helm had been pried off Sir Ralph's head. His face was white, and blood had pooled in his helmet from a wound in his neck. His men tried to revive him without success. Bending over him, his fingers searching for a pulse, his squire solemnly pronounced Sir Ralph Warren dead.

The trumpeter blew a short fanfare, alerting all to his announcement.

"The champion, and victor of the mortal combat between Sir Ralph Warren of Cater's Hill, fighting for England and King Henry, and Lord Rhys of Trevaron, fighting for Wales and Owain Glyndwr, is Lord Rhys of Trevaron."

Wild cheers broke out on the Welsh side. A stir like a rising wind passed over the English ranks as their fallen champion was carried back to his wagon.

Jessamyn cradled Rhys's head on her skirts, sponging blood from his face. She offered him a cup of wine, handed to her by one of his men. What now? Nervously she scanned the English ranks, expecting them to charge the unprepared Welsh soldiers. As she waited, the first drops of rain began to patter on her upturned face. To her amazement the English soldiers packed up their arms, and grumbling loudly about the rain, they moved farther downhill to seek cover. Jessamyn could hardly believe they were going to allow this hard-fought victory to stand.

One by one, the groups of soldiers moved back the way they had come, heads down against the increasingly heavy rain. Today's battle had been Sir Ralph Warren's; they had no stomach for further contest. Back to their comrades they went, toiling along the road, heads hunched against the rain which drove hard from the west.

The Welsh troops were equally amazed. They allowed the English soldiers to go without harassment. Finally, the remnants of the small Welsh army were left alone on the hill to retrieve their dead and wounded.

Rhys smiled at Jessamyn and reached up with his cold steel gauntlet to touch her bright hair.

"Well, by God, I'm either still alive, or died and gone to heaven," he remarked, looking at her lovely, tear-stained face, and finding it the most beautiful sight he had ever seen.

"Come, let me get you out of the rain, sweetheart. Can you walk?" she asked anxiously as Rhys stirred, groaning with the effort of sitting up.

Every bone in his body felt as if it were broken. Rhys was convinced that he must have been one enormous bruise. Blood still trickled inside his sleeve, and the fabric of his jambeson was stuck to his wounds, painfully tearing loose with every movement. Eagerly his men came to his aid, cheering him, carefully patting him on the back, for they knew he had just suffered a terrible ordeal.

As Rhys struggled painfully uphill, supported by several stalwart archers, he raised his hand to show them he was still alive, still fit to command. A great

435

cheer broke out as his men greeted him when he was taken back to the wagons.

The heavy rain drummed against the wagon's canvas roof as Jessamyn bathed and bandaged Rhys's wounds. She gasped in horror when his men took off his armor and she saw one great gash beneath his arm, another on his shoulder. The myriad cuts and bruises of combat she bathed with soothing tinctures before applying salve and bandaging them. Men more used to treating battle wounds showed her how to clean and pack his deep wounds to stop the bleeding.

She wept for the need to hurt him. Rhys gritted his teeth and groaned deeply as they packed the wounds with clean linen, fighting the pain as he tried to stay conscious. He sipped generously from the pain-killing cup Jessamyn had brewed over the campfire, and after several pauses in the operation, he was able to continue.

When Rhys was patched up well enough for travel, he decided that they should head for Wales. They were too vulnerable to attack to stay where they were. He had already lost too many men to be able to successfully ward off a second attack.

Rhys still found it hard to believe Ralph Warren was dead. When he had been staggering in the mud, his strength virtually spent, the reminder of what Warren had done to Jessamyn drove him on, producing superhuman effort. It was the fire of hatred which gave him the upper hand as he fought in a weary stupor, delivering ineffectual blows as he tried to hang on to consciousness, fighting to avenge Jessamyn.

The rain gradually stopped as they splashed along the country lanes, bogged down in puddles and besmirched by mud.

During the night Rhys ran a fever and Jessamyn

anxiously nursed him, crouching beside him in the wagon where she sponged his head with cool water, and offered him sips of sallow willow tea in an effort to break his fever.

Jessamyn dozed fitfully through the long night, the next day and the following night, jerking awake each time Rhys cried out to sponge his brow and force down sips of tea to ease his pain. When she finally slept, neither hooting owls nor the distant rumble of thunder disturbed her sleep, so weary had she grown through the long ordeal.

Jessamyn awoke to a bright morning sun. To her amazement she saw Rhys, clear-eyed, leaning against the side of the wagon, ravenously tearing apart a thick hunk of bread and cheese, and washing it down with sweet ale purchased from a nearby tavern.

"Rhys, you're better!" she cried in delight. "How do you feel?"

"Like Hell," he announced cheerfully, his mouth full. "But I'll live, thanks to you. I always knew you'd be invaluable when we went into battle."

"I never expected to take you up on the offer," she said, smiling at him as she leaned over to kiss his stubbly cheek. "You mustn't overdo things. And I have to dress your wounds."

He grimaced. "I was afraid of that. Tell me, did you think I was going to lose the fight?"

She had to admit to the truth. "Yes. He's fought in so many tourneys, whereas you . . ."

"Have never even entered the lists. I'm only good for killing men in a free-for-all . . . go on, say it."

"Well, I did feel you were mismatched. And I was terrified you wouldn't win."

"Me too."

"What!" Round-eyed she stared at him in surprise. "But you looked so confident . . . and acted foolhardy! Oh, Rhys I thought . . ."

"Playing for time, love, hoping Glyndwr would come to our rescue. We'd have been slaughtered to a man if we'd continued to fight them in a pitched battle. I only hoped Warren honored his chivalric vows enough to keep his word to treat you well when I was gone."

Tears trickled down her cheeks as she gently embraced him, ever mindful of his painful wounds. The warmth of his mouth was a sweet delight she had never thought to taste again.

"Oh, Rhys, I've never prayed so hard in my life. Let's take you home."

"No."

She recoiled at his gruff answer. "Surely you're still not intending to go into battle for Glyndwr, not like this? You'll be killed."

"Are you ordering my days now, woman?"

His stern voice caused her a stab of unease, but she valued his safety more than her regard for her own person.

"I am," Jessamyn declared firmly. "You're under my care. And you won't fight again until you're well."

"Good—that's all I wanted to hear."

Amazed, she stared at him, seeing his mouth twitch, for he could no longer keep a straight face. Then he began to chuckle at her shocked expression.

"Jessamyn Dacre, you haven't changed much, despite all your sweet talk to the contrary. Will you still have me, weak as a kitten?"

"You've no need to ask that. Of course I'll have you."

"Then let's be about our journey. We've a way to go before we're done."

"You'll do no such thing. There'll be no hard riding. Trevaron's a long way off."

"Who said anything about Trevaron."

Puzzled she put her hand to his brow, thinking his fever had returned to muddle his thinking. His flesh felt cool to the touch. He kissed her wrist, and traced the pounding blue vein beneath the surface with his tongue.

"No fever . . . yet you're talking in riddles."

Rhys wrapped his good arm about her and drew her against him. "I've a mind to wed you without more delay, Jess. We're going to Curlew to relieve the garrison."

She gasped with mingled shock and delight. "You're not well enough to fight."

"Who said I was going to fight. By all accounts, the troops have grown fat and lazy. Now that Sir Ralph's dead, I'll make them an offer. Give up Curlew and live—keep it and die. I'm sure they'll see the wisdom of surrender."

"You've so few men. How can you hope to beat them?"

"We'll take Griffith's men with us. The lads have gathered banners as souvenirs; we'll float them aloft for Jackson to see, tricking him into thinking we're just a sampling of what's to come. We'll threaten him with the rest of our army, only a few hours' march away."

"It might work."

"Oh, come—where's your faith? It has to work. Having little stomach left for fighting, when he sees our captured English banners, he's bound to surrender. Arden Hughes said that half the time, they don't even pull up the bridge, and the winch is rusting and badly maintained."

She kissed his face, surprised that he was already

planning strategy, having barely recovered from his grueling contest of arms.

"You're an amazing man," she whispered, tracing her finger over his swollen lip. "That must be why I love you so much."

Chapter Twenty-four

A bitter wind whistled through chinks in the manor's windows, but in the stone-walled keep, a roaring fire and many charcoal braziers kept the cold at bay.

The Lord and Lady of Trevaron and their tenants were making merry at a splendid Christmas feast. The walls were hung with boughs of evergreens. Bunches of holly and mistletoe festooned the great, stone hearth and the red-covered tables were adorned with tendrils of ivy and gilded fir cones. A troupe of brightly garbed mummers had presented a lengthy farce of ribald content, and Jessamyn concluded that it was probably as well she did not understand Welsh sufficiently to translate much of it.

A boar's head, surrounded by spiced crabapples, was ceremoniously paraded through the Hall before being set in the place of honor before the lord and lady. Steaming platters of roast venison, lamb, and beef followed, the servants carrying them in merry procession around the tables before taking them to the High table. Other servers followed, bringing dishes of roast turnips laced with honey, garlic-scented beans, fish and meat pasties, jugged hare, and baked fish—until the feast table groaned beneath the weight of their Christmas bounty. Much wine and ale had already been consumed during the mummers' performance and many of the guests were already tipsy.

After a lute and harp had sweetly carolled a Christmas tune, Rhys held up his hand for silence. The guests complied as best they could, smiling benignly upon their handsome young lord arrayed in a scarlet doublet with a glinting gold chain around his neck. Beside him sat his beautiful lady, her gown of shimmering peacock blue silk edged with marten, her bright auburn hair coiled about her dainty ears and fastened inside gold net cauls.

"I want to propose a toast to my dear wife, Jessamyn," Rhys said, raising his wine cup high for all to see."

To a man, the guests rose to drink the toast, cheering the lovely English lady who had come from so far away to marry their lord. And a second toast was drunk to their lord, who was still as besotted with his lady as he had been on the first day they set eyes on her.

"Tomorrow we'll hold a ceremony in our newly completed chapel to re-pledge our marriage vows."

A cheer greeted this announcement, for the common folk saw a second feast forthcoming out of this celebration. The chapel had been finished in record time, at their lady's behest, in thanks for Lord Rhys's miraculous recovery after his mortal combat with the English knight. By his bravery,

442

Lord Rhys had saved the Welsh army from defeat. Already this great feat of arms had been enshrined in song and fable, and was fast becoming the most popular selection in the bards' repertoire.

Rhys clasped Jessamyn's hand, urging her to rise and stand beside him. He picked up his cup and, turning to the assembly, smiled proudly, his arm about his wife's waist.

"One final toast—will you join me in welcoming my heir, who'll be amongst you some time in the spring?"

Gasps of delight, laughter, and resounding cheers, greeted their lord's welcome news. The tenants clapped and stamped their feet, greatly pleased to learn Trevaron would soon have an heir.

Rhys indicated that the guests should return to their meal and his tenants soon set about their feast with renewed appetites.

"Oh, Rhys, they're as pleased as we are," Jessamyn remarked in surprise, surveying the sea of beaming faces at the lower tables. "Tomorrow we'll finally be married by a priest here in Wales. It'll do my soul good to have it done. Just think—this will be our third ceremony. There's no possible way you can squeeze out of this marriage."

"And of all those ceremonies, this will be the most meaningful," Rhys assured, taking her hand and pressing his lips in her palm. "Our handfasting was for them, Curlew was for you, this will be for me— and our babe."

Smiling, he placed his hand over the swelling in her abdomen and, as if it knew its father, the babe gave a resounding kick. Surprised and pleased to have such immediate recognition, Rhys smiled fondly at Jessamyn and bent to kiss that mound of silk. Slightly embarrassed by his action, Jessamyn quickly raised his head.

Patricia Phillips

"Happy Christmas, *cariad*. May there be a long lifetime of Christmas feasts to follow."

Jessamyn rested her head on his shoulder, her eyes welling with tears of happiness. Now that she had regained control of Curlew, Rhys had promised they would divide their year between his lands and hers, administering to their tenants and holding lordship courts to settle disputes in both Trevaron and Curlew. She could still hardly believe that his daring plan had worked. When Captain Jackson saw their sea of assorted banners and his men failed to pull up the bridge, he had readily capitulated. He considered himself fortunate to have been able to ride away unharmed. They had merely crossed the drawbridge and walked inside the castle. Because of Rhys's plan their child could now grow up with a shared heritage, being heir to both Curlew and Trevaron.

"If this babe's a girl instead of a boy, do you know what I'll call her," she said, suddenly struck by the surprising thought their coming heir might be female. In all the time they had talked about the babe they had always assumed it would be a boy. Jessamyn rather fancied a sweet little girl whom she could teach to follow in her ways.

"No, what will it be? The choice is yours."

"Rose—in memory of her conception," she whispered, knowing that he understood by the sudden light in his brown eyes and his swift, answering smile.

Jessamyn fingered the plaited corn symbol inside her chatelaine, given to her by Meggy Hughes. When next they visited Curlew, she would tell Meggy her gift had worked miracles. And Jessamyn smiled as her handsome husband pressed his mouth against her cheek. This Christmas their love had come full circle.

BRIMMING WITH PASSION...
BURSTING WITH EXCITEMENT...

UNFORGETTABLE HISTORICAL ROMANCES FROM *LEISURE BOOKS!*

The Magic by Robin Lee Hatcher. Destined for a loveless marriage to a virtual stranger, Cassandra Jamison finds herself instead swept aboard a notorious pirate ship and into its captain's arms. How can she hope to resist the most devastatingly seductive man she's ever encountered?
_3433-6 $4.99 US/$5.99 CAN

Ryan's Enchantress by Connie Harwell. When tomboy Susan Bradford meets her handsome new neighbor, she is shocked to realize that she longs for his tender caresses, longs to wipe the mocking grin off his face and show him how much of a woman she can be.
_3436-0 $4.99 US/$5.99 CAN

Fleeting Splendor by Julie Moffett. Trapped in a marriage of convenience with broodingly handsome Nathaniel Beauchamp, Alana MacKenzie makes the surprising discovery that love can sometimes blossom in the most unexpected places.
_3434-4 $4.50 US/$5.50 CAN

LEISURE BOOKS
ATTN: Order Department
276 5th Avenue, New York, NY 10001

Please add $1.50 for shipping and handling for the first book and $.35 for each book thereafter. PA., N.Y.S. and N.Y.C. residents, please add appropriate sales tax. No cash, stamps, or C.O.D.s. All orders shipped within 6 weeks via postal service book rate. Canadian orders require $2.00 extra postage and must be paid in U.S. dollars through a U.S. banking facility.

Name _____
Address _____
City _____ State _____ Zip _____
I have enclosed $_____ in payment for the checked book(s).
Payment <u>must</u> accompany all orders.□ Please send a free catalog.